BROKEN SKIN

Stuart MacBride has gone from asking people if they 'want fries with that' to project-managing vast IT projects for the oil industry. Somewhere in the middle he managed to make money out of dressing up as a woman, doing voiceovers, graphic design, working offshore, and very boring things involving websites. He failed the interview to become a funeral director.

His first book, *Cold Granite*, was shortlisted for the International Thriller Writers' best debut novel and won the Barry Award for best first novel. The follow-up, *Dying Light*, became an instant top-ten bestseller. Stuart MacBride won the 2007 Dagger in the Library, awarded for a body of work.

Stuart lives in north-east Scotland with his wife Fiona, cat Grendel, and a vegetable plot full of w

Vis

D1492823

'Stuart MacBride goes straight for the jugular with a tight, thrilling novel' *Glasgow Herald*

'This is Ian Rankin on Speed . . . the humour is black, the violence is apalling, the language is, well, realistic, the entertainment is unflagging. I hunger for the earlier novels' *Adelaide Review*

'An impressive debut . . . an edge-of-your-seat page-turner' *Publishers Weekly*

'A cracking new writer on the crime scene who hooks you from the first page and never lets you go. The action is ferocious and the pace unrelenting' *Northern Echo*

'Compelling reading' *Telegraph*

'A gritty, roller-coaster, in-your-face thriller' *Aberdeen Press and Journal*

'MacBride is a confident writer . . . does a good line in black humour and has a nose for the macabre.' *Scotsman*

'The story is violent and bloody; some of the crimes are vicious and MacBride doesn't hold back on the details. But there is plenty of dark humour, and a warmth to the portrayal of the police officers which lightens an otherwise grim tale by this very talented writer' Susanna Yager, *Sunday Telegraph*

By Stuart MacBride

Cold Granite
Dying Light
Broken Skin

STUART MACBRIDE

BROKEN SKIN

HARPER

Harper
An imprint of HarperCollins*Publishers*
77–85 Fulham Palace Road,
Hammersmith, London W6 8JB

www.harpercollins.co.uk

This paperback edition 2008
1

First published in Great Britain by
HarperCollins*Publishers* 2007

Copyright © Stuart MacBride 2007

Stuart MacBride asserts the moral right to
be identified as the author of this work

A catalogue record for this book is
available from the British Library

ISBN 978-0-00-785561-2

Typeset in Meridien
by Palimpsest Book Production Limited,
Grangemouth, Stirlingshire

Printed and bound in Great Britain by
Clays Ltd, St Ives plc

Mixed Sources

Product group from well-managed
forests and other controlled sources
www.fsc.org Cert no. SW-COC-1806
© 1996 Forest Stewardship Council

FSC is a non-profit international organisation established to promote the
responsible management of the world's forests. Products carrying the FSC
label are independently certified to assure consumers that they come
from forests that are managed to meet the social, economic and
ecological needs of present and future generations.

Find out more about HarperCollins and the environment at
www.harpercollins.co.uk/green

For Fiona
(third time's the charm)

Without Whom . . .

Researching a book is always fun – especially when people are prepared to open up and let you into their worlds of expertise. In writing *Broken Skin* I needed some pretty specialist information about the BDSM scene. The people who shared their secrets with me don't want to be named, but they know who they are and I thank them.

I also want to thank everyone at Grampian Police who answered all my stupid questions with clever answers: Sergeant John Souter (CCTV); Inspector John Soutar (Control); Chief Inspector Jim Bilsland; Bruce Duncan and Zoe in the IB; and Fingerprint Expert Gary Dempster. An extra special nod goes to PC Derek Bain, who put up with more than most – thanks!

And once again I owe a debt of gratitude to that lovely guru of all things post mortem: Ishbel Gall. She knows more about dead bodies than anyone I've ever met.

These are the people responsible for anything I've got right: anything I've got wrong is my own silly fault.

More thanks go to Philip Patterson – still the best friend and agent a bearded write-ist could have – Luke, Isabella, and everyone else at Marjacq scripts; my editorial team of spoon-wielding Berber ninjas, AKA the brilliant Jane Johnson and Sarah Hodgson; the superb Amanda, Lucy, Andrea, Fiona, Kelly, Clive, Wendy, Damon, Leisa, Dom and the rest of the team at HarperCollins for doing a stunning job; Kelley Ragland at St Martin's Press for all her help; and James Oswald for everything not nailed down.

I also want to thank Ian Burdis who donated a large sum of money to the Juvenile Diabetes Research Foundation so that his partner, Debbie Kerr, could be a character in this book. Two other real people who feature are my old friend Alexander Clark (who was invaluable for IT info), and John Rickards who writes excellent crime novels, when not appearing in my slightly twisted ones. Needless to say, Debs, Alex and John have let me get away with murder ;}#

And lastly, but not leastly, I have to thank my naughty wife Fiona. Not everyone would put up with this kind of thing . . .

SEX

1

Up ahead the woman stops. She stands on one leg under the streetlight, rubbing her ankle, as if she's not used to wearing high heels. Number seven: a wee Torry quine on her way home after a night out on the pish, staggering along in her fuck-me heels and miniskirt, even though it's February in Aberdeen and freezing cold. She's a looker. Curly brown hair. Upturned little nose. Nice legs, long and sexy. The kind he likes to feel struggling beneath him as he makes the bitch take it. Shows her who's boss.

She straightens up and teeters off again, mumbling away to herself in a little alcoholic haze. He likes them drunk: not so drunk they don't know what's happening, but drunk enough that they can't do anything about it. Can't get a good look at him.

Dirty bitches.

She lurches past the NorFish building – spotlit for a moment in the sweeping headlights of an articulated lorry – across the roundabout and onto the cobbles of Victoria Bridge, crossing the dark, silent River Dee into Torry. He hangs back a bit, pretending to tie his shoelace until she's nearly all the way over. This part of town isn't his usual hunting ground, so he has to play it carefully. Make sure no one's watching. He smiles: the dark, grey street is deserted – just him and lucky Number Seven.

A quick jog and he's right behind her again. He's fit, doesn't even break a sweat in his Aberdeen Football Club tracksuit, complete with hood and black Nike trainers. Who's going to look twice at a man out for a jog?

Torry's bleak in the late February night – granite buildings stained almost black with grime, washed with piss-yellow streetlight. The woman fits right in: cheap clothes, cheap black leather jacket, cheap shoes, cheap perfume. A dirty girl. He smiles and feels the knife in his pocket. Time for the dirty girl to get her 'treat'.

She turns left, heading off the long, sweeping curve of Victoria Road onto one of the side streets, where the fish processing factories are. Probably taking a shortcut back to her horrible little bedsit, or the house she shares with mummy and daddy. He grins, hoping it's mummy and daddy – she should have someone to share her pain with when this is all over. Because there's going to be a *lot* of pain to share.

The street's deserted, just the back end of an

empty eighteen-wheeler parked opposite the oriental cash and carry. It's all industrial units here, silent and dark and closed for the night. No one to see them and call for help.

The woman – Number Seven – passes a skip full of twisted metal, and he speeds up, closing the gap. Her heels go click-clack on the cold concrete pavement, but his Nikes are silent. Past a couple of those big plastic bins overflowing with discarded fish heads and bones, grimy wooden pallets slapped on top to keep the seagulls out. Closer.

Out with the knife, one hand rubbing the front of his tracksuit, stroking his erection for luck. Every detail stands out bright and clear, like blood splashed on pale, white skin.

She turns at the last minute, eyes going wide as she sees him, then sees the knife, too shocked to scream. This is going to be special. Number Seven will get to do things she's never dreamed of, not in her darkest nightmares. She—

Her arm flashes out, knocking the knife away as she grabs his tracksuit and buries her knee in his groin hard enough to lift him off the ground.

He lets out a little squeal and she closes his mouth with a fist. Black concentric circles chase a hot yellow roar and his knees give way. The pavement is cold and hard as he collapses, curls up around his battered testicles, and cries.

*   *   *

5

'Jesus . . .' DC Rennie peered at the man snivelling away on the cracked pavement among the fishy stains. 'I think you broke his goolies. I heard them pop.'

'He'll live.' PC Jackie Watson forced the man over onto his face, cuffing his hands behind his back. He groaned and whimpered. Jackie smiled. 'Serves you right, you dirty little bastard . . .' She glanced up at Rennie. 'Anyone looking?' He said no, so she kicked the guy in the ribs. 'That's for Christine, Laura, Gail, Sarah, Jennifer, Joanne, and Sandra.'

'Jesus, Jackie!' Rennie grabbed her before she could do it again. 'What if someone sees?'

'You said no one was looking.'

'Yeah, but—'

'So what's the problem?' She stood, glowering down at the crying man in the AFC tracksuit. 'Right, Sunshine, on your feet.'

He didn't move. 'Oh for god's sake . . .' She grabbed his ear and hauled him upright. 'Rennie, you want to . . . ?' But DC Rennie was busy on the radio, telling Control that Operation Sweetmeat had been a success – they'd caught the bastard.

2

Aberdeen Royal Infirmary was spreading like a concrete tumour. For years it'd been in remission, but lately it had started to grow again, infecting the surrounding area with new wings of concrete and steel. And every time he saw it, Detective Sergeant Logan McRae's heart sank.

Stifling a yawn he crumpled up the thin plastic cup his vending-machine coffee had come in and dropped it in the bin before pushing through the brown double doors into the heady bouquet of disinfectant, formalin and death.

The hospital morgue was a lot bigger than the one down at Grampian Police Force Headquarters and a lot more cheerful. A small stereo in one corner of the large, brown room pumped out Dr Hook's greatest hits, the music almost drowning out the sound of running water as it gurgled down a drain on one of the dissecting tables. A woman in a green plastic apron, surgical scrubs and white Wellington boots was packing an old lady's organs back where they'd come from, to the tune of *When You're in Love with a Beautiful Woman*.

Logan's unidentified male was lying on his back on a hospital gurney, eyes taped shut, skin as pale as wax paper. They'd left all the surgical tubes and lines attached for the inevitable post mortem: it made the body look abandoned. Mid-twenties, short blond hair, thin, but well muscled, as if he'd been addicted to the gym. His lower limbs and abdomen were smeared red, a long row of hurried stitches marking where they'd sewn him back together again after the surgeon finally admitted defeat. Death: one, NHS Grampian: zero.

The woman stuffing the old lady looked up and saw Logan peering down at the man's naked body. 'Police?' He nodded and she pulled off her mask, frizzy red hair escaping from underneath her surgical cap. 'Thought so. We've not bagged him up yet.' Stating the obvious. Not that there was much chance of getting any useful forensic evidence off the body now. Not after it'd been contaminated in the A&E lobby, examination room, and operating theatre.

'Don't worry about it, I can wait.'

'OK.' She picked the old lady's ribcage up off a stainless steel trolley and fiddled it back into place, then started to close up.

He watched her for a moment before asking: 'Any chance you could take a quick look at our John Doe here?'

8

'No bloody chance! You got any idea what the Hormonal Bitch Queen would do to me if she found out some lowly APT played with the corpse before she got her icy little fingers on it?'

'I'm not asking you to do a full post mortem, but you could, you know,' shrug, 'take a look?' He tried on his best smile. 'Otherwise we're going to have to wait till tomorrow afternoon. Sooner we know, the sooner we can catch whoever did this. Come on, just a quick external examination – no one will ever know.'

She pursed her lips, frowned, sighed, then said, 'OK. But you tell anyone I did this and you're going in one of those bloody freezers, understand?'

Logan grinned. 'My lips are sealed.'

'Right, give me a minute to finish up here and we'll see what we can do . . .' Ten minutes later the old lady was sewn closed and back in a refrigerated drawer. The APT pulled on a fresh pair of gloves. 'What do we know?'

'Shoved out of a car at A&E, wrapped in a blanket.' Logan hoisted up the plastic bag full of bloodstained fabric they'd given him upstairs. 'We'll do a full forensic on the clothes, but could be a hit and run. Driver flattens some poor sod, panics, bundles them into the back of the car and abandons them at the hospital.' He watched as the anatomical pathology technician started prodding the cold flesh, muttering 'hit and run' under her breath in time to the music.

'Don't think so.' She shook her head, sending

a stray Irn-Bru-coloured curl bouncing. 'Look—' she hooked a finger into the side of the man's mouth, pulling it back to expose the teeth, still wrapped around the ventilation tube, 'incisors, canines and premolars are broken, but there's no damage to the nose or chin. An impact would leave scarring on the lips. He's bitten down on something . . .' She stroked the side of the dead man's face. 'Looks like some sort of gag, you can just see the marks in the skin.' Logan's blood ran cold.

'You sure?'

'Yup. And he's covered with tiny burns. See?' Little circles and splotches of angry red skin, some with yellowing blisters in the middle. Oh God.

'What else?'

'Dermal abrasions, bruising . . . I'd say he's been roughed up a bit . . . More marks on the wrists, like he's been strapped to something. It's too thick to be rope. A belt? Something like that?'

That was all Logan needed: another body who'd been tied up and tortured. He was about to ask her if there were any fingers missing when she handed him a pair of gloves and told him to give her a hand turning the body over. It was a mess of dark, clotted blood, reaching from the small of the back all the way down to the ankles.

The APT slowly scanned the skin, pointing out more burns and contusions as she went, then prised the corpse's buttocks apart with a sticky screltching sound. 'Bloody hell.' She stepped back, blinked, then peered at the man's backside again.

Dr Hook started in on *If I Said You Had A Beautiful Body (Would You Hold It Against Me?)*. 'The only way this was a car accident is if someone tried to park a Transit van up his backside.' She straightened up, peeling off her latex gloves. 'And if you want anything more, you're going to have to ask a pathologist, 'cos I'm not opening him up to find out.'

Grampian Police Force Headquarters wasn't the prettiest building in Aberdeen: a seven-storey block of dark grey concrete and glass stripes – like an ugly Liquorice Allsort – jaundiced with pale yellow streetlight.

There was a lot of indignant shouting coming from the front lobby, so Logan gave it a miss. One look through the part-glazed door was enough for him: a large woman with grey hair and a walking stick was giving Big Gary on the front desk an earful about police harassment, prejudice and stupidity. Bellowing, 'YOU SHOULD ALL BE ASHAMED OF YOURSELVES!' at the top of her lungs. He took the stairs instead.

The canteen was in the post-midnight lull: just the sound of pots and pans clattering in the sink and a late-night radio station turned down low to keep Logan company as he sat slurping his cream of tomato soup, trying not to think about the dead man's ruptured rear end.

He was finishing up when a familiar figure grumbled her way up to the service counter and asked for three coffees, one with spit in it. PC Jackie Watson – she'd changed out of the rape-bait outfit she'd worn to work that evening and back into the standard all-black uniform, her hair returned to its regulation bun. She didn't look very happy. Logan sneaked up behind her while she was waiting, grabbed her round the middle and went, 'Boo!'.

She didn't even flinch. 'I could see you reflected in the sneeze guard.'

'Oh . . . How's it going?'

Jackie peered over the counter at the little old man fumbling about with the coffee machine. 'How long does it take to make three bloody cups of coffee?'

'That good, eh?'

She shrugged. 'Honestly, I'd be quicker swimming to Brazil and picking the bloody beans myself!'

When the three cups finally materialized, Logan walked her back down to interview room number four. 'Here,' she said, handing him two of the paper containers, 'hold these.' She peeled the plastic lid off the third, howched, and spat into the frothy brown liquid, before putting the lid back on and giving it a shake.

'Jackie! You can't—'

'Watch me.' She took the other coffees back and pushed through into the interview room. In the brief moment the door was open, Logan could see the huge, angry shape of DI Insch leaning back against the wall, arms crossed, face furious, and then Jackie banged the door shut with her hip.

Intrigued, Logan wandered down the corridor to the observation room. It was tiny and drab – just a couple of plastic chairs, a battered desk and a set of video monitors. Someone was already in there – ferreting about in his ear with the chewed end of an old biro: DC Simon Rennie. He pulled the pen out, examined the tip, then stuck it back in his ear and wiggled it about some more.

'If you're looking for a brain, you're digging in the wrong end,' said Logan, sinking into the other seat.

Rennie grinned at him. 'How's your John Doe then?'

'Dead. How's your rapist?'

Rennie tapped the monitor in front of him with the ear-end of his biro. 'Recognize anyone?'

Logan leaned forward and stared at the flickering picture: interview room number four, the back of Jackie's head, a scarred Formica table, and the accused. 'Bloody hell, isn't that—'

'Yup. Rob Macintyre. AKA Goalden Boy.' Rennie sat back in his seat with a sigh. 'Course, you know what this means?'

'Aberdeen doesn't stand a chance on Saturday?'

'Aye, and it's bloody Falkirk. How embarrassing is that going to be?' He buried his head in his hands. 'Falkirk!'

Robert Macintyre – the best striker Aberdeen Football Club had seen for years. 'What happened to his face?' The man's top lip was swollen and split.

'Jackie. She did a Playtex on his balls too: lift and separate . . .' They sat in silence for a minute watching the man on the screen shifting uncomfortably, taking the occasional sip from Jackie's spit-flavoured coffee. He wasn't much to look at – twenty-one years old, sticky-out ears, weak chin, dark spiky hair, a single black eyebrow stretched across his skinny face – but the little bugger could run like the wind and score from halfway down the pitch.

'He come clean? Confess all his sins?'

Rennie snorted. 'No. And his one phone call? Made us ring his mum. She was down here like a bloody shot, shouting the odds. Woman's like a Rottweiler on steroids. Aye, you can take the quine out of Torry, but you can't take Torry out the quine.'

Logan cranked the volume up, but there was nothing to hear. DI Insch was probably trying one of his patented silences again: leaving a long, empty pause for the accused to jump in and fill, knowing that most people were incapable of keeping their gobs shut in stressful situations. But not Macintyre. He didn't seem bothered at all. Except by his crushed gonads.

DI Insch's voice boomed from off camera, crackling through the speakers. *'Going to give you one more chance, Rob: tell us about the rapes, or we'll nail you to the wall. Your choice. Talk to us and it'll look good in front of the jury: shows remorse, maybe gets you a shorter sentence. Don't and they'll think you're just a nasty wee shite who preys on young women and deserves to go down for the rest of his life.'* Another trademark pause.

'Look,' said Macintyre at last, sitting forward, wincing, then settling back in his chair again, one hand under the table. He'd not been in the limelight long enough to lose his Aberdeen accent yet, all the vowels low and stretched. *'I'll say it again, slowly so you'll understand, like. I was out for a wee jog. Keepin' fit fer the match Saturday. I didn't rape anyone.'*

Jackie got as far as, *'You had a knife—'* before Insch told her to shut up. His bulk loomed into the frame, leaning on the tabletop with both fists, his bald head glinting in the overhead lights, obscuring Macintyre from the camera.

'Yes you did, Rob – you followed them, you jumped them, you battered them, you raped them, you carved up their faces—'

'It wasnae me!'

'You took trophies, you daft sod: necklaces, earrings, even a pair of knickers! We'll find them when we search your house.'

'I never did nothin', OK? Get that intae your fat, thick heid. I NEVER RAPED NOBODY!'

'You really think you're going to walk away from this? We don't need your confession, we've got enough on you—'

'Know what? I've had enough of cooperatin' with the police. I want tae see ma lawyer.'

15

'We've been through *all this: you get to see a lawyer when I say so, not before!'*

'*Aye? Well you might as well send out for more coffee then, 'cos it's gonnae be a long night. And I'm no sayin' anythin' else.'*

And he didn't.

3

Rob Macintyre's arrest had come too late to make the first edition of the *Press and Journal* – Aberdeen's local paper – but it was on the Scottish bit of the early-morning TV news. A dour-faced newswoman stood outside Pittodrie football stadium in the dark, talking to a small knot of shivering fans. Asking their opinion on the whole superstar-striker-as-marauding-rapist thing. God knew how the BBC had got onto the story so quick.

The supporters, all dressed in bright-red, replica AFC football tops, backed their hero all the way: Macintyre was a good lad; wouldn't do anything like that; it was a fit-up, the club needed him . . . And then it was on to a house fire in Dundee. Logan sat in the lounge, yawning, drinking tea and listening to some lopsided freak from Tayside Police telling the public how important it was to check the batteries in their smoke alarms. And then the travel, weather, and back to the London studio.

17

An entire country's news squeezed into eight minutes.

Logan's unidentified male wasn't due to be post mortemed till ten am – nearly three hours away – but there was a shedload of paperwork to be filled in first.

He finished his tea and went to get dressed.

The morgue at FHQ shone with an antiseptic fervour. Sparkling white tiles covered the walls and floor, glinting cutting tables sat beneath polished extractor fans, the room lined with pristine work surfaces. Logan changed into the compulsory white over suit with hood and blue plastic booties before pushing into the sterile area. The guest of honour was already laid out, flat on his back in all his pasty, bloodstained glory while an IB photographer clicked and flashed his way around the body, documenting everything as another technician used sticky tape to remove any trace evidence he could find. A slow-motion dance complete with disco strobe.

Doc Fraser was slumped over one of the other cutting tables, a copy of the P&J spread out on the stainless-steel surface in front of him. He looked up, saw Logan walking in and asked him for an eight letter word beginning with B.

'No idea. Who's SIO?'

The pathologist sighed and started chewing on the end of his pen, 'God knows; I'm just corrob-orating today. The Fiscal's about somewhere, you can ask her if you like. No one tells me anything.'

Logan knew the feeling.

He found the Procurator Fiscal out in the viewing room, pacing back and forth, looking as if she was talking to herself until he saw the little Bluetooth headset attached to her ear. 'No,' she said, fiddling with a palmtop computer, 'we need to make sure the case is airtight. I don't want to be fielding questions when I'm working on my tan. Now what about those Bridge of Don burglaries? . . .' He left her to it.

It wasn't long before the answer lurched through the morgue doors, hauling at the crotch of her SOC coveralls and coughing as if she was about to bring up a lung. DI Steel, their senior investigating officer. A five-foot-nine, wrinkly, middle-aged disaster area, smelling of stale cigarette smoke and Chanel Number Five. 'Laz!' she said, grinning as soon as she clapped eyes on Logan, 'This no' a bit fresh for one of your corpses? Thought you liked them a bit more ripe?'

Logan didn't rise to it. 'He was found outside A&E last night, bleeding to death. No witnesses. Something horrible's happened to his backside.'

'Oh aye?' The inspector raised an eyebrow. 'Medical horrible, or "I was hoovering naked and fell on a statue of Queen Victoria" horrible?'

'Queen Victoria.'

Steel nodded sagely. 'Yeah – I wondered why they gave me this one. We about ready to get started? I'm bursting for a fag.'

Doc Fraser looked up from his crossword, pulled the pen out of his gob and asked Steel the same question he'd asked Logan. The inspector cocked her head on one side, thought about it, frowned, then said, 'Buggered?'

'No, it's got an S in it. We're waiting for Dr MacAlister.'

DI Steel nodded again. 'Ah, it's going to be one of *those* post mortems.' She sighed. 'Come on then, Laz: let's hear it.' So Logan talked her through the statements he'd taken last night while the victim was in surgery, then the paperwork that had come down from the hospital with the body. 'What about the CCTV?' she asked when he'd finished.

'Nothing we can use. The car's number plates are unreadable – probably covered with something – driver wore a hooded top and baseball cap.'

'Ah, thug chic. Got a make on the car?'

'Fusty-looking Volvo estate.'

Steel blew a long, wet raspberry. 'So much for an easy case. Well, maybe Madame Death can tell us something, presuming she ever bloody gets here!' Ten minutes later and the inspector was threatening to start singing *Why Are We Waiting?*

Dr Isobel MacAlister finally lumbered into the morgue at twenty past ten, looking flushed. She ignored DI Steel's derogatory round of applause and cry of 'Thar she blows!' and scrubbed up, needing help to get into her cutting gear, the green plastic apron stretched tight over her enormous stomach.

'Right,' she said, clicking on the Dictaphone, 'we have an unidentified male – mid to late twenties . . .'

It was weird watching a heavily pregnant pathologist at work. Even weirder: the thing growing in her womb could have been Logan's, if things had turned out differently. But they hadn't. So instead of being filled with paternal pride, he was standing here watching Isobel slice up yet another dead body, feeling a strange mix of regret, and relief. And then nausea as she got her assistant to heft out the corpse's urogenital block for her.

They finished with tea and biscuits in the pathologists' office, with Isobel sitting behind the desk and complaining about the heat, even though February was putting on its usual performance outside the window, hurling icy rain against the glass.

'Looks like something pretty big's been repeatedly forced inside him,' she said, checking her notes, 'between four and five inches in diameter, and at least fourteen inches long. The sphincter's extensively damaged and the lower intestine was torn in four places. He lost too much blood, pressure dropped, heart stopped. Death was due to severe shock. There was nothing the hospital could have done.' She shifted in her seat, trying to get closer to the desk, but her pregnant bulge got in the way. 'Some of the burn marks on the torso have a crust of wax, but there's half a dozen cigarette burns too. Most of the contusions are superficial.'

DI Steel helped herself to a Jaffa Cake, mumbling, 'What about the ligature marks?' with her mouth full.

'Looks like thick leather straps with metal buckles. There's quite a bit of chafing about the edges, so I'd say he struggled a fair bit.'

Steel snorted, sending crumbs flying. 'Well, you would, wouldn't you? Someone turns your arse inside out.'

That got her a scowl and a chilly silence. 'I'll need to wait for the blood toxicology to come back,' Isobel said at last, 'but I found a significant quantity of alcohol in the stomach and partially digested pills as well.'

'So, whoever it was got him pissed and doped-up first, then strapped him down and buggered him to death with a Wellington boot. And they say romance is dead.'

Isobel's scowl got twenty degrees colder. 'Any other *startling* insights you'd like to share with us, Inspector?' Steel just grinned back at her and polished off another biscuit. Then the Procurator Fiscal confirmed that they'd be treating this case as murder, before telling them all about her upcoming holiday to the Seychelles. A substantive depute would be in charge while she was away soaking up the sun and cocktails, but they were to try not to break the girl, or there'd be trouble when she got back – looking pointedly at

DI Steel. The inspector pretended not to know what she was talking about.

'Bloody hell!' Steel said as they ran up the stairs from the morgue to the rear podium car park, sploshing through ankle-deep puddles, making for the back door to FHQ. 'Why can't they open the internal door when it's pishing with rain?' There was only one indoor route through from the main building to the morgue, but it was reserved for victims' relatives and the Chief Constable. The rank and file had to brave the weather.

She shook herself like a terrier, then ran a hand through her unruly hair, spraying water onto the linoleum. At forty-three she looked sixty-five – wrinkled, pointy face, saggy neck like a turkey, hair designed to startle old ladies, fingers stained a fetching shade of nicotine yellow. 'Come on,' she said, leading the way towards the lifts, 'you can get the teas in while I have a fag. And get some bacon butties too – I'm starving. Bastard post mortem went on for *ages*.'

Logan backed into DI Steel's office, balancing two mugs of tea and a couple of tinfoil parcels on a manila folder. The inspector was standing with her back to the door, staring out of the open window, a cigarette smouldering away between her fingers – completely ignoring the ban on smoking in the workplace – the bitter tang of Benson & Hedges curling out into the rain. 'You know,' she said, as

Logan eased the door closed and dished out the refreshments, 'oh, ta . . . sometimes it pisses me off that Fatty Insch gets all the big cases: all the high-profile stuff, like this serial rape thing.' She peeled open her tinfoil-wrapped buttie, eating and smoking and talking all at the same time. 'And then I see that shite and think, thank Christ.'

Logan joined her at the window. Down in the front car park there was a clump of outside-broadcast vans. A little knot of cameras and journalists were sheltering under umbrellas in the steady downpour, the occasional flash illuminating the concrete and granite like lightning. 'Rob Macintyre.'

'Aye: Robby Bobby "Goalden Boy" Macintyre. Could Insch no' find someone else to be his bloody rapist? Macintyre's a local sodding hero.' She took a huge bite, sending a cascade of white flour spilling down the front of her charcoal-grey suit. 'Tell you, it's a PR disaster waiting to happen. Little bugger's got his publicist working overtime making sure everyone stands up and tells the world what a great guy he is and how he'd never do anything naughty like rape seven women at knifepoint . . .' She sucked the last gasp from her cigarette and flicked it out into the downpour. Logan couldn't tell for sure, but it looked as if she was aiming for the man from Sky News. It was too far down to tell if she got him or not.

She took another bite and chewed thoughtfully. 'We get a nice, juicy murder and Insch gets a world of shite.' She shrugged. 'Still, rather him than us, eh?'

'I'm getting the media department to run off some "Do you know this man" posters for our body,' Logan said, 'and I got the report on his clothes back from Forensics.'

A long, silent pause. Then, 'Well, tell me what they said for God's sake, can you no' see I'm busy?' She settled back behind her cluttered desk, put her feet up, and lit another cigarette, blowing a long stream of smoke at the ceiling.

'Right.' Logan opened the manila folder and skimmed through it, making for the conclusions at the end. 'Blah, blah, blah, here we go: they think the blood in the clothes and blanket are all from the same person – blood type matches, but the mobile DNA thing's on the blink, so we've had to send samples off to Dundee to be sure. They're pretty certain it's all his though.'

'Genius.' She rolled her eyes. 'They tell us anything we *don't* already know?'

'They got fibres from the blanket he was wrapped in, so if we get a suspect they can run a match, but—'

'But bugger all that'll help us actually find out who he is.'

'Interesting thing is the list of clothing.' Logan handed over the report and the inspector pursed her lips, reading, then rereading it.

'Come on then, Miss Marple,' she said after the third time through, 'dazzle me with your brilliance.'

25

'Trousers, sweatshirt and blanket. No socks, no underwear, no jacket. No personal effects – no keys, no coins, not even an old hanky. He's been naked and someone's dressed him as quickly as possible, emptied his pockets, bundled him into the car and—'

'Oh for God's sake.' Steel threw the report back across the table at him. 'Of course he was bloody naked, you don't bondage someone up and bugger them to death fully dressed, do you?'

'Oh. Well, no, I suppose . . .'

She watched him squirm for a moment, then grinned. 'See, this is why they pay me the big bucks.'

'Anyway,' he could feel a blush creeping up his cheeks, 'the killer probably wrapped him in the blanket to keep blood off the car seats, but the thing was soaked through. The back seat will be saturated.'

'Which is no sodding good to us unless we find the car. Get the labs to see if they can do something with the number plate on that surveillance tape. And set up a briefing: couple of dozen uniform, some CID, you know the drill. And we'll need a HOLMES suite, and an incident room, and . . .' She frowned. 'Anything I've forgotten?'

Logan sighed – as usual he was going to be left doing all the work. 'Press release.'

'Bingo!' She beamed. 'Press release. And while you're at it, see if they can get us a slot on the news as well – we'll stick up the victim's face, you ask people to phone in, and I'll chat up that girl does the weather . . .' The inspector stared off into the distance for a happy moment, then snapped back into the here and now. 'I've got some calls to make.' She made wafting gestures, 'Go on, shoo, out, run along, go. Bugger off.'

Logan picked up his half-drunk cup of tea and left her to it.

4

Three twenty-nine pm – the car park round the back of Brimmond Hill. Alpha Nine Six scrunched to a halt between two huge waterlogged potholes, windscreen wipers going full-tilt in the rain. The top of the hill was lost in the low cloud, the gorse, heather and bracken battered and dripping. The driver pulled on the handbrake. 'What do you think?'

'Rock, paper, scissors?'

'OK . . . one, two three . . . shit.' Scowling out of the windscreen at the downpour. 'Best of three?'

'No.'

'OK, OK . . . bloody hell . . .' The driver cracked the door open, letting in the roar of the rain, drowning out the constant background chatter of the radio. He pulled on his waterproof jacket, turned the collar up, pulled his hat down low over his ears, and jumped out of the car, swearing as he ran across to the burnt-out wreck opposite, trying to avoid the puddles.

The patrol car window wound halfway down, and the PC in the passenger seat shouted, 'Well?'

Grumbling, the driver clicked his torch on and peered into the blackened shell. There wasn't much left: the skeletal remains of seats, their wire frames caked with lumps of grey and black ash; dashboard reduced to a buckled sheet of sagging metal; the tyres a slough of vitrified rubber. All the glass was gone. He ran the torch's beam round the inside, just in case. Anything in there was long gone. 'Nothing. Just a crappy old Volvo no one loves any more.'

Steel was back at her office window, peering out at the cluster of journalists and TV cameras far below when Logan returned from getting everything organized. 'Briefing's at four,' he said, slumping into the threadbare visitors' chair. 'You've got sixteen uniform, five CID and about eight admin. And I got the IB to take a good head-and-shoulders shot of the body with his eyes open, they're going to touch it up on the computer so he doesn't look so dead.' Logan yawned, but Steel didn't seem to notice, just sparked up another cigarette and went back to blowing smoke out into the rain. 'Press release will be ready about . . .' he checked his notes, 'five, but they don't think they can get you on the news tonight. Not with this Rob Macintyre thing going on.'

She nodded. 'No room on the box for two Aberdeen stories eh? Shame . . .' She sighed. 'I'd have loved to show that blonde weathergirl what a real wet front looks like . . . Still, the circus down there's getting geared up for something. Want to go watch? If we're lucky that grumpy, fat bastard Insch will punch someone.'

It was too damp for a real media frenzy, instead they all huddled under their umbrellas, pointing cameras, microphones and digital recorders at the FHQ car park as a black BMW pulled up and a smug-looking bastard climbed out into the rain and a barrage of questions. Sandy Moir-Farquharson, defence lawyer extraordinaire: tall, well-dressed, with greying hair, a slightly squint nose, and a junior to hold his brolly for him. Rob Macintyre got out of the back seat and bounced along beside him, grinning from ear to ear – despite the swollen lip Jackie had given him – in a very expensive-looking charcoal-grey suit, his trademark ruby earstud twinkling in the camera lights. It was a blatant rip-off of other, much more famous foot-ballers from the English leagues, only Macintyre's was red, Aberdeen Football Club's team colour. Finally a large, grey-haired woman emerged from the car wearing a triumphant, satisfied smile – the one who'd been shouting at Big Gary last night.

Standing beneath an umbrella purloined from the lost and found, Logan grimaced. 'This doesn't look good.'

DI Steel snorted, arms crossed, face screwed up

tight. 'Never does when Hissing Bloody Sid's involved.'

The lawyer raised his arms and the crowd of journalists fell quiet. 'I am delighted to say that the court has agreed to give my client Mr Macintyre the opportunity to challenge these ridiculous charges in a court of law.'

'Wonderful,' Steel dug in her pockets and came out with a packet of cigarettes, 'we're prosecuting the little sod, and he's making out it's all *their* idea!'

'Mr Macintyre's innocence,' said the lawyer, 'will be proved beyond a shadow of a doubt, and Grampian Police will be forced to put an end to their hateful campaign to ruin his reputation once and for all. We can only assume that someone up there,' he pointed at the looming black-and-white hulk of FHQ, '*really* doesn't want Aberdeen to win the Scottish Premier League!' That actually got a laugh. And then the questions started, all of them fielded by Sandy Moir-Farquharson before his client could open his mouth: 'Will you be playing this Saturday against Falkirk?' 'What does your fiancée say about all this?' 'Is it true you've been offered a place with Manchester United?' Only one journalist asked about this not being the first time Macintyre had been accused of rape, but Sandy ignored her, answering a much more cuddly question about Macintyre's upcoming marriage instead. The only person who seemed to have noticed was Macintyre's mum, who spent the rest of the conference scowling furiously at the woman who'd dared to bring up her son's past.

The lawyer took a couple more questions, then led a smiling Macintyre – and his mum – back to the waiting BMW. They disappeared in a flurry of flash photography. DI Steel took a long sniff, then spat out into the rain. 'Slimy wee shite. And we thought Insch was in a bad mood before. He'll be fucking apoplectic now.' She set a lighter to her cigarette, the smoke getting trapped inside the brolly. 'Speak of the devil . . .'

Insch strode down Queen Street, coming back from the Sheriff Court, face set in an ugly line, his huge, fat body barely shielded from the rain by a massive golf umbrella. Someone stepped out in front of him – thin, bearded, glasses, looking furious – and the inspector paused, then grabbed the man by the arm and steered him in through the main doors to FHQ. Logan caught, 'It's him isn't it? Why the hell are you letting him go? What's wrong with you people—' before the doors shut.

Steel stayed outside to finish her fag while Logan hurried in out of the rain to make sure everything was ready for the briefing, keeping his head down as he passed Insch and the angry man, not wanting to get involved. Ignoring the inspector as he promised to put Macintyre away for a long, long time.

Four o'clock and the briefing room was full of men and women in uniform, a handful of detective constables in suits, and an overweight detective sergeant eating cheese and onion crisps. There was still no sign of DI Steel so Logan did the roll call. Then the introduction. Then the background. He was just launching into the CCTV footage when she turned up with the Assistant Chief Constable in tow. Trying not to look as pissed off as he felt, Logan got one of the CID blokes to turn off the lights. 'Right,' he said, pressing play as Steel and the ACC found seats, 'this was taken at twelve minutes past ten last night.'

The large screen behind his head flickered and the entrance to Accident and Emergency appeared. An ambulance sat in front of the doors, lights off and nobody home. Then a ratty old Volvo estate shuddered to a halt, half mounting the kerb, the driver an indistinct blob behind the steering wheel. The blob unclipped its seatbelt, wrenched the door open and leapt out of the car. Logan hit pause and everything stopped. 'Blue jeans, black trainers, grey hooded top, dark green baseball cap.' The face was invisible, hidden in the cap's shadow.

'The car's number plate's been purposely obscured – probably with electrical tape – so all we have is make and model. I've put out a lookout request for a blue or green Volvo estate: the details are in your briefing packs.' He paused and looked around the room, trying to make eye-contact with as many people as possible. 'The backseat's soaked in blood, so the killer will either try to hide the vehicle, or get rid of it. We need to find it first!'

He pressed play again and the hooded figure sprinted round the front of the Volvo, opened the rear passenger door, and dragged the dying man from the back seat. Then jumped back into the car and got the hell out of there.

'This,' said Logan as the picture became a fuzz of static and white lines, 'is the camera at the security barriers . . .' The screen settled into a shot of a bright orange booth with a uniformed old man in it, reading a newspaper. He looked up, smiled and waved as the Volvo slowed down. The driver wound down his or her window and slipped the ticket into the machine. A brief pause, the barrier slid up, the Volvo drove off, and the guard went back to his paper.

'So we have a witness. If you turn to the back of your pack, you'll find an e-fit.' Logan switched off the video and clicked on the projector. Behind him a computer-generated identikit picture sprang onto the screen: round face, big moustache, glasses and a neatly trimmed goatee. 'According to our security guard the suspect has an Irish accent—' A uniformed constable stuck up her hand. 'Yes?'

'Northern or southern Irish?'

'He says it was like that thick priest on *Father Ted*, so southern. Our suspect was calm enough to exchange a few words about the weather, even though he's just dumped someone who's bleeding to death outside A&E.'

Logan hit the button and the e-fit disappeared, replaced with a post mortem photo of the dead man's face. 'This is our victim. And this is what the killer did to him . . .' Click – and everyone in the room squirmed.

Logan worked his way to the end of the briefing, finishing up with everyone's teams and assignments, then DI Steel creaked to her feet and told them all the Assistant Chief Constable wanted a word. 'Now then,' said the ACC, going for a friendly smile, 'as you know, the health of our officers is of primary importance to us all . . .'

When at long last everyone was gone, Steel slumped into a chair at the front of the room, head back, groaning at the flickering fluorescent lights. 'God, that man's hard work.'

'I had to start without you.'

Steel nodded. 'I saw. Well done you. Top of the class. I would've been on time, but the rotten sod was hanging about outside the women's toilets. Pervert. Had to tell him what we were up to.' She worked a hand under her jacket and fiddled about in her armpit. 'Concerned about the health of their officers . . . If they think I'm going to take part in their stupid "Fit Like" programme they can kiss my sharny arse!'

Logan finished tidying up. 'Where do you want to start?'

Steel checked her watch, thought about it, then said, 'A large white wine. And some chips. And some fags. Nearly knocking off time.'

'But—'

'Look, the papers will run the victim's photo

and the killer's e-fit tomorrow. All the dentists' surgeries will be closed by now so we can't start searching dental records. We're *no'* going to get an ID tonight. The only thing left to do is get the incident room set up, and the admin officer can do that. You and me are going for a pint.'

'But—'

'That's an order, Sergeant.'

'Yes, ma'am.'

Archibald Simpson's used to be a bank before it became a pub. A huge granite edifice on the east end of Union Street, complete with Corinthian pillars, portico, ornate ceiling, shiny brass fittings, chandeliers, and cheap beer. Being just round the corner from FHQ it was the standard police drinking hole after a hard day's sodding about in the rain.

Steel made Logan get the first round in, taking her usual seat in the aisle just off the main banking floor, in the corner, under the television. One large white wine, two portions of chips, and a pint of Stella. What he really wanted was to go home and get some sleep, but if he did that the inspector would sulk and he'd end up lumbered with all the crappy jobs on the investigation. So he stayed and talked shop, listening to her moan on about her other cases, like the dead tramp they'd found in Duthie Park – natural causes, but no one knew who the hell he was – and the series of housebreakings in Tillydrone, Bridge of Don, and

Rosemount. And the man flashing his undercarriage on Guild Street. By the time the chips arrived she was moaning about her girlfriend Susan and how she was always on at her to get a cat, but Steel knew it was just the warm-up act for a baby and she wasn't ready for that kind of commitment.

They got more drinks and the day-shift started squelching in, the pub slowly filling up with off-duty police men and women. Logan knew most of them by name – well, except for some of the younger ones – but he'd only ever seen one of them naked: PC Jackie Watson, marching towards them, bearing beer, a scowl, and tomato sauce flavour crisps.

She plonked herself down next to Logan and offered the crisps round. 'Jesus, what a shitty day.'

'And hello to you too.' Logan grinned at her: the effects of two pints on a nearly empty stomach. 'We saw Hissing Sid outside the courthouse.'

Jackie scowled. 'Little bastard. How come every bloody case he's involved in has to have a press conference on the steps outside FHQ? You know *anyone* else who does that?'

Logan shrugged. 'He's a media whore.'

'Aye,' said Steel, polishing off her drink, 'he's a whore, but we're the ones getting screwed the whole time. Anyone for another?' She took their orders and stomped off to the bar, leaving Logan and Jackie alone.

'Can you believe he had the cheek to say I

assaulted his rapist bastard client while he was cuffed and on the ground?' Jackie scowled. 'And get this – they're saying he was only out jogging. He approached me to "ask directions".' She even made little sarcastic quote-bunnies with her fingers. 'With a knife. Can you believe that?'

Logan knew better than to say anything, just sat there and nodded. Letting her rant. 'And the bloody media! According to them he's already been found innocent! Bastards. And the bloody search team couldn't find their arses with both hands and a map. All through Macintyre's house and not one bloody trophy. No knickers, no jewellery, nothing. Not a bloody thing!' There was more, but Logan gradually tuned it out. Jackie just needed to let off a bit of steam: get it out of her system.

Jackie was still going strong when DI Steel wobbled back to the table with a handful of glasses. The inspector clinked them down on the tabletop, with an apologetic, 'I forgot what everyone wanted, so I got whiskies.'

And slowly, but surely, they all got very, very drunk.

5

Wednesday morning's half-seven briefing was a lot more painful than Tuesday's, but at least this time Logan got to slouch in a seat at the back of the class, while DI Steel grumbled her hungover way through the day's assignments, finishing off with a subdued chorus of, 'We are not at home to Mr Fuck-Up!' The whole team joined in, trying to make Logan's head split in two.

Three cups of coffee later and he was beginning to feel slightly less terminal, even if he was bored out of his pounding skull. The incident room was busy, everyone still all excited and determined to get a quick result, the walls lined with maps and pin-boards and post mortem photographs. The local papers had been full of speculation about Rob Macintyre, but Steel's unknown body had still managed to make the front page of the P&J. They'd printed the touched-up morgue photo, the killer's e-fit, and a story that somehow managed to make it all sound like Grampian Police's fault.

Which wasn't surprising, considering who wrote it: Colin Miller, the *Press and Journal*'s star reporter. He certainly knew how to hold a grudge.

Sighing, Logan folded the paper and dumped it in the bin. So far the response had been lacklustre, only about a dozen people had phoned in claiming to know who the dead man was. No one had recognized the killer yet. But all that would change as soon as the press conference went out on the lunchtime news; then they'd be swamped. Televised appeals always brought the nutters out in droves. Still, you never knew . . .

'Hoy, Laz.'

Logan looked up to see a thin man in a sergeant's uniform and huge Wyatt Earp moustache. Sergeant Eric Mitchell, peering over the top of his glasses and grinning like an idiot. 'Your "lady friend" about?'

Logan frowned, suspicious. 'Which one?'

'Watson, you daft sod. Is she about?'

'Back shift, won't be in till two.'

'Aye, well you might want to tell her to call in sick . . .' he tossed a rolled-up copy of the *Daily Mail* onto Logan's lap, winked, then sauntered off. Whistling happily to himself.

But before Logan could ask what was going on, DI Steel plonked a pile of files on the table in front of him. 'This bloody thing's killing me,' she said, fiddling with her bra strap. 'Get a couple of uniforms to go through these, OK? See if we can't find someone on the dodgy bastards list who matches that e-fit. Then you can go chase up that dental records lot.' She gave up on the strap and started hauling at the underwire. 'And while you're at it—'

'Actually,' said Logan, cutting her off, 'I thought I might go out and follow up a couple of those possible IDs for our victim. You know: show willing for the troops.' Which had the added advantage of getting him away from the inspector before she could think up any more crappy jobs for him to do.

Steel thought about it, head on one side, focusing on a spot between Logan's ears, as if she was trying to read his brain. 'OK,' she said at last, 'but you can take . . .' she did a slow turn, pointing at a constable in the corner, scribbling something up on the incident board, 'yeah, take Rickards with you. Do the poor wee sod good to see the outside world. Might stop the short-arsed bastard whining for a change. He's—'

'Inspector?' It was the admin officer, waving some more paperwork at them.

'Oh God,' Steel groaned and then whispered to Logan, 'cover for me, will you? I'm dying for a fag.' She turned and told the admin officer she had an urgent meeting with the ACC to get to, but DS McRae would deal with whatever it was. Then made herself scarce.

With a sigh, Logan accepted the sheets of paper.

He signed for a CID pool car – one of the many scabrous Vauxhalls in the FHQ fleet – and made

41

Constable Rickards drive, so he could slump in the passenger seat and doze. At least he was starting to feel a little better now. After the whisky they'd gone onto vodka, then some weird little bloke had tried to chat Jackie up, and they'd all had a good laugh at him, and then it was more beer, tequila, and then . . . it was kind of blurry until they were standing outside the kebab shop on Belmont Street. And when they finally got home, Jackie had fallen asleep in the toilet.

Logan ran a hand over his face, stifling a yawn – he was getting too old for this . . .

Yesterday's rain had gone, leaving the city sparkling clean. Everything glowed in the light of an unseasonably warm February sun, glinting back from chips of mica trapped in the pale grey granite. Rickards drove them down Union Street, heading for a small semi-detached in Kincorth – a blob of houses on the south-side of the city – and an old woman who claimed to know the dead man from the papers.

'So,' said Logan, as the PC swung the car across the King George IV bridge, the water sparkling like sharpened diamonds on either side, 'you were in on that big brothel raid in Kingswells last week?'

Rickards mumbled something about a team effort.

'Kinky dungeon, wasn't it?' said Logan, watching a pair of seagulls fighting over an abandoned crisp packet. 'Whips and chains and nipple-clamps and all that?'

'Ah . . . er . . . yes . . . it . . . erm . . .' Rickards blushed, the twisted line of scar tissue that snaked up the middle of his top lip standing out white against red, as if someone had tried to give him a hair lip with a broken bottle. Logan smiled – it looked as if the constable wasn't exactly a man of the world. He resisted the urge to take the piss, and went back to watching the world go by.

The old lady's house was three-quarters of the way down Abbotswell Crescent, with a view out across the dual carriageway, over the Craigshaw and Tullos industrial estates. Lovely. Especially with Torry in the background, the sunshine and blue skies fighting a losing battle to make it look attractive.

Fifteen minutes, two cups of tea and some Penguin biscuits later, they were back in the car.

'So much for that.' Logan called DI Steel with the bad news, only to be given another two addresses: one in Mannofield, the other in Mastrick. Both of which were equally useless.

Rickards squirmed in his seat, as if his underwear was trying to eat him. 'So what now?'

Logan checked his watch: coming up for eleven. 'Back to the station. We can—' His mobile phone went into its usual apoplexy of bleeps and whistles. 'Hold on.' He dragged it out. 'Hello?'

'Where the hell are you?' DI Steel, sounding annoyed.

'Mastrick. You sent us here, remember?'

'Did I? Oh . . . Well . . . in that case, why haven't you finished yet?'

'We have. We're just heading back now.'

'Good – press conference is at twelve. We're going to be on the lunchtime news. And when I say 'we' I mean you too. Don't be late. And you can check out another address on your way in – woman phoned to say the dead guy lives next door with his parents. And remember: if you're no' back here by twelve, I'll kill you.'

Logan took down the address and hung up with a groan. 'Change of plan – we've got one more stop to make.'

Blackburn was more like a building site than a dormitory town: sprawling developments of tiny detached houses crammed into minuscule plots of land, spilling away to the north and west, costing an arm and a leg, even though it meant living like a battery chicken. The address Steel had given them was for the second-last house in a half-completed cul-de-sac that didn't even have a proper road yet, just a thin layer of rutted tarmac covered in drying mud and potholes, the rumble of earthmovers battling for supremacy against the screech of circular saws and the bang of nailguns. Everything was slowly disappearing beneath a pale cloud of cream-coloured dust.

Number seven was a four-bedroom 'executive villa' built on a postage stamp. Logan got Rickards to ring the doorbell while he stared out over the rolling hills to the north. Wondering how long it would take the developers to carpet them in more houses.

The door was answered by a flushed-looking woman in baggy T-shirt and jogging bottoms, balancing a small child on one hip. 'Hello?' Sounding slightly nervous.

Logan went for a reassuring smile as the woman's kid stared at him with open mouth and wide blue eyes. 'Mrs . . . ' he checked his notes, 'Brown? Hi. You phoned us this morning about this man?' Logan held up the photo.

She nodded. 'I *think* so. He sort of looks like the guy next door's son. Jason I think it is.' The toddler wriggled and she shifted him, bringing him round till he was sitting in the crook of her arm, clutching her hair and peering out at the policemen on the doorstep. 'He's looking after the house while they're on holiday.'

'You're sure it's him?' Logan handed her the picture and she bit her bottom lip.

'I . . . It looks a lot like him . . .' Nervous giggle. 'I asked Paul and he said it might be . . .'

'When did you last see Jason?'

She shrugged. 'It's been kind of hectic. Couple of days?'

'OK.' Logan took the photo back and the child began to squeal. 'What's Jason's last name?' Having to speak up over the noise.

'Sorry: we only moved in three weeks ago, everything's still in boxes.' She bounced the child up and down, making cooing, 'Who's Mummy's big boy?' noises. 'Maybe the site office would know?'

'Thanks for your help.'

Logan and Rickards went next door, tried the bell, peered in through the front window – a pristine living room with tasteful furnishings and paintings on the wall – then walked round the house. The back yard was a morass of mud flecked with grass seed, a solitary whirly standing in the middle like a marooned antenna, the yellow plastic cable sagging and empty. There was nothing in the garage either, just a dark black splot of leaked motor oil.

Rickards walked back to the unfinished road, staring up at the house's empty windows. 'What do you think?'

'Much the same as every other sighting we've had today – bloody useless.' Logan climbed back into the car and checked the time. 'Jesus, it's twenty to twelve! Come on, we'd better get a shift on: Steel will kill us if we're late.'

6

They made it back to the station by the skin of their teeth. The room was already filling up: television cameras, journalists, and photographers staking out their territory among the rows of folding chairs, all eyes focused on the raised stage and table at the front. 'Thought you was never going to turn up!'

Logan turned to find DI Steel standing directly behind him, fiddling with a packet of cigarettes, turning them round and round in her hands, like nicotine prayer beads. 'You get anything from those addresses?'

'Nothing.'

'Bugger.' The cigarette packet got a few more twists.

'Problem?'

Steel shrugged, looked over her shoulder, then back at the gathering mass of reporters. 'Just could do with a swift result on this one. We're keeping a lid on the cause of death, but you know what this place is like: sooner or later, someone's going to say something stupid.' She paused and sneaked a glance at Logan. 'Course, you know all about that.'

'And what's *that* supposed to mean?'

'Nothing, nothing.' She backed off, grinning. 'Who cares what the *Daily Mail* says anyway? Shite, there's the ACC . . . ' Logan watched her go, wondering what on earth she was talking about.

The briefing started at twelve o'clock prompt, and as the ACC launched into his 'thank you all for coming' speech, Logan let his attention wander. He wouldn't be needed until they threw the thing open to questions and probably not even then. So instead he scanned the assembled journalistic horde, looking to see if he recognized anyone. Colin Miller was sitting in the third row, face like a wet fart, mumbling into a small digital recorder. Probably getting ready to give Grampian Police another kicking in tomorrow's P&J. There were a couple of others Logan knew from previous conferences, and some he recognized from the telly, but his eyes kept going back to Miller, his surly expression, and his black leather gloves. Not exactly playing the happy expectant father. The reporter looked up from his Dictaphone and saw Logan watching him. He scowled back, obviously still blaming Logan for the loss of his fingers, as if *he'd* been the one wielding the poultry shears . . .

The ACC threw the conference open to questions and the moment was gone.

*   *   *

As soon as they were finished, Logan hurried down to the incident room. Steel was the second person to make cryptic comments about the *Daily Mail* and Logan wanted to know why. The copy Eric had thrown at him was still sitting where he'd left it, so Logan skimmed quickly through the paper, looking for DS Logan McRae Screws Up Again! but not finding it. What he did find was a centre-page spread titled, Police Hound Aberdeen Striker! with a big photo of Rob Macintyre's ugly face and an article charting his meteoric rise to fame; describing Grampian Police's investigation as part of 'an ongoing campaign to cripple Aberdeen Football Club's only chance of winning the Scottish Premier League'.

'Macintyre (21)', the paper said, 'was an obvious target for desperate women: young, successful, wealthy, and going all the way to the top!' But that wasn't the bit DI Steel and Sergeant Eric Mitchell had been dropping hints about.

It was a pull-out quote, big white letters on a bright red background: Of Course He's B****y Guilty – The Little S*** Attacked Me! attributed to PC Jackie Watson (28) with a couple more choice sentences further on in the article about how 'little b******s like him should be banged up for life'. Logan groaned. No wonder Eric said Jackie should call in sick – she was in for one hell of a bollocking when she reported for duty. He glanced up at the clock on the wall. Which would be in about fifteen minutes. 'Crap!'

He dialled the flat, hoping to God she hadn't left for work yet. She hadn't.

Jackie picked up the phone with an angry, *'What?'*

Too late. 'You've seen the paper then?'

'I've seen the lounge! We're living in a bombsite!'

'Oh God . . . Look, do you remember talking to a journalist?'

'What? I've got to get ready for—'

'It's in the *Daily Mail*: "Of course he's bloody guilty – the little shite attacked me". Sound familiar?'

There was a moment's silence from the other end of the phone and then the swearing started. Lots and lots of swearing. *'Bastard never said he was a journalist!'*

'Who?'

'That greasy little fuck in the pub last night – remember? I told you he bought me a drink, was all "oh, I saw you on the telly", and "what a great job you policewomen do" and "can I have your phone number?" Bastard!'

'You know what's going to happen, don't you?'

'Count Bloody Dracula.'

'Eric thinks you should call in sick.'

Jackie laughed. Short and hollow. *'Fat lot of good putting it off will do . . .'*

'No, I suppose not.'

'So what we got?' DI Steel loomed over Logan's shoulder, peering down at the report in his hands, her breath reeking of stale cigarettes and extra-strong mints.

Logan sighed and started ticking things off on his fingers: 'Sixty callers say they know who our victim is, but none of them agree. We've got seven teams of two going through them. As for the suspect, there's five men on the sex offenders' list who look like the e-fit: two rapists, one paedophile, a flasher, and guy who sexually assaulted a priest.'

'Yeah?' Steel smiled, 'Makes a change from them molesting choirboys I suppose.'

'Don't think any of them are likely though: flashers are all mouth and no trousers; the victim was too old to be of interest to a paedophile; both rapists only attacked women; and the priest fiddler's just come out of Peterhead, so he's under a supervisory order. According to his handlers he was locked up in his hostel when our guy was dumping his victim outside A&E.'

She stared off into the middle distance for a bit, then said, 'Better interview them all anyway. Even the priestophile. If nothing else it'll look like we're doing something.' Steel lowered her voice to a whisper. 'You heard from Watson yet?'

'No.' As soon as Jackie signed in she'd been escorted straight up to Professional Standards.

'Shame you can't get that Weegie journo of yours to cover for her.' But the days of Colin Miller doing favours for Logan were long gone.

'So, you want me to get those guys picked up?'

Another thoughtful pause, then, 'No. Let's go

see them. If I'm no' in the office this mornin' I can't have my medical for that stupid "Fit Like" programme.' She twirled her cigarettes in her hand. 'Put it off for long enough and they might forget all about me.'

It took the inspector fifteen minutes before she was fed up with the first rapist. And only seven before she leaned over and whispered, 'How about we accidentally kick the shite out of him?' at the second's house. And the flasher wasn't up to much, not after DI Steel shouted, 'Let's see it, then!' as soon as they'd been let in through the front door. Iain Watt was probably taller than he looked, standing hunched into himself, thinning brown hair, cardigan, overweight, mid thirties. The archetypal Mr Nobody, living in a big empty house on Don Street that overlooked the main route students took between the halls of residence and Aberdeen University. As Steel stood at the lounge window, a handful of young women sashayed past, laughing and joking, all long hair and unexplored curves. Logan could have sworn he heard her groan.

'So, how's it work?' she asked, when the students finally disappeared round the corner, 'you see them coming, nip out and flash them a glimpse of your "turgid member"? That it?'

'I . . .' Watt wouldn't meet her eyes, just kept staring at the spotless sheepskin rug in the middle of the room, 'I've had counselling . . . I'm on pills.'

'Yeah? Can't get it up any more, eh?' She drew the curtains, plunging the room into darkness, leaving just a sliver of light that fell across Watt's bald spot. 'If I hear so much as a rumour about someone showing their willy off down here, you're not going to need pills. I'm going to permanently fix you with the toe of my boot. Understand?'

He blushed, head still down. 'I haven't . . . I haven't felt the need. I had counselling.'

'Yeah, you said.' She stood in silence for a moment. 'So why did you do it then?'

Logan could see the beads of sweat starting to form on the man's forehead. The silence drew out and the beads joined up, trickling down the side of Watt's face. 'I . . .' He cleared his throat. 'I don't know what you're talking about.'

'We know.' The inspector's voice was soft, almost sorrowful.

'I . . .' His eyes darted towards the door, then back to the sheepskin. 'But, I . . .'

'Come on, don't make me do this the hard way.'

He buried his head in his hands and started to cry. 'I didn't mean to!'

Logan threw Steel a questioning look, but she just shrugged. Whatever the guy was confessing to was news to her. 'Why don't you tell us all about it, Iain?' asked Logan, 'You'll feel better if you can tell someone.'

Slowly, Watt stood, biting his bottom lip, tears and snot dribbling down his face, mixing with the sweat. His round shoulders shivered as he led them through into the kitchen, snivelling, 'I didn't mean to, I didn't . . .' over and over again. And Logan began to seriously worry about whatever it was Watt had done.

The hunched man reached for a kitchen drawer, but Logan got there first, clamping his hand down over Watt's. Just in case it was full of knives. 'Tell you what,' he said, keeping his voice low and calm, 'why don't you let me get that for you? You just stand back . . . Good.' Logan pulled a pair of latex gloves from his jacket pocket and snapped them on, before easing the drawer open. Inside was a flashlight, a packet of AAA batteries and a pair of blood-soaked women's underwear. The kind Laura Shand was supposed to have been wearing when Rob Macintyre raped her. The kind Macintyre was supposed to have taken as a trophy.

DI Steel said what they both were thinking: 'Oh fuck.'

7

The car park was in shadow, the February sun hidden behind the grey and black bulk of FHQ. Dark and cold. 'This is going to be a nightmare,' said Steel, when Logan came out to tell her Watt was processed and ready for interview. She sighed, letting loose a pall of cigarette smoke. 'Tell you, Insch is going to blow a fucking gasket . . . Still,' she straightened up and flicked the last inch of her fag under the Chief Constable's BMW, 'no' really our problem right now.' She sniffed thoughtfully, then told Logan to go dig up everything they had on Laura Shand: interview transcripts, medical reports, the lot. She wanted to read up on Watt's victim before they interviewed him.

Which was why Logan ended up outside DI Insch's incident room. According to the records department, the inspector had the files signed out – working on the prosecution case and trying to pin everything on Rob Macintyre. Taking a deep breath, Logan marched in.

It was one of the biggest incident rooms in the place, but it was virtually empty, just a couple of admin officers packing the remnants of Operation Sweetmeat away into brown cardboard filing boxes, clearing the place out for the next major enquiry. And there, perched on the edge of a groaning desk, was DI Insch. He was massive: a big fat man with a shiny bald head and hands the size of shovels, his suit stretched to bursting point. He looked like an angry pink caterpillar about to outgrow its skin, as he shovelled chocolate-covered raisins into his mouth.

Logan cleared his throat and said, 'Excuse me, sir, I need to borrow the Laura Shand file.'

Insch stopped chewing and swung a baleful eye in Logan's direction. 'Oh aye?' his voice a deep, bass growl, '*Why?*'

Oh God, here we go . . .'Er, we've arrested someone who claims to have attacked her.' Logan added a 'sir,' for good measure.

The inspector levered himself off the desk and scowled. 'Don't be stupid, Macintyre attacked her.'

'Yes, well . . .' Think fast! 'This guy's probably lying; we just need to make sure. You know, to prove he had nothing to do with it . . . which he can't have if it was Macintyre . . .' Starting to ramble. 'So, if I could just have the file, sir, I'll get out of your . . .' DON'T SAY HAIR! 'Way.'

'Who is it?'

Logan could feel his fixed grin starting to slip. 'Iain Watt, he's just a flasher. It's probably nothing

. . .' He watched as DI Insch's eyes contracted to little black coals in his angry, piggy face.

'It better be.' But he handed the file over anyway.

Somehow Logan got the feeling it would be pushing his luck to ask if the inspector knew what Professional Standards had done to Jackie.

Six thirty-eight and interview room number five smelt of fear and stale sweat. Iain Watt sat on the other side of the scarred table, his white SOC suit making scrunching noises every time he moved. He fidgeted and fiddled while he told Logan and DI Steel about his time in therapy and how Dr Goulding thought he'd been making excellent progress . . . Not looking at the clear plastic evidence pouch sitting on the table in front of him. The one with Laura Shand's knickers in it: pink with grey pigs, stained with dark brown dried blood.

'If you're making such bloody good progress, how come you had these in your kitchen drawer?' asked Steel, poking the evidence bag.

'I . . .' Watt hung his head. 'I used to see her walking sometimes. In Seaton Park . . . I . . .' He cleared his throat. 'Can I have a glass of water?'

'No. Now tell us about her.'

Silence.

Then, 'I thought about it for ages . . .'

More silence.

'I'll bet you bloody did.'

'No! Dr Goulding's been telling me how I have to make contact with women, try to forge a meaningful relationship. Change the way I think about them. Not just . . . you know . . .' He took a deep shuddering breath. 'I just wanted to say hello to her. That's all. Just "hello", maybe, "nice day, isn't it?" and maybe she'd say hello back and it would be nice and we'd be having a conversation and it would be all right and . . .' Watt's eyes slid across the blood-spattered material. He licked his lips. 'And I thought about it for weeks. How Dr Goulding said I had to make the first move. And I practised in front of the mirror and it was all perfect . . .'

Another pause, broken only by the metallic whirr of the tapes going round in the recording unit – audio and video, immortalizing the moment for posterity. Logan leaned forward in his seat. 'But it didn't go to plan, did it, Iain?'

Watt shook his head. 'I said, "hello, nice day isn't it?" and she didn't say anything. She just kept walking. Like I wasn't even there . . .'

Steel sighed. 'So you attacked her.'

'No! No, I thought maybe she misheard. Maybe I had my fly down by accident, you know? Accidentally?' He looked from Steel to Logan, searching for understanding. 'But, but I hadn't . . . she didn't like me. She didn't want to talk to me. I'd reached out, just like Dr Goulding said I should . . .'

Steel tried again. 'So *then* you attacked her.'

'No. I went home and had beans on toast. Then I read the paper. And they were saying about this guy who goes after women with a knife and how he . . . how he has *sex* with them. Sex . . . And I thought . . . I . . . I went out and waited for her . . . She wouldn't even say hello . . .'

'Shite. Could he no' have just been making it up?' DI Steel stood, smoking by the open window in her office. Outside, the sun was setting: gilding the granite spines of Marischal College with sparkling light, deep blue shadows creeping in around the edges, ready to smother it all.

'I've called Laura Shand,' said Logan, from the other side of the desk. 'She's going to come in and make a formal ID.' He tried to look nonchalant. 'Are you going to tell DI Insch?'

'What, that we've buggered his case?' Steel sighed, then examined the glowing tip of her cigarette. 'I should probably give these things up. Then again . . .' she took a long, deep drag. 'Fuck it.' She pulled out her mobile and fiddled with the buttons, before holding it to her ear. 'Insch? . . . Yeah, it's me Steel . . . Uh huh, I told him to get the files . . . Uh huh . . . No. Watt's copped for it. Macintyre didn't rape Laura . . . Hello? Insch?' She pursed her lips and blew a kiss at her phone, before switching the thing off and sticking it back in her pocket. 'He hung up.'

'Oh . . .' Logan could see what was coming, and didn't want to be anywhere near when it did. 'Er, Inspector, if you don't need me, I think I'd better—' A loud bang from somewhere down the corridor outside Steel's office, like someone slamming a door. 'You know,' he stood, inching his way towards the exit, 'I should go get an ID book made up and—' Too late.

The door burst open: DI Insch, looking very, very angry, his face swollen and red. He poked a fat finger at DI Steel. 'What the hell do you think you're playing at!'

She sighed, took one last puff on her cigarette and threw it out of the window. 'My job, OK? I don't like it any more than—'

'You had no right interviewing—'

'Watt confessed. His story matches Laura Shand's—'

'HE'S LYING!' Little white flecks of spit flew in the evening light.

'Oh grow the fuck up.' Steel slumped into her tatty office chair. 'And close the bloody door: you want the rest of the station to hear you acting like an arsehole?'

It took an obvious effort, but DI Insch, still scarlet and trembling with rage, stepped into the small office and closed the door behind him. Trapping Logan inside. 'Did it *ever* occur to you,' said Insch, through gritted teeth, 'that your flasher's just confessing for the attention! He's an exhibitionist, remember?'

'Then how come everything matches? Eh?' Steel leant forward and waved Laura Shand's file at him. 'Not just one or two things, *everything*! He had her bloody panties in a kitchen drawer!'

'Oh, really? Well that's *convenient*, isn't it? You get an arrest and my whole case gets screwed. You cast doubt on Laura Shand's rape and—'

'We didn't do it on sodding purpose! I was just fishing – trying out the old "we know you've been naughty" bit – and he fell for it. Could have been anything, flashing, stolen radios—'

'The Shand MO was identical!'

Steel threw her hands in the air. 'He read about it in the papers: man plus knife plus woman equals sex.' Emphasizing each and every word: 'He – had – her – knickers – in – his – kitchen! He raped her!'

'He . . .' Insch scowled. 'He must have seen it happen. He watched Macintyre rape her, and then he took the knickers. Something to remind himself—'

'Give it up.' Steel sighed and ran a tired hand across her wrinkly face. Pulling it out of shape. 'For Christ's sake: Macintyre might have raped the others, but he didn't do Laura.'

'But—'

'NO! Get it through your thick head: he didn't do this one!'

Insch loomed over her desk, voice low and menacing. 'Who the hell do you think you're talking to?'

'You!' Steel shoved her chair back and stood, leaning in close until her nose was inches from Insch's. 'You've been a right miserable cunt for months now! Whatever's eating your fat arse *it's not my bloody fault!* So stop taking it out on the rest of us! Watt raped Laura Shand – END OF STORY!'

Insch actually went dark purple for a moment, then turned on his heel and stormed off, slamming the door behind him hard enough to make Logan's fillings vibrate.

FHQ was eerily silent in the wake of Insch's storming out. There was barely a whisper as Logan left DI Steel's office and wandered back to his little cubicle in the CID room. It took him nearly twenty minutes to check his email and make up an identification book for Laura Shand to look at when she came in – Iain Watt's face hidden amongst pictures of eleven others from the Scottish Criminal Records Office database. It was a formality more than anything else: with Watt's confession and the forensic evidence, he'd be on the first bus back to Peterhead Prison, whether she could identify him or not.

And then Logan really couldn't put it off any longer: he called the front desk and asked Big Gary where Jackie was.

'*No idea.*' Was the reply. '*She went to Professional Standards first thing, but they can't have fired or suspended her, or they'd've had me in there as her Federation rep.*' There was a faint slurping sound, as if Gary was in the middle of a mug of tea. '*Probably just a smack on the wrists.*'

'Yeah . . . thanks Gary.' Logan hung up and tried her mobile: it rang and rang, then beeped over to voicemail. There was no point asking Professional Standards – they wouldn't tell him anything – so he went for a walk instead, wandering the corridors and asking if anyone had seen PC Watson.

He found her in the basement records room, where the old files went to die, sorting through the ancient unsolved investigations and swearing under her breath – a constant, violent monologue about what would happen if she ever got her hands on that bastard from the *Daily Mail*. She dumped a dusty box onto the concrete floor and yanked the lid off, glaring at the contents.

Logan closed the door behind him and wandered over. 'Hey you.' She looked up, still glaring and he backed off a couple of paces, hands up in surrender. 'Whoa, whatever it is, I'm sorry!'

Jackie went back to scowling at the open box. 'Can you believe this shite?' She hauled out an ancient bundle of files held together by an elastic band so old it was beginning to flake away in brittle brown shards. 'Half these bloody things don't even match the sodding inventory. Lazy bastards . . .'

'You OK?'

She shrugged and started scribbling down a list of the contents into a large notebook. 'I mean, look at it. Not like it's hard to keep track of what's in a bloody box, is it?'

'Jackie?'

'I mean, some of this stuff goes back thirty, forty years! Why the hell couldn't they do it properly in the first place?' Throwing the pile of files back in the box, the vitrified rubber band shattering into a thousand pieces. 'Fucking thing!'

'Jackie. It's OK.'

'Get the prehistoric bastards out of retirement and make them come down here and inventory their own bloody case files.' She dragged another bundle out and began scribbling in her notebook again. 'Should have solved them in the first place! Who cares about some daft sod getting beaten up twenty years ago – it's not like we're going to catch whoever did it any time soon, is it?' There were angry tears, glinting at the corners of her eyes.

'Jackie!'

'They talked to me like I was a fucking child! OK? Like I'd done it on purpose! Like I was just some stupid bloody woman who couldn't keep her big mouth shut!'

'Come here.' Logan helped her to her feet, then wrapped her in his arms.

8

The shit hit the fan, first thing Thursday morning – Logan could smell it as soon as his copy of the *Press and Journal* was delivered at ten past seven. TOLD YOU I DIDN'T DO IT! was the headline, above a photo of Rob Macintyre's ugly, big-eared head. Logan read the article in the kitchen, his cup of coffee going cold beside him. There was a brief account of how DI Steel and local police 'hero' DS McRae had charged a known sex offender with one of the rapes Macintyre was supposed to have committed, leaving the footballer in the clear. According to the paper, Macintyre's legal team were going to the Sheriff Court to have the whole case abandoned. And last, but not least, was a nice big quote from Sandy the Snake telling everyone how this just went to prove that his client had been the victim of a cynical campaign by Grampian Police.

Logan didn't need to look at the by-line to know who'd written it: Colin Bloody Miller rides again.

He noticed for the first time that the word 'hero' Miller always attached whenever he mentioned Logan in the papers now came in ironic single quotes. Grimacing, he sluiced the last filmy remnants of his morning coffee down the sink and went to work.

DI Steel wasn't there, so Logan had to start the morning briefing without her. Again. She slouched in five minutes before the end, complaining about having to go see the ACC first thing. Logan finished up then looked expectantly at her. 'Anything you'd like to add, Inspector?'

'Damn right . . .' She held up a clenched fist. 'We are not at home to Mr Fuck-Up!' Silence. 'Come on people, we're not leaving here till you do it. We are not at home to Mr Fuck-Up!' And this time everyone joined in, Logan trying not to groan as Steel went into her, 'I can't hear you!' routine. Eventually she'd had enough and told them all to get their backsides in gear. Logan hung back as they filtered out.

'Did you see the paper this morning?'

Steel nodded. 'Why do you think the ACC hauled me into his office? The Fiscal goes off on holiday with a lovely cast-iron case against Macintyre and twenty-four hours later it's falling apart.'

'They've still got the other six rapes to do him on.'

'Phffff . . .' She pulled out her cigarettes and

stared morosely into the packet. 'Yeah, but this thing with Watt's going to make a jury itchy: we were wrong about Laura Shand, who's to say we've not fucked up the other ones too? And all the time Rob Macintyre will be sitting there like an ugly wee angel with Hissing Sid polishing his halo for him.' She shook her head. 'Tell you, Insch might be a grumpy fat bastard, but I'd no' wish that case on anyone.'

She pulled herself out of her seat and performed an elaborate stretch, ending with a grimace. 'If anyone asks I'm off for a fag. You got anything on this morning?'

'Laura Shand's coming in at ten for the ID. Other than that: nothing.' It wasn't until the words were out that he realized his mistake. Steel now had an excuse to give him something to do.

'Good, you can go chase up the IB for those results on Watt's house, see if the little sod isn't responsible for more of Macintyre's victims. And while you're at it, get some more bodies on that e-fit, someone *must* know who he is!' She stopped for a moment and had a thoughtful scratch. 'And chase up whatever slack bastard's going through the dental records; tell them to get a shift on. This is a murder investigation, no' a slumber party!'

The constable responsible for coordinating the dental records search was sitting behind a small desk in the corner of the incident room, surrounded by piles of paper. PC Rickards, phone clamped to one ear while he scribbled something down on a form. Logan waited till he'd hung up. 'Well, any luck?'

Rickards scrunched up his face and sighed. 'Needle in a haystack. Most of these dentists have about three thousand patients on their books, and the inspector wants me to check every dental practice from Dundee to Peterhead. It's taking forever.'

'You'll get there.' Logan turned to leave, but Rickards grabbed his sleeve.

'Er, sir . . .' lowering his voice to a whisper, 'I was wondering about the victim . . .' A blush started at the white collar of his police shirt, rapidly turning his face the colour of boiled ham. 'Does . . . does he have a scar on his backside?'

Logan frowned. 'Hang on.' He went and dug the post mortem report out of the filing cabinet, flicking through it to the exterior examination. There were two diagrams of the body: front and back, marked up with the burns, cuts, ligature marks, contusions, and scars.

'Well?' Rickards asked.

'Left or right cheek?'

The PC thought about it for a moment. 'Left.'

'Got it in one.'

'Then I think I know who he is.'

9

DI Steel had her feet up on the desk, a cup of coffee in one hand, and an unlit cigarette bobbing about between her lips as she spoke. 'So how come Rickards recognizes this guy's arse then? He been there?'

Logan shrugged. 'Says he saw it on one of the DVDs they confiscated from that brothel raid. He's getting it out of evidence now.'

'Excellent. Nothing like a spot of hardcore porn in the morning to set you up for the day!'

They convened in the board room, Rickards fighting with the DVD player while Steel examined the case. '*James Bondage*?' She peered at the small print on the back, holding it at arm's length to get it in focus. 'Hey, this is shot in Aberdeen! Brilliant! Never knew we had our own dirty film industry.'

The constable sat back on his haunches and smiled as the TV flickered into life. 'They do quite a few titles. Not bad actually, once you get past the accents. They . . .' He drifted to a halt as he turned and saw the look on DI Steel's face. Then he went bright red. 'I mean, that's what the guys we arrested said. Em . . .' He coughed, fidgeted, then said, 'We're, em . . . ready to go . . .'

'I'll bet you are.' Steel plonked herself down on the end of the conference table as the screen faded to dark blue, then there was a copyright notice, and a warning that this presentation had been rated R18 by the British Board of Film Classification. And then the production company logo appeared and Logan couldn't help laughing: CROCODILDO FILMS LTD! featuring what could only be described as a rampant, battery-operated reptile. And then the titles started, along with a thinly-veiled pastiche of the James Bond music.

Rickards stabbed the buttons on the remote control, and everything whirred into fast forward: sports car, house, what looked like Balmedie beach, people whizzing about at sixty-four times normal speed. Suddenly the screen filled with pink and the inspector shouted, 'Play! Press play!', but Rickards didn't.

'It's coming up in a minute.'

'But I want to see *this* bit!' More cars, a fancy house, a brunette in a bikini, a fat man with a goatee, and then more pink. 'Oh come on! Let us see something!'

'Just a . . . this is it!' Rickards hit play and the jerking figures settled into something more recognizable. And explicit. It was clearly meant to be a take-off of the old 'Secret Agent is captured and tortured for information before being left alone to escape' routine. Only this time the man in the tuxedo was being strapped, face down, onto a customized massage table by a very busty redhead in a rubber nun's outfit. And then spanked. 'Here . . .' said Rickards, tapping the screen as the nun ripped James Bondage's trousers and pants off. 'The henchman.' A figure emerged from the shadows – mid-twenties, short blond hair, dark glasses – dressed like a priest.

The man pulled off his shades and said, *'There's no point in resisting, Mr Bondage, you will tell us everything!'* as the nun stopped spanking and pulled on a neon-blue strap-on. Rickards hit pause and everything stopped. 'See – it looks just like him!' He held up one of the IB's touched-up morgue photos. Logan had to admit he had a point.

'What about the scar?'

PC Rickards hit fast forward again, much to DI Steel's displeasure. Pink, more pink, figures whooshing about, and play: the priest-henchman thrusting away at the back-end of the nun while the front end was busy with Mr Bondage's erection. In, out, in, out, in, out – freeze. Caught mid-stroke the crescent-shaped scar was easy to spot. Rickards looked expectantly at them. 'Well, what do you think?'

Logan checked the post mortem file: the victim's scar was identical to the one currently filling the television screen. 'It's definitely him.'

'So who is he?'

Logan didn't think it was possible, but Rickards actually went redder as he said, 'According to the credits he's called Dick Longlay.'

'Aye, that'll be bloody shinin'. "Dick Long Lay"? Porn star name if ever I heard one. Might as well call himself "I've got a huge cock".' She squinted at the DVD case again. 'You got an address for this lot?'

Rickards nodded, and Steel stared at him for a moment, before saying, 'I'm not bloody clairvoyant: where are they?' Rickards told her and she smiled. 'Well, get a shift on then! I fancy a trip to Crocodildo Films.'

'You sure this is the right place?' Steel took two steps back and stared up at the small industrial unit, hidden away down a small alley off Hutcheon Street. The sign on the wall said CLARKRIG TRAINING SYSTEMS LTD.

PC Rickards checked his notes again. 'Should be. It's their registered office anyway.'

Inside it was all potted plants and framed shots of oil rigs and people posing with safety equipment. Two large, ancient-looking projectors sat on mahogany plinths in the middle of the floor, locked away in matching glass cases, like an exhibit at the Natural History Museum. The receptionist – a bloated woman in her sixties – put down her copy of *Hello* and smiled at her visitors. 'Can I help you?' Like someone's mum putting on a posh voice for the telephone.

Logan flashed his warrant card. 'We need to speak to someone about . . .' he paused, not quite sure how to ask her about Crocodildo Films. She looked like the type that would shock easily. 'Er . . .'

'Oh for goodness sake,' said Steel pushing past him. 'We want to talk to someone about the porn.'

'Aye?' said the receptionist, dropping the posh voice. 'Hud oan and I'll give the boss a bell.' She punched a number into her switchboard, listened to it ring for a while, then a pop and crackle came from the speakerphone and a less than happy voice said, *'Oh for God's sake: what now? I told you we're filming!'*

The receptionist puffed up. 'Alexander Lloyd Clark! Don't you dare talk to your mother like that!'

A pause, then a long-suffering, *'What can I do for you, Mother?'*

'You've got visitors.'

'Can you tell them to sod off? I'm busy. If they—'

DI Steel leaned over the desk and shouted, 'It's the police.'

Another pause. *'Mum, have you got this on speakerphone again? How many times do I have to tell you—'*

'We need to talk to you, Mr Clark.'

'Is it about the break-in? Because it's about bloody time!'

Steel mouthed 'break-in?' at Logan, but he just shrugged. 'No, it's about—'

'*Look, come back tomorrow. I'm busy today. Make an appointment. I—*'

Steel cut in before the receptionist could get out the diary. 'Listen up Sunshine, you can either assist us with our enquiries, or I can arrest your pornmongering arse and drag it down the station. Up to you.'

'*Oh, bloody hell. OK, OK, I'll come back to the office.*'

A broad smile slid across the inspector's face. 'No, you stay where you are and we'll come to you.'

'*Fine, OK, whatever . . .*' He gave them the address – a container yard in Altens – then hung up.

Steel beamed. 'Always wanted to see a porn film getting made. Think they'll let me audition?'

Altens wasn't exactly scenic: a collection of industrial units on the southern edge of the city; hideous oil company buildings; storage yards; vans selling fast food; and the abandoned back ends of articulated lorries, some stacked with lengths of drilling pipe, others carrying nothing more than a couple of greasy coils of blue rope. They found the film crew set up by a stack of the huge metal containers used to transport goods offshore. Lights, cameras, and not a lot of action.

'Which one of you's Clark?' Steel shouted. Nearly everyone pointed at a large bloke in a massive padded jacket, woolly hat and greying goatee beard, drinking something from a polystyrene cup – the steam coiling up around his strange little rectangular glasses. He wasn't quite as big as DI Insch, but it was close. The man froze, as if he'd been caught doing something naughty, then pulled on an ingratiating smile.

'Zander Clark, with a Z,' he said, sticking out a gloved hand. 'Hi. You must be . . . ?'

'The police. So . . .' she looked at the camera, the lights, and then the small cluster of people huddling round a script, 'when does the shagging start?'

A spray of coffee exploded from Zander's lips. 'Shh!' He grabbed Steel by the arm and led her away. 'We're shooting a safety training course, OK? I don't want my client finding out I do adult films on the side.'

'No' proud of them, eh? I can understand that: I've seen one.' She hauled out the James Bondage DVD.

'Actually,' said Zander, straightening up to his full height, which had to be at least six three, 'my films have won awards all over Europe, thank you very much. I just like to keep my businesses separate.'

'Worried your client's going to ditch you if he knows you do stuff about nuns buggering secret agents?'

He scowled, looking more petulant than angry. 'You said you wanted to see me.'

'Oh, aye.' She held the DVD up again. 'This bloke, Dick Longlay: who is he?'

Zander took the case off her and squinted at it.

'Jason,' he said at last. 'Jason Fettes, I gave him his big break.'

'Spit-roasting a nun?'

'Look, do you have a problem with something? Erotic films too "real" for you? Just because you've never had sex in your life it doesn't mean—'

Logan cut him off before things got ugly. 'When did you last see Mr Fettes?'

The large man treated Steel to a scowl, then turned his back on her. 'A couple of weeks ago: had to get him in to do some foley work on his last film. Bloody sound was appalling.' He waved at a cadaverous man with a boom mike and a bored expression. 'I swear to God I'm going to fire his skinny arse if he doesn't pull his socks up.'

'Jason.'

'Oh, right, right. Yeah, I use him quite a bit. He was in *James Bondage*, the sequel: *From Rubber With Love*, a couple about a plumber – well, you have to, don't you? It's tradition. *Harriet Potter and the Chamber of Filth*, *Jamie and the Magic Crotch*, and, of course, *Crocodildo Dundee*. I won the XRCO Best Film for that.' Glowing with pride. 'In fact, he's going to be in my new one too: *Down-Hole Tools*. It's about this accident investigator who goes offshore, only to discover that Amazonian Viking women have come back from the past and are making all the guys on the rig have sex with them until they die! It's going to be huge.'

'I see . . .' said Logan, trying to keep a straight face. 'And do you have an address for Jason?'

'Not on me . . . .' Frown. 'Cults I think . . . No, wait, he's just moved. Blackburn. His mum and dad bought one of those new houses.'

Logan tried not to swear.

'So are you telling me,' said Steel, twisting round in the passenger seat so she could glare at Logan in the back, 'that you daft buggers were at the guy's address yesterday morning and didn't say anything?'

Up front, Rickards went bright red, but kept his eyes on the road and his mouth shut. So it was down to Logan. 'It's not our fault! The woman wasn't even sure she recognized him! And anyway, what was all that about back there? You didn't have to antagonize him.'

'Aye, well,' Steel shrugged, 'I was all fired up to see some steamy, explicit sex, instead of which they're all buggering about with bloody forklift trucks.' She turned back to face the front. 'Besides, he shouldn't have been such a big fat bastard: reminded me of Grumpy Insch.'

The blue sky was a thing of the past by the time they arrived at the housing development. A pall of grey-purple cloud hung overhead, a cold wind whipping through the half-built houses, their roof joists sticking out like ribs picked clean of meat. 'Bloody hell, it's freezing!' said Steel, clambering out of the car and onto the dusty road. 'Rickards: go find out if the neighbour's seen Jason Big Dick since Monday – We'll look like a right bunch of tits if it's not him.'

As the constable scurried off next door, Steel lit a cigarette, stuck her hands deep in her pockets and trudged up the path to the silent house.

The place was just as deserted and locked up as last time, but the inspector insisted on peering in every window, leaving boot-prints in the empty flowerbeds and finger marks on the glass. They'd got as far as the garage before Rickards returned with the news that no, the neighbour hadn't seen Jason again and would they all like to come in for a cup of tea?

'Too bloody right I would!' said Steel, sooking the last puff from her cigarette before grinding the butt out on the pale brick walls. 'Freezing me nipples off here.'

Logan tried not to picture it. 'I'll go see the site office, they might . . .' He trailed off as a large red Citroën pulled into the drive, the back full of suit-cases and boxes.

The driver killed the engine, took one look at Rickards standing there in his police uniform, and climbed out. 'Bloody hell!' He was in his early fifties with lots of pink scalp showing between the grey hairs. 'It's those little vandals from the village again, isn't it? I've told the builder they need to get some bloody security sorted out, but will they listen to me? No! We go away for two bloody weeks . . . What have the little bastards done now?'

Logan and Rickards looked at DI Steel. This was one of those times where rank was a burden rather than a privilege. Senior officer on site got to break the bad news, those were the rules. But the inspector wasn't playing by them. 'Go on then, Sergeant,' she whispered, 'you're up. Be gentle though, eh?'

Wonderful. 'We're not here about vandalism, sir.' Logan pulled the IB's touched-up morgue photo out of his pocket and handed it over. 'Do you recognize this man?'

That got a long-suffering sigh and a weary, 'What's he done?'

'I'm afraid I have some very bad news for you.'

10

They left PC Rickards in the lounge with Jason's mother. She was just sitting on the couch, silent and still, as if she wasn't really there. Mr Fettes was doing slightly better: bustling around the kitchen, apologizing for the smell as a small terrier did ecstatic circles about his legs, barking and wagging its tail. He picked the dog's dish off the mat by the washing machine and rinsed it under the tap, telling them what a good boy Wee Jock was for only going in the kitchen, when he could have crapped all over the house if he'd wanted. Left here alone for two and a bit days. Really it was remarkable, when you thought about it. What with Jason not being here to feed him, or let him out. What with Jason being . . . The tin opener clattered to the floor. Mr Fettes curled in on himself and cried.

DI Steel wrapped an arm around the sobbing man's shoulders and steered him to one of the chairs at the kitchen table. 'Here, why don't you let me feed the wee lad, eh? You sit there, and afterwards I'll get us a nice cup of tea.' She threw a glance in Logan's direction, silently mouthing the words 'go have a poke about'.

Jason's room was easy enough to find: a double bedroom on the second floor with a computer desk in the corner and an Ikea bookshelf full of science fiction and fantasy novels. No posters on the walls, but a lot of framed photographs – Jason with friends, Jason at the beach, Jason in America with a pretty dark-haired girl . . . There wasn't a single photo in here that didn't feature his face. Posing for posterity. Logan slipped on a pair of latex gloves and eased the wardrobe door open. The clothes looked as if they might have been expensive once, now becoming slightly tatty with wear.

There was nothing much in the pockets: a few receipts from Burger King, a handful of nearly illegible notes scribbled on the back of napkins, some lint and three ribbed condoms. He tried the bedside cabinets: socks, underpants, handkerchiefs, more socks, a small silver key, a collection of cheap-looking pornographic magazines, and a handful of Crocodildo DVDs. Logan stuck them on top of the computer desk and peered under the bed. A small set of free weights, a plastic storage thing full of T-shirts, and a long metal chest. Padlocked. The key from the bedside cabinet fit perfectly.

Logan took one look inside. Whistled softly. Then locked it up again.

The computer desk was a mess of CDs and bits of paper. There were a couple of letters from Equity, the actors' union, regretfully informing Jason that his application for membership was being declined as he'd not been employed for his 'adult films' on a suitable contract. A handful of pages ripped from the *Stage* with auditions circled in red ink. And right at the bottom of the pile: a parking ticket. Logan gave it a cursory glance, about to stick it back where he'd found it when he saw the number plate. It was far too old to be the red Citroën parked in the driveway, and he knew it wasn't in the garage. He called Control, asking for a lookout report to be put on the vehicle. There was a brief pause on the other end of the line, complete with the clickity clack of a keyboard being pounded, and then, *'OK, so that's a lookout request for a blue Volvo estate, registration number—'*

'What?'

'The number plate, it belongs to a blue Volvo estate.'

Logan sighed. Of course it did.

He found DI Steel standing outside the back door, having a fag and staring out at the lowering clouds, her breath indistinguishable from the cigarette smoke in the cold morning air. She looked tired and old. 'Sorry, Laz,' she said, as he stepped out into the cold, 'I just couldn't face telling someone else their kid's dead. Some DI, eh?' She sighed, then took another deep drag on her cigarette. 'One hundred and sixty-seven. That's how many times

I've broken the news. I was working it out just now. A hundred and sixty-seven people.' Another sigh. 'What a bloody job. We must be mad . . .'

'I found something in Jason's room. The car he was dropped off in – looks like it was his.'

'Shite.'

'Yup. There's a computer as well. I've told Mr Fettes we're going to need to take it and a couple of other things down to the lab for analysis.'

'The poor sod had no idea his wee boy was making porn films. Makes you think, doesn't it?'

'You want Rickards to stay here with them?'

'What?' She frowned, dragged back from a thoughtful pause. 'Better no'. He's no' been trained, so Christ knows what he'd come out with. Get a Family Liaison officer out here. We'll nip back to the station soon as they arrive.'

They drove back to FHQ with Jason's computer, the long metal chest from under his bed and his collection of pornography all stuffed in the boot of the car. Mr Fettes sat in the back with DI Steel – coming in to formally identify his son's body. Down in the morgue viewing room, he took one look at Jason, said, 'He looks so small . . .' and asked to be taken home. All in a voice that was little more than a whisper. Steel got Alpha Six Nine to give him a lift.

Upstairs, the incident room was nearly empty, just a couple of PCs answering the phones while everyone else was off to the canteen for lunch.

Logan had signed everything they'd taken from Jason's room into evidence, then out again, so they could go through it on one of the desks by the window. Steel went straight for the porn, examining the DVDs and reading out choice quotes from the cover blurbs in her best theatrical voice. Then came the magazines. They weren't exactly high class, but they were explicit. And they all featured Jason Fettes.

'Bloody hell,' said Steel, holding up a two-page spread of their victim, two unidentified women and a man in a rubber mask, 'he's got a porn collection full of his own face. Narcissistic little onanist, isn't he?' She stuck the magazine back on the pile. 'What's in the box?'

Logan unlocked it and showed them.

'Fuck me!' The inspector reached in and pulled out a full-length rubber suit with built-in arms, legs, gloves, and booties, all in matt black. She poked a latex-gloved finger through a little hole in the crotch. There was an identical one round the back. 'Think he got this at Marks & Spencer?' There was a matching moulded, black rubber hood with tiny little holes for the nose and eyes in the box as well as a collection of bats, paddles, gags, and strange pink things: most of which were battery-operated.

Logan peered at a weird, mushroom-shaped object. 'What the hell's this?'

'Butt plug,' said Steel and Rickards, both at the same time. Then the constable went bright red.

'OK, Sherlock,' the inspector grinned at him and pulled a small black plastic case out of the box, 'seeing as your specialist subject is sexual deviancy: what's this?' She clicked it open, exposing a jumble of wires, pads and a controller.

Rickards went from red to deep scarlet. 'It's an electrostim set.'

'Yeah?' she looked genuinely surprised.

'You . . . it gives you . . . the electricity . . . for heightening . . . ahem.'

'Good is it?' She pulled the controller out and started poking at the buttons.

'It . . . well, it depends . . . I . . .'

Logan came to the constable's rescue. 'At least this explains the strap marks we found on Jason's body.'

'Hmm?' Steel put the controller back in its case and snapped the thing shut again.

'Well, he's obviously heavily into the bondage scene. Someone picks him up, takes him home and ties him up, only it goes too far – the guy panics and dumps him outside A&E. It was an accident.'

'An accident? How do you *accidentally* bugger someone to death?'

'You know what these bondage lot are like,' said Logan, pointing at the contents of Jason's hope chest, 'one minute it's tying each other up for a bit of light spanking, and the next it's whips, chains, nipple-clamps and butt plugs.' He might have been imagining it, but he got the feeling

Rickards was scowling at him. 'And let's face it: if you're going to kill someone, there are better ways of doing it. You've already got the guy tied up and gagged, why not just strangle him? Or put a plastic bag over his head. And why rush him to the hospital afterwards?'

Steel scowled, obviously trying to come up with an alternative scenario. 'Oh bloody hell,' she said at last, 'so much for my nice juicy murder.' And then she stomped off to tell the ACC.

PC Rickards waited till she was gone before he spoke. 'You know, just because Jason was different it doesn't make him a pervert!'

Logan stared at him. 'Oh – my – God, you're one of them aren't you? You're into all this bondage stuff!'

'I . . .' The constable's face blossomed with beet-root-coloured embarrassment and then he stormed off, leaving a grinning Logan to pack Jason Fettes' collection away.

'Right, settle down you lot!' DI Steel stood at the front of the briefing room while Aberdeen's finest made themselves comfortable. 'We now have an ID for our victim.' She nodded to Logan and he hit the button. Behind the inspector the screen filled with a smiling face, snapped on a beach somewhere a damn sight warmer than the north-east of Scotland. 'Jason Fettes, AKA: Dick Longlay.' That got a laugh and the inspector let it die down before continuing. 'He made dirty movies for

Crocodildo Films, which is how our very own PC Rickards was able to identify him.'

A sudden barrage of wolf whistles and off-colour comments were thrown in Rickards' direction – the constable looked mortified. He went even redder when Steel started talking about Jason Fettes' bondage set. 'So,' she said, as Logan clicked the screen onto a picture of the rubber romper suit, laid out on the incident room floor, 'we need to start asking around the sex shops and wherever else it is the bondage crowd hang. Like Ellon. And Westhill.'

While the inspector spoke, Logan kept an eye on Rickards: it seemed as if he was about to say something, but thought better of it.

'Current theory: this was a sex game gone wrong, so Fettes probably went home with this person of his own free will. There's no blood at the victim's house, so they must have gone to Mr Moustache's bondage bachelor pad.' Click and the e-fit appeared.

'We're pretty sure the victim was contacted through this site . . .' Steel paused, waiting for Logan to catch up – the image behind her changing to a pink and black website called 'BONDAGEOPOLIS!'. 'Fettes had an advert on there, the IT guys found a copy on his hard drive . . .' She paused and dug out a printout from the briefing pack, reading aloud: 'Real life porn star seeks switch for no-holds-barred action.'

It was DC Rennie who stuck his hand up. 'What's a switch?'

'Well,' said Steel, 'let's ask our resident sexpert.' She stared at PC Rickards, until he came out with, 'It's a BDSM term: someone who can be either dominant or submissive. Top or a bottom.' Blushing furiously as most of the room started making 'bottom' jokes.

'OK,' the inspector tipped the embarrassed constable a wink, 'that's enough out of—' Rennie's hand was up again. 'What now?'

'BDSM?'

'Bondage, Domination and Sadomasochism. Pay attention, for God's sake. See Constable Rickards afterwards if you want a demonstration.' More laughter. Gradually a sense of order returned, but the rest of the briefing was marked by giggles and sniggering. Now that this was 'death by misadventure' rather than murder, it didn't seem quite so . . . serious. When Steel called the meeting to a close, Rickards was the first one out the door.

'You should go easy on him,' said Logan as the last few people wandered off, 'I get the feeling he's not exactly seeing the funny side.'

'Oh for God's sake!' She rolled her eyes and dug out a packet of cigarettes, shaking them, then peering inside. 'What is it with bloody prima donnas in this place? OK, OK, I'll talk to him. Can I at least have a fag first?'

While the inspector was off sacrificing a lung to the gods of nicotine, Logan went looking for Jackie, finding her in the same place as yesterday: covered in dust, down in the basement archives.

'How's it going?'

She looked up and shrugged. 'Same shite, different day. You?'

'I got to tell someone their son had been killed.'

'Shite too, then.' She scribbled something in her notebook then slid a set of case files back on the shelf. 'You hear about Macintyre? Hissing Sid's got him an interim hearing. Says he has "new evidence". We've got to present tomorrow.'

'Tomorrow?'

'Tomorrow.' Jackie slammed another box down on the concrete floor. 'Unbe-fucking-lievable isn't it? Things you can get away with if you're famous.' She yanked the lid off and dropped it at her feet. 'I tell you, if that slimy lawyer bastard gets Macintyre off I'm going to make his life a living hell. Him and Macintyre both.'

Logan believed her. 'You want to go get something to eat tonight? We could try that tapas bar on Union Street? Get a bit squiffy? Go home and fool around?'

'"Squiffy"? What the hell is this, *Five Go Mad in Mastrick*? I don't get "squiffy"; I get paralytic, shitfaced, drunk. Maybe tipsy at a push.' She grinned at him. 'But the rest of it sounds fine.'

Only Logan never got that far.

Half past seven and the rain was coming down like icy nails, bouncing off the rutted car park floor, misting in the headlights as Logan pulled up and killed the engine. The sun had set long ago, leaving behind a cold, bleak night; Brimmond Hill was a dark mass looming above them, only the winking red lights on the transmitter at the summit giving any indication of where the top was. And even then it was lost in the downpour most of the time. Alpha Two Zero was parked at the far end, blue and white lights rotating lazily, made fuzzy by the rain.

DI Steel sat in the passenger seat, listening to it drumming on the car roof. 'Buggering arsemonkeys. We're going to get soaked . . .' She pulled out a crumpled packet of cigarettes, automatically offering one to Logan, before remembering he didn't any more and lighting one up herself. She pointed her lighter at the burnt-out hulk sitting between the two cars. 'They sure it's his?'

Logan nodded, coughed, then rolled down his window, letting the smoke out. The steady hiss and clacker of rain hitting the gorse bushes, heather and potholes oozed in. 'The silly sods found the thing on Tuesday, didn't put two and two together because it wasn't blue.' Which was fair enough, the burnt-out hulk was an off-grey-brown colour, mottled with black. 'They only ran the chassis number this afternoon so they could issue a fixed-penalty notice to the owner for dumping it here. Someone recognized Fettes's name.'

Steel swore. 'We could have had an ID two bloody days ago!'

Logan just shrugged.

Someone clambered out of the patrol car opposite, turning up his collar and hurrying towards them, the rain drumming on his peaked cap as a dirty, battered-looking white Transit van bumped its way into the car park. The constable bent down and stuck his head through Logan's open window. 'You want us to cordon off the scene before the IB get started?' he asked, dripping.

Steel squinted at him through the smoke. 'No bloody point now, is there? Everything'll be washed away! Why the hell didn't you call it in when you found the sodding thing?'

The constable shrugged. 'Don't look at me: I was off sick!'

'Fine, yes, go. Cordon to your heart's content.' She scowled as he scurried off. 'Fat lot of bloody good this'll do us: damn thing looks like a charcoal briquette. You imagine any forensic evidence lasting through that, and all this?' indicating the torrential rain.

'Not really, no. But at least now we know that whoever did it is local.'

Steel nearly choked on her fag. 'Come on then, Miss Marple, astound me.'

'They spotted the Volvo on Tuesday night, yes? That means it was dumped and burned on Monday night/early Tuesday morning. Whoever did it was able to get home from here without a car.'

Grudgingly, Steel admitted he had a point – Brimmond Hill wasn't exactly the middle of nowhere, but it was close – anyone setting fire to the car they drove up here would be facing a long, *slow* trek into town. 'Kingswells?' It was on the other side of the hill.

'Maybe, but you'd break your neck in the dark if you didn't know where you were going.'

'Aye, well,' she said, as three IB technicians swore their way out of the dirty white van and started fighting with the blue plastic scene-of-crime tent, trying to get it up over the scorched wreck, 'there's no need to look so damn pleased with yourself – it doesn't get us any closer to catching him, does it?' She rolled down her window and pinged the last tiny nub of her cigarette out into the rain. 'Beginning to wonder if this whole case isn't a waste of time. Isn't like Fettes was battered to death, is it? He was into kinky sex. It went wrong. He died.' She closed her eyes, pinched the bridge of her nose, and sighed. 'The poor sod on the other end didn't do it on purpose, did they? Can you imagine having to live with that on your conscience?'

There was silence as they watched the IB getting drenched trying to protect trace evidence that probably wasn't there any more.

'This is such a bloody waste of time,' said Steel at last. 'Come on, let's get the hell out of here. If they find anything they'll call us.'

They didn't.

11

Quarter to nine in the morning was far too early to be hanging about outside a licensed sex shop on Crown Street, waiting for it to open. But Logan didn't have any choice – this was where DI Steel wanted to be. She was sitting in the passenger seat, munching her way through a packet of Bacon Frazzles, a tin of Irn-Bru sitting on the dashboard in front of her. A thin drizzle misted the windscreen, slowly turning the granite tenements a darker grey to match the sky. Logan yawned, covering his mouth with the back of his hand, then settled down into his seat, wondering if it'd be OK to have a quick nap. Steel poked him in the shoulder. 'Heads up,' she said, pointing through the windscreen at a small bald man with glasses, all bundled up against the cold, carrying a big bunch of keys.

The shop was discreet, just a frosted window with the words SECRET TIMES etched on it in powder pink. The little bald bloke hunted through his keys, then squatted down and took the padlock off the roller grille covering the entrance. They waited until he'd unlocked the front door before climbing out of the car and into the cold drizzle.

Inside, Secret Times was lined with videos, DVDs and moulded latex. Mr Bald was in the process of peeling off his coat. 'We're no' open till ten,' he said, without a smile.

'Now is that any way to greet a valued customer, Frank?'

'Eh?' The man took off his rain-misted glasses, polishing them on the corner of his cardigan, before putting them back on again. 'Inspector Steel! How nice t'see you again.' This time he did smile, showing off a huge number of perfect white teeth, as if they'd come out of a packet. He cast a quick look at Logan, then back to Steel, lowering his voice to a stage whisper: 'I've no' got that *thing* in for you yet. They say it's still out of stock.'

Steel shook her head. 'I'm no' here about that, Frank. I need to know if you've seen this bloke.' She waited for Logan to pull out a copy of the e-fit picture – baseball cap, round face, glasses, huge moustache, goatee beard.

The bald man took the picture and frowned at it. 'Fit's he done?'

'None of your business. Recognize him? He'll be one of the BDSM crowd.'

Frank peered some more then handed it back. 'Nope. But we get a few of them in here; you want I should ask around?'

'Couldn't hurt.' She turned to leave then froze on the doorstep, turning back. 'And try lighting a fire under your supplier, eh? I'm in my sexual prime here, no point wasting it, is there?'

They tried the other licensed sex shops in Aberdeen, then had to make a last-minute dash back to FHQ for a meeting Steel had forgotten about with the Detective Chief Superintendent in charge of CID. 'If anyone asks,' she said, jumping out of the car, 'we were detained questioning a suspect, OK?' And then she was gone, scurrying into the building, complaining about not having time for a cigarette all the way.

Logan parked the car.

Up in the incident room, things carried on as normal – occasional telephone calls from public-spirited idiots claiming to have seen a blue Volvo estate, others who said they knew who the man in the e-fit was, some with alternative IDs for Jason Fettes, and a couple who actually claimed to have seen him shopping in Boots that morning. Even though he was still lying in a refrigerated drawer down in the morgue.

Logan sat with the admin officer, a skeletally thin woman in her mid-forties, going through the reams of actions churned out by the Home Office Large Major Enquiry System, and assigning them to the available officers. After that he went through the progress reports. And then, with nothing else needing his attention, wandered off to the archives to see how Jackie was getting on. Only she wasn't there.

Up at the reception desk, Big Gary looked at him as if he'd been dropped on his head as a child. 'She's in court, you idiot – they've got that special hearing thing for Macintyre.'

'Sodding hell.' He'd forgotten all about it.

'If you hurry, you can still go cheer on your beloved.' Gary dunked a KitKat in his huge mug of tea, then sooked off the melted chocolate. 'Eric says she's next up.'

Court One was a lot busier than normal – the public galleries crammed with people here to see Sandy Moir-Farquharson trying to get Rob Macintyre off with rape. The place always made Logan think of a converted cinema: magnolia walls, balcony and stalls, the screen replaced by a tall wooden platform topped with pillars and a portico, and above all that the royal coat of arms keeping watch over the proceedings. Even if it was covered with elastic bands, presumably pinged up from the floor below when the court was empty and no one was watching. An oval podium sat in front of the bench, the court clerk and his assistant on one side facing the unwashed masses, the prosecution and defence on the other – looking up at the Sheriff in his robes and silk drop.

Normally all this would have been done in a little room round the back, behind closed doors, but the defence had requested a hearing in open court and to everyone's surprise Sheriff McRitchie had agreed. According to station gossip it had something to do with his being a lifelong Dons fan in search of an extra season ticket.

Hissing Sid was in full flow as Logan sneaked in the back doors and found a seat at the end of a row, right behind DC Rennie. The constable was wearing his 'court appearance' suit – the one that always made him look like the accused, rather than a police witness.

Logan inched forward and whispered in Rennie's ear: 'How's it going?'

The constable turned and gave him a pained look. 'Not good. I thought Insch was going to tear Hissing Sid a new one when he started banging on about police bias and harassment.'

Logan pointed at the dock where Jackie glowered down at Sandy the Snake as he postured and played to the court. 'How's she doing?'

'Well . . . she's not hit anyone *yet*.'

'Oh.'

'So, you see, Milord,' said the lawyer with a flourish, 'every time Grampian Police have investigated my client they have been forced to drop the charges, because the malicious claims of these women have been proven groundless. My client is an irritation to Inspector Insch and his ilk: an innocent man they can't "fit up" with—'

The prosecution was on her feet like a shot. 'Milord – I must object!'

Sandy didn't even wait for the Sheriff to rule

on it, just smiled his oily smile and apologized. 'I merely meant that while we all have our crosses to bear, Grampian Police seem to have their axe to grind . . . '

Logan scanned the court. It didn't take long to make out the huge, angry figure of DI Insch, looking as if his head was about to explode. He was going to be a nightmare to deal with after this. Rachael Tulloch – the deputy fiscal left in charge while the PF was off sunning herself on a beach in the Seychelles – wasn't looking any happier, sitting at the central desk next to the prosecution scribbling furiously while Moir-Farquharson put on his one-man show.

The lawyer held up a clear plastic evidence pouch so everyone could see the contents. 'Can you identify this item, Constable Watson?'

Jackie nodded. 'It's the knife Macintyre attacked me with.'

The lawyer smiled. 'That would be for a *jury* to decide, Constable. You say he attacked you with this knife, but your labs couldn't find a single fingerprint from my client on it. Could they?'

'He was wearing gloves.'

'So you have no proof at all that this knife belongs to my client, or that he'd ever used it?'

'He attacked—'

'Please answer the question, Constable."

'We . . . we have no *empiric* evidence, but—'

'You have no evidence.' He turned and faced the Sheriff, smiling up at the man. 'they have no evidence, Milord. My client was out jogging in preparation for tomorrow's match against Falkirk and stopped this woman to ask for directions. *She* attacked *him*.'

'That's a load of—'

'Constable!' Sheriff McRitchie waggled his gavel at her. 'I will not warn you again!'

Jackie shut her mouth and seethed.

'Thank you, Milord. You assaulted Mr Macintyre, didn't you, Constable Watson? Even after you had nearly crippled him, cracked two of his teeth, and had him handcuffed on the ground – you assaulted him!'

'Boll . . .' she stopped herself. 'I restrained him: that was all!'

'You kicked him in the ribs, it's in the photographs!' Hissing Sid held the glossy eight-by-tens up as proof.

'He fell. Ask DC Rennie.'

'You've been warned for excessive force before, haven't you, Constable?' And that was how it went for the next five minutes: he attacked Jackie's credibility as a witness, made her out to be little more than a thug with a warrant card. She looked ready to throttle him by the time he was finished.

'Milord,' he performed a slow pirouette, and pointed at the footballer, sitting all prim and proper like a good boy, holding his mum's hand, 'Robert Macintyre is an upstanding member of this community, a hero to many, an inspirational figure to children everywhere, a man who works tirelessly for local charities. We all heard Constable Watson admit that there is *no evidence* against my client. I've shown that the identifications obtained from these so-called "victims" are flawed to say the least. Let's not forget that Grampian Police were adamant that Laura Shand was attacked by Robert Macintyre, yet now we find that someone else has confessed to that crime. And most important of all: my client has an alibi for each and every night these rapes are supposed to have taken place. Milord, given all these *facts*, I have to ask why this frivolous and malicious case is being pursued. Surely it behoves the Procurator Fiscal's office to cease these proceedings before they waste even more of the taxpayers' money.'

The Sheriff pursed his lips, cogitated for a moment, then asked the Deputy PF if she had anything to add at this point. Rachael Tulloch didn't look happy as she stood to say she'd have to consult with her superiors. She'd pulled her long, frizzy, not-quite-red hair back in a severe ponytail and it was beginning to unravel along with her case.

There was an exasperated sigh, then the Sheriff called for a half-hour recess.

Jackie marched down from the stand, glaring at Hissing Sid the whole time. The lawyer just turned his back on her and shook the hand of his smiling client. 'Can you believe this shite?' she demanded, back at the prosecution bench. 'Where the hell did Macintyre get an alibi from?'

'His bloody fiancée,' said the Deputy PF, groaning. 'She now swears blind he was with her every night. Why does stuff like this always have to happen when the PF's away?'

Jackie stared at the footballer with his expensive suit and sticky-out ears. 'He's going to walk, isn't he.' It wasn't a question.

The Deputy PF scowled and dug out her mobile phone. 'Not if I have anything to do with it.'

Logan slumped in the visitor's chair on the other side of DI Steel's desk, while the inspector battered away at her computer keyboard. 'Oh, cheer up for God's sake,' she told him, 'it's not the end of the world, is it?'

He shrugged and went back to staring out at the grey granite bulk of Marischal College. The misting drizzle had given way to heavy rain, bouncing off the jagged spires, hammering down on the black tarmac streets and concrete pavements. Drenching the just and unjust alike.

'You know,' Steel stopped typing for a moment, 'I remember when Macintyre was a kid, wee bugger was never out of trouble, but you could always rely on his mum to lie for him.' Putting on a broad Aberdonian accent for, '"Oh, no, he couldnae hiv burnt doon yer man's sheddie, he wiz with me a'night!"'

'Arson's a long way from rape. And it's his fiancée this time, not his mum.'

'Aye, well, you've got to start somewhere,

haven't you?' The inspector finished typing with a flourish. 'Right, they've cut our manpower budget, but I think we can still do this if we concentrate on the bondage scene and porn merchants.' She smiled and hoicked her feet up onto the desk, scattering a small pile of reports. 'I tell you, Laz, I've got a really good feeling about this one. We're going to get a quick result. I can feel it in me water.'

VIOLENCE

Three weeks later.

12

Logan skidded to a halt, scanning the empty street. Nothing but parked cars, a skip full of builders' rubble, and the rain. No sign of Sean Morrison, or any of his nasty little friends. Shite. He did a slow turn, trying to figure out where the wee bugger had got to. He'd been right behind Sean all the way down North Silver Street; nearly lost him in Golden Square when some idiot in a people carrier reversed out without looking; and now Logan was standing halfway down Crimon Place with blood all down the front of his suit, and Sean Morrison was nowhere to be seen.

It was all residential on the right-hand side of the street – flats at one end and small terraced houses at the other, their granite walls contrasting with the dark-glass-and-concrete office units opposite. Logan was pretty sure Sean hadn't gone into one of the houses and it was unlikely he'd be welcome in any of the business premises. Not looking the way he did.

The cathedral car park went straight through to Huntly Street, and so did a small path down the side of the GlobalSantaFe building, but Logan had seen Sean sprinting past them onto Crimon Place, the little eight-year-old's arms and legs going fifteen to the dozen.

That left the King's Gate car park at the far end, but there was no way Sean could have got there so fast. He was hiding somewhere.

Gritting his teeth against the stitch in his side, Logan jogged forwards, pulling out his mobile phone to call for backup. It rang and rang and rang . . .

A drenched, knackered-looking policewoman staggered to a halt at the far end of the street, face flushed, panting and shiny as the rain drummed on her peaked cap and black waterproof jacket.

Still waiting for Control to pick up, Logan shouted, 'You see him?'

She shook her head. 'No . . . not . . . not a sign . . . Little bastard can run . . .'

A voice crackled in his ear – Control telling him the switchboard was buggered and— Logan cut the man off and told him to get a patrol car to Crimon Place right now. Sean Morrison had gone to ground. He snapped his phone shut and started back up the street, yelling, 'Check the cars!' to the constable at the far end. He peered underneath and between the vehicles as he went, splashing through puddles, the cold rain bouncing off the road, pavement, BMWs, Porsches, clapped-out Fiestas, Rovers . . . soaking through Logan's stained suit, plastering his hair to his head as he searched for the child.

'There!' It was the policewoman who spotted him. 'Behind the skip!' Sean Morrison – eight years old, four foot two, bloody nose, wearing jeans and a red AFC hooded top – grabbed a length of wooden banister not much smaller than a cricket bat from the debris filling the skip, swinging it as the constable lunged for him, catching her right in the face. She grunted and jack-knifed, both feet leaving the ground as she fell, leaving a spray of bright scarlet hanging in the air, glowing against the low, blue-grey clouds. Logan froze for a moment, and so did Sean, watching as she battered onto the wet tarmac, then the eight-year-old looked up at Logan, turned, and legged it.

For a moment Logan was torn between checking the constable was OK and grabbing the little bastard who'd clobbered her. He sprinted after the boy.

Sean Morrison was fast all right, but his little legs weren't nearly as long as Logan's, plus he was still carrying his makeshift club. He made a hard right, skidding on the wet road, trendy trainers sending up a spray of rainwater as he leapt the kerb and hammered round the side of the Boys' Brigade Battalion with Logan hard on his heels. And then he suddenly stopped, swinging his chunk of banister.

Logan had just enough time to get his arms up, covering his face before the wood cracked into it. But it was still enough to make him stop dead, slipping on the wet ground and hitting it hard as his legs went out from underneath him. The breath rushing out of his lungs, fire screeching across his scarred stomach. And then Sean was swearing, calling him a dirtymotherfuckingcuntbastard as he swung the wooden weapon again, smashing it down on Logan's back, then more swearing – something about a splinter – and the banister went flying. Smash. A car alarm shredded the rainy air. Then a trainer crashed into the top of Logan's head. He curled into a ball, protecting his stomach as a foot stomped down on his ribs. Making them creak. The little thug took three steps back, took a run up and slammed another foot into Logan's back.

Sean was about to do it again, when a pained, angry shout cut across the blaring car alarm: 'CUMB HERE YOU LIDDLE BASDARD!'

Logan opened his eyes in time to see Sean Morrison turn and begin to run. 'No you bloody don't!' Lashing out with a hand, he grabbed the eight-year-old's ankle, sending him crashing to the ground. More swearing. Logan lurched upright, staggered sideways and fell against an Alfa Romeo with a smashed front windscreen, clutching his head as the policewoman skidded to a halt. Everything was lurching in and out of focus in time to the ringing in his ears.

The PC's face was a mess of blood, one eye already swollen shut, her nose flattened and misshapen, scarlet bubbles popping from her nostrils as she grabbed Sean Morrison by the scruff of the neck and hauled him off the ground. 'You're fugging nicked!'

She turned, asked Logan if he was OK, then suddenly went very pale. *Clatter* and Sean Morrison hit the ground in a tangle of arms and legs. The eight-year-old scrambled to his feet as the constable stared open-mouthed at the knife hilt sticking out of her neck, just between the stab-proof vest and her collarbone. Her hands fluttered, bright red spilling down her chest, her eyes locked onto Logan's, imploring . . . Then she went down like a sack of tatties.

Logan caught her just in time to stop her head cracking open on the pavement. Easing her down he grabbed the Airwave handset on her shoulder and shouted, 'Officer down! Corner of Crimon Place and Skene Terrace! Repeat, Officer down!'

He cradled her head in his lap as she twitched and moaned. Fresh blood soaking into his trousers as Sean Morrison ran away.

Four hours later and Logan was standing in Accident and Emergency, getting an update from a male nurse with a hairy mole. The PC was lucky still to be alive, the knife had nicked the brachio-cephalic vein – one millimetre to the right and the last sixty seconds of her life would have been sprayed all over the pavement and Logan. She was still critical, but stable.

Outside, the rain had eased up a bit as the day

had grown colder, not enough to snow yet, but it'd probably get there soon enough. Logan dug out his phone and switched it back on. Six messages. The first was Jackie trying not to sound worried as she asked about his run-in with Sean Morrison. Then it was Rennie telling him how that missing old-age pensioner they were looking for had being sighted in Turriff, and then Big Gary wanting Logan to keep him up to date with the PC's condition. Apparently there was still no sign of Sean Morrison. Logan thought about just deleting Steel's messages, but listened to them anyway:

The first was pretty much her standard whine these days, *'Bloody ACC's been down here again! Why haven't we arrested anyone for Jason Fettes's death? His bloody parents have been banging their gums in the papers again. Jesus, it's no' like we didn't try, is it? No' our fault their kid was a dirty bondage boy . . .'* Some muttered swearing. *'And why haven't we caught anyone for those break-ins yet?'* Whinge, whinge, whinge. *'Tell you: next time that pointy-headed bastard comes down here I'm going to shove one of Fettes's butt plugs right down his throat! See how he likes—'* There was more, but Logan just deleted it.

The second message was a bit more up to date, *'What the hell do you think you're playing at? He was eight! How could you let him get away? What the . . . Hold on, I've got someone on the other line . . .'* and then silence. Beeeeeep. New message: *'Where was I? Oh, aye – Eight! Fuck's sake . . .'* Then some

110

coughing. *'Anyway, the hospital called about the bloke your wee villain attacked: punctured lung. It's no' lookin' good. I've got a press conference set up for quarter to six, so get your arse back to the station!'* Beeeeeeep.

Logan groaned. His head was throbbing, the skin tender and swollen where Sean had kicked it. His ribs ached from being stamped on. His suit was stiff with dried blood. Right now all he wanted to do was go home, take a couple of the pills he'd been given after an embarrassing examination – *'You were beaten up by an eight-year-old? Seriously? Hey, Maggie, come see this!'* – climb into a long hot shower, curl up and feel sorry for himself until Jackie got back from her shift. And then get her to feel sorry for him too. Instead of which he had to be at a press conference in – he checked his watch – just over half an hour. Muttering curses, Logan slouched back into A&E and went in search of one of the PCs stationed at the hospital to give him a lift.

The natives were getting restless as Logan limped into the media briefing room – rows of cameras and hungry faces from the national press, waiting for the main course to get to the table. 'Where the bloody hell have you been?' DI Steel: an unlit fag in her mouth, clicking a cheap, petrol station lighter on then off, then on, then off. DC Rennie trailed along behind her like a nervous spaniel.

'Hospital.' Logan pointed at the inspector's cigarette. 'They'll throw a fit if you light up in here.'

'Jerry Bloody Cochrane – silly sod went and died on us, so now every bastard under the sun wants to know what we're going to do about it.' She pulled the cigarette from her mouth and stuffed it back in the packet. Then took it out again. 'Shite – why the hell did I have to get this sodding case, why couldn't Fatty Insch have it instead? He should be used to PR disasters by now. I don't need any more horrible cases . . .' she trailed off as she finally noticed Logan's suit and shirt were clarted in dried blood. 'Oh fucking hell! Could you no' have changed? We're on in seven minutes!'

'I was at the hospital!'

'Fuck. Fuck, fuck, fuck . . .' She screwed her face up, then stared at DC Rennie. 'Right, the pair of you: find somewhere quiet and swap clothes. You're both about the same size.' Rennie opened his mouth to complain, but the inspector beat him to it. 'NOW!'

There was no one in interview room number three so they used that – Logan grimacing his way out of his shirt, jacket and trousers while Rennie stripped down to his Fred Flintstone boxer shorts, took one look at Logan's bruised ribs and scar spangled stomach and said, 'Bloody hell – you look terrible.'

Logan couldn't muster up the energy to scowl at him. 'Thanks a heap.'

He got back to the briefing room with thirty seconds to spare and limped up to DI Steel. 'Happy now?' he asked, making it clear that he wasn't. If he sat down too quickly, there was every chance he and his borrowed trousers were going to part company. She gave him a quick once-over.

'You'll do. But could you no' have combed your hair? You look like a burst bloody mattress.' Which was rich coming from her. Logan did his best with his fingers. Steel nodded. 'Better. Did you get—' The doors at the far end of the room banged open and the Chief Constable marched in. 'Oh bollocks – God's here.' Deep breath. 'Right, remember: we are not at home to Mr Fuck-up . . .'

The table was longer than usual, set up so there'd be room for a Family Liaison officer and a pale, sixty-eight-year-old woman with puffy red eyes and trembling hands: Mrs Cochrane, the victim's wife. Logan waited for her to sit down before taking his place next to DI Steel, lowering himself carefully into his chair, trying not to aggravate his bruised ribs or split Rennie's trousers.

'Right,' the Chief Constable stood, his silver hair glowing like a shampoo commercial in the bright television lights, 'before we start today I want to make one thing crystal clear: Mrs Cochrane has had a terrible shock today. She's lost her husband of nearly fifty years. She's here because she wants to help us catch those responsible. But the first person I hear making inappropriate comments or asking tactless questions is going to get thrown out on their ear and barred. Do I make myself clear?' There was an uncomfortable silence. The CC nodded. 'Good.' And sat down again.

'Today, at eleven minutes past twelve a pregnant woman shopping in the St Nicholas Centre was accosted by a gang of children, ranging from six to nine years old. They tried to steal her purse, but she resisted, so they subjected her to a vicious assault. Mr Cochrane went to intervene on her behalf . . .'

Logan didn't need to listen to the rest, he'd been one of the first ones on the scene – having nipped out to buy a sandwich and bag of crisps from Markies for lunch. Hearing the screams, running through the jumpers and trousers into the shopping centre, just in time to see Sean Morrison help himself to the old man's wallet and scarper. Calling for backup, running over to the victim, trying to staunch the bleeding. Telling the store detectives to keep pressure on the knife wound till the ambulance got there, then chasing after the little bastards. And not catching them.

He listened to Mrs Cochrane make an impassioned plea for anyone who knew where her husband's killers were to come forward and tell the police, tears sparking in the harsh media spotlight, running down her pale, lined cheeks. And then the Chief Constable thanked her for her bravery and threw the briefing open to questions.

Mostly it was the usual: 'Do you have any suspects?' 'Are you anticipating any arrests?' Then the woman from Sky News asked the Chief

Constable about the trial of Iain Watt: was he going to be charged with the other rapes supposedly committed by Rob Macintyre?

The Chief Constable glowered at her – the 'Granite City Rapist', as the papers had started calling Watt, was a something of a sore point. And with that, the press briefing was brought to an abrupt close.

13

The sun was hot enough to turn the car into a microwave oven, but when Logan clambered out into the late February morning it was so cold his nipples instantly pointed due north. His back was killing him: the bruises where Sean Morrison had kicked and battered him spreading like green and purple ink on wet blotting paper. King's Gate stretched downhill from the King's Cross round-about on Anderson Drive to where they used to film *The Beechgrove Garden*, and the view from the top of the hill was stunning – a slice of Aberdeen: grey granite shining in the sunshine, dark slate roofs, church spires, the North Sea glittering like a vast, deep-blue sapphire, a neon-orange supply vessel slowly making its way south towards the harbour. Just a shame it was bloody freezing.

'Jesus Effing Christ!' DI Steel stamped her feet, swore, dug out a cigarette and lit it, the smoke whipped away by the icy wind. 'My fridge is warmer than this!'

Logan ignored her, looking down the street at the Morrison residence – a large granite two-storey job with a huge BMW 4x4 sitting outside. Not exactly the type of place you'd expect a nasty, thieving, murderous little bastard like Sean Morrison to come from. Parked cars lined either side of the road – many of them containing bored-looking journalists, cameras and notebooks at the almost ready. No one seemed to have noticed that the inspector and Logan had arrived yet. 'You want me to get started?' he asked, one hand rubbing the small of his aching back. The painkillers they'd given him last night were about a fifth of the strength he was used to – might as well have been Smarties for all the good they were doing. At least they would have tasted better.

Steel shivered, hands jammed deep into her armpits, puffing away on her cigarette like mad. 'Give us a minute . . . I only get one fag this morning and I'm going to bloody well enjoy it if it kills me.'

Logan sighed and made a show of checking his watch. 'Nearly half eight – we're going to have to get a shift on if we're going to make the PM.'

'Nicotine patches my arse . . .' The inspector squinted into the bright sunshine 'Anyway, think I'm going to give this one a miss. Not like we don't know what killed the old guy, is it?'

'Suppose not.' He watched the bright orange supply boat disappear behind the tombstone slab of St Nicholas House. 'What do you want to do about Jason Fettes?'

'What about him? The whole bloody thing's dead in the water. No one's got any idea who did it, and no one cares either. Except the bloody parents and those fuckers at the P&J.' Colin Miller leading another 'campaign for justice' as an excuse to give Grampian Police an extra kicking. The inspector scowled, cigarette smouldering away between her lips. 'We've got no evidence, no witnesses and no bloody clue.'

'I know, but you're supposed to do an update for the ACC today, remember?'

'Is that today?' Steel swore. 'Tell you, between that, this thing, and those bloody housebreakings, my crime statistics look sodding awful. Still,' the cigarette was flicked out into the middle of the road, where it got crushed beneath the wheels of a number twenty-three bus, 'at least we're guaranteed a quick result *this* time.'

Logan had heard that one before.

They marched down the pavement, making for the Morrisons' front door where a lone uniformed officer stood looking cold and miserable. They were still one house away when a baldy wee man appeared in front of them, clutching a digital recorder. 'Ken Inglis – Radio Scotland. Inspector, have you found the boy yet?' It was as if someone had dropped a dead zebra in a tank of piranha: as soon they smelled blood there were reporters everywhere.

'No' yet,' said Steel in a sudden barrage of camera flashes. 'But we are pursuing several lines of enquiry. Now if you'll excuse—'

'*ITN News*: is it true Morrison's been in trouble with the police before?'

'I really can't comment on any—'

'Has Constable Nairn recovered consciousness yet?'

'Joanna Calder – *Guardian*: How worried are you for the boy's safety?'

Steel gave the uniformed PC guarding the Morrisons' house a wave and he shambled into action, forcing his way through the cameras and questions, holding them back and keeping them there, so Logan and Steel could get to the front door. Right at the very edge of the pack, dour-faced civilians stood, glowering after them. None of them carried placards yet, but it would only be a matter of time.

Logan leaned on the bell.

Inside, chez Morrison was like an advert for furniture polish. Everything gleamed. Logan stood by the fire, roasting the backs of his legs, while Steel sat on the couch, working her way through a china mug of tea and a couple of digestive biscuits. Mrs Morrison was on the other sofa looking plump, startled and a lot older than she should have at thirty-two, while her husband paced, wringing his hands, flipping from worried to angry to apologetic and back again. 'Sean's never done anything like this before!' he said, and the inspector snorted.

'I should bloody hope not! Knifing seventy-year-old men and police officers isn't something you want becoming a habit.'

Logan tried a slightly less confrontational approach. 'And Sean's not been home since yesterday?'

The mother shook her head, curly brown hair bouncing around her oval face. Puffy, pink eyes sparkling with tears. 'He went out to school in the morning and we haven't seen him since! All night! What if something's happened to him? What if he's hurt?'

Steel put her mug down on the coffee table. 'I think we need to be more concerned about him hurting other people.'

'He's a good boy!'

'He's just killed someone!'

The father scowled at her. 'He's only eight.'

'And Jerry Cochrane was seventy-two, but he's still dead. And we're bloody lucky he didn't kill that policewoman too! Your darling wee son is a—'

Logan cut her off before she could say anything else. 'Mr Morrison, have you checked the outbuildings in case Sean snuck back last night?'

'Fat chance of *that* happening with all those bloody journalists camped out on our doorstep! It's like a—'

'Mr Morrison—'

'Yes. *Of course I checked*, and so did your damn search team – twice last night and once this morning.'

'And you can't think of anywhere else he might have gone? A friend, or a relative: anything like that?'

'Why aren't you out there looking for him? It was below freezing last night! He's only eight! He—' The phone rang and Mrs Morrison's eyes went wide, bottom lip trembling. Backing away from the thing. Her husband just stared at it.

Steel gave it five rings before asking, 'You going to answer that, then?'

'Er . . . yes . . .' Mr Morrison licked his lips, wrung his hands, and picked up the phone. 'Hello?' He recoiled back from the earpiece, then slammed the handset back down into its cradle.

'Let me guess: wrong number?'

'They've been calling ever since it was on the news. About the . . . the old man getting hurt. They say terrible—' The ringing started again. This time Steel was the one who grabbed the phone, slopping a wee tidalwave of tea on the coffee table in the process.

'Aye?' she demanded, 'Who's this?' Then listened, face screwed up in concentration, as if she was trying to place the voice. 'Listen up, shite-face, this is the police. You call here again and I'm gonnae find out where you live, come down there and ram my boot so far up your arse you'll be tasting athlete's foot powder for a month!' She held the phone away from her ear. 'Hung up, fancy that . . .' Then she punched 1471 into the handset, repeating the automated voice as it recited the caller's number, so Logan could write it down. She smiled at Mr Morrison. 'We'll send a patrol car round: give her a hard time. You in the phonebook?' The man

121

nodded. 'Aye, well,' said Steel, putting the phone back and picking up her tea again, 'change your number and go ex-directory.'

'We can't . . . What if Sean calls?'

'Calls? He's got a mobile?'

The mother and father exchanged a worried look, then Mr Morrison said, 'We don't believe children should have them. You know: brain tumours.' He collapsed into an armchair, looking on the verge of tears. 'He could be anywhere . . .'

Just to be on the safe side, Steel sent Logan off to check the shed and garage again, while she stayed inside in the warm with another cup of tea. The search team had been thorough – the garage was a mess, everything piled up in one corner. Paint tins, boxes of household junk, three sets of skis, one windsurfer, more junk. Logan peered into all the cupboards, under the work top, into the chest freezer, but Sean wasn't there. And he wasn't in the shed either, or hiding in the garden.

Logan went back inside and searched every room, including the washing machine and tumble drier – you never knew what an eight-year-old kid could fit inside if it put its mind to it. Nearly an hour after he'd started, Logan clambered down from the attic, coughing from the dust, little bits of rock wool insulation sticking to his suit.

DI Steel was standing there waiting for him. 'Well?'

'Nothing.' He wiped a hand over his face, trying to get rid of a cobweb.

'Ah well, it was worth a go.'

They marched out through the knot of journalists and back to the car, ignoring the shouted questions, keeping their heads down till they were safely ensconced in the scabby CID Vauxhall Logan had signed for. Steel squinted out through the windscreen at the Morrison house. 'What do you think,' she asked, 'he going to come home?'

Logan nodded and turned the engine over. 'You should have seen his room; kid's got more stuff than I do. Parents must spoil him rotten. One night out in the cold and he'll be desperate to get home.'

'Are you mental? He just knifed an old man and a policewoman. He's no' Christopher Bloody Robin. I think the vicious little bastard's got somewhere to lie low . . .'

'Well, he can't stay hidden for ever,' said Logan, pulling away from the kerb and pointing the car back towards FHQ, 'he only got fifty quid from Cochrane's wallet and it's not like he can actually spend it – can't be a single person in Aberdeen who doesn't know what he looks like by now.' They'd tried telling the media that Sean was just a missing child, released his picture and asked anyone who saw him to come forward, but one of the witnesses from the St Nicholas Centre spotted the photo on the news, rang up the *Daily Record* and ID'd Sean as the kid who'd knifed Jerry Cochrane. And the press had a field day – EIGHT-YEAR-OLD KILLER!, THE NEW FACE OF EVIL!, SCHOOLBOY KILLS OAP! – it had made every second-edition front page in Scotland and quite a few south of the border too. 'We could try following his mates; someone's got to be getting food to him?'

She thought about it for a moment, head on one side, chewing on the inside of her cheek. 'Nah, that'll take for ever. If I was him I'd be on the first bus south to London, or Brighton, or some other godforsaken hole.'

'He's eight.'

'Blah, blah, blah. When did you last have anything to do with kids, eh? Eight's the new thirteen. Oh, they look like butter wouldn't bloody melt, but they're smacked out their tits half the time trying to get each other pregnant.' She pulled out her cigarettes, shoogled the packet, then put it away again with a sigh. 'Let's get the little bastards picked up and dragged down to the station: give them the fright of their lives. See if one of them'll shop him. And you'd better check the CCTV for the train and bus station too. And get some uniforms down there to speak to the drivers . . . Oh, and when you've got that lot organized, you might as well do that update report on Jason Fettes. No point sitting about twiddling your thumbs all day, is there?'

By the time Logan had finished doing the inspector's job for her, the first of Sean Morrison's 'little chums' was sitting in interview room number two with her father. There was an unpleasant smell of stale socks and ancient coffee with an underlying whiff of sour garlic, slowly marinating everyone present. DI Steel sat back in her cheap, plastic chair and stared at the little girl sitting opposite. Natalie Lenox: eight years old; long, dark brown hair; pale face; all her fingernails bitten down to tiny nubs; a furious scowl pulling at her chubby features. Her father was a bigger version of the same thing, only without the hair. He glowered as Logan wheeled a trolley with a TV and video on it into the corner and plugged them in. 'I want my lawyer present.'

Steel sighed. 'We've been through this. *Twice.* No lawyer.'

'Then I'm not saying anything more.'

'That's fine with me, keep your trap shut and I'll speak to Natalie instead.'

'She's not saying anything either.'

The inspector put on her most charming smile, which wasn't saying much. 'If you continue to be obstructive Mr Lenox I'll have you replaced by an appropriate adult, how about that?'

'You can't do that!'

'Want a bet? Natalie here was involved in the murder of a seventy-two-year-old man, I think—'

'She had nothing to do with it!' He poked his child in the shoulder. 'Tell them, tell them you had nothing to do with it.'

'I hid nuthin' to dae with it.' The kid's accent was broad Aberdonian, and as sullen as her mashed-potato face. 'Nuthin'.'

'Uh huh.' Steel told Logan to start the tape. 'Then how do you explain this?' The screen flickered, a jagged line of static creeping upwards, revealing the inside of the Union Street end of the St Nicholas Centre. People wandered past, laden down with shopping bags and baby buggies, and then a pregnant woman lurched into view, carrying a huge handbag and a plastic carrier from The Body Shop. She'd just passed the lottery booth when half a dozen children arrived – most wearing hooded tops, keeping their faces shielded from the camera. The inspector hit pause. 'Bottom left, the girl in the green top.'

She hit play and the girl darted forward, banging into the pregnant woman hard enough to make her drop her handbag. The woman staggered, the girl helping her stay on her feet, grinning up at her, mouth going twenty to the dozen. It was Natalie Lenox – her fat little face and long hair clearly visible on the screen – probably apologizing for being so clumsy while two of her friends helped pick up the nice lady's things. Helping themselves to her purse in the process. Sean Morrison handed the bag back with a modest tilt of the head, but the pregnant woman wasn't buying it. She grabbed him by the sleeve and started shouting.

'I . . .' Natalie's father licked his top lip and tried

again. 'So she bumped into someone. That's not a crime.'

'This isn't the first time. We've had about a dozen other complaints of bags, wallets and purses being stolen. All the victims remember being banged into by a little girl and her friends. Want to bet they recognize Natalie when we show them her picture?'

On the screen Sean lashed out, catching the pregnant woman on the side of the head, sending her crashing to the ground. She didn't let go, so he put the boot in. And that was when Jerry Cochrane ran into shot. At the sides of the picture shoppers stopped to stare as the old man hauled Sean off the woman. Holding him by the scruff of the neck, shouting. Sean hit him. And the old man hit him back, smack: right across the nose. And that's when it happened – the flash of a knife blade, and a startled expression on Jerry Cochrane's face. He sat down hard, letting go of Sean. The eight-year-old started laying into the old man with fists and feet, while a gathering crowd of shoppers looked on in shock. And then all the kids were at it, punching and kicking. Steel hit pause, so they could all see Natalie Lenox kicking Jerry Cochrane in the head.

'So,' said Steel, 'still think she had nothing to do with it?'

Mr Lenox, went very pale. 'I . . .'

Steel switched the TV off. 'I want to know where Sean Morrison is. And I want to know now.'

The little girl just scowled at them.

Her father swallowed hard. Then skelped her over the back of the head. 'Tell them!'

Nothing.

'Put it this way,' said the inspector, 'you're probably looking at a spell in a young offenders' institution. Locked up with all the other nasty little boys and girls. No mummy and daddy to look after you and buy you nice things.'

'They . . . they can't send her to prison! She's only eight!'

Logan shrugged. 'That's the legal age of criminal responsibility in Scotland, Mr Lenox. Vicious attack like that, a man dead. She's likely to get four, maybe five years. She'll be a teenager by the time she gets out. You'd be surprised how much they can change.'

'Oh God.' Mr Lenox covered his mouth with a shaking hand. 'It'll kill her mother!'

'Unless she helps us catch Sean Morrison. Then maybe we could have a word with the Procurator Fiscal, convince her that Natalie wants to make amends . . . ?'

'She does! You do, don't you?'

But Natalie just glared at her father, hot, angry tears making her eyes shine. Like Sean Morrison's knife.

14

'Jesus,' said Steel slouching back against the interview-room wall, clutching a half-empty cup of coffee to her chest. 'I've interviewed mass murderers with more humanity in them.' She shivered. 'Thank God I never wanted kids . . . Creepy little fuckers.'

So far they'd had three of Sean Morrison's gang in for interview and not one of them was prepared to spill the beans on his whereabouts. But they each came attached to a hysterical, panicking parent who had no idea what their darling child had been up to. Until they saw the CCTV footage.

The inspector swirled the filmy-brown liquid around in her mug. 'You know, when I was a kid we respected our elders . . . Well, maybe no' *respected*, but you knew if you gave some old fart lip they'd tan your arse for you. And then they'd tell your mum and dad, so they could do the same.' She nodded sagely, and took another gulp. 'Speaking of arses, have you seen Rennie?'

'Why, what's he done?' And suddenly Logan thought of a container yard in Altens. He frowned, trying to figure out why.

'Nothing, that's the bloody problem, I . . .' she trailed off, staring at Logan. 'What: you daydreaming about my creamy white thighs again?'

'Zander Clark.'

'Who?'

'The guy who runs the porn studio – he didn't ask what Jason had done. When we asked him who the guy on the DVD was. He didn't ask.'

'Aaaaaaaand?'

'Well,' Logan shrugged. 'Everyone always asks, don't they?'

'No' always.'

'But—'

'You're kidding, right? I mean, it's a bit Miss Marple, isn't it?' She laughed, a throaty sound that rattled a bit towards the end. 'You want me to summon Professor Plum, Miss Scarlet, and Colonel Mustard to the dining room for you?' Logan didn't dignify that with a reply. 'Oh, come on,' she said at last, 'it's Friday night: I'll buy you a nice pint of beer, OK? Nearly going home time anyway.'

'What about the search teams?'

'What about them?' And then she remembered. 'Bollocks. It'll be dark in half an hour won't it? And all the useless buggers will be back here wanting debriefed.' She groaned. 'You do one half and I'll do the other, OK? We could still be in the pub by seven.'

Logan held up the tiny pack of rubbish painkillers the hospital had given him for his battered head and bruised ribs – there were only a couple left. 'I'm not supposed to be drinking.'

'Aye well, *my* doctor says I'm no' supposed to smoke, drink, or chat up his receptionist, but it doesn't bloody stop me, does it?'

The search teams started trickling in around six, with not a lot to show for seven hours out in the freezing cold February air. No one had seen Sean Morrison. He wasn't hiding in anyone's shed, garage, or gazebo. They'd even had a team go through the Robert Gordon school buildings looking to see if Sean had gone to ground where he was meant to go to school. 'According to the head,' said a blue-faced PC, wrapping herself round a mug of hot chocolate, 'he's no' exactly a regular visitor. Started bunking off about six months ago. Became really disruptive. Bullying, theft, swearing . . . Right wee shite by all accounts. Had the parents in about a dozen times, but it never made any difference.'

'Yeah?' Logan ran a hand over his chin, feeling the stubble begin to scritch beneath his fingers. 'His dad told us Sean's never been in trouble before this.'

The PC snorted. 'Aye, well, he's lying then.' She shifted from foot to foot. 'Er, is there anything else, sir, or can I go change?' adding, 'Karaoke tonight.' by way of an explanation. Logan wished her luck and moved onto the next team's report.

DI Steel finished first, not surprisingly – they'd be lucky if she even skimmed the forms before telling the officers to bugger off to the pub. 'Right,' she said, hands deep in her trouser pockets, 'we all done for tonight?'

. Logan shook his head. 'Still need to sort out the teams for tomorrow. And I was thinking: we should get a POLSA, start looking in the parks and woods.' And if they had a Police Search Advisor, Logan wouldn't have to do all the co-ordination and logistics for a change. 'Maybe his mother was right and he's lying in a ditch somewhere. He's been in all the papers, suppose someone recognized him and decided to avenge Jerry Cochrane?'

'Oh God, that's all we need.' Steel screwed up her face and swore. 'This was supposed to be a nice easy case – we know who did it, we've got it on tape, we've got forensic, we've got witnesses . . .' The only thing they didn't have was Sean Morrison.

Logan stood at the front of the briefing room, feeling slightly sick. He wasn't the only one: half the team looked terminally hungover. And he'd been sensible – called it a night after the first round of flaming Drambuies, but not before he'd been subjected to DI Steel belting out *D'Ya Think I'm Sexy* at Café Bardot's late night karaoke session. It wasn't a performance he'd be forgetting in a hurry. Unfortunately.

Right now she was introducing the team to their brand new Police Search Advisor – a tall, thin sergeant with droopy eyes and a pronounced chin, who launched into a detailed description of today's search pattern, locations, teams and all the other things that weren't Logan's problem any more.

'Right,' said the inspector when the POLSA was finished, 'even though Sean Morrison's an evil wee bastard, he's only eight. He's no' been home in two days and it was below freezing both nights. Chances are he's holed up somewhere warm with a bottle of vodka and a stack of porn, but he could just as easily be freezing to death under a bush. So keep your eyes open!' She made them all repeat the DI Steel pledge of allegiance: 'We are not at home to Mr Fuck-Up!' then let them get on with it.

'Do you want to go front up Morrison's father again?' Logan asked while the troops filed out of the room.

'You go: and take Rickards. I'm sick of him moaning on about how everyone takes the piss out of him the whole time. I've got an audience with His Holiness the Chief Constable, have to con him into thinking this case is no' a huge, flaming disaster . . .' She dug a packet of nicotine gum from her pocket, popped a couple of pieces in her mouth then chewed, grimacing. 'We'll be fine.

We'll find Morrison today, lock him up, and all will be right with the world again. Just as long as the CC doesn't want to know about all the other cases I've still not solved.'

A lid of dove-grey had settled over the town, leeching the colour out of everything, the pale granite buildings merging with the monochrome sky. Rickards made it all the way from the station to School Hill before he started complaining about all the jokes he'd had to put up with since that first Jason Fettes briefing. Logan tuned him out, watching the pedestrians and traffic, looking for an eight-year-old boy in an AFC hooded top.

Rickards was still moaning when they pulled onto King's Gate, parking uphill from the Morrison house in order to find a space.

'Look on the bright side,' Logan told him, 'at least everyone thinks they're just taking the piss. Imagine what would happen if they actually knew you were in the scene.'

The constable scowled at him. 'I am *not*!'

'Oh come off it – you really expect me to believe you recognized Jason Fettes's backside after catching a glimpse of it on a seized DVD? You must have seen it dozens of times to remember it that clearly.' He unclipped his seatbelt and climbed out into the grey morning. Yesterday's spectacular view was gone; all the elements were still there, but they were dull and cold. The sea was the colour of clay, a dark smudge beneath a darker horizon. Sooner or later it was going to pee with rain.

Rickards scrambled out after him. 'I . . .' the constable blushed, then shuffled nervously, not making eye-contact. 'You . . . you didn't tell anyone, did you?'

'Of course I didn't! You can dress up in rubber and spank each other till you're blue in the face, far as I'm concerned it's nobody's business but your own.'

'Wish I'd never come forward with that bloody ID . . .'

Logan stopped and stared at him. 'You really mean that?'

He sighed. 'No. Fettes didn't deserve to be an unidentified body.'

'No one does.'

The crowd of journalists outside the Morrison place had grown since yesterday – there were even a couple of outside-broadcast vans, their satellite dishes brushing the skeletal beech trees that lined the road. A clot of protestors had formed around the gate, some had even made their own placards: SHAME!, JUSTICE FOR JERRY! and KIDS SHOULDN'T KILL! They should have looked indignant and self-righteous, but instead they just looked cold, huddled around a thermos of tea, complaining about the weather. They mustered up a bit of shouting and posturing when Logan and Rickards appeared, playing up for the assembled media. Logan got the constable to cut a path for him, ignoring the cameras and microphones being jammed in his face. Keeping up a constant stream of 'no comment' until they were safely inside the house.

Mr Morrison was in the darkened lounge, looking five years older than he had yesterday. Dark circles lurked beneath his eyes, his face pale and fish-like. As soon as the Family Liaison officer showed them through he was on his feet, wringing his hands. 'Is . . . have they . . .' unable to ask the question.

'We haven't found him yet,' said Logan, motioning for the man to sit in one of his own armchairs, before sending PC Rickards off to make the tea. 'I just need to ask a couple of follow-up questions.'

'Do they . . .' a nervous cough, 'do they think he'll still be OK?'

'We hope so, Mr Morrison. From what I can tell Sean's a resourceful wee boy.' That seemed to calm his father a bit, but not much. 'We spoke to his headmaster yesterday: he says Sean started causing problems six months ago.'

'Oh.'

'But you led us to believe that he'd never been in trouble before.'

'Ah, yes . . .' Mr Morrison stared down at his hands. 'You see, his mother . . . well, she worships the ground Sean walks on. She . . . well, we've probably spoiled him a little, but . . .' he shrugged.

'Six months ago. What happened?'

'September? He stole another boy's bag.' Morrison

stared at the drawn curtains, shutting out the thin daylight and photographer's lenses. 'He'd never done anything like that before . . .' A sigh. 'Then he punched someone. Stole some dinner money. Started playing truant. We nearly ended up in court. Lucky he didn't get expelled.'

Logan settled onto the couch. 'He ever tell you why?'

The man laughed, short and bitter. 'No. Well they don't, do they? Parents are always the last to know. One minute they're fine and the next you're having to apologize to some distraught mother because your kid's just bitten theirs. Came back from Guildford and he was like a different wee boy . . .'

'Guildford?'

'Well, we – I mean Gwen and I – went to Guildford. Gwen's dad was going in for a double bypass. Her mum was a mess. We didn't want Sean to come in case, you know . . . in case the surgery went wrong.'

Rickards came through with the tea, plonking three mugs down on the coffee table. He hadn't managed to rustle up any biscuits. 'So,' Logan helped himself to a mug, 'who did Sean stay with when you were away?'

Mr Morrison opened and closed his mouth a few times, then said he didn't really know. It'd been one of Sean's classmates. 'Gwen will know, but she's asleep . . . the doctor gave her something to help—'

'It's important, sir.'

'Yes,' he pulled himself out of his chair, and went back to wringing his hands again, 'yes, of course. I'll go . . . ask.'

The name didn't match any of those on Sean's list of 'friends' – according to Mrs Morrison, Sean hadn't spoken to the boy for months; he used to visit all the time, but they'd not seen him since they got back from visiting her mother and father. 'But you know what boys are like,' she'd said, sounding groggy, full of sedatives, 'one minute they're the best of friends, the next they've forgotten each other exists.' She still had the address, though, which was how Logan and Rickards ended up outside a large granite box of a house on Hamilton Place. A wee boy could have run down here in seven or eight minutes.

'Uh huh,' said Logan, staring up at the place, his mobile phone clamped to his ear, 'how many?'

'Mother, father and three children: boy and two girls.'

'Anyone got any priors?'

There was a pause as the voice from Control checked with the PNC. *'Nope . . . Well, the father was done for drink driving seven years ago, but nothing since.'*

'OK, thanks for—'

'They did report a series of break-ins starting five months ago . . . Oh, and some vandalism in September, October . . . right the way through till Christmas. Broken windows, paint on the doors, that kind of thing. Hang

on and I'll cross-reference it . . .' A longer pause, and this time Logan could swear he heard crisps being surreptitiously crunched. *'Unlucky: looks like it was just them. No other reported incidents of vandalism in Hamilton Place. Couple of stolen bikes down the other end and—'*

'That's fine. Thanks,' said Logan before he was given the complete criminal history of the street. He stuck the phone back in his pocket. Just after ten on a Saturday morning – if they were lucky, the whole family would still be at home.

The front door was opened by a balding man in his mid-thirties. A little older than Sean Morrison's dad and a lot heavier round the middle. He took one look at Rickards standing there on his doorstep, and said, 'About bloody time you showed up: we called Thursday!'

Logan couldn't help himself. 'Thursday?'

'Thursday! The window! Don't you lot even *speak* to each other? Or did they just send you out to arse about and waste our time like the last ones? Well?'

Typical: Control was getting ready to list every crime and misdemeanour in the area going back to 1906, but they couldn't tell him there was an open call at the address he was asking about in the first place. 'We're not here about the window, Mr Whyte; we're here about Sean Morrison.'

And at that the bald man's face clouded over. 'We have nothing to say about that little b . . . about him.'

'He was your son . . .' Logan checked his notes, 'Ewan's friend, wasn't he?'

'That was a long time ago.' Mr Whyte stepped back as the first specks of rain began to fall, making tiny water blisters on the bright-blue door.

'Right up till six months ago.'

'About that.'

'Same time you started reporting acts of vandalism?'

He started easing the door closed. 'Look, I've told you we don't want to talk about that Morrison child. Ewan hasn't had anything to do with him for months. Now if you'll excuse me, I have to go—'

'This will only take a moment, sir.' Logan stuck his foot in the crack, keeping the door from shutting. 'And you wouldn't want people to think you refused to help us catch Sean Morrison, would you? It might look like you were protecting him.'

Whyte scowled and swore, but he let them in.

15

Mr Whyte scuttled about the living room, picking up toys and colouring books and piling them on the coffee table, obviously flustered at being outmanoeuvred. Logan let his gaze wander around the room: eclectic ornaments; an upright piano; photos of various sea-and-sand holidays. A large dining room lay through an open archway with a conservatory tacked onto the back, littered with stuffed animals and bits of brightly coloured plastic. Through the glass he could see a remarkably well-tended garden complete with koi pond and waterfall. Very flash. An old man was out in the drizzle, taking a pair of pruning shears to a massive clump of honeysuckle, cutting it back to the bone. Which was not an image Logan wanted to dwell on.

Whyte ran out of things to stack on top of one another, and said, 'I suppose you expect a cup of tea,' with enough distaste for Logan to suspect that it would arrive with spit in it. A Jackie Watson special.

'Actually, sir, I think we're fine. Why don't you and I talk about Sean Morrison?'

The man sank into a floral-patterned armchair. 'He's been nothing but trouble. I knew he'd end up hurting someone! That poor old man . . . you should bring back flogging.'

Logan nodded. 'Next time the Crown Office asks, I'll be sure to let them know. He wasn't trouble to start with though, was he?'

Whyte shifted in his seat. 'I always knew—'

'Then why did you let him stay here when his parents went down to Guildford last September?'

'Yes . . . well . . . he was a lot better behaved then.'

'But not after.'

'Look, I've no idea, OK? He was fine one day and the next he was all sullen and wouldn't do anything. We tried taking him bowling, carting, the pictures, even bloody LaserQuest. And all he'd do was mope about and sulk.'

'While he was staying here?'

'Of course while he was staying here. He just kept getting worse; three weeks we had him and it was a nightmare.' He checked his watch. 'Look, is this going to take long? I've got to get the girls ready for ballet.'

'Why did he change?'

'How should I know?' sounding a bit defensive. 'Like I say, he was fine one minute, and the next: boom. Something must have happened at school – a bully, or a teacher, or maybe he did really badly in a test.' He stood, running his hands through what was left of his hair. 'Look, I'm *really* going to have to go. If the girls aren't there for the start of the lesson they send them home. You don't even get a refund.'

'OK, I'd like to speak to your wife, if she's about.'

'She takes Ewan to five-a-side football on Saturdays.' He turned and shouted up the stairs, telling his 'little princesses' to get their tutus down here or they were going to be late. A stampede of tiny elephant feet rumbled down from the first floor, bringing two little girls in pink ballet costumes and duffel coats with it. They were only five, jumping up and down while their dad tried to coax them into their Wellington boots.

The girls took one look at Rickards, squealed, and hid behind their father's legs, peering out at the strange policeman in their house. 'Don't take it personally,' said Whyte, shooing his ballerinas towards the front door, 'they don't like men in uniform – you should see what they're like with the postman. Come on girls, last one in the car's a stinky!'

'Well,' said Logan, handing Mr Whyte a Grampian Police business card, 'if you can think of anything else, let me know. And I'll need to speak to your wife and son too.'

'Yes, yes, OK fine.' He stuffed the card in his pocket without looking at it, then hurried them out into the rain. 'Molly, darling, put your seatbelt on properly, or the nasty policeman will arrest you!'

'It's the kid, isn't it?' said Rickards as the Whytes' car reversed out of the drive, both little girls staring at him as if he'd grown horns. 'Doing all the vandalism.'

Logan nodded. 'Bit of a sodding coincidence if it isn't . . . and I'll bet Whyte knows it too. Which makes you wonder why Sean Morrison's dad played dumb: Whyte would have been round there like a shot, shouting the odds. Only natural.'

'Doesn't want to admit his kid's a horrible wee bastard?'

'Bit late for that, isn't it?' They climbed back into the CID pool car, Logan watching the rain make ripples on the wet windscreen, until they were suddenly wheeched away as Rickards started the engine and turned the wipers on.

'Where now?'

'Hold on a minute.' Logan dug his phone out and called Control again. 'Those vandalism reports from Whyte: Hamilton Place, did he say he suspected anyone?'

There was a pause on the other end of the line, the plastic clatter of computer keys, then, *'No names . . . fingerprints didn't turn up anything either – always wore gloves . . . window . . . car . . . fish . . . window again . . . No match on anything. Investigating officer thinks it's got to be someone with a grudge.'*

'There's a surprise. And the last report was on Thursday night?'

'Nine pm.' The same day Sean Morrison stabbed two people. Logan thanked her and hung up, then sat drumming his fingers on the dashboard.

'Sir?'

'Back in a sec.' He climbed back out into the rain, leaving Rickards in the car as he made his way down a little path at the side of the Whytes' house, through a tall gate and into the back garden.

The koi pond was like pewter, droplets of water making it shimmer. The gardener had finished the pruning; now he was on his knees, digging away at a flowerbed with a small trowel, ignoring the thin rain. 'Bit early for that, isn't it?' asked Logan, walking up and putting on his best friendly smile.

'Never too early to get the garden in order.' Traces of an Aberdonian accent, but not much.

Logan pointed up at the house. 'You work for the Whytes for long?'

The old man settled back on his haunches, grimaced, and stuck the trowel in the flowerbed, peeling off a pair of mud-crusted gardening gloves. 'I don't work for them. I'm Daniel's father.' Mr Whyte senior levered himself up to his feet with a grunt.

'You lived here long?'

'Eight months. Ever since my Mary died. The house was too empty without her.'

Eight months – that explained why he wasn't on the database as living at the address. 'So you were here when Sean Morrison stayed?'

'Terrible, isn't it? He was such a lovely wee boy, I can't believe he'd hurt anyone.'

'Your son thinks he's a vicious little monster.'

The old man gave a sad smile. 'Yes . . . well . . . Sean Morrison is the spitting image of Daniel's little brother. Daniel was always jealous.' He sniffed and stared at the pond where a golden shape swam beneath the surface. 'It was our own fault: Mary and I spoiled Craig. We shouldn't have, but he was such a beautiful child.' There was silence in the garden. 'Mary was never the same after . . .' Mr Whyte senior gave an embarrassed cough. 'Yes, well, no point in dwelling on it now.'

It might have been the rain misting his eyes, or it might have been a tear. Either way Logan left him to his memories.

DI Steel was sitting behind her desk when Logan backed into her office carrying two mugs of tea. She had a big wet stain over her left boob and a scowl on her face. 'Where the hell have you been?'

'You wanted to see me?' Trying not to stare at the inspector's damp patch.

'Aye, fifteen minutes ago . . .' She threw a sheet of A4 at him: a memo from the Chief Constable himself. Logan read it, muttering along under his breath until he got to the bombshell.

'Oh . . . Well, it could be worse.'

'How?' Steel pulled the office window open, then went rummaging for her cigarettes. 'How could it be worse?'

'Look, I'm sure he's going to—'

'Why the hell did they have to lump him on my team?' Cigarettes found, the hunt for a working lighter began. 'He's going to be a bloody nightmare!'

So that was why she'd wanted him to drop everything and rush up to her office: so she could whinge about DI Insch being assigned to 'facilitate her caseload'. Logan sighed. 'Well, you could give him those house break-ins to look after, or the Fettes investigation?'

'Are you kidding? You know what he's like – he'll try and take over the whole lot. *I'll* end up working for *him*!' The lighter went, scrrrrrit, scrit, scrit, then she hurled it at the bin in the corner. 'Fucking thing . . . If I wanted "help" I'd have asked for it.' Which was the starting point for a fifteen-minute-long rant ending with, 'You'll have to look after him.'

'Me?' Logan sat bolt upright. 'Why me? Give him Rennie, or Rickards!'

But DI Steel just shook her head. 'Sorry Laz: can't do that. Rennie'd be like kicking a kitten, and Bondage Boy would enjoy it too much. All that abuse, he'd never get any work done.' She took a slurp from her mug. 'So you see: it has to be you. You're young, you'll get over it.'

16

Detective Inspector Insch wasn't the sort of person you wanted to get on the wrong side of. Which was unfortunate, because he didn't seem to *have* a right side any more. Logan took a deep breath, then knocked on the inspector's door, having spent an unhappy twenty minutes in the canteen trying to figure out how to keep him busy without actually having to work with him.

A deep, rumbling voice sounded on the other side of the door. 'Enter.' All the warmth of a butcher's bandsaw. Insch's office was larger than Steel's and a lot tidier, with framed theatre posters on the walls: local musical productions of *Kiss me Kate*, *Chicago* and a handful of pantomimes. Some of which featured the inspector in various ridiculous costumes. Pride of place had been given to *The Mikado* in a big mahogany frame on the wall facing Insch's desk.

The huge man looked up at Logan, said, 'Oh,

it's you,' then went back to hammering away at his keyboard with fat, angry fingers.

'DI Steel thought I should come up and—'

'Where the hell do they get off telling me to work for *her*?'

Logan slumped into one of the inspector's visitors' chairs and prepared himself to be whinged to, but Insch just ground his teeth for a minute, then went back to punishing his keyboard.

When there was nothing else forthcoming, Logan held up a couple of manila folders. 'I brought you the case files for those housebreakings. There's—'

'I don't care.' The inspector stabbed the return key then pushed his chair back, staring at Logan over steepled fingers. 'Tell me about the dead body.'

'Which one: the tramp's, the old man who got stabbed Thursday, or the porn star who got buggered to death?'

'The last one. And *try* to bear in mind the victim was a human being, Sergeant.'

And suddenly Logan felt very ashamed of himself. 'Sorry, sir.' That was DI Steel's influence – he'd definitely been working with her for too long. He told Insch everything they knew about Jason Fettes, from his parochial porn career to his rubber bondage suit. Keeping it professional and objective.

Insch listened in silence, stuffing fruit pastilles into his mouth and making the occasional note on small yellow Post-its. 'What about this website: Bondageopolis?' he asked when Logan had finished. 'You get onto Fettes's ISP?'

'It's a local company – they've turned over Fettes's emails and there's nothing in there that looks like it's connected with his death. But from the list of favourites on his computer, we think he's got at least one hotmail account and maybe a couple of yahoo ones as well.'

'And?'

'They're all anonymous – you don't have to give any real details. Could sign up as Osama Bin Laden and no one would bother to check. And Fettes was careful, seems to have cleared his cache pretty regularly and didn't get the browser to remember usernames or passwords.'

'So you can't just log in as him.'

'Nope. I got the IT department to go through his emails and see if he might have forwarded anything to himself from his anonymous accounts. They've got a couple of possibles, but it's taking forever to get anything sorted out with the free email people. Not only do we have the data protection act to deal with, everything has to go through their head offices in the States. It's a nightmare.'

Insch leaned forward, resting his huge elbows on the desktop, staring down at his collection of Post-its. 'OK, bring me the files – updates, interviews, PM notes, everything. Even the HOLMES actions. We'll go through them this afternoon.'

'Yes, sir.' So much for keeping the inspector at arm's length.

By the end of the day they'd mapped out the whole investigation and DI Insch hadn't snapped at Logan once. Which was something of a record these days. 'Tomorrow morning,' said Insch, frowning at his watch, 'I want you to get the team together and we'll do a re-start briefing. Where the hell is that idiot Rennie?'

'No idea, sir.'

'Well, if you see him, tell him I want him at the Arts Centre by half-six at the latest, or his bollocks are going to be hanging from my car keys!' And with that he was gone.

Logan let out a sigh of relief. Insch was a lot more work than he used to be. Still, at least it was time to go home. He was in the middle of signing out when DI Steel found him. 'Heading off early are we?' she asked, treating him to an imperious sniff.

'My shift finished twenty minutes ago, so no.'

'Well, well: at home to Mr Grumpy are we? How was Fatty Insch, he snap your bra strap and chase you round the desk?'

'He wants the Jason Fettes case.'

Steel looked surprised. 'Bondage, sex shops, and seedy internet chat rooms? Doesn't sound like him. Still, what the hell: he's welcome to it, one less thing for me to worry about. You offer him them break-ins as well?'

'Wasn't interested.'

She sighed. 'Me neither. You don't want them, do you?'

'No, not really, I—'

'Actually, that's no' a bad idea, give you an excuse to get away from Inspector Fat Bastard now and then.'

'But—'

'Nope, my mind's made up. You can have Rickards, dirty little squit that he is. Just drop me an update report every couple of weeks and we'll be fine. Don't worry, I'm no' expecting you to actually solve them.'

Somehow that didn't make Logan feel any better.

Drizzle drifted down from the sky in lazy waves, making the streetlights glow like fireflies the length of Union Street. Logan turned his collar up and hurried home, before it could seep all the way through to his skin. The flat was ominously silent when he got in. By quarter to seven there was still no sign of Jackie, which probably meant she'd gone straight to the pub after work. It was becoming something of a habit – ever since the Macintyre rape trial fell to pieces. Logan tried calling her, but her mobile went straight to voice-mail. So that meant he'd have to fend for himself, or face another night in the pub. He checked the kitchen cupboards, then the fridge and decided on a trip to the nearest Chinese carryout.

He was locking the front door when the flat's phone started to ring. Cursing, he let himself back in, just in time to cut the answering machine off mid-flow. 'Hello?'

'Who's this?' The familiar voice of Big Gary.

'Who do you think it is? You phoned me, remember?'

'Aye, but you could've been Watson's fancy piece. He sounds affa like you.'

'Very funny. What do you want Gary?'

'DI Insch: can't get hold of him, his mobile's off, so you're next in line.'

'No I'm—'

'Aye, you are. I asked Steel and she says you're working for him now.'

Bloody DI Bloody Steel. Logan sighed. 'What's up?'

'We just got a call in from Tayside Police – they've had a rape that's a dead match for your Rob Macintyre case.'

17

The sound of a piano being tortured greeted Logan as he pushed through the Arts Centre's main doors. According to the posters up outside in the huge, columned portico, there was supposed to be a series of Samuel Beckett plays on this week, but *Waiting For Godot* had a big CANCELLED sticker across it. Which explained how Insch had managed to get hold of the Arts Centre – calling everyone in for a special rehearsal, even though it was a Saturday night. Normally a production wouldn't get to set foot on the stage until a day or two before the run. And from the sounds of things, Insch's *Mikado* was nowhere near ready for that.

Logan sneaked in through the doors to the theatre – burgundy carpet, mahogany panelling, rows and rows of empty seats facing a stage that was bedecked with some of the lumpiest people Logan had ever seen, mostly wearing jeans and sweatshirts. And down in the front row of seats was DI Insch, addressing his cast: 'Again, from "I'll tear the mask from your disguising" and please, for the love of God, watch for the beat!'

Logan stood and watched them for a minute, trying not to laugh. DC Rennie was in the middle of the men, overacting and throwing his hands about like a demented windmill. This time the chorus were *almost* on time with their bellowing. Insch made them do it again. Logan really didn't want to have to suffer it a third time through, so he marched up and tapped the inspector on the shoulder.

'Sorry to interrupt, sir, but Control called: Tayside Police have been on the phone . . .' Insch listened to what little information Logan had, before turning and telling the people on stage that they were going to go over this bit until they got it right, or it killed them. He didn't care which. Leaving them in the not-so-careful hands of the pianist he steered Logan out into the corridor.

'Get back there and find out if they got any forensic evidence. We've not destroyed Macintyre's DNA sample yet – if we can get a match he's screwed. In fact, get Tayside to email up every-thing they've got. I'll be finished here in . . .' he checked his watch, then looked back at the double doors as a ragged cacophony marked another ill-fated adventure into the world of Gilbert and Sullivan. 'We'll still be here by the time you get back.'

Listening to the noise coming from the stage, Logan got the feeling he could come back the same time next year and they'd still be bloody awful.

The last page chugged into the printer's out tray. According to Tayside Police there was no sign of forensic evidence: no hairs, no flakes of skin, no semen, nothing. But the MO was a perfect match for Rob Macintyre: a lone woman, walking home at night takes a short cut through a darkened street and is jumped from behind. Forced to the ground at knifepoint, cut and raped by a man with an Aberdonian accent. Just like every attack they'd tried to pin on Macintyre. And like all the other Macintyre cases, there was nothing connecting the footballer to the crime.

Logan stuffed the printouts into a manila folder and headed back to the Arts Centre. It had taken nearly an hour and a half to get everything emailed up from Dundee, and by the time he got back to the theatre, Insch was in the middle of his standard motivational speech – the same one he gave to incident rooms after telling them all how crap they were and that they should be ashamed to call themselves police officers. 'Now go get cleaned up and I'll see you in the pub.' He forced a smile. 'Good work tonight, people!'

Insch watched them all troop off stage chattering excitedly, then sank down into one of the theatre seats, put his head in his hands and muttered quiet obscenities.

Logan gave him a couple of minutes. Then, 'Got those files you wanted, sir.'

The inspector looked up, wearing a grimace of artistic pain. 'You're not a big theatregoer, are you, Sergeant?'

'Not as such, sir, no.'

Insch nodded thoughtfully. 'Nights like this, I don't blame you.' He sighed. 'OK. Let's see what you've got.' They spread the printouts from Tayside Police on top of the grand piano in the orchestra pit: blood analysis, medical reports, before and after photos of the victim, and a blurry identikit picture of the attacker. It could have been anyone.

'Nikki Bruce, twenty-three, she was on her way home from a night out with friends. She was sick outside the nightclub, so the taxi driver refused to take her. Walked home alone along Broughty Ferry Road. That's where he attacked her.'

The inspector scowled at the photos – before, Nikki had been a good looking young woman with bright eyes and a mischievous smile. The 'after' picture was completely different: one eye swollen shut, the other bright red with burst blood vessels, her nose flattened and off to one side, her mouth crooked and puffed-up, the lip split, three or four teeth missing, her whole face covered in bandages, surgical padding and bruises. It was hard to believe this was the same person.

'And where,' he asked, 'was Macintyre when all this happened?'

'Thought he wasn't a suspect any more.'

Something disturbingly like a growl rumbled deep within Insch's throat. 'Like hell he's not.' He pulled out his mobile and called the Procurator Fiscal, looking for a warrant to drag Macintyre in for questioning. And from the sound of things not getting very far. 'No . . . no . . . he's . . . of course it's him! It's his MO, he's . . . no, we don't . . . but . . .' He placed one massive hand on the pile of paperwork and crushed it into a ball. 'Yes, I understand . . . no . . . of course. Thank you for your time.' Insch hung up, slipped the phone carefully in his pocket, then hurled the printouts at the stage. 'FUCK!' Sheets of paper flared white in the footlights' glow, then slipped back onto the grey-painted floor. A few fluttered down into the orchestra pit. Logan held his breath and waited for the inspector to start taking it out on him.

Instead, Insch screwed his face up, stuck two fingers against the throbbing side of his neck and hissed air in and out through his nose. The trembling subsided and Insch's breathing returned to normal, his face slowly losing its dark purple tinge.

'Er . . .' Logan knew he was probably going to regret asking this, 'are you OK, sir?'

'The PF,' said Insch, his voice eerily level, 'feels that without any evidence directly linking Macintyre to the rape, we can't bring him in for questioning or it'll just look like harassment. If we want to speak to him, we'll have to go round and ask him *nicely*.' The calm act was starting to crumble a bit at the end. 'But right now, I need a drink.'

A patrol car roared by on Broad Street while Logan followed the inspector's massive bulk down a steep flight of stairs to the Illicit Still's subterranean bar. They'd had to walk past FHQ to get here, Insch wrapped up in a brooding silence, while Logan tried to uncrumple the files and get them back into some semblance of order. The pub was about the same distance from headquarters as Archibald Simpson's, but wouldn't be full of off-duty policemen. Which was why Insch had chosen it for this post-rehearsal get-together. Inside, the place looked like it had been designed by someone with a serious banister fetish – they were everywhere, carving the place up into little seating areas, full of students and people with trendy haircuts.

Logan followed Insch up to the bar. 'What do you want to do about Macintyre then?' he asked while the inspector ordered their drinks, then sent the barman hunting for crisps and peanuts.

'We go see him. Smile politely. Ask our questions. And figure out how to nail the ugly wee bastard. See if we can get the ACC to authorize a low-key surveillance operation. Macintyre's going to go out again sooner or later . . .' Somehow Logan doubted they'd get permission: if the PF was leery of the case, the Assistant Chief Constable wouldn't touch it with the shitty end of a pointy stick.

The *Mikado* crowd were through in the snug –
a smaller room up a little flight of stone steps from
the main bar, with slightly fewer superfluous
banisters. Rennie was holding court for a trio of
women. All three of them threw their heads back
and laughed like drains as he reached the punch
line of a particularly dirty joke. Grinning like an
idiot, he looked up and saw Logan. 'Hey, come
meet Sophie, Anna and Liz! They're my naughty
schoolgirls. Come on, scoot up, Liz, let the man
park his bum.' Rennie did the introductions,
playing up Logan's 'police hero' credentials for his
fellow thespians. 'You catch any of the rehearsal?'

Logan turned to check the inspector wasn't
within earshot. 'Only the motivational speech bit
at the end.' A little white lie.

'Oh yeah,' Rennie nodded sagely, 'we sucked
big time tonight. Arse from elbow the whole way.'

Anna, or Liz – Logan wasn't sure which –
slapped the constable on the shoulder. 'Cheeky
bugger! Anyway, Debs was brilliant.' Pointing at
a serious-looking woman sitting on the edge of
the group, deep in conversation with DI Insch. It
took Logan a moment to recognize her: dark, wavy
hair; rosy cheeks; she looked nothing like the
bitch-faced harridan she'd been playing on stage.

One of the other two rolled her eyes. 'Debs is
always brilliant. But Erick . . .'

'Oh God, don't get me started on *Erick* . . .'

Every discussion seemed to revolve around the
various shows they'd been in and who was

sleeping with whom. And Logan didn't have a clue who they were talking about.

He finally escaped one hour and three pints later. Every time he tried to get out of there, Rennie would lurch back from the bar with another round. Eventually he'd had to fake a date with Jackie in order to escape. It wasn't that they were bad people, he just didn't have anything in common with any of them. Well, except for DI Insch and DC Rennie, and he got enough of them during working hours.

The closest he'd got to a normal conversation was with the 'brilliant' Debs about New Zealand and *The Lord Of The Rings* films, and even then it was all about actors and scenery and scripts. Much more interesting was the contents of her handbag, which Logan got an unscheduled peek at when she went rummaging for a hankie after spilling a glass of white wine down herself: compact, lipstick, mobile phone, Ian Rankin paperback, tampons, breath mints, and what looked like a set of fur-lined handcuffs. It took all sorts.

Midnight. A clunk and bang from the front door, then some random giggling and Jackie burst into the bedroom. Logan groaned as the overhead light snapped on, dragging him from sleep and poking its fingers in his eyes. He pulled the duvet up over his head and listened to Jackie bumping into things. Click and the room was in darkness again, then a cold body leapt in beside him and tried to warm its hands on his naked chest. 'Aaagh – get off – horrible woman!' Jackie just giggled and snuggled in closer. Logan gasped. 'You smell like a brewery!'

'Yup, I've been *drinking*.' She snorted and stuck her cold nose into Logan's neck. 'I've been very, very naughty, you may have to spank me.'

'Your feet are freezing.'

'Ooh, I love it when you're all manly . . .' And then she jumped on him.

Ten past seven and DI Insch's morning briefing was in full swing, the inspector rumbling out his instructions from the front of the room, one huge buttock perched on the edge of a desk, popping chocolate raisins into his mouth between sentences. Like a big, pink eating machine. This investigation had been stagnant for too long. There were going to be some changes. Or he was going to kick everyone's arse for them.

Not that there were many arses to kick – when the case had been downgraded from murder to kinky sex gone wrong, the team had been cut by more than two thirds and stuck in one of the smaller incident rooms. Now it was just Insch, Logan, DC Rennie and a handful of uniforms. And even then Logan was only part time.

'Where do you think you're going?' asked Insch as Logan tried to sneak out at the end.

'Those break-ins. You didn't want the case, so I've been lumbered with it.'

Insch shook his head. 'Not today you're not – you've got some homework to do.' He handed over a plastic bag.

'What's this?' said Logan, peering inside at Jason Fettes' narcissistic porn collection.

'This is what Steel should have done in the first place. Go through that lot and see if you can find a match for the guy who dropped Fettes off at the hospital. Maybe they worked together.'

Now that Insch mentioned it, it did sound bloody obvious. But it meant Logan would have to spend the whole day watching a dead man having sex, which didn't exactly sound like a bundle of laughs. Especially not after watching his post mortem. 'Yes, sir.'

'And don't take too long about it either – we're seeing Macintyre at ten and I want you there in case I need someone to talk me out of strangling the little footballing bastard.'

Logan was about to complain that two and a half hours probably wasn't enough time to watch six DVDs and go through eight pornographic magazines. But Insch cut him off with a fat finger. 'If you're thinking of having a whinge, don't. There's no one here to talk me out of strangling *you*.'

18

There was no way he was going to get through all of Fettes' porn collection by ten on his own, so Logan grabbed Rickards and commandeered a tiny room full of abandoned box-files and evidence bags. It had nicotine-yellow ceiling tiles, peeling magnolia paint on the walls, and a fluorescent light that buzzed and flickered, but it was the only place free. Now all they needed was something to watch the DVDs on.

'Got an idea . . .' Rickards disappeared off, leaving Logan in the cramped and messy space.

Swearing quietly to himself, Logan started stacking things in the corner. By the time the constable returned he'd cleared enough space to work in.

'Don't tell anyone, OK?' said Rickards, dumping an archive box on the tabletop. 'Sergeant Mitchell thinks I'm taking them upstairs for more finger-print tests.' Inside there were new-looking laptops and one of those little photo printers.

Logan was impressed. 'Where did—'

'Part of that brothel raid. They were doing live internet sex shows with their punters.' He started plugging things in. 'We can take screen-grabs from Fettes' porn films and print them out.' The machinery whirred and beeped into life, and the constable nodded happily.

'Not as daft as you look then.' Logan selected one of Fettes' DVDs at random.

Rickards grinned. 'Thank God for that, eh?'

By ten o'clock they had a small stack of printed-out porn stars. It'd been easy enough to whiz through the films on fast forward, pausing every time a new face appeared, taking a screen shot, printing it out, then cranking up the speed again. Not surprisingly a lot of the same people popped up in nearly every film, but three of them actually bore a vague resemblance to the e-fit. If you squinted and ignored the whole goatee beard thing.

Logan made sure they all had the names of their films scribbled on the back then went off in search of Insch.

Rob Macintyre's football salary had bought him a large granite house in one of the more exclusive streets off the swankier end of Great Western Road, and a brand new silver Porsche 911 to park outside it, reflecting back the gunmetal skies. According to the DMV computers the twenty-one-year-old also had a Merc and an Audi estate. All with personalized number plates. Logan got the feeling Macintyre was probably spending money as fast as he earned it. Playing Aberdeen's 'look at my car – see how successful I am!' game.

Insch's muck-encrusted Range Rover looked decidedly out of place. The inspector sat in the driver's seat, staring up at the house, crunching his way through a packet of Polo mints. 'You see what they said in the paper this morning?'

'Same as usual: you'd think they'd get tired of kicking us by now.' P&J front page headline: POLICE CAN'T CATCH 8-YEAR OLD KILLER! Colin Miller again, banging on about how Grampian Police couldn't find their backsides with both hands, let alone Sean Morrison. Even for Miller it was vitriolic stuff.

Logan cracked his window open, trying to let some fresh air in. The whole car stank of wet dog. 'What the hell are we supposed to do – search the whole city by hand? Just because he's eight, doesn't mean he's . . .' A scowl had settled onto the inspector's face. 'What?'

'Not your missing bloody child: the Dundee rape!' He shook his head and lumbered out of the car. 'Well, come on then – we don't have all day. Mr Macintyre has kindly granted us a whole twenty minutes of his time and I don't want to waste it sitting here listening to you whine!'

A surprisingly pretty brunette let them into Macintyre's home – she had a distracting amount of cleavage on display, a gold and ruby pendant nestling between her breasts, an engagement ring the size of a gobstopper, and legs like a pole-dancer's. A stereotypical footballer's wife in training. She couldn't have been much more than four months pregnant – the bulge artfully framed by her low-slung trousers, cropped, low-cut T-shirt and open blouse, a ruby-pierced bellybutton sparkling invitingly. 'I don't know why you can't just leave him alone!' she said, marching down the hall ahead of them. 'He's never harmed anyone! You should be out catching real crooks, not harassing my Robert . . .'

Inside, the place was like an Ikea advert: all minimalist lines and pale wood, arty photographs, prints, seashells and strange little glass things in wooden frames. Nothing looked *real*, as if the whole house had been bought from a catalogue in one go, rather than built up over the years. It was soulless. Logan had been expecting more bling.

Macintyre was sitting in the front room, feet up on the coffee table, can of coke in one hand and a phone in the other, chatting away in broad Aberdonian. Macintyre's fiancée growled, 'Feet!' at him and he snatched them back to the carpet as if he'd been scalded, covered the mouthpiece and apologized to his beloved. Logan had never actually met the man before, only seen him in court, on television, or on the pitch at Pittodrie. For a moment he tried picturing the ugly wee sod pinning that poor woman from Dundee to the ground while he carved up her face.

If it *was* him, then Jackie was right: the footballer needed a stiff bloody kicking. He watched
as Macintyre went back to his phone call, laughing
– not a care in the world. And there, to see things
remained that way, was Sandy Moir-Farquharson,
standing with his back to a huge tropical fish tank,
wearing an expression that made Logan want to
check the soles of his shoes in case he'd trodden
in something.

'Ah,' said Insch, 'Mr Far-Quar-Son,' pronouncing
the lawyer's name wrongly in a childish attempt to
wind the man up, 'Macintyre didn't tell us you'd
be here. How *nice* to see you.'

The lawyer sniffed. 'Spare me your amateur
theatrics, Insch, I'm not in the mood. You are here
because my client wants to make sure you don't
jump to any of your usual idiotic conclusions about
this Dundee attack. You are *not* here to interro-
gate, belittle or browbeat Mr Macintyre, is that
clear?'

The inspector's face darkened, 'You don't tell
me how to question a suspect!'

'Please, try and get this through your swollen,
shiny pink head: Mr Macintyre is – not – a –
suspect. Your last pathetic attempt to fit up my
client was thrown out of court, remember? And
furthermore—'

A clatter at the door and Macintyre's mother
backed in, wheeling a hostess trolley with tea
things and little cakes on it.

'Now, now,' said Macintyre, the words long, flat

and Doric, as his mum handed out the cups and saucers. 'Gie the mannie a break, he's only deein' his joab.' Without the phone clamped to his lug Logan could see Macintyre's ruby earstud twinkling away, red like his fiancée's pendant, the colour of AFC. The colour of fresh blood. And for the first time, Logan got the feeling Macintyre was laying it on a bit thick – playing the good-natured, parochial Teuchter for the nasty policemen. Macintyre pointed Insch at an expensive-looking couch. 'Yoooo ask away Inspector, I'll dee ma best ta help ye.'

Hissing Sid didn't look too happy about it, but he didn't say anything as DI Insch sat, pulled a sheet of newsprint from his jacket pocket and laid it on the spotless coffee table in the middle of the room, smoothing it out so that the headline was facing the footballer: COPYCAT RAPIST STRIKES IN DUNDEE! 'I'd like to know where you were on Friday night.'

'Easy – I wis with Ashley, wizn't I, baby?'

Logan watched her right hand flutter to the gold chain round her neck, the one with the shiny red ruby dangling from it. She nodded. 'Yes, he was with me all night.' Then she dazzled them with her smile. 'Snored like a bandsaw too.'

'Dinna listen tae her,' said Macintyre. 'I dinna snore!'

'Yes you do, you—'

Insch cut in across this charming domestic scene. 'Where? Where did you spend the night?'

'In bed.' – Macintyre.

'In town.' – Ashley, both speaking at the same time. She blushed and threw a pillow at her husband to be. 'We went out for a couple of pints, got a takeaway and spent the rest of the night here.'

'That's right,' said the mother, bringing round the Bakewell tarts and Tunnock's tea cakes. 'I wis here when they came back.'

Insch stared at her. 'Don't tell me he still lives at home with his mum.'

'*I* live with *him*. This is my Robby's hoose, bought it outright: nae mortgage. How many sons can dae that?'

Insch made them tell him which pub they'd gone to, and which carryout as well. Logan wrote it all down, knowing he was probably going to get lumbered with checking their alibis.

'And if that's all, Inspector,' said the lawyer, 'I think my client has been generous enough with his time. If you have any further questions you will submit them to me in writing and I will pass them on.'

'Oh you think so, do you?' Insch pulled himself from the couch's leathery embrace and loomed over the lawyer, using his bulk to intimidate the man. Moir-Farquharson didn't even flinch.

'Any attempt on your part to contact my client directly will be treated as harassment. Given your recent behaviour I don't think we'll have any trouble getting a court order. Do you?'

* * *

The explosion happened in the car outside – DI Insch railing and swearing with the doors closed and the windows rolled up, while Logan stood outside on the pavement, not looking forward to the trip back to the station. Finally Insch calmed down, doing the same pulse-taking, deep-breathing exercise Logan had seen last night in the theatre. And then the passenger door popped open and Insch told him to get into the car: they didn't have all day.

The traffic was unusually heavy for a Sunday morning, and the inspector kept up a muttered, murderous commentary as he threaded the car back towards the station.

'Er . . .' said Logan, 'are you OK, sir?'

Insch turned a baleful eye on him and said no he bloody well wasn't. Then there was an uncomfortable silence. Logan tried a different tack.

'Fettes's collection – we've got three possible matches from the DVDs.'

A grim smile slid onto the inspector's fat features. 'Have we now? Names?'

'All made-up, porn-star ones.' He pulled the three glossy photo-style printouts from his pocket and handed them over. 'We'd have to ask the guy who directs the things.'

Insch clamped the screen grabs against the steering wheel, glancing at them as he drove. 'You see,' he thrust the pictures back at Logan, suddenly in a much better mood. 'I'm on the case less than twenty-four hours and we're already making progress.' He pulled the car round, following Logan's directions to ClarkRig Training Systems Ltd. 'Check the side pocket will you, should be some toffees in there . . .'

Zander Clark's mum was polishing the reception desk when Logan and Insch walked in. 'Wow,' she said, staring at the inspector, 'you're a big one, aren't you?'

'Is your son in?' asked Logan, before she got them all into trouble.

'Eh? Oh . . . yes, yes. We don't normally work Sundays, but he gets a bit obsessed when he's working on something new. You go right on through.' She pointed at a dark blue door leading off the reception area. 'They're filming though, so *shhhhh!*'

The indoor studio was long and wide, the sort of place you could park four or five double-decker buses in and still have room for a pipe band. They'd built a film set in here – what looked like a small section of an oil rig's accommodation block – three cabins with bunk beds, a shower and a stretch of corridor, all with powerful television lights hanging overhead. Only Logan was pretty certain they weren't shooting a safety film. Not unless it was 'how to avoid catching sexually transmitted diseases from Viking lesbians'.

Both Logan and Insch stood frozen to the spot, watching as a man in dirty orange overalls walked in on two bleached blondes – hair in pigtails, unfeasibly round breasts – making friends with a double-ended rubber willy and some lubricant. A bloke with a Steadicam walked around the newcomer, stopping just behind him, focusing on the bed and the Viking ladies.

'Aaaaaand, cut!' Zander Clark, stood up from behind a monitor and marched onto the set. 'Brian, that was perfect. Claire, Gemma: I still need more energy from you, darlings.' He plonked himself down onto the bed next to them. 'Remember – this is you celebrating life! You've been in the ice caves of Ragnarok for five hundred years, but now you're out: you're free!'

The girls exchanged a look. 'Aye, well,' said one, 'it's no' easy celebratin' life wi' a dildo up yer—'

'Ragnarok,' said Insch, his deep bass rumble echoing off the bare warehouse walls, 'is an event, not a place.'

The sound man looked up, saw them standing there, then bonked the director on the shoulder with his boom mike. 'You got visitors.'

'Oh for goodness' sake!' Zander threw his hands in the air. 'This is a *closed set!* You're not supposed to be in here!' He stopped and stared at Logan. 'Do I know you?'

Insch nodded. 'Show the nice man your warrant card, Sergeant.'

Zander snapped his fingers. 'Of course – you were with that inspector woman, weren't you: ugly, wrinkled old boot, thought erotic films were beneath her. You here about my break-in this time?' The director stuck out his hand to Insch. 'Zander Clark, with a Z.' Logan had been right: the director wasn't *quite* as big as the inspector, but it was close. Without the beard, hair and glasses they'd be very fat, pink, peas in a pod.

Insch took his hand and squeezed, making the man wince. 'We need to talk to you about some of your employees.'

'Oh, right . . .' Zander retrieved his hand and stuck it under his arm, before turning and shouting back at the set, 'Take ten, people. You're doing *great* today!' He sounded a lot more convincing than Insch had last night with his theatre crowd. 'Honestly,' said Zander, dropping his voice as the ladies on the bed unplugged themselves and climbed into fluffy pink dressing gowns, 'it's like juggling cats some days.'

Insch nodded. 'I know what you mean. And I'll bet half of them can't remember their bloody lines either.'

Zander smiled, hooked his arm through Insch's and led him over to a trestle table with thermos flasks, pastries and sandwiches on it. 'God, if I had a pound for every time I've had to re-shoot a scene because of that! The only things they get even *vaguely* right are "ooh" and "ahh" and "harder!" Try getting them to say anything more complicated and you're at it all day. Are you in the arts, Inspector?'

'Local stuff. Mostly musicals. A bit of panto-mime, I—'

'That's it!' He slapped Insch on the back. 'I *knew* I'd seen you somewhere before: two years ago – *Aladdin*. You were Evil Uncle Abanaza. Brilliant.'

'Well, I wouldn't—'

'Just you stop right there! You brought an emotional resonance to the role, and that's not easy with the little buggers in the audience shouting, "He's behind you!" the whole time.'

Logan wandered off before they could start discussing motivation and method acting: panto versus porn.

The cast and crew had split up: the sound, camera, make-up and lighting people hanging out in one of the fake cabins while the actors went round the back to smoke cigarettes and talk about *EastEnders*. He tried them first. 'Excuse me.'

The Viking ladies turned to him in unison. Up close it was easy to see the layers of foundation hiding bad skin, the slightly squint features. Pale, plain women done up to look like something they weren't. And Mr Orange Boiler Suit wasn't exactly an oil painting either. 'Sorry, darlin',' said Gemma, flicking a chunk of ash off the end of her fag, 'we're kinda workin' right now, so we canna do the whole *fan* thing. OK?'

Logan pulled out his warrant card again. 'Coincidence: I'm working too.'

The girls took a step back, but Mr Boiler Suit squared his shoulders – he couldn't have been much over five foot three, but Logan supposed 'height' wasn't the measurement they'd hired him for. Not standing up anyway. Boiler Suit scowled. 'You heard her, we're *working*!' He flexed his muscles and gave Logan his best hard-man impersonation. 'Now clear off out of it!'

Logan stared at him, until the man looked away, then shuffled backwards to stand with the Vikings. 'You recognize any of these men?' Logan handed over the three screenshots from Jason's porn collection.

'Hey,' said the man, peering at one, then flipping it over, reading the film name off the back, 'this is me! Wow . . . Claire, you remember *Cumlamity Jane*?'

Claire groaned. *'Fastest Dildo In The West*: couldnae walk straight for a week!' Boiler Suit handed over the printout and she laughed. 'You used to be such a porker, Brian!'

Logan checked the e-fit – without the extra weight round the face he looked nothing like the man in the picture. But Logan asked him where he was the night Fettes died anyway.

'Eurodisney. Two weeks with the girlfriend and her kid. Pissed down the whole time.' It'd be easy enough to check.

'And what about the other two?'

Gemma ID'd the man in *From Rubber With Love*: 'Frank Garvie – I think he's somethin' in computers now . . . Oh and this een,' she held up the last printout, 'Mat McEwan, he's deid. Took an overdose at Christmas. Shame, he was nice.'

Logan thanked them for their time, then went

and asked the camera crew the same questions, just in case, but the stars seemed to be telling the truth. Insch and Zander were laughing about something when Logan got back to the food table, both of them drinking coffee and stuffing their faces with Danish pastries. 'You see,' said the director in a shower of pastry flakes, 'it's all about challenging expectations. It doesn't have to just be sex, sex, sex – there should be a real emotional message to it as well. It has to have some heart! That's why I don't do gonzo films. No freak sex, nothing that degrades women, no violence,' another bite, 'OK, there's a bit of spanking in the bondage stuff, but it's all safe, consensual, and straight.'

Insch opened his mouth, but Logan butted in before he could say anything. 'What about James Bondage: the nun with the strap-on?'

'Oh, please, that's straight. Kinky, but straight. I don't do gay porn.'

'No? What about the two girls then? Your Vikings.'

Zander smiled indulgently, patting Logan on the shoulder. 'Girl-on-girl isn't gay, it's *erotic*.'

'Yes . . . well . . . I've identified the guys from Fettes's porn collection: one's dead, one's here, and the other quit the business about a year ago.'

Zander peered at the screenshot. 'Oh, Frank. Yes . . . got performance anxiety after a while. The spirit was willing, but the flesh was floppy. Works for an IT company in the Bridge of Don now. Used to do our website. I've got his business card around here somewhere if it helps?' Insch told him that it would, and the director led them back through to the reception area, copying Garvie's home and work addresses down onto a compliments slip. 'Look, I've got to get back to it, but before you go,' Zander rummaged about in a cardboard box under the desk, coming out with a DVD. '*Crocodildo Dundee*, my masterpiece. I'd really like to know what you think. It's so nice to actually talk to someone about the *art* for a change.'

He showed them to the front door, shook Insch's hand, then did the same with Logan, winking as he did. 'Remember, Sergeant: kinky, but straight.'

19

Insch made Logan drive: he was too busy reading the blurb on the back of his new DVD. 'You know,' he said as Logan wrestled the Range Rover through the Sunday lunchtime traffic, 'I always wanted to work in films. OK, maybe not this kind of thing, but proper movies with cameras and lights and clapperboards . . .'

Logan had never heard the huge man sigh wistfully before. 'You not think he's a bit suspect?' he asked, edging out into the traffic on King Street, 'Everything he does has anal sex and dildos in it. He's obsessed.'

'So?'

'Jason Fettes: internal bleeding, torn sphincter, prolapse . . . ?' He squeezed in between a bus and a filthy grey lorry. 'Plus when Steel and I asked him if he could identify Fettes's photo he didn't ask "what's he done"?'

Insch frowned, then rummaged about in the glove compartment, letting loose an avalanche of sweetie wrappers. 'Not everyone asks.' He popped a toffee into his mouth. 'You've been hanging round with DI Steel for too long. It's rotted your brain.'

There was no response at Frank Garvie's flat, so they tried his work address instead. Aberdeen Science and Technology Park sat in a little belt of green, surrounded by trees, in the Bridge of Don, the car parks virtually empty except for a handful of vehicles and a family of deer grazing on the grass verges. Garvie's office was a couple of rooms in a wing of Davidson House, a starfish-shaped building at the furthest end of Campus One. He didn't look much like a porn star – balding, slightly podgy, clean shaven, shirt and tie. No sign of the raven-and-skull-tattooed backside Logan had seen bobbing about in *From Rubber With Love*. It wasn't that kind of office.

Everyone else was away for lunch, so they had the room to themselves: a collection of cubicles decorated with plants, plastic Darth Vaders, and Dilbert cartoons. The blinds drawn to keep the low sun from glaring back off the computer screens. Garvie's smile was nervous as the inspector lowered himself into one of the office chairs and made a show of looking round the room. 'So: not in the porn business any more then?'

'Er . . . no . . . And I'd rather people didn't know about it, OK? I've got a good job here.'

'In IT.'

'The money's a lot better, I get overtime on the weekends. And . . . well, you know . . .'

Insch just sat and stared at him, letting the silence grow. It didn't take long before Garvie felt uncomfortable enough to start talking again. 'I couldn't do it, OK? Get an erection. I couldn't get it up. You try screwing two women in front of half a dozen people, with cameras and sound men and someone shouting instructions the whole time – it's not easy.' He folded his arms, bit his bottom lip, then said, 'Plus there . . . Look, it . . .' An embarrassed cough. 'You've heard of gay-for-pay, yeah? Well . . . I was the other way round.'

'And no one else knows.'

Garvie hung his head, mumbling, 'A couple of friends. Not my parents or the guys I work with. So . . . I'd rather you didn't . . .' He shrugged. 'You know.'

'Don't worry, sir, we're the soul of discretion. Aren't we, Sergeant?'

That meant it was Logan's turn: 'Where were you on Monday night, four weeks ago?'

'Four weeks? Erm . . .' He checked his *Star Trek* calendar. 'At home? I think? Monday I usually go out role-playing, but I was in bed with something.'

Insch smiled. 'And does "something" have a name?'

Garvie blushed. 'There wouldn't be any point . . . I still can't . . .' He cleared his throat. 'I'm impotent.' Staring hard at Captain Kirk fighting Spock in some sort of arena.

181

'I see. And is there anyone who can confirm that you were in bed, alone?'

'Not unless my cat counts. What am I supposed to have done?'

'Do you know a Mr Jason Fettes?'

Garvie didn't even take time to think about it: 'No.'

'Really?' Logan held up one of Fettes' DVDs. 'That's funny because he was in *From Rubber With Love* too. See?'

'Well,' Garvie kept his eyes on Kirk and Spock, 'with films you don't always get to meet everyone who—'

'You did a double entry with him and a girl called "Misty". He was on the bottom. So to speak.'

Silence. 'I'd rather not talk about it.'

Insch found an open packet of Skittles on the desk and helped himself. 'Tough.'

'He . . .' Deep breath. 'Look, I'm really not comfortable discussing this, OK? I mean, I saw that thing in the papers—'

'But you didn't come forward and tell us who he was?'

'I *wanted* to . . . but . . .'

Silence.

Dark circles were beginning to form beneath Garvie's arms, the smell of second-hand curry oozing out of him like a malodorous fog. Fidgeting in his seat, he stared up at the ceiling tiles, then down at his hands, then back to his *Star Trek* calendar again. Anything to avoid making eye-contact with DI Insch or Logan. He couldn't have looked more guilty if he'd tried.

'I . . . I didn't think it would make any difference . . .' Garvie ran a hand over his damp forehead, then wiped it dry on his trouser leg. 'We worked together a couple of times, that's all.'

'And did you ever see him socially?'

Squirm. 'I . . . no . . . well . . . ehm . . .' His cheeks bright red. 'We . . . he . . .' Gulp. 'We met at a couple of . . . parties.'

'What kind of parties?'

'BDSM . . . BDSM parties.'

Insch frowned. 'What the hell is a—'

Logan answered that one for him, 'Bondage, domination and sadomasochism. Far as we can tell Fettes was pretty active in the scene.'

There was an uncomfortable pause, then Garvie cleared his throat, fidgeted some more, and finally said, 'When I started having . . . problems, I . . . well . . . sometimes it helped. The . . . it's not . . .' He gave up. 'We used to go to parties in Ellon, or Cults. Westhill a couple of times. They'd have a Black Room, usually just a bedroom you know, with beanbags and stuff? The windows taped over, no lights. I had this sweet dark red, full-body rubber suit, custom made – a Kastley, top of the range . . . Doesn't fit any more . . .' Garvie paused and took a deep breath. 'It's meant to be anonymous, but I knew what Jason . . . Sometimes he and I . . .' he trailed off and shrugged.

'You're saying Jason was gay.'

Garvie almost laughed. 'It's not like that. Gay, straight . . . it's . . . it's not like that. You wouldn't understand.'

'So you and Jason would meet up at bondage parties and have sex. Why did you tell us you'd never met him?'

'Why do you think? I never hurt him, OK?'

Logan leant across the desk and laid an understanding hand on Garvie's arm. 'Not even if he asked you to? Wanted you to be his "top"? Is that what happened, Frank? Did he ask you to hurt him and it just got out of hand?'

'No! See: I knew you'd do this! I didn't do that to him.'

'Accidents happen, Frank. We can understand that.'

'It wasn't me! I've not seen Jason for over a month!'

'He died four weeks ago.'

Garvie shoved his chair back and lurched to his feet. 'IT WASN'T ME!'

'Calm down, Frank—'

'You can't pin this on me! I didn't do anything!' He wiped the sweat from his face. 'It's not fair!'

'Not fair?' Insch turned on him, 'I'll tell you what's not bloody fair – a young man lying in the morgue while some sick bastard gets away with murder. THAT'S not fair!'

Garvie backed away, trembling. 'I want a lawyer.'

'I'll bet you do. Sergeant, escort Mr Garvie to the car please. We're going for a little ride.'

They put Garvie in the back of Insch's Range Rover and stuck the child locks on, the inspector driving them back into town while Logan rode with the ex-porn star. Making sure he didn't get up to anything. The sky had darkened – wind whipping white froth off the steel-grey North Sea, as they took the Beach Esplanade.

A handful of hardy souls were out braving the elements with their dogs, marching along the top path, their coat-tails whipping about their legs. The Kings Links golf course was nearly deserted, and so was the road, just the clump and bump of potholes and the occasional whimper from their 'guest'. The man was terrified, hunched up and trembling, eyes darting left and right, sweat beading on his forehead. Not big on small talk.

'You know,' said Logan, trying again, 'it doesn't have to be this hard, Frank, all you need to do is talk to us. OK?'

Garvie inched away from him until he was hard against the other door without so much as a word. Logan sighed and watched the scenery go by instead, looking down the embankment at the side of the road as the golf course gave way to a driving range. There was a dilapidated old pitch-and-put between there and the road: a manky collection of four rusty white anchors and some little concrete lumps, all glowing in a shaft of golden sunlight.

A wee boy was whacking a golf ball about on the patchy grass, completely oblivious to the brooding clouds and howling wind. Logan envied him, it would be nice to be that innocent again and un—
'Stop the car!'

Insch didn't need to be told twice: he slammed on the brakes. The Range Rover screeched to a halt and Logan yanked the door handle. Nothing happened. 'Bloody child locks!'

'What the hell is going—'

'Let me out!'

'Sergeant?'

Logan mashed his thumb down on the electric window button, sticking his hand through the gap and opening the door from the outside. Insch unbuckled himself, shouting, 'What's wrong?' as Logan leapt from the car and started running hell for leather down the steep slope towards the large white-painted anchor that marked the northern edge of the pitch-and-put course, yelling back over his shoulder: 'It's Morrison! Call for backup!'

He nearly lost it jumping over a gorse bush, slithering on the grass on the other side, just managing to stay upright by flailing his arms in circles. The kid had his back to Logan – completely oblivious – bent over his putter, trying to get his ball into a two-foot length of ancient drainpipe. He looked up at the last moment, just as Logan barrelled into him, sending them both crashing to the ground. The wee boy screamed as Logan pushed his face into the damp grass and dragged the handcuffs out, breathing hard. 'Sean Morrison . . . I'm arresting you . . . for the murder of Jerry Cochrane—'

Someone was shouting in the background.

'—and the attempted murder of PC Jess Nairn. Hold still! You do not have to say anything, but it may harm your defence if you fail to mention—'

Angry voices getting closer. Sean struggling beneath him. Logan put his knee in the small of the child's back. Trying not to take too much satisfaction from the yelp of pain. That would teach him to go kicking policemen in the head.

'—when questioned something you later rely on in court—'

'GET OFF HIM!'

'—Anything you do say will be given in evidence.' Logan pulled out his warrant card and flashed it at the furious-looking man running across the pitch-and-put course, an angry woman following close behind. 'Police – stay back everything's under—' A fist connected with his cheekbone, snapping his head round. Logan crashed into the grass, struggling to get up as the man leapt on him. Another fist caught him on the side of the head. The world roared in his ears, and the sound of a woman screaming something.

Logan grabbed a handful of the man's groin and did his best to crush it. Twisting at the same time. The guy's face went purple and a thin sliver of spit dribbled from his lips as Logan shoved him off, staggered to his feet and kicked him in the backside, sending him sprawling. Logan stumbled, caught himself, and sat down hard on the wheel of the fake cannon-mount-thing between the second and third hole. 'What part . . .' he puffed, mouth full of the coppery taste of fresh blood, 'what part of "Police, stay back" didn't you understand?'

'You bastard!' The woman spat at him.

Logan picked up his warrant card from the grass at Sean Morrison's feet, and shoved it at her. 'Police!' He leant forward, hands on his knees, trying not to throw up. She ran to the small boy, crying, pulling him to his knees, kissed him on the cheeks and forehead, then stood, marched over to Logan and smacked him one.

She had a better right hook than the man. 'You dirty bastard! You dirty, fucking bastard!' Another punch, but this time Logan was ready for her, grabbing her arm and yanking her off balance. She went crashing into the metal ramp between the cannon wheels, tumbling over it to lie spread-eagled on the third hole. Groaning.

'What the hell is wrong with you people?' Logan lurched to his feet. 'I'm a policeman! This is a murder suspect! Ow . . .' The inside of his mouth ached: he'd taken a chunk out of his cheek. He spat a glob of blood out onto the ground at his feet as Insch's Range Rover screeched to a halt by the abandoned hut, where they used to rent out the pitch-and-put golf clubs in the open season.

The inspector jumped out and plipped on the locks – leaving Garvie handcuffed in the back – lumbering across the course with surprising speed.

'Did you get him?'

Logan nodded. 'Over there.' He winced and explored the inside of his mouth with a finger. One of his teeth was loose.

Insch hauled the kid to his feet. The eight-year-old murderer wailed and moaned and blubbered, snot and tears streaming down his face. Logan pulled his finger out and stared. 'Fuck.'

It wasn't Sean Morrison.

20

The Chief Constable's office was full of unhappy
faces – DI Insch and DI Steel sitting opposite one
another in the visitors' chairs while 'God' himself
sat behind the desk, drumming his fingers lightly
on the formal complaint lodged by the wee
boy's family. Count Nosferatu – AKA Inspector
Napier, the ginger-haired, parrot-faced, miser-
able-bastard head of Professional Standards –
lurked by the window, scowling at Logan as he
went through the events leading up to the
current fiasco. They'd kept him waiting outside
for nearly an hour while they decided what they
were going to do about him. Big Gary was here
too, in his official capacity as Federation rep,
which meant it was serious. They were probably
going to fire him.

Logan could feel Napier's hooded eyes boring
into his back like a set of steak knives. The
inspector had gone out of his way to make life
difficult ever since the 'Mastrick Monster' case;

screwing Logan over had become something of a pet project for him. He'd be loving this. Logan got to the part where the family started threatening lawsuits then finished. Now the only sound in the room was the radiator, pinging away to itself beneath the window, and then the CC said, 'You really, *genuinely* believed he was Sean Morrison?'

'Yes, sir.' Maybe he'd be lucky and get off with a suspension?

'And you used force because you thought the child was violent?' The CC steepled his fingers. 'An eight-year-old boy?'

'Sir, last time we ran into him he stabbed a policewoman in the throat. And he'd just killed—'

'And you let him get away.' Napier – his voice like a sliver of ice. 'If it weren't for your . . . "condition" Constable Nairn wouldn't have had to rescue you, would she, Sergeant?' Logan didn't answer that. The inspector sneered. 'Surely even *you* should have been able to subdue an eight-year-old child!'

The CC held up a hand and Napier went quiet again. 'You understand that we're going to get hauled over the coals on this one, don't you, Sergeant? Not only have Grampian Police failed to catch an eight-year-old murderer, we're also going round assaulting children and their families at random.'

'They attacked me! I was just—'

The Chief Constable kept on talking. 'Do you

have any idea how incompetent that makes us look, Sergeant?'

Logan had thought it was a rhetorical question, but the CC stared at him until he answered. 'I thought it was Sean Morrison.'

A sigh. 'And that's the only reason we're not suspending you. But for God's sake – next time you get the notion to arrest a small child, try and pick the right one!'

If anyone asked, he'd say he was concentrating on the three million break-ins DI Steel had lumbered him with, but if he was being honest, Logan was hiding in the cramped little room he'd commandeered to watch Jason Fettes' porn collection, having a bit of a sulk. The Force Medical Officer had given him a couple of cold packs for his bashed head, but they didn't seem to be doing much good. He still ached.

Bloody parents: what the hell did they think they were doing, dressing their bloody kid up like Sean Morrison? It wasn't as if the kid's description wasn't plastered all over the papers and television news . . .

He sat and stared at the laptops Rickards had purloined from the evidence store. Then started swearing. If anyone found out they'd been using the damn things to watch dirty DVDs he'd be right back up in front of Napier again and the pointy-faced bastard would get another shot at making life difficult. Logan was rummaging about under the desk, trying to untangle the wires and plugs, when the door battered open and a huge shadow loomed into the room. Insch.

'What the hell are you doing down . . . never mind. Get your coat – the PF likes Garvie as a suspect. He and the victim knew each other, they're both into bondage, they've had sex together – or whatever it is these freaks do – and Garvie's impotent.' Logan stuck his head out from beneath the desk, just in time to see a cola cube disappear into the inspector's mouth. The huge man sooked thoughtfully. 'That says sexually frustrated to me. Garvie gets himself one of those jumbo-sized strap-on things, ties Fettes up, and gets carried away. Suddenly there's blood everywhere and a last-minute rush to the hospital.'

'So we need to get a search warrant and—'

Insch held up two sheets of paper. 'Signed and sealed. We're just waiting for the IB to get their backsides in gear.' He smiled, the buzzing striplight flickering off his bald head. 'What did I tell you: Steel couldn't crack it in four weeks and I've done it in less than a day.'

Garvie's flat was nothing special from the outside – two bedrooms on the second floor of a four-storey building in Danestone, a sprawl of boxy homes on the north bank of the River Don. Winding cul-de-sacs, yellow brick, and pantiles. Huge metal pylons marched through the middle of the place, like Martian tripods frozen on their way to war. Garvie's building sat in the shadow of one, a faint electrical buzzing just audible through the open kitchen window. The flat was done up in classic geek chic: the lounge housed a complete collection of *Star Trek*, *DS9*, *Voyager*, *Next Generation*, *Enterprise*, *Buffy the Vampire Slayer*, *Stargate*, *Farscape*, *The Simpsons* and a stack of Japanese Anime; PlayStation, Xbox and TiVo hooked into each other and a collection of fancy speakers; one wall dominated by a huge screen, the projector bolted to the roof above the door; and a single black leather couch. The spare bedroom was done out as a study with a collection of computers and stacks of books and comics. The latter all sealed away in individual plastic sheaths, as if Garvie was afraid they'd catch something.

The bondage gear was in the master bedroom, taking up one side of the built-in wardrobe, the custom-made dark red rubber suit hanging next to a variety of leather harnesses, straps, paddles and flogging whips. 'Houston, we have lift off . . .' said one of the IB technicians, emerging from the bottom of the wardrobe with a large black phallus. It was at least a foot and a half long, standing out in sharp contrast to its finder's white paper over suit. It went in a large evidence bag. Next out was a familiar pink mushroom shape.

Insch got as far as, 'What the—' before Logan jumped in with 'Butt plug.' The inspector stared at him.

'I . . . er . . . DI Steel told me about them when

we found one in Fettes's bedroom.' Feeling a blush rising up his cheeks, suddenly uncomfortably hot in his SOC outfit.

Garvie's porn collection was alphabetically ordered in a small bookcase next to the bed – a handful of his own films, and a collection of American and Dutch hardcore gay porn. Hidden away at the back of the sock drawer was a collection of unlabelled video tapes and two ancient seventeen-millimetre film canisters. One marked THE BUTLER'S REVENGE, the other FESTIVE FROLICS in faded brown script.

'You know,' said Logan as they were bagged up, 'somehow I don't see Garvie being the old-fashioned projector type . . .' And he was right – they searched the whole place from top to bottom but there was no sign of any device that would play anything that old. 'He's got something dodgy in there.' Logan asked the IB guys to take the canisters out and open them, expecting a nice juicy haul of drugs. Disappointed when they turned out to contain exactly what it said on the tin – old rolls of brittle, black and white film.

'Never mind,' said Insch, as they were sealed back up again and returned to their bags, 'I'm sure you'll get something right soon. Law of averages.' Then he clomped off to stand on the doorstep and eat Chewits, leaving Logan to keep an eye on the IB team as they started sampling the bedclothes and carpet for blood and semen stains.

* * *

An hour later and they were back in the car, watching the last of the evidence bags being loaded into the back of the IB's filthy-white Transit van. 'This makes no sense,' said Insch, as Logan started the car, 'there should be blood everywhere. Even if Garvie's got kinky rubber sheets, there'd be a trail between the bedroom and the front door . . .' He stared off into the middle distance for a bit. 'Check all the hotels and B&Bs – see if anywhere rents rooms by the hour to the bondage crowd. Flash Fettes and Garvie's photos about: I want to know if anyone put them up that night. And get a door-to-door done here too. Was Fettes a regular visitor?' The inspector went rummaging in the glove compartment again, coming up empty. 'Sod it. Well, come on, Sergeant, back to HQ, we haven't got all bloody day.'

21

The flat was warm when he got home, the TV competing with the kitchen stereo for who could make the walls shake more. Jackie was through in the bedroom, pulling a pair of old black jeans on over a thick pair of tights. She didn't hear him the first time, so he had to shout it again: 'YOU GOING DEAF IN YOUR OLD AGE?'

'What?' she looked puzzled for a moment, then zipped up her jeans. 'It's that moron downstairs, he's been on a Whitney Houston binge since I got home.' She stopped, and ran a hand across Logan's battered cheek. 'That's some wallop you got . . . Big Gary said they didn't fire you.'

'Napier wasn't happy about it.'

'Napier's never bloody happy.' Jackie pulled on her thick, padded, black jacket, then dug a woolly hat out of the top drawer. It was black too.

'Going somewhere?'

She nodded, stuffing her curly hair into the hat. 'Rennie's been shooting his mouth off about this

Mikado thing all day. I bet him twenty quid he'd be dreadful, so I'm going to the rehearsal to heckle.' Jackie paused, hunting through her coat pockets till she found a pair of black padded gloves.

'You look like a cat burglar.'

'Thanks a heap.' She pulled on her gloves, then frowned at him, head on one side. 'You want to come?'

'No: I've seen them. Your twenty quid's safe.'

'Thought so. Don't wait up, OK? I'm going to the pub afterwards, and you know what Rennie's like when he gets a drink inside him.' And then she was gone.

Monday morning was cold and clear, the sky tainted pale blue with pre-dawn light as Logan walked Jackie up the hill to the Castlegate, making for FHQ and a seven o'clock start. Her nose and ears were bright red by the time they reached King Street, breath streaming out behind them, frost sparkling on the pavements. She stifled another yawn – breaking the scowl that had been creasing her face since the alarm went off at six.

'So what time *did* you get in then?' he asked, trying not to think about the story in that morning's P&J. The one titled, POLICEMAN ATTACKED MY CHILD!

Jackie buried her hands deeper into her coat pockets. 'No idea. Late. And you were right – they were bloody awful. Easiest twenty quid I ever made.' She didn't even crack a smile.

'You want to talk about it?' Logan asked.

'What, the rehearsal?' Shrug. 'Bloody disastrous—'

'You've had a face on all morning.'

'Don't be stupid.' They stopped, waiting for a break in the traffic so they could hurry across the road and down the little alleyway at the side of the Tollbooth and the side entrance to FHQ. 'It's Macintyre, OK? We let the raping bastard get away with it and now he's attacking women in Dundee.'

'Might not be him.'

'Are you kidding? Of *course* it's him, dirty little fuck.' She stepped out onto the road as the lights changed. 'And where is he? In prison? No, he's sodding about in his expensive house and expensive cars with that pregnant bitch fiancée of his. How the hell can she give him an alibi? She's got to *know* he's guilty!'

They kissed goodbye in the shadow of the morgue, then Jackie stomped off, still cursing Rob Macintyre under her breath, while Logan made his way up to the Jason Fettes incident room.

DI Insch's morning briefing had a triumphant feel to it, even if it did start nearly an hour late. The inspector perched on a desk at the front of the room, telling everyone about Frank Garvie: the ex-porn star was due to appear in court at half eleven, where the Procurator Fiscal would ask for him to be held for trial without bail. But it wasn't likely to happen. 'Officially, this isn't a murder investigation,' said Insch, his voice booming in the small room, 'but we're going to treat it like one. It might *look* like an accident, like a sex game gone wrong, but Garvie's got guilty written all over him. He strapped Jason Fettes down and rammed something so far inside him he ruptured the intestinal wall. Fettes broke his own teeth biting down from the pain. He died in agony. We need to know where Garvie took his victim.'

The trouble with asking bed and breakfast establishments if they rented out rooms by the hour for illicit sexual liaisons was that they all said 'No.' Accommodation in the city was at a premium anyway – most places made quite enough exploiting the oil and service companies, without having to cater for that kind of thing as well. So Logan was given the task of trolling round the carpet warehouses, looking to see if any of the hundreds of Aberdeen B&Bs had replaced carpets recently, trying to get rid of suspicious bloodstains.

It was a complete waste of time: if the owners had woken up to find one of their rooms drenched in blood they would have called the police. Stood to reason. But DI Insch was adamant, and Logan didn't see any point in arguing – it would just get him shouted at.

He grabbed Rickards and signed for a leprous Vauxhall, making the constable drive. The morning sky was crystal blue, one side of the street bathed in sunshine, the other shivering in frigid shadow.

Rickards took them up Schoolhill, stopping at the lights to let a troop of schoolchildren swarm across the road, dressed up in their Robert Gordon uniforms: the boys in charcoal-grey trousers, the girls in kilted, tartan skirts, dark blazers marking the cut-off line for untucked shirts and squint ties. Nearly all of them had mobile phones clamped to their ears.

The lights changed to green, a couple of stragglers meandering past without a care in the world. Finally Rickards pulled away, drifting past the crowds of identically dressed kids milling about outside the Robert Gordon's gates – determined not to go through until the very last minute. Enjoying their freedom. Logan turned to watch them. 'Stop the car.'

'What?'

'Pull up over there.' Pointing at the grey slab of Aberdeen Art Gallery.

Rickards did as he was told.

They marched through the crowds, making for a small knot of children by the statue of the school's eighteenth-century founder. There were five of them, laughing and pushing a small ginger-haired girl around. Logan grabbed the ringleader by the scruff of the neck – a boy, seven or eight years old, in expensive sunglasses. The laughter stopped dead. 'Still not learned your lesson?'

'Getoffme! Getthefuckoffme!' Flailing his arms around.

Logan pushed him towards Rickards, before he

could do any damage. The constable got a good double handful of jacket, stopping the kid from doing a runner. No longer the centre of attention, the little girl slipped away.

'Peter, isn't it?' asked Logan as the kid struggled. 'You carrying a knife, like your mate Sean?'

The child's face was every bit as ugly and petulant as it had been in the interview room on Friday – one of Sean's little posse. 'My dad says I don't have to tell you fuckers nothing!'

'Good, you can keep your mouth shut while we search you.'

The struggling got more violent and Rickards tightened his grip as the boy screamed, 'POLICE BRUTALITY!' at the top of his lungs. 'You can't search me! I've not done nothing!'

'I have reason to believe you may be carrying a concealed weapon. That means I have the power to search you. We can—'

'He touched my arse!' Wriggling, looking back at PC Rickards. 'He's a pervert! CHILD ABUSE!'

'Shut up and empty your pockets.'

'Think you're so fucking hard, don't you? Sean kicked your arse! Soon as this fucking paedo lets go I'm gonna kick it too!'

'Your mum and dad must be so proud. Hold him.' Logan started with the jacket: an iPod, a portable game station, a bag of crisps, and a mobile phone. 'What have we here?' Logan flicked it open and clicked it on, the screen lighting up with a picture of a naked woman. The keypad wasn't locked. 'You got a receipt for this, Peter? Not stolen is it?'

'Fuck you!'

Logan called up the built-in phone book and scrolled through it till he found what he was looking for: SEAN – MOBILE. The phone his parents had sworn blind he didn't have. He punched 'call' and held the thing to his ear, listening as it rang, and rang, and rang, and—

'*Pete?*'

'No. You remember me, Sean?'

The kid in Rickards' hands squirmed and writhed, shouting, 'It's the pigs! Sean, it's the fucking police!'

Silence from the other end. Not the sound of a dead line, but of someone very scared, trying to breathe softly.

'Sean, the policewoman's going to be OK. You can come home.'

'Don't fucking listen to him, Sean! Don't—' Rickards clamped a hand over the kid's mouth.

More silent breathing.

'Your mum and dad are worried about you, Sean.'

'*I . . .*'

Logan waited for him to say something else, but that was all he got. 'Come on, Sean, tell me where you are and we'll come get you. It'll be OK.' He left a long pause. Still nothing. Time to try something else. 'You've kept it inside for a long time, haven't you, Sean? What happened six months ago?' A sharp intake of breath on the other end. 'Don't you want to talk to someone about it?'

And the line went dead.

Logan closed the phone and told Rickards to un-gag Sean's mate. 'Where is he?'

A furious scowl. 'I'm telling my dad! I'm telling the teachers! You're fucked! They'll fire you and—'

'He's gone, hasn't he: London? Edinburgh?'

Something cunning passed across the kid's features, then he said, 'Yeah. Yeah, he's gone. London. You'll never find him.'

The first peal of bells from St Nicholas Kirk rang through the cold morning air, sounding nine am and the kids began to drift away to class. Logan took a note of Sean's number and tossed the phone back to the sour-faced child, telling Rickards to let him go. The eight-year-old scrambled for the mobile, catching it just before it hit the pavement.

Back in the car, Logan settled into the passenger seat and told Rickards to do a quick one-eighty at the roundabout, keeping his eye on Sean's friends. Expecting one of them to make a break for it, bunk off and go see the eight-year-old murderer. But one by one they shuffled in through the gates and were gone.

'Damn.' Logan frowned, watching the school go slowly by. Insch or Steel? Insch or Steel . . .'Right,' he said, not really liking either alternative, 'back to the station.'

Constable Rickards looked appalled. 'But the inspector—'

'I know. He'll blow a gasket. You drop me off, then go round the carpet places. Not like you can't handle it on your own, is it?'

'Well, no . . .'

'And you can check out Macintyre's alibi too.' Logan dug out the notes he'd made at the footballer's house yesterday – the pub and the takeaway – and handed them over. 'But if you find anything, you call me first!' And with any luck Insch would never know Logan had dumped him for DI Steel.

22

'What do you mean, you spoke to him?' Steel looked as if someone had tried to comb her hair with a ferret. She sat behind her desk, feet up, cigarette dangling out of the side of her mouth, a small drift of ash falling from the tip down the front of her blouse, like dandruff.

Logan smiled. 'Searched one of his little friends – he had Sean's number programmed into his mobile.'

Steel scowled. 'His bloody parents swore blind he didn't have one!'

'And he's still in Aberdeen too. The kid claimed Sean had run off to London, but he's not as good a liar as he thinks.' He pulled out the hastily scribbled note with Sean Morrison's mobile number on it, and passed it over.

'Ya wee beauty . . .' She picked up her phone and started to dial. Listening in silence as it rang, then hung up. 'Voicemail.'

'My guess is he's only going to take calls from numbers he knows. But now we can—'

Steel was already dialling again – getting on to Control to set up a GSM trace on Sean's phone. She covered the mouthpiece with her hand. 'Get on to the incident room, I want all search teams converging on . . .' Silence for a moment, as she waited for the information. 'Cragiebuckler . . .' A small area on the west of the city, between Rubislaw and Mannofield. 'Hazledene Road!' She slammed the phone down. 'We've got him!'

Tracking someone through their mobile phone wasn't one hundred per cent accurate, but at least they had Sean Morrison pinned down to within fifty metres. A patrol car sat at either end of the quiet road, and more blocked off the surrounding streets, just in case Sean tried to leg it through the back gardens, while a team of twenty uniforms went door to door. He wasn't going to get away this time.

Steel marched up and down the pavement, scratching away nervously at her shoulder as the search teams reported in. Nothing, nothing, nothing, nothing— 'Inspector!' A PC, waving from the open front door of a house just up the road.

She hurried over, looking hopeful. 'You found the little bastard?'

He shook his head, holding up a clear evidence pouch with a mobile phone in it. 'He's not here.'

Inside, the house was a mess: crisp packets, comics, unwashed plates and mugs, half-empty tins of beans, the discarded shells of microwave ready meals, the drained contents of the drinks cupboard stacked up under the window . . . and no Sean Morrison. They turned the place upside down, searching every cupboard and wardrobe, under the beds, the attic, then did the same thing to the large garden shed.

Steel stood in the middle of the garden and swore. 'Where the hell is he?'

'Looks like he broke in through the upstairs bathroom window.' Logan pointed to where the woodwork was scuffed, the paint scratched around the catch. 'Been living on duty-free booze, microwave pizzas, and anything else he could find in the freezer.'

'FUCK!' Steel kicked a plastic tipper truck the length of the lawn, sending it crashing into the fence. 'If you'd just taken the bloody number instead of calling him this morning, he'd still bloody be here!'

'I didn't know he'd run!' Logan backed away towards the house but she followed him, ranting and swearing all the way.

'Course he'd bloody run! What the fuck's wrong with you?'

Logan had got as far as the kitchen door. 'If it wasn't for me we wouldn't even know he'd been here!'

'Don't you *dare* try and twist this round!' she followed him into the house – the fully fitted kitchen smeared with spilled food and empty cartons.

208

A granite worktop stopped Logan's retreat. 'Look, it's not like I did it on . . .' He stopped, looking down at a full, partially congealed Seedy Sanchez Pot Noodle, sitting next to the toaster. He picked up the plastic container. It was still warm.

'Four bloody days we've been looking for this wee shite, and you—'

'He's only just gone.' Logan pressed the Pot Noodle on Steel, then upended the kettle into the sink. The hot water steamed as it hit the piles of unwashed dishes. 'When you called he didn't recognize the number. He dumped the phone and legged it.'

Steel looked down at the container of noodles in her hand and all the wind seemed to go out of her sails. There was an embarrassed silence. 'Aye . . . well . . .' She dumped the carton into the filthy sink and slumped back against the fridge. 'Sorry,' rubbing her forehead, 'shite . . . I *really* thought we were going to get him this time . . .' Sigh. 'Tell you Laz, every case I've got is going nowhere. I am the queen of crap.' She groaned. 'How the hell am I going to explain this to the CC?'

As the PCs trooped out of the house, Logan took one last look at the lounge. Sean Morrison had been living like a feral animal, breaking into someone's home and making himself a nest. Whoever's house it was, they were going to be in for a nasty shock when they got back. There was a large framed photo over the fireplace, husband, wife, two point four children and a golden retriever. The kids were wearing the familiar dark blazers and grey flannel trousers of Robert Gordon's – the same school Sean went to. 'How did he know?'

'You still in here?' DI Steel, standing in the hallway, looking depressed and fiddling with her shoulder again, muttering, 'Sodding nicotine patches . . . don't work for shite . . .'

'How did Sean know he'd be safe? Look at this place: he's been living here for days. What if the family came home?'

'What?'

Logan grinned. 'I think I know how we can find him again.'

They stood outside in the sunshine, Steel fidgeting impatiently while Logan listened to Big Gary listing off names and addresses on the other end of the phone. Logan thanked him and hung up, telling the inspector 'Mr and Mrs Struther.' He pointed at the house they'd just left. 'They've taken the kids to Alicante for a fortnight. Their eldest is in Sean's class. According to the school there's three other families on holiday during term time: MacKenzie, Duncan and Burnett. Sean's breaking into places he knows are empty, where he can raid the booze cabinet and the freezer.'

Steel closed her eyes, raised her face to the high, blue sky, and said, 'Oh, thank God.'

Logan checked his watch. 'We've got one address in Rosemount, one in Cults and one in

Kingswells. Kingswells is too far without transport, and all the buses have his picture up anyway. Cults is possible, but it's a hell of a hike. Rosemount's only a fifteen-minute walk.'

'Aye, unless he's nicked a bike.' Steel pulled out her phone and called Control, telling them to get a couple of unmarked cars to each of the addresses. 'Laz,' she said, when it was all organized, 'if I ever turn straight, you're getting a freebie!'

Two hours later and DI Steel's stomach was growling from the passenger seat. 'Where the hell is he?' She rummaged through her pockets, swore, and slumped back in her seat. 'Nip out and get us some fags, will you?'

Logan groaned. 'He'll be here, OK? Where else is he going to go? Anyway, thought you were cutting back.'

'Don't you bloody start.' She puffed up her cheeks and let out a long, slow breath. 'You had your assessment yet then?'

'Nope.'

'Lucky bastard.' She did her puffer fish impersonation again. 'I'm bloody starving . . .' The house on Whitehall Place was silent and empty, curtains partially drawn. 'Maybe we should check the place again? Maybe he's already inside?'

'He can't be – we'd have seen him.'

She pulled an Airwave handset out and demanded an update from the team watching the back gardens, getting nothing but complaints from the PCs about having to stand around in the cold. She stuffed the thing back in her pocket. 'Where *is* he?'

'Maybe he'll wait till it gets dark?'

Steel swore. 'I'm not sitting in this bloody car till the sun goes down. Come on,' she climbed out into the cold afternoon, 'let's go find a nice public-spirited citizen to make us a cup of tea.'

Mrs McRitchie lived right across the road and wasn't the kind of woman to leave it at just a cup of tea. She backed into the lounge, carrying a tray loaded down with macaroni cheese. 'Hope you're hungry!' she said, clattering it down on the coffee table.

'Did you . . . ?' DI Steel raised an eyebrow, staring at the plates. 'Chips! Alice, you're a star!' She slathered the lot in black pepper, salt and vinegar, before shovelling it into her mouth. Mumbling, 'God, I needed that,' as she chewed.

They had a perfect view of the house opposite, the one Mr Burnett and family had abandoned for a fortnight in the Seychelles. 'You see,' said Steel, taking a slurp of tea, 'much better than sitting in that bloody car.'

Logan checked his watch. 'Going to be another four hours before sundown. Five till it gets really dark.'

'And?' Mouth full of chips.

'Well, I've got stuff I need to do for Insch.'

Steel waved her fork dismissively. 'Screw him:

212

we're out in the field, the CC thinks we're doing something "proactive", we're warm, comfy, got good food, and nothing to do but relax till Sean Morrison shows up. It's no' often we get a chance like this.' She scooped up another glistening mound of pasta and cheese sauce. 'Enjoy it while you can.'

She probably had a point, but Logan was already beginning to feel guilty about abandoning Rickards to chase up the carpet places on his own. As soon as he'd finished lunch he'd call and see how the constable was getting on.

When the macaroni cheese was all gone, followed down by a slice of Dundee cake and more cups of tea, DI Steel settled back into an old leather armchair with a copy of the P&J. And five minutes later she was fast asleep.

Logan dug out his mobile phone. 'Rickards? Yeah . . . no, no sign of him yet. How you getting on?' Not very well by the sound of things. According to the constable, half the places he'd visited were bleating about the Data Protection Act and the other half took forever to get anything useful out of their ancient, creaking computers. So far nothing matched the list of B&Bs.

Logan told him to stick with it, hung up, and went to get himself another cup of tea.

The phone call he'd been dreading came not long after three. DI Steel snored gently in an armchair, the paper draped over her like a newsprint blanket, an afternoon matinee of *High Noon* on the television while Mrs McRitchie sat on the couch, scribbling away in a Sudoku book. Logan excused himself, and took the call in the bedroom upstairs, where he could keep an eye on the street while DI Insch shouted at him.

'Where the hell have you got to? I told you to go round the carpet places!' God alone knew how he'd found out. Logan passed on Rickard's update in the hope it would mollify him. It didn't. *'Get your arse back in gear – I want a completed list by the close of business* today!*'*

'I can't, sir, we're on stakeout—'

'Stakeout? Get some bloody uniforms to do it – we've got Garvie to put away!'

' But Steel's ordered me to—'

'Oh, I see, when she *gives the orders you jump to it, but when I—'*

'How did the hearing go this morning?' Trying to distract him, but the inspector wasn't having any of it. Instead Logan got a two-minute rant on how he was letting Jason Fettes and his family down. Logan sighed, put the phone on mute, and tried to think pleasant thoughts while Insch complained.

'And for your information,' said the inspector at last, *'the greasy little sod got bail. He's out there now!'*

'You've got someone following him?'

There was a pause, then, *'Of course I've got someone following him: I might be a Teuchter, but I'm not a bloody idiot!'*

'I didn't mean—'

'He'll go back to where he had Fettes sooner or later. He knows we're on to him: he'll want to get rid of any evidence.' He was starting to sound a bit calmer. *'Tomorrow I want you in my office first thing, understand? You're supposed to be working for me, not Steel.'*

'Yes, sir.' As if he had any say in the matter.

'And if you hear from Watson – I want to see her too. Soon as there's any bloody work to be done round here, everyone disappears.'

And the line went dead.

Half-four and the light was beginning to go. The sky slid into sunset, grey clouds laced with violent pink, looking like hot coals against the glowing blue. Children meandered home from school, some in groups, some on their own, breath streaming out behind them in the cold evening air. None looked like Sean Morrison.

'What d'you think?' asked Steel, standing at the living room window, staring out at the street.

'Soon.' At least Logan *hoped* it would be soon. 'If I was him I'd wait till everyone was settling down to dinner. They're all distracted, not paying attention as he breaks into their neighbours' house . . . Over there!' A young boy, dragging his heels, meandered up the street, dressed in the familiar grey and dark blue school uniform.

Steel squinted, the wrinkles around her eyes deepening to heavy folds. 'He's no' wearing jeans *or* an AFC hoodie.'

'He changed – Sean knows we're looking for him, we've got his description up all over the place. So he steals a school uniform from the Struther place. Just another kid on his way back from a hard day's learning.'

'I *suppose* so . . .'

They watched the little boy stop to tie his shoelace, then wander straight past the Burnett place and on up the road. 'Maybe he's casing the joint? Just—'

'It's no' him.'

'No, wait, he'll be back in a minute . . .' Logan drifted to a halt. The wee boy had stopped four houses up. The front door opened and a woman's voice called out – something about fish fingers – the kid scuffed his way inside. Clunk, and he was gone. 'Damn.'

Six o'clock and the sky was dark as a bruise. The occasional car drifted past the window where Logan and Steel waited, but other than that the street was quiet. 'He's got to show soon,' said Logan, shifting from foot to foot, trying for optimistic.

'I dunno . . .' Steel sighed. 'Knowing my luck he's buggered off for good this time. I'm beginning to think I'm fucking jinxed—' A light blossomed in the windows across the road and the inspector stood transfixed. Someone was in the Burnett house. 'Got ya, you dirty wee bastard!' She grabbed her phone and started calling round the teams. 'Who saw him? How'd he get in? . . . What you do: fall asleep? . . . Yes . . . I know it's cold . . . No . . . Look, it's no' exactly been a picnic for us either . . . No! Wait till I give the word.' She closed her phone, cutting whoever it was off. 'Moaning bastards.'

'They didn't see him then?'

'Pah.' She snorted and pulled her shoes back on. 'How half of them pass basic training is beyond me.' They thanked their hostess, then hurried across the road, making for the front door, DI Steel with her phone out, telling the teams to get into the Burnetts' back garden.

'What do you want to do about entry?' asked Logan as they crept up to the front door – a pair of uniformed constables were already waiting for them, looking charged up, stab-proof vests on, extendible truncheons and pepper-spray at the ready.

The inspector shrugged. 'We've got a warrant for Sean's arrest . . . if anyone asks we're in close pursuit, OK?' She turned to the burliest constable – a woman with legs like tree trunks. 'Kick it down.'

BOOOOOM! And the woodwork juddered. One more kick and the lock splintered out of the surround, sending shards of broken wood flying into the hallway as the front door slammed open and bounced off the wall. PC Burly shouted, 'POLICE, NOBODY MOVE!' and charged in, her partner hot on her heels.

A crash from the rear of the house, 'POLICE!', and the sound of heavy boots battering their way in through the back door.

Steel grinned. 'Cracks me up every time they do that.'

23

They went through the place from top to bottom and back again: there was no sign of Sean Morrison.

The inspector stood in the immaculate lounge and swore a blue streak. 'How the hell could we miss him? He's a wee boy, no' fucking Houdini!' She spun round, glowering at the team who'd been watching the back garden. 'You! You let him sneak past, didn't you!'

They backed off in unison, mumbling about how they didn't see anyone and it was cold and dark and they were *sure* Sean hadn't got past them . . . That just made Steel rant louder.

Logan slouched through to the darkened dining room, looking to get away from the inspector's tirade before any of it got turned in his direction. He pulled out his phone and slumped in one of the chairs, sitting in the dark, dialling Jackie's number from memory. She'd be home by now, wondering where the hell he'd got to. Eight rings and it crackled onto the answer phone: Jackie's voice telling him they were both out fighting crime or getting drunk, but he could leave a message after the beep. He hung up.

How on earth did Sean Morrison manage to sneak past half a dozen policemen? It just didn't make any sense. It was almost as if— The standard lamp in the corner suddenly bloomed into light, making the polished silverware glint.

'Oh sodding hell . . .' The lamp was plugged into one of those timed switches – the Burnetts must have set it up to make the place look as if it was still being lived in. Deterring burglars and making an arse out of the police. Sean Morrison was never in the house at all.

Groaning, he pulled himself to his feet and switched the damn thing off, plunging the room into darkness again. Logan stood at the window, wondering how quickly he could slope off after the impending bollocking, drown his sorrows in a bottle of wine and a Chinese takeaway. Steel was going to blame him for this, he could feel it. He'd been so *sure* the eight-year-old would come here . . .

There was someone standing on the other side of the road, staring up at the house. A small boy wearing jeans and a heavy, padded jacket, a rucksack over his shoulder. Mouth hanging open. Sean Morrison.

Logan dashed into the hall, shouting, 'He's outside!' exploding out of the front door and down the steps. Sean only hesitated for a second and then he was off. Logan tore after him, hearing muffled cries from inside as others joined the chase, feet pounding the pavement.

Sean screeched round the corner onto Westfield Terrace. The rucksack went flying, as the wee boy lightened the load. A flash of black at Logan's shoulder – a PC catching up as they ran up the small street, closing the gap.

There was a car parked halfway on the pavement: Sean jumped onto the bonnet, to the roof, then made a huge leap for the six-foot-high stone wall behind, scrabbling into someone's back garden. The PC was first to the wall, hauling himself over as a security light stabbed the darkness.

Breathing hard, Logan followed him, landing in a clump of conifers, staggering out just in time to see the constable make a grab for Sean's trouser leg as the child disappeared over the next-door fence.

Sean screamed.

'Come back here, you little bugger!' The PC yanked Sean back into the garden. They went down in a tangle of limbs and swearing. Then a loud yelp, and the PC let go, holding his left wrist in his right hand, staring at the gash across his palm. Fresh blood glowed neon-red in the security spotlight. 'Aaaaagh!'

Sean scrambled away, swearing, crying, holding a glittering kitchen knife. Staring at the PC, then up at Logan as a policewoman cleared the wall, crashed into a decorative border and went sprawling across the lawn. The eight-year-old murderer snarled, waved the knife and backed against the fence, eyes darting round the garden. 'Fuckers! Fucking bastard fuckers!'

A window opened at the back of the house and an old man stuck his head out, yelling that he was calling the police.

'It's over, Sean.' Logan put on his understanding, approachable voice. 'Come on, put the knife down. I know you don't want to hurt anyone else.'

'Fucking KILL YOU!' Tears ran down his cheeks, a silvery trail heading south from both nostrils. Bottom lip trembling. 'Kill you . . .'

Behind him, Logan could hear the policewoman groaning to her feet as another uniformed officer crashed into the garden. 'You don't have to run any more.'

'Fuckers . . .' The knife's point wavered, dipping towards the churned-up grass.

'Shhhh, it's OK, Sean, it's OK.'

The policewoman marched straight up and sprayed Sean Morrison in the face with pepper spray. 'That's for Jess Nairn, ya wee shite.'

They could have heard the boy's screams in Peterhead.

'They'll sting for a while, but the swelling'll go down soon enough. No' that it'll make much odds

222

where he's goin'.' Doc Wilson, slouched against the corridor wall, hands in his pockets, face like a bank holiday weekend – long and dreich. He gave a dramatic sigh. 'I'm seein' one of them oncologists tomorrow morning . . .'

Logan nodded, not really wanting to get drawn into Doc Wilson's world of misery again. 'Is he well enough for questioning?'

The doctor thought about it then shrugged. 'Doesn't really matter, does it?' He pulled himself off the wall, picked up his medical bag and slumped off, mumbling to himself all the way.

'Well,' said Steel when Logan got back up to her office, 'what did Doctor Doom and Gloom say? He show you his tumour?'

'No permanent damage. You can interview Sean if you want. And Big Gary says the kid's dad's downstairs shouting the odds: police brutality, human rights, legal action. The usual.'

She checked her watch. 'Twenty-seven minutes till show time . . . what do you think, worth a punt?'

'Up to you.'

She rubbed a nicotine-stained finger along the bridge of her nose. 'What the hell: get them into an interview room. If nothing else we'll put the fear of God into the wee bugger.'

Interviewing Sean Morrison was like interviewing a breezeblock. He just sat on the other side of the table, sullen and silent, scowling at the camera.

His face was swollen and red, like a bad case of sunburn, eyes the colour of beetroot. Still tearing up from the pepper spray. He wouldn't even confirm his name.

Mr Morrison sat next to his son, one arm wrapped around the little thug's shoulders, trembling with anger. 'I demand you take my son to the hospital!'

'No – and I'm no' telling you again,' said Steel. 'He's been checked over by the duty doctor, he'll be fine.'

'He's in pain! Look what your storm troopers have done to him! LOOK!' Clutching Sean's red chin, leaving white fingerprints behind when the child shook him off. 'He's only eight!'

Steel slammed her hand down on the table, making the plastic cups of tea and coffee tremble. 'Listen up: your innocent little darling tried to stab two police officers tonight. One's up in A&E getting his hand stitched back together. Then there's the policewoman he stabbed in the throat and THE OLD MAN HE KILLED!'

'We demand to see a lawyer.'

Logan tapped the inspector on the shoulder and whispered in her ear, 'Seven fifteen – press conference in five minutes.'

She stood, scraping her chair back from the table, staring at the father. 'You're here at my discretion Morrison. I can have you replaced by a social worker, like *that*.' Snapping her fingers under his nose. 'I've got him on CCTV killing the old man. I've got a police witness to him stabbing Constable Jess Nairn. I've got even more witnesses to him trying the same thing on tonight. I've got the knives; I've got his fingerprints. I don't *need* a confession.'

She gave Logan the nod and he said, 'Interview suspended at seven sixteen.'

Steel leant on the table, engulfing Sean Morrison's father in a wave of stale cigarette breath. 'He's going to "secure accommodation" till he's sixteen – it's like a children's home, but they lock the little bastards up – then he'll go to a young offender's institution till he's twenty-one. Then he'll go to prison. If he's lucky he'll be out in time for his thirtieth birthday. You want to make it easier for him? Maybe cut his sentence? You get him to talk.'

Everyone was waiting for them, the Chief Constable sticking his hand over the microphone and whispering something to the inspector as she settled into her seat – probably something about what a great job she'd done, because she smiled happily – and then they got the press conference underway. Logan sat back in his chair and listened as the CC announced Sean Morrison's capture, then opened the floor for questions. First up: 'Why did it take Grampian Police four days to catch an eight-year-old boy?' Then, 'Will there be a public enquiry into the handling of the investigation?'

It was Colin Miller who asked the question

Logan had been dreading: 'Is it true Sean Morrison was assaulted durin' his arrest?'

Steel gritted her teeth. 'No it isn't.'

'Then why did neighbours report a child "screaming in pain" when it took place?'

The inspector launched into an explanation, but the press had tasted blood. Wasn't it true that DS McRae had assaulted a young boy at the beach yesterday? Were officers looking for revenge after PC Nairn was stabbed by Morrison on Thursday? Was there an institutionalized vigilante culture in Grampian Police?

The Chief Constable didn't let it go on for too long. The press conference was brought to a close and everyone 'invited' to leave.

'Bunch of bastards!' said Steel, in the corridor afterwards. 'What the hell happened to "well done" and "for she's a jolly good fellow"?'

Logan stepped out of the way as the CC stormed past, closely followed by the Press Liaison Officer. 'Don't think God's very happy about it either.'

Steel watched the man disappear through the double doors. 'Bugger the lot of them. Come on: we're going to the pub. I think we deserve a pat on the back, even if no other bastard does.'

Logan clunked the drinks down on the sticky, beer-spilled table and dumped half a dozen packets of crisps in the middle. There was a feeding frenzy as Steel and two uniforms from the team that had grabbed Sean Morrison fought over the tomato sauce flavour. Three rounds into the evening and the conversation had drifted from work to football and Rob Macintyre's hat trick against St Mirren at the weekend. Everyone tactfully ignoring the rape allegations in favour of the four-one final score. DI Steel threw her hands in the air, staring over Logan's shoulder, back towards the bar, shouting, 'Just in time!' at the constable who'd tackled Sean in the garden. He had one hand swathed in white bandages. 'Laz!' the inspector bellowed, 'Laz, go get that man a drink! On me! Double whisky!'

Logan was still waiting to get served when he felt a tap on his shoulder. He turned, expecting to see Steel, or Jackie, but it was PC Rickards, dressed in tatty jeans, a pornographic T-shirt, and a scruffy jacket. 'Er . . . sorry to bother you, sir, but Sergeant Mitchell said I'd probably find you here.'

'You want a drink? Steel's buying – we caught Sean Morrison.' Logan knew he was grinning like an idiot, but he couldn't help it.

Rickards looked uncomfortable. 'I just wanted to tell you I'd gone through all those carpet places – no one's sold anything to a B&B for months. Sorry.'

'Not your fault, it was always a long shot . . .' Logan frowned. 'Wait a minute, didn't your shift finish about three hours ago? Have you been hanging around the station waiting for me all this time?'

'What? No, no. God.' He pulled a face. 'I mean,

how sad would that be? Urgh . . .' Going slightly red. 'I had a couple of hours to kill, so I've been reading through some of those break-in reports. You know, see if I can spot a pattern.'

'In that case you definitely deserve a drink.' Logan caught the barman's eye and ordered Steel's double whisky then turned to ask Rickards what he wanted.

'No, really, sir, I can't—'

'Yes you can. Pint?'

'I . . .' Rickards was going red again. 'Everyone keeps taking the piss. Ever since that bloody briefing – it's all innuendo and double entendre and bloody "suits you, sir!" Some bastard's even been posting condoms through the grille in my locker. I'm bloody sick of it.'

Logan ordered him a pint of lager. 'Look, if you let them get to you they'll keep on doing it. They like to get a reaction, that's all. Come on – one pint's not going to kill you, is it?' He took the drinks from the bar and handed Rickards his pint. 'That's an order, Constable.'

Rickards cracked a twisted smile. 'Yes, sir.'

It was quieter outside, standing under the columned portico at the front of the pub, staying out of the wind, waiting for Jackie to pick up the flat's phone. It rang through to the answering machine, so Logan tried her on her mobile. Ringing and ringing and ringing and . . .'*Hello?*'

'Hey, we caught him!'

'*What?*' sounding distracted.

'Sean Morrison, we caught him.'

'*Oh, yeah, I heard on the news. Cool . . .*'

'We're in the pub, want to come?'

A pause, then, '*Oh, no, I can't – you remember my friend Janette? Her fiancé's just dumped her, she's in a right state, so I'm kinda stuck.*'

'Oh,' trying not to sound disappointed, 'well, that's OK. Don't worry about it.'

'*Sorry . . . Look, don't wait up for me, I've no idea when I'm going to escape. Probably not till late. She's a nightmare when she gets started.*'

A bendy bus thundered past, narrowly missing a barely dressed young woman and her Neanderthal boyfriend. Logan watched them hurling abuse at the driver.

'*Look, she's coming back from the toilet, gotta go.*'

'OK, I . . .' But she'd already hung up.

Logan stood on the top step, looking down at the phone in his hands. Then closed it up and went back inside.

24

First thing Tuesday morning and Logan was in DI Insch's office, listening to the big man grumble about not getting enough resources to make a murder case against Frank Garvie. They still hadn't found anywhere he could have taken Jason Fettes to kill him: he didn't own or rent any other property; wasn't looking after anywhere for an ageing relative, or a work colleague; and the B&B idea was a complete dead end. So all they had was the large black dildo found in Garvie's closet. Yes it was clarted with DNA, but none of it belonged to Jason Fettes.

The inspector scowled and tore open another family-value-sized bag of jelly babies. 'The PF's not happy,' he said, ripping the head off a little pink infant, 'says we're not going to get a conviction without forensic evidence . . .' A handful of tiny figures disappeared into Insch's mouth, to be chewed unhappily. 'And I've got this bloody stupid terrorism thing today. Like I don't have enough to deal with!' He dragged a copy of that morning's *Scottish Sun* from his in-tray and slapped it on the tabletop. MACINTYRE SAYS, 'I'LL SUE!', above a photo of the ugly footballer and his well-dressed lawyer, Sandy Moir-Farquharson. COPS CATCH KILLER KID was relegated to a tiny sidebar. 'Bad enough we get slapped with an injunction for harassing him, but now the raping wee bastard thinks he's got a case for libel and slander!' Little flecks of spit sparked in the overhead lights. He ground his teeth, turning a delicate shade of angry scarlet, then stared over Logan's shoulder at the big framed *Mikado* poster. Fuming. 'What about his alibi for Friday night?'

'I got Rickards to check it out: Macintyre and his fiancée left the pub at nine, went to the take-away, picked up a chicken chow mein, beef in black bean sauce—'

'I didn't ask for the bloody menu!'

'Sorry, sir. They left the carryout at half nine.'

Insch gave him a grim smile. 'Nikki Bruce was attacked between midnight and quarter past – plenty of time for the wee shite to get down the road to Dundee and catch her coming out of the nightclub.'

'Only his fiancée swears he was with her all night. And we've got nothing that proves otherwise, so—'

The inspector's smile vanished. 'Exactly whose side are you on, Sergeant?'

Logan didn't answer that and Insch scowled at

him, letting an uncomfortable silence grow, before grabbing the Fettes case file off his desk and tossing it across the Formica. 'I want you to go through everything we seized from Garvie's flat – find me a connection.'

Rickards was waiting for him in their tiny, makeshift incident room when Logan lurched in, carrying a huge box from the evidence locker. The constable helped him get it up on the desk, eyeing the contents suspiciously. Everything was covered in a patina of black and white fingerprint powder, sealed away in individual evidence bags. Logan pointed at the open box. 'Need to go through this lot for DI Insch. And before you say anything: I know, OK?'

'Oh God . . .' Rickards pulled out a stack of DVDs with titles like *Deutsche Mannliebe* and *Knechtschaftgummijungen* with a lot of half-naked men on them. Some of whom were wearing leder-hosen. 'We've not got to watch this lot, have we?'

Logan patted him on the shoulder. 'Not *we*, you. I've got to go chase up the IB about those servers.'

'Give us a chance!' said the middle-aged man in the SKATE OR DIE T-shirt, his desk littered with laptops, mice and scribbled-on Post-it notes. 'We're still going through that stuff from the brothel raid. No way we'll get anywhere near your stuff for at least a week.'

Logan didn't like the sound of that. 'What about

Dundee – thought they were supposed to be the computer experts.'

That got a shrug. 'Big fraud case – ETSA four weeks minimum.'

'ETSA?'

'Estimated Time Sodding About.' He picked up an old Biro from his pigsty desk and stuck it in his gob, sooking distractedly. A placebo cigarette.

'Insch will throw a wobbler if we don't get this done soon as.'

Skate Or Die swore. 'Marvellous. Finnie in one ear, Insch in the other. What a bastarding week . . .'

'Could you not just take a quick peek?'

'No! Finnie's on my neck as it is.' He pulled the pen from his mouth, automatically flicking nonexistent ash on the floor. 'Well, maybe . . . Look, I'll see what I can do, OK? No promises.'

It was better than nothing.

Nine am and Logan decided it was about time Rickards had a break. He dragged the constable up to the canteen and bought him a cup of tea and a rowie with jam. Both disappeared in record time. 'You got many more to go?' asked Logan as Rickards wiped his greasy hands on a paper napkin.

'Six.' He pulled off his glasses and rubbed his eyes. 'Highspeed, hardcore, German gay porn is even less fun than it sounds . . .'

'Talking about your personal life again?' It was DC Rennie, with a croissant and a cup of fancy coffee. He sat down with a grin. 'Tell you, I was this close—'

'I'm not gay!' Rickards jumped to his feet. 'Fucking hell, what's wrong with you bastards? You know what? I have more sex in a month than you get all year!' He leant over the table to poke Rennie in the shoulder, as the whole canteen went quiet. 'With women! It's BDSM, OK? Just because you don't fucking understand it, doesn't make it gay!' And then he stormed off.

Rennie sat there with his mouth hanging open, and slowly conversations started back up again. 'I was only kidding.'

'Yeah, well . . . He's a bit touchy.'

'You think?' Rennie ripped a bite out of his croissant and washed it down with a mouthful of coffee. 'I didn't *mean* anything by it. Just taking the piss.' He stared at the empty doorway. 'Is he really into all that leather and spanking?' Rennie grinned. 'He's probably on the phone right now to his mates in the bondage mafia. I'll wake up tomorrow morning and there'll be a horse's head in a gimp mask lying on top of the duvet.'

'Think you might have overreacted a bit there?' asked Logan back in their grubby little incident room, sitting a fresh mug of tea down in front of Rickards and his protruding bottom lip.

The constable scowled up at him. 'Did you tell them? I trusted you and—'

'Of course I didn't! Rennie was just pulling your

234

leg. No one knew. Well, not till you shouted it all over the canteen . . .'

Rickards opened his mouth to say something and froze, realization dawning in his horrified eyes. 'Oh fuck.' He buried his head in his hands.

'Congratulations.' Logan patted him on the back. 'You've just come out of the bondage closet.'

It was nearly lunchtime before they got to the bottom of Frank Garvie's porn stash, and by then Rickards was beginning to come to terms with his outing. The DVDs were all what they claimed to be, the videos homemade – Garvie in his dark red rubber romper suit, sometimes with friends, but mostly alone. The only things Rickards hadn't tried were the two canisters of old seventeen-millimetre film. Logan cracked open *The Butler's Revenge* and examined the case. According to the Identification Bureau's audiovisual team it was probably Victorian and there was nothing in the station that could handle film stock that old. Not that it mattered: anything illegal in there would be well past its sell-by-date. There was nothing here to tie Frank Garvie to the corpse of Jason Fettes.

Rickards picked up one of the ancient film canisters. 'Er . . . sir,' he said, turning it over and reading the title, *Festive Frolics*, 'I think these are stolen . . .' He dumped it on the desk, then went squirrelling in a stack of paperwork on the floor by the radiator, coming up with a handful of forms, mumbling to himself as he flicked through the pages. 'Here:

three canisters of vintage Victorian erotic films stolen from ClarkRig Training Systems. Knew I recognized them.' He smiled, proud of himself. 'Told you I'd been reading the reports.'

Logan checked the list of stolen property – Rickards was right. Zander Clark, Aberdeen's premier pornographer, had reported the films missing in amongst a host of other antique sex toys and outfits, with a few computers, mobile phones and digital video cameras thrown in for good measure. A slow smile spread across Logan's face.

He dialled DI Insch's number, but it went straight through to voicemail, so he tried Steel instead. Voicemail again. One more go – the Control Room, where a woman with an almost impenetrable Banff accent told him that both inspectors were in the Terror Readiness Review and wouldn't be gettin' oot till aifter six. Logan hung up, tapping the phone against his chin. 'I think,' he said at last, 'that you and I should go pay Mr Frank Garvie a visit. See if he can explain why he's got stolen Victorian pornography hidden in his sock drawer.'

But first they were going to take a wee detour and test out a theory.

Zander with a Z was in the editing suite, a huge insulated mug of coffee sitting alongside a plate of stovies, dark disks of pickled beetroot leaching purple into the potato. People in hard hats lurched back and forwards on the screen in front of him as the director fiddled with the console. He didn't even look up as Logan and Rickards entered. 'With you in a minute . . . this is an important scene . . .'

'When do the naked Viking women arrive?'

The large man punched a button and the people froze in place. 'They don't,' he said, winding it back and pressing play, staring intently at the finished product. 'Perfect!' He rewarded himself with a massive forkful of stovies, chewing as he spoke. 'This is *Safety First! A guide to container management.* Lot of people don't bother with plot and narrative when they do this kind of stuff, it's just one stupid scene after another. "Don't do this, don't do that" . . . *My* safety films have theme and subtext. That's why they win awards.'

'Yes . . .' Logan pulled one of the ancient film canisters out of Rickards' hands. 'We were wondering if you recognized this.'

Zander's eye went wide. '*The Butler's Revenge*! You caught the bastard!' He reached forward and grabbed the other one from the constable. 'And *Festive Frolics*!' he stopped, looking slightly puzzled. 'What happened to *Kitty-Cat Katy* and all the other stuff?'

'*Kitty-Cat* . . . ?'

'*Katy*. It's a woman who comes on dressed as a cat and licks herself. One of those old Victorian circus acts. Contortionist pornography from eighteen ninety-eight. Very, very rare.' He held the films against his chest, cuddling them. 'You do have them, don't you? The rest of the stuff that was stolen?'

'We're currently pursuing several lines of enquiry.' Which usually meant, 'we don't have a sodding clue' so it was nice to able to use it legitimately for a change. 'We'll need to hold on to them for a while as evidence,' he said and Zander's face fell. 'But you'll get them back.'

The director nodded. 'At least you've found them . . . Tell you what,' he bustled out into the reception, coming back with a couple of DVD cases, 'I felt kinda guilty you didn't get one last time. Here: best thing I ever did.' He gave Rickards his own copy too: *Crocodildo Dundee*.

Logan turned the thing over in his hands, and there on the cover – hamming it up behind the heroine's long, bronzed legs – was Jason Fettes, dressed like a gangster. Which was the real reason for their visit. 'You never asked us what he'd done.'

'Who?' Zander's smile slipped an inch.

'Jason Fettes, AKA Dick Longlay, you never asked what he'd done.'

'No?'

'You knew, didn't you?' Logan stuck the DVD in the deep pocket of his overcoat and settled back against the mixing desk, arms crossed, giving him DI Insch's patented silent technique.

'I . . . well . . . it all depends what you mean by "knew" . . . I mean.' He cleared his throat. 'Look,

I knew Jason was into other stuff. That's all! I didn't know he was dead or anything. I get a bit obsessive when I'm working on a film.'

'Other stuff like BDSM?'

A blush rushed up Zander's cheeks. 'He was . . . renting himself. For sex.'

'Was he now?'

Another jiggly nod. 'He was so desperate to get out to Hollywood and try being a proper actor. Had this screenplay he was working on . . . You'd be surprised how many people want to sleep with a genuine porn star, even in Aberdeen.' An uncomfortable pause. 'We used to get emails through the Crocodildo website.'

Logan stayed silent, watching as Zander Clark, porn producer, started to sweat.

'I . . . I wasn't his pimp, if that's what you're thinking! I never had anything to do with that! We just treated everything as fan mail and forwarded it on. Really!'

'And did you keep copies?'

'No! Nothing. Deleted everything. It wasn't anything to do with me, or the company. If Jason wanted to make a bit of money sleeping with deluded, middle-aged ladies that was his business . . .' He started picking at the side of his thumb with the nail on his index finger. 'Seriously, I don't know anything else.'

'I want the email address you forwarded them on to.'

'Sure, sure, no problem, always happy to cooperate with the police.' Going for jovial bonhomie and overshooting the mark by about a mile.

'You see,' said Logan as the fat man hurried off to get it for them, 'sometimes even Miss Marple gets it right.'

25

Garvie wasn't at work, where a frosty-faced man in jeans and a polo shirt told Logan in no uncertain terms what he thought of the police harassing innocent men until they had to be signed off for stress. So they tried the ex-porn star's flat in Danestone. The sun was hidden behind the building, casting a long, blue shadow across the frost-bleached grass and glittering grey tarmac. Rickards leant on the bell again and again, until finally an upstairs window cracked open and a bleary face peered out. 'Go away!'

Logan put on his best, friendly smile. 'Come on Frank, let us in: it's freezing out here.'

'I'm not well.' And it looked like he was telling the truth: dark purple bags under his eyes, a day's worth of blue-grey stubble stretched across his double chin and pallid cheeks.

'I can get a warrant if you like?'

The man's face went even paler, then disappeared. Thirty seconds later a low buzzing sound came from the door lock. They pushed through into the stairwell, marching up to the third floor. Things had changed in the twenty-four hours since they'd searched Garvie's apartment. Now the word PERVERT!!! was sprayed across the front door in dripping scarlet paint.

Garvie hurried them into the flat, slamming the door and locking it behind him. The tiny hallway stank of disinfectant and the lingering taint of burning paper and excrement. They settled in the dark lounge, curtains drawn, the only light coming from the huge projection screen, with one of the starships *Enterprise* whooshing across it. Garvie hit pause and the music stopped. Up close Logan could see a line of fresh bruising wrapped around the ex-porn star's throat. As if someone had tried to strangle him. Garvie slumped down onto the large black leather sofa, knocking over two empty wine bottles that clunked and rattled on the laminate floor. 'Is this going to take long?' He couldn't even look at them.

'Depends on you, sir.' Logan settled into a matching black armchair. 'We . . .' he trailed off. 'That new?' Pointing at a stainless steel hook bolted to the ceiling. He couldn't believe he hadn't noticed it before.

Garvie barely glanced at it. 'No. What do you want?'

'Tea with milk would be nice. Rickards, do the honours would you?' The constable nodded, and headed off into the kitchen. Soon the sound of drawers and cupboards being opened and closed filtered into the living room. 'We've got a problem, Frank,' said Logan, holding up the Victorian film canisters. 'When we searched your house we found these.'

Garvie's eyes flashed up, then back down to his lap. 'I don't know anything about those.'

'They were in your bedside cabinet with your home movies and socks. Ring any bells?'

'I . . .' And then he was silent again.

'They're stolen property. Someone broke into ClarkRig Training Systems and made off with these and a number of other items from your ex-employer's private collection. Bit of a coincidence that, isn't it?'

Garvie stared at the films. 'I didn't steal them!'

'Come on Frank, you knew Clark had these, you knew what they were worth, you broke in and—'

'I bought them!'

Logan sat back, looking sceptical. 'Bought them?'

'From a guy. In the pub. I . . .' he coughed, cleared his throat, and tried again. 'I knew they were Zander's. I was going to give them back to him. I just . . . didn't get round to it . . .'

'And does this guy in the pub have a name?'

'I . . .' Garvie's eyes went back to his curry-stained jogging bottoms. 'I never met him before.'

Logan stood, shaking his head sadly. 'You've got to be one of the worst liars I've ever seen.

Frank Garvie, I'm arresting you for possession of stolen goods, you do not have to say anything—'

'Ron! Ron Berwick. He sometimes sells stuff round the pubs in Bridge of Don – has a place outside Balmedie. I didn't have anything to do with it, I swear!'

'Where outside Balmedie?'

And Garvie told them everything.

The afternoon was crisp and clear, frost still dusting the shadowed grass and skeletal brambles like icing sugar. Up above, the eggshell-blue sky faded to hazy white on the horizon, a thin, dark blue line marking the sea, just visible from the small clump of houses nearly eight miles north of Aberdeen. They'd been a farm steading at one point, a wide, horseshoe-shaped, single-storey granite barn for cattle or pigs, but someone had turned them into six terraced houses with lots of varnished wood and dormer windows, a row of single garages sitting off to the left. According to Control, Ronald Berwick lived in the end house, with his wife, three kids and a Labrador.

'Er, sir,' said Rickards, wriggling in the driver's seat of their scabby CID Vauxhall, watching as half a dozen firearms-trained officers piled out the back of an unmarked filthy-white van, 'is this not a bit . . .' He pointed at the men and women scurrying towards Ronald Berwick's house, dressed all in black: black body armour, black scarves wound round their faces, bulky black helmets on their heads, bent nearly double over their black Heckler and Koch MP5 machine pistols, Glock nine millimetres strapped to their hips. 'Well . . . over the top?'

'No.' It had taken some doing to convince the inspector running the control room to let him have a firearms team, but there was no way Logan was going to have a repeat of what happened last time he'd raided a property for stolen goods. He never wanted to attend another police funeral, let alone be responsible for one.

Two of the black-clad officers flattened themselves on either side of the front door, a third standing ready with the hand-held black battering ram, while the others hurried round the back. A wee boy's face appeared in the window of one of the houses opposite, nose pressed against the glass, eyes wide. A metallic bleep came from Rickards' Airwave handset and the lead officer's voice crackled into the car: *'Team One – we are in position.'*

Another bleep: *'Team Two – aye, we're roond the back. Nae sign of any bugger.'*

Logan gave the word and the door was battered off its hinges, falling into the hallway while the three SAS-style bobbies charged inside, shouting, 'POLICE! ON THE FLOOR NOW! NOBODY MOVE!' Five minutes later the head firearms officer appeared where the front door used to be and gave the thumbs up. And all without a single shot being fired.

Berwick's home smelled of fresh paint. There wasn't a single picture on the walls, the lounge carpet covered with newspapers, a stepladder stood by the electric fireplace, open tins of magnolia sitting next to it. A shout came from the back of the house, 'I said keep your hands where I can see them!' followed by a terrified shriek.

Logan hurried through the lounge into a small hallway where a black-clad, gun-wielding PC was pointing her machine pistol in through an open door. 'I'm not going to tell you again!' Someone inside whimpered. Peering round the door Logan saw a terrified man in his early thirties sitting on the toilet, trousers round his ankles, bare legs trembling, face pale, eyes screwed shut, and hands in the air.

'Ronald Berwick?'

'Please don't kill me!'

Logan told the constable to lower her weapon. 'When you've finished up there Mr Berwick, I'd like a word with you in the kitchen. And don't forget to wash your hands.'

The kitchen-come-dining-room was just as bare as the rest of the house, as if someone had stripped the life out of it. A large, American-style fridge sat in the corner, humming away quietly to itself without a single magnet or kid's drawing to break up the monotony. The walls were equally spartan: no calendar, no knick-knacks, no flowers, nothing.

Ronald Berwick was marched through from the bathroom at gunpoint and forced to make nine cups of tea: six for the firearms squad, one each for Rickards and Logan, and one for himself. He even managed to produce a packet of Penguin biscuits. 'There we go,' said Logan as the man jittered his way into a seat at the kitchen table, 'how you feeling?'

Berwick stared at him. 'I was having a crap and someone kicked the bathroom door in and stuck a machine gun in my face, how the hell do you think I'm feeling? Scared the shit out of me.'

Logan tried not to smile. 'I've got a warrant to search these premises for stolen goods.'

The man groaned. 'Great. First Margaret, now this.' He sagged forwards till he was hunched over his mug, staring gloomily into the depths muttering, 'Fucking fuck, fuck, fuckering fuck . . .'

They went through every room in the house, but there was no sign of stolen Victorian sexual ephemera. 'OK,' said Logan after one of the firearms officers stuck their head down from the loft hatch to tell him there was nothing in the attic, 'let's try the garage then.'

They trooped outside. The little boy who'd watched them break down Berwick's front door had been joined by his younger sister, staring at the policemen as if they were the most exciting thing to happen round here for ages. By the time Berwick had led Logan and his team to the last garage on the row they were bustling out the door, desperate not to miss a single moment.

Logan let Rickards do the honours, unlocking the red garage door and hauling it up. Inside it was like Aladdin's cave for electrical appliances, none of them in their original packaging. There were boxes full of digital cameras, DVD recorders, iPods, laptop and desktop computers, silverware, picture frames, candlesticks, DVDs, CDs, jewellery, digital camcorders . . .'Good God!' Logan was impressed in spite of himself. 'How many houses did you have to knock over to get all this?'

Berwick suddenly found his shoes of all-consuming interest. 'I've never seen these things before in my life.'

'Oh, come on. You know fine well we can just cart all this stuff down to the station and check it against our burglary reports. Everything in here's going to be clarted in your fingerprints. Why not save us all the trouble and tell us who you stole them from? It'll look much better for you in court.'

There was a moment's silent contemplation, then a long-suffering sigh. 'Fuck. Who told you?'

'Give us the addresses and I'll make sure the PF knows you cooperated.'

'It was Margaret, wasn't it? Vindictive bitch. Not bad enough she takes my kids and everything in the building society, *no*, she's got to shop me to the bloody police too.' He stood, watching Rickards squeeze his way into the garage glory hole. 'You married, Inspector?'

'Detective Sergeant,' said Logan. 'And no.'

Berwick nodded. 'Good. That's where the

248

fucking trouble starts. You go out and do your best to put food on the table. Keep a roof over their heads. Then she starts going out at night on her own, when she's supposed to be looking after the kids. "Visiting friends". Lying bitch.'

Deep in the garage, Rickards pulled a box from the pile and rummaged about in it, coming out with a translucent, purple dildo. 'Sir, I've found something!'

Logan groaned. 'Put on a pair of gloves for God's sake!'

'Course, you know what she was doing, don't you?' said Berwick, as Rickards snapped on a pair of latex gloves and started hefting out various items of sexual apparatus. 'She was screwing the guy who came to install our broadband. There's me, risking life and liberty to keep her in hair dye and French classes, and she's off shagging some internet geek.' He seemed to shrink. 'And get this, when I confront her, she's the one who acts all hurt! How dare I follow her! What happened to trust? She's shagging someone else and I'm getting a bollocking for not trusting her . . . Fucking women.'

Rickards held a round metal canister aloft. '*Kitty-Cat Katy*!'

'I go out on a job and when I come back she's gone. Took the kids and everything else that wasn't nailed down. Hired a removal truck: you believe that?' Berwick sniffed, watching the PC in his garage happily digging through the stuff from

Zander Clark's Victorian porn collection. 'Found a note in the kitchen: "I've left you. Mother always said I could do better, so now I have."' He shook his head. 'Tell you, never trust a bloody woman, they'll fuck you over every time.'

It was well after six but Logan was still sitting in DI Steel's incident room, surrounded by ever expanding piles of paperwork, filling in all the forms that came with actually solving a burglary. Rickards was on the other side of the desk, trying to match up the list of items collected from Ronald Berwick's garage with the properties he said he'd stolen them from. They hadn't recovered everything on the burglary reports, but then Logan hadn't really expected to. In his experience most people padded out their claim with at least two things they'd never owned in the first place, but always fancied – figuring the insurance company wouldn't mind treating them. And Berwick had been flogging stuff down the pubs to finance his redecorating binge.

Logan put the finishing touches to another set of forms and sent them to the laser printer in the corner, creaking his way out of his chair to go get them when the machine had finished squeaking and whirring. 'How many's that?' he asked, stapling the new sheets together and adding them to the pile.

Rickards looked up from his screen. 'I've done twenty.'

Logan nodded, then checked his watch. 'So we should be finished about . . . seven, half-seven?' He stifled a yawn. 'After that, we're going for a pizza. Not often—'

'Sorry, sir,' the familiar, telltale blush was working its way across Rickards' face. 'I've got a . . . ehm . . . meeting to go to tonight.'

'Yeah?' Logan slumped back behind his desk and called up the next burglary report. 'Let me ask you something,' he said, starting in on the form, 'what kind of people are into that kind of thing?'

'Well . . .' the constable cleared his throat, going an even deeper shade of embarrassed scarlet. 'It . . . we . . .' The door clattered open and a look of relief bloomed on Rickards' face, until he realized it was DI Steel standing in the doorway with hair like a startled grey squirrel, two patches of dark blue shadowing the armpits of her blouse.

'Well?' she demanded, 'Is it true?'

Logan nodded, pointing at the steadily growing pile of completed forms. 'Sixty-two break-ins.'

'Sixty-two? Ha – that's nearly all of them! You try to fit him up with the rest?'

'Yes, but he's not having any of it. They're probably his, but he's sold the stuff, so we've got no evidence.'

'Ah well, can't complain I suppose. Sixty-two . . .' She stuck her hands in her pockets, and beamed happily. 'All those burglaries cleared up and wee Sean Morrison in custody; my crime

251

statistics'll look bloody brilliant this month. Right, soon as the paperwork's done we're goin' out on the toot. My treat. You me and Spanky.'

The constable sent Logan a panicked look. 'Spanky . . . ?'

'Actually, ma'am, Rickards was just telling me he has to go see his mum tonight, so it'll just be you and me.'

Steel actually looked disappointed. 'Aye? You sure Spanky? Clearin' up sixty-two break-ins needs a celebration . . .' She left a long enough pause for Rickards to change his mind, but the constable just blushed furiously and apologized instead. She shrugged. 'Ah well, means more beer for us.'

An hour later and Rickards was long gone – hurrying off to get rubbered up, or whatever it was he did with his BDSM mates, grinning from ear to ear because Logan had told him he'd done an excellent job today, carefully downplaying Steel's new pet name for the constable. After all, knowing what the inspector was usually like, 'Spanky' was getting off lightly. Logan pulled the final report from the printer, powered everything down, flicked off the lights, yawned, and headed downstairs to the main reception desk. It was quiet and empty, so he let himself in the side door, heading round the back of the two-way mirror, where Big Gary was busily slurping his way through a vast mug of coffee and getting chocolate digestive crumbs all over a copy of the *Evening Express.*

'Mmmmphmm mph?' he asked as Logan helped himself to a biscuit.

'No idea. I've been on days non-stop for a week now and I'm knackered.'

Big Gary washed down his mouthful with a slug of coffee. 'Your shift pattern's for shite, you know that, don't you?' He pulled a thick ledger from the shelf. 'Take three days off and then you're on nights Saturday.' He gave Logan a big fat wink. 'And that puts you back in step with the lovely Miss Watson.'

Logan smiled. 'About bloody time too.' It'd be nice to spend some time together for a change. He checked his watch – she was on days, so that meant she'd be home right now. Maybe he could swing her an invite to Steel's burglary celebration? He dug out his mobile and called the inspector – from the sound of things she was already in the pub.

'*Laz!*' Probably on her second whisky. '*Where are you?*'

'Just finished, I—'

'*Good. Get your arse over here!*'

'Do you mind if Jackie joins us tonight?'

'*Why would I mind? Hell, for sixty-two break-ins I'd even buy Rennie dinner.*' The sound of someone shouting, '*Yay!*' in the background.

Smiling, Logan hung up and called the flat, getting the answering machine. Again. He tried

Jackie on her mobile. 'How'd you like to come to dinner with me and DI Steel? She's buying.'

There was a small pause, then, *'I'd love to, but I can't. Janette called: she's locked herself in the bathroom with a bottle of vodka and a photo album, so that's my evening screwed again. Tell you, if I ever get my hands on her bloody fiancé, I'm going to wring his sodding neck.'*

'Oh . . .' Logan frowned, trying to picture Janette and coming up empty. 'You *are* remembering about tomorrow night though, aren't you?'

'Tomorrow . . . Oh shite!' She swore for a bit, then asked, *'No way we could put it off till next week?'*

'It's her fifty-fifth birthday party, so no.'

'You don't even want to go!'

'No, but I have to. And you know what she'll be like if you don't show.'

More swearing. *'OK, OK, we'll go to the stupid party. Jesus. Happy now?'*

'Not especially.' He tried being reasonable, 'Look, we don't even have to stay for all of it, we can—'

'Fine. Whatever. I've got to go.' And the line went dead.

Logan went to the pub.

26

The next morning DI Steel looked even more dreadful than usual; sitting very still in one of the Chief Constable's visitors' chairs, pretending to pay attention as the man told her, Logan and PC Rickards what a great job they'd all done. 'It's not often we get sixty-two crimes wiped off the books in one day,' he said, leaning back against the windowsill, high, grey cloud scudding past behind him. 'Even the papers have laid off us for once.' And he was right: the front page of that morning's *Press and Journal* was all about a local property developer turning up at Aberdeen Royal Infirmary with both legs broken.

It might have been Logan's imagination, but Rickards seemed to be fidgeting more than usual, shifting about in his seat, trying not to wince. As if he'd got piles. 'Now,' said the CC, gifting them all a broad smile, 'if we can just get to the bottom of this Fettes case it'll be back to business as usual!'

Steel nodded carefully, and mumbled something about DI Insch doing a fine job in that department. 'Excellent.' The Chief Constable settled back behind his desk. 'So, I take it we're building a nice airtight case?'

'Aye, well,' Steel's voice sounded like a cross between Darth Vader and a belt sander, 'obviously I've got a bit more supervising to do, but Insch has my complete confidence.' Making sure she could claim the credit if he succeeded and blame him if he didn't.

'I see. Well, given the recent "difficulties" I want you to be hands-on with this one, Inspector. I don't want it turning into another disaster like Rob Macintyre.' He picked up a silver letter opener, holding it by the point, as if he was about to throw it at someone. 'Oh, and DS McRae,'

Logan got the feeling something nasty was coming. 'Yes, sir?'

'It's not often I have to consider suspending and commending the same officer in one week. I'll be keeping an eye on you.'

'Er . . . thank you, sir.' But Logan wasn't entirely sure if he'd just been praised or threatened.

Logan and Rickards didn't even get as far as the stairs before disaster struck in the shape of DC Rennie. 'Been looking all over for you! Detective Inspector Insch requests the honour of your company, at your earliest possible convenience.'

'What did he really say?'

'Get your arse up to the incident room pronto, and bring Bondage . . .' he stopped himself, gave a small 'ahem' and tried again, 'and bring PC Rickards with you.'

Logan shook his head. 'No way: we're not even supposed to be here.' If it hadn't been for DI Steel phoning up at half eight to tell him to come get a pat on the head from the Chief Constable, he'd still be in his bed, sleeping off last night's celebratory curry and late-night drinks. 'I'm back . . .' he worked it out on his fingers, three days off: 'Saturday.'

Rennie put on a pained smile. 'He did say ASAP, sir.'

Logan sighed. 'Of course he did.'

DI Insch was deep in conversation with the admin officer when Logan and his band of merry policemen marched in. They hung around by the incident board, waiting for the inspector to finish. It didn't take Rennie long before he started telling them all about how great it was being in *The Mikado* and how Sophie, Anna and Liz were all over him. 'Tell you,' he said, 'I play my cards right I'm in for a threesome. Four if I'm lucky!'

Rickards snorted. 'You've never had a threesome before?'

'Well . . .' Rennie shifted from foot to foot on the dirty, grey-green carpet tiles. 'No.'

'So,' said Logan, changing the subject before anyone asked him, 'how's it going: rehearsals . . . and things.'

'Better. Still not great, well, except for Debs.

The rest of us are lumbering about the place like bloody Tellytubbies.'

Logan laughed. 'Yeah, Jackie said you were a bit "challenged".' Rennie looked puzzled, so he explained, 'The rehearsal on Sunday? When you lost your bet? Twenty quid?'

'Nah,' Rennie shook his head. 'Rehearsals are Monday, Wednesday and Friday. You sure she . . . oh, *Sunday*, oh, yeah. Right, Sunday.' He slapped his forehead. 'Course. You know me: no brains. Sunday. Yeah.'

'Rennie, get your backside over here!' – DI Insch, glowering over the top of a report. The constable trotted across the room, there was some muttered discussion, and then he was off out the door on a new errand. Insch thrust the report back to the admin officer and creaked his massive frame off the desk. 'Sergeant McRae, I've been calling you all morning.'

Logan nodded. 'We were with the CC, sir, and you know what he's like if a mobile goes off while—'

'In my office, Sergeant, and bring your constable with you.'

The inspector waited till they were all in his room, then told Rickards to close the door. He settled into the large black leather chair behind the desk and stared at them in silence. 'Where,' he said, 'is my status report from yesterday? It should have been on my desk first thing this morning.' Prodding the wood with a huge sausage-like finger.

'We had a large number of burglary reports—'

'I don't care. I sent you to do a job, I expect you to bloody well do it!' His face was starting to take on that horribly familiar florid tinge.

Rickards broke the golden rule and answered back: 'That's not fair! We solved sixty-two burglaries yesterday, got a commendation from the Chief—'

'Did I ask for your opinion, Constable?' The words coming out low and dangerous.

Rickards straightened his shoulders, drawing himself up to his full five foot five. 'With all due respect—' Logan kicked him in the shin before he could get himself into any more trouble. The constable snapped his mouth shut as Insch worked himself up into a full fit of righteous fury.

'Don't you ever *dare* "with all due bloody respect" me, Rickards. You've got something to say: say it!' He stood, towering over the constable.

'No, sir, sorry sir. Nothing.'

'SAY IT!

Logan closed his eyes and hoped to God that Rickards was bright enough to keep his big mouth shut. He wasn't. 'Sir, we cleared up a lot of crimes yesterday. We used our initiative – the CC said we were a credit to the force!'

'Did he now?' Insch had finally progressed from scarlet pink to dark purple, and Logan's eyes were inexorably drawn to that throbbing vein in the fat man's forehead, as if a worm was burrowing away under the skin. 'Understand this, Constable: when I say frog, you jump. You do not backchat,

259

you don't "with all due respect" and you don't whinge. You say "how high" AND YOU BLOODY JUMP!'

He swung a huge finger at Logan. '*You* should know better!'

'Yes, sir.' There was no point arguing, it would just prolong the bollocking; much easier and quicker to roll with the punches.

The fat man checked the pulse at the side of his neck, and rumbled his way back into his seat. 'What happened yesterday?'

Logan gave Insch the short version: Garvie buying stolen porn from a man they later charged with sixty-two burglaries. 'And according to Zander Clark, Fettes was acting as a male prostitute; selling middle-aged ladies the chance to sleep with a bona fide porn star. He got email offers through the Crocodildo website, they were forwarded to this hotmail address.' Logan handed over the compliments slip the director had given him.

Insch took it with a grunt, pulled out the Jason Fettes case file, and flipped through the paperwork till he found the IB report on the victim's computer. 'Bloody typical! It's not even on the list of email addresses they gave us.' He slammed the folder shut. 'Get onto them: I want everything sent to, or from, that address in the last six months. Garvie must have been in touch with him. Then find out what's happening with those bloody servers! And if you see Watson, tell her I want a word.' He sat back in his seat and flicked on his computer. 'Well, what are you waiting for? Move it!'

At least Rickards had enough sense to wait until they were well out of earshot before he started complaining. 'Why the hell did we have to just stand there and take it? We're not children! You didn't even—'

'Because I know what he's like, OK? There's no point arguing with Insch right now, it only antagonizes him and he's in a foul enough mood as it is.'

'But he's not supposed to—'

Logan held up a hand, cutting him off. 'You've not worked with a lot of DIs, have you? They all *say* they've got an open-door policy and you can come to them with anything and everyone's opinion is valid, but when push comes to shove, it's all bollocks. This is their show. If an investigation goes tits up, they're the ones get reamed for it, not us.'

'That still doesn't give him the right to treat us like shit!'

'True, but I'm not going back in there to argue the toss. Are you?'

Talking to the IB's pet nerd involved a ten minute rant from Mr Skate Or Die on how no one understood how difficult it was to do forensic computing properly and was it his fault the Dundee labs were up to their ears? When Logan passed on Insch's demands, it just set him off again.

By the time Logan finally got around to signing out, all he wanted to do was go back to the flat, crawl into a hot bath and forget about DI Grumpy Bastard Insch. Big Gary was on the desk again, cup of tea in one huge paw, the other wrapped around a raisin whirl. 'Where the hell have you been?' the large man asked, mouth full of pastry. 'I've had Insch on my arse all morning looking for you, turn your bloody phone on!'

Logan stuck two fingers up and scribbled his signature into the book. 'Day off, remember? And for your information, I was upstairs getting a commendation from the Chief Constable.'

'Ah,' Big Gary wiped an imaginary tear from his eye, 'it's a proud moment for us all. Still, switch on your phone: I'm not your secretary.' He handed over a wad of barely legible messages, all saying things like: PHONE INSCH! and WHERE THE BLOODY HELL ARE YOU? Logan scrunched them up and dropped them in the nearest bin, before pulling out his phone and switching it back on again. The thing was full of increasingly irate messages from Insch, and Logan went through them, deleting as he went. Last but not least was a grumpy-sounding one from Jackie, reminding him to pick up a present and a card for tonight, before setting off on a truncated rant about Rob Macintyre being on the radio this morning, telling everyone how much he'd suffered at the hands of Aberdeen Police's hate campaign. *'And the little shite's got himself a book deal! What sort of idiot—'* then the message abruptly ended. Logan deleted it too. This thing with Macintyre was turning into an obsession; every day something else set her off and Logan would be treated to another lecture about how the footballer needed stringing up by the balls. He was getting sick of it.

Sticking the phone back in his pocket, he headed off into town, looking for the sort of present a woman in her mid-fifties wouldn't complain about too much.

He was in the middle of buying some kind of elephant wind-chime thing when his phone started up: the Ice Queen, AKA Dr Isobel MacAlister. *'He didn't come home! Last night! He didn't come home!'*

Logan handed over his credit card and the young woman behind the counter started wrapping. 'Isobel, I don't—'

'Colin! He didn't come home!' She was on the verge of tears, which wasn't like her at all.

'Maybe he's out on assignment? Visiting—'

'He would have told me!' There was a pause, and then her voice dropped to a whisper. *'You know what happened last time . . .'*

'I'm sure it's nothing, he—'

'You have to find him!'

Trying to keep the exasperation out of his voice, Logan accepted the plastic bag with his gift-wrapped elephants inside it and promised to do what he could.

263

27

Two hours later Logan marched into the Globe Inn on North Silver Street, pulled a stool up to the bar and ordered a pint of Stella and a cheese and onion toastie. 'You know,' he said, as the barmaid went off to phone his order through to the kitchen, 'she's doing her nut in down the morgue. It's upsetting the corpses.'

Colin Miller, golden boy reporter on the P&J, tireless campaigner against Grampian Police in general and Detective Sergeant Logan McRae in particular, turned a bleary, bloodshot eye in his direction and told him to fuck off. He wasn't a tall man even by PC Rickards' standards, but he more than made up for it in width. What had been a lot of muscle was beginning to soften and settle into middle-aged spread on the father-to-be. His usual suit was missing – replaced by jeans, heavy tartan shirt, scuffed leather jacket, and the heady stench of alcohol. He clasped the pint of beer on the bar in front of him with black-gloved hands.

There wasn't so much as a flash of gold or silver about the man. Not like him at all. *And* he hadn't shaved.

'Come on, Colin, she's worried about you. You don't come home all night; she thinks something horrible's happened.'

'Aye? Like fuckin' last time, you mean?' The words were slurred and broad Glaswegian. He held up his hands, wiggling the fingers so Logan could see the joints that wouldn't move any more. The rigid parts showing where prosthetic plastic replaced flesh and bone.

'Colin, she's worried about you.'

'None of yer bloody business. Interferin' wee fuck.'

Logan sighed. 'Look: I'm sorry, OK? For the *thousandth* time: I'm sorry! I didn't mean for it to happen. It wasn't on purpose. What the hell else am I supposed to say?'

'How 'bout you don't say another fuckin' thing.' Miller stood, threw back the last mouthful of beer, and banged his empty glass down on the bar top. 'I don't fuckin' need you, "Mr Big Police Hero",' poking Logan in the shoulder. 'So just sod off an' leave me alone.' The reporter turned on his heel and staggered into a marble-topped table, before righting himself and lurching towards the toilets.

Logan pulled out his mobile and called Isobel back, telling her, 'He's OK. Just a bit drunk.' Then hanging up before she could start asking questions or hectoring him. Just to be on the safe side, he switched the thing off again.

The cheese toastie arrived just as Miller came marching back to the bar and ordered another pint of heavy and a double Highland Park. The whisky glittered like amber in the glass as it was set before him.

'How about I call you a taxi and get you home?'

'How 'bout you fuck off instead?'

Logan picked up his toastie – the pale bread imprinted with a scallop pattern of golden brown – and broke it on the diagonal, fingernail-crescents of white onion poking out between the slices. 'Here.' He slid the other half over to Miller.

The reporter stared down at the triangle of bread. 'This doesnae make us fuckin' even.' But he picked it up and ate it anyway, carefully wrapping the half toastie in Logan's napkin, so as not to get any grease on his gloves. Fastidious even while pished. 'How'd you know I'd be here?'

'You're not the only one who finds stuff out for a living.'

'Yeah. Suppose not . . .' There was a pause, broken by someone putting an old Deacon Blue song on the jukebox. They listened in silence. 'I'm no' ready for a bairn.' Miller said at last, squinting one-eyed at his own ragged reflection in the mirror behind the bar. 'Can barely look after myself . . .' he paused, rolling the empty whisky glass back and forth in his gloved hand. 'And Izzy – Jesus, she's terrified of no' workin' any more. That they'll get some other bird in tae hack up the deid bodies while she's away bringin' up junior. She'll no' see her beloved morgue ever again . . .' A thoughtful pause, then a mouthful of dark brown beer. Then a belch.

'Come on, you'll make great parents.'

Miller didn't even look up. 'What the hell would you know?'

'True.' Logan smiled. 'But it's what you're supposed to say, isn't it?'

The reporter nodded, swaying on his bar stool. 'Aye . . .'

'Come on, Colin, time to go home.'

Logan called for a taxi and poured the reporter into it, flashing his warrant card at the driver before he could start moaning about not wanting to clean vomit out of his upholstery. He needn't have worried: as soon as Miller's head hit the seat he was out like a light, snoring gently as they drove the five-minute trip to Rubislaw Den. At the other end, Logan paid the man and hauled Colin out into the overcast afternoon.

Dr Isobel MacAlister's love nest was a lot bigger than Logan's one-bedroom flat. Three storeys of very expensive granite in Aberdeen's moneyed district, the road packed with flashy sports cars and huge four-by-fours. He rummaged about in Miller's pockets until he found the keys, then let them in through the front door.

A wailing chorus of bleeps erupted in the small hallway. Miller fumbled his way to a small side cupboard and punched in the disarm code. Zero – Five – One – Zero. Isobel's birthday, fifth of October. Logan supposed it was her way of making sure the reporter never forgot.

'Got it put in . . . put in after the thing . . .' Colin held up his hands and wiggled them at Logan again. 'Just in . . .' a small 'ulp'ing noise, a worried look, then a couple of deep breaths. 'Just in case, like.' He lurched off towards the kitchen, calling, 'Come on, got some . . . Laga . . . Lagavulinin, linin, in . . .' over his shoulder.

'You sure you wouldn't rather have a nice cup of coffee?' Logan asked, following him.

'Whisky, whisky, whisky . . .' Two tumblers came from the cupboard next to the kettle, ringing like tiny crystal bells as Miller fumbled them onto the kitchen table, then went hunting for the bottle. Logan stuck the kettle on.

'You know, Laz,' said the reporter, from the depths of the pantry, 'I used to . . . used to really like you . . .' He emerged, twisting the cork off the top of a half-empty bottle of single malt. 'You was always a bit . . . bit of an arse, like, but you . . . you was my mate.' He slumped into one of the chairs by the kitchen table, scowling. 'Why'd you have tae fuck it up?'

'It was an accident, Colin.' Logan raided the dishwasher for a mug, heaping it with instant coffee and sugar, before topping it up with boiling water. 'I never wanted it to turn out the way it did. You know that—'

'Tada!' The reporter whipped his right glove off, dropping it on the tabletop. The third finger was missing its top two joints, the pinky everything above the second segment. The stumps pink and shiny. 'Fucking things itch . . . itch like a bastard sometimes.' He screwed up one eye and peered at the bottle of whisky, carefully slopping a huge measure into each glass. Then pulled off his other glove, revealing another pair of shiny stumps, rubbing them against his stubbled chin.

Logan placed the coffee in front of him, but the reporter ignored it. Colin picked up one of the huge whiskies instead and held it aloft in a toast, 'Here's tae sunny Aber-fuckin'-deen.' He waited for Logan to raise the other glass then clinked them together. 'Sheep-shaggin' bastards!'

Twenty minutes later and Logan was locking Isobel's front door and popping the key back through the letterbox, leaving Miller snoring away on the couch in the lounge. Two things were certain: Colin would have one hell of a hangover tomorrow, and Isobel would kill him. There but for the grace of God . . . Logan smiled and headed back into town.

He didn't even get as far as the Queen's Cross roundabout before his phone started ringing: an irate DI Insch wanting to know where the hell he'd got to. 'It's my day off, sir, I'm—'

'Where are you?'

'What? Queen's Road, heading back into—'

'*Hold on . . .*' There was some muted conversation Logan couldn't make out, but finally the inspector came back on the line: '*Stay where you are, there's a patrol car coming for you.*'

'But—'

'*We're going to Dundee.*'

Insch sat in the back with Logan, passing him sheets from the Macintyre rape case while the dual carriageway south flashed past the car's windows. The traffic cop driving seemed to be making an attempt on the land speed record, overtaking everything else on the road: saloons, hatchbacks, sports cars, and lorries. 'I still don't see why we have to drop everything and rush down the road,' said Logan, accepting another victim statement.

The inspector scowled at him. 'You *want* Macintyre out there raping more women? Sooner we catch him the sooner he's off the bloody streets.'

Fair point. Logan scanned the statement, having difficulty taking it in. 'You sure we'll be back in time? Only I've got—'

'For the last time, yes! You'll make your bloody party. Now pay attention,' he poked the sheets in Logan's hand with a fat finger, 'Christine Forrester: Macintyre's last Aberdeen victim.'

Logan skimmed the form. 'Jesus.'

'He gets worse with every one.' It had taken the surgeons seven hours to stitch Christine

Forrester's face and neck back to something approaching normal. The attached photograph was enough to make Logan look away, not certain if he was feeling sick because of the picture, or because he was trying to read a whole case file in the back of a police car flying down the road at ninety miles an hour as the sun set.

'So,' he said, turning the eight-by-ten face down, 'why me?'

Insch grumbled something and pulled out a big bag of tiny gummy bears. 'I'd take Watson, but she had to go shoot her bloody mouth off to the papers. Now if I have her anywhere near the investigation everyone will say it's a witch hunt.'

Logan watched a handful of little jelly figures disappear, trying not to imagine them screaming as the inspector chewed. 'You're convinced it's Macintyre.'

'Course it's bloody Macintyre.' The words barely audible through all the dying bears.

Logan nodded. Insch was just like Jackie: unable to see past his own obsession. It didn't matter what the inspector said: it was still a witch hunt. He kept his mouth shut and went back to the case file.

Dundee's Ninewells Hospital was huge, a labyrinth of corridors and interconnected buildings, the familiar smell of disinfectant and the buzz of fluorescent lighting depressing the hell out of Logan as he marched behind Insch down the stairs and along the corridor to the neurology ward. A middle-aged woman in white and green sat at the nurses station, peering over her specs at a clipboard festooned with forms, a huge box of chocolates lying open beside her. Insch helped himself to one, then said, 'Nikki Bruce?'

The ward sister looked up. 'You relatives?' her voice going up at the end in a classic Fife lilt.

The inspector showed her his warrant card. 'Police, we—'

'Aye, I know. Nikki's expecting you.' She stood, only coming up to the middle of Insch's enormous barrel chest, and led them down the corridor to a small, private room. 'She's had a tough time of it – a lot of pain. Don't tire her out.'

Helium balloons bobbed gently in the airconditioning: glittering metallic things with teddy bears and kittens on them, GET WELL SOON cards pinned to the cork board over the bed, but no flowers. Nikki was propped up with crunchy white NHS pillows, her features hidden in the shadows, an intravenous drip in her arm and a pair of white iPod headphones in her ears.

Insch cleared his throat and sank himself into the high-backed chair by the bed – the one for patients – leaving Logan to fetch a creaky plastic seat from the corner. There was a flicker of movement, as if Nikki had only just realized they were there. Then she sighed and clicked off her music with a trembling, bandaged hand.

The inspector asked her how she was doing, in

a voice so full of sympathy Logan almost didn't recognize it. 'I'm really sorry,' the big man said, 'but we need to ask you some questions. Are you still OK with that?'

A nod. As Logan's eyes adjusted to the darkened room, he could see the difference a couple of days had made. Nikki's bruises had blossomed until her whole face was puffy and dark, fresh surgical padding covering the wounds he'd read about on the way down, a faint tinge of yellow and tiny red dots leaking through the white gauze, marking the path of her attacker's knife. When she spoke her voice was small and painful, crying as she answered the inspector. Telling him about the birthday party at the nightclub, drinking too much. Not remembering anything till she was being sick in the taxi rank. Trying to walk home. The knife. His body. The blood . . . Her words made Logan feel ill all over again – how the hell could someone *do* this to another human being?

When it was over Insch apologized again, placed a hand on her shoulder and promised he'd do everything he could to catch the man responsible. Then they left her alone with her pain and her grief.

There was a man in a suit waiting for them at the reception desk: rough features and hands like shovels. He had CID written all over him. 'Well?'

Insch helped himself to another chocolate from the nurse's box. 'Nothing conclusive. But it sounds identical to Macintyre's MO, everything fits.'

'We knew that – we told *you* that!' The man's Dundee accent coming out loud and proud. 'We didn't ask you down here to tell us what we already bloody know.'

'Listen up, Sunshine,' said Insch, stepping up close, using his bulk to force the man back a step, voice low and menacing, 'I've got six women in Aberdeen who've been attacked by this bastard. This is not a game, or a pissing contest. Understand?'

'Who the hell are you calling "Sunshine"?' The man bristled, shoulders back, chest out. 'It's Detective Chief Superintendent Campbell to you, or "sir", one of the two. Do *you* understand?'

Insch was starting to go scarlet, but he managed to say, 'Yes . . . sir. Sorry, sir.'

'That's better.' DCS Campbell turned to Logan, 'That the case file?' sticking out his hand.

Logan looked at Insch, got the nod, and passed it over. 'From the victim photographs it looks like he's escalating. Won't be long until he kills someone.'

'Brilliant,' said the DCS, skimming through the folder, 'you Teuchter bastards train him then let him loose down here. Thanks a fuckin' heap . . .'

'You know,' Logan was probably going to regret this, but someone had to say it, 'it might not be Rob Macintyre. It could still be a copycat.'

Campbell turned a cold eye on him. '*Really*, Sergeant? Any other *startling* insights you'd like to share with us?' Logan could think of a few involving the DCS, his mother and a horse's arse, but he kept his mouth shut. 'Aye,' said Campbell, slapping the Macintyre file shut and stuffing it under his arm, 'thought not. Well, we'll take it from here, and if we need anyone to state the bloody obvious I'll give you a call. Meantime, try and keep your raping wee shites to yourselves. Understand?'

Insch looked as if his head was ready to pop as he said, 'We'll do our best.'

The road back to Aberdeen was one long stretch of dark, winding dual carriageway and it flashed past at the same speed as before – twenty miles over the legal limit as PC Stirling Moss put his foot to the floor. 'I'm sorry,' said Logan as they roared past an eighteen-wheeler on its way north to Asda, 'I was just trying to be objective.'

Silence. Then, 'I don't need you undermining me in front of craggy-faced dickheads like Campbell!'

'I wasn't trying to—'

'It was Macintyre, OK? You saw what he did to that girl. She's twenty-three and he's scarred her for life. Not just on the outside. What he did to her will *never* heal.'

Logan couldn't think of an answer to that, but then Insch didn't seem to want one. The inspector folded his massive arms over his chest and closed his eyes. Up front, the driver clicked on the radio and seventies rock and roll sounded through the car as it ate up the road and the miles from Dundee.

Jackie didn't appear back at the flat until nearly quarter to eight. She stomped her feet in the hallway, muttering curses under her breath, clambering out of her huge padded jacket then draping herself over the radiator, complaining about the weather. 'Not supposed to snow till the weekend . . .' Her nose was AFC-red. 'Make us a cup of coffee, will you?'

'Where have you been? It's nearly eight!' Logan followed her through into the lounge where she kicked off her shoes and stood with her back to the electric fire, holding one foot inches from the glowing bars. 'You'll get chilblains.'

Jackie didn't seem to care. 'Steel was looking for you. Something about a PF review for the Morrison case tomorrow?'

'Wonderful.' So much for a day off. 'Anyway, come on, you need to get a shift on if you want a shower before we go: taxi's booked for eight.' He picked up her discarded boots and carried them through to the hall, calling back over his shoulder, 'Got a card and a sort of elephant wind-chime thing.'

'Oh Christ, that's not tonight, is it?' There was a pause and then some swearing. 'Why the hell does it have to be tonight?'

'Because it's her birthday. Let's not do this again, OK?'

'I was only saying.'

Shaking his head, Logan left her to it and went to get ready.

Twelve minutes past eight and a car horn brayed from the street outside. Logan peered through the curtains: there was a taxi sitting in the middle of the road. 'About bloody time. Jackie, you ready?' No reply. He picked up the parcel and birthday card, then stuck his head out into the hall. Empty, but he could hear her in the bedroom, talking to herself. 'No, I can't. Got to go to this stupid bloody birthday thing . . . no . . .' Logan's hand froze over the doorknob, listening. 'Yes . . . Look I was at it all last night, *and* the night before. I'm knackered, OK?' A longer pause, then, 'Nah, he doesn't suspect a thing. Look, it'll have to be tomorrow . . . Yeah, me too.' The phone beeped as she hung up.

Logan backed away, staring at the half-open bedroom door.

Another honk on the taxi horn and Jackie emerged into the hall, pulling on her coat. She froze for a moment, seeing him standing there. Then said, 'Well, come on then, thought we were in a hurry.'

The birthday party wasn't as horrible as Logan had been expecting: it was much, much worse. Jackie kept checking her watch, as if she had somewhere better to be, and Logan watched her grumbling her way through the party like a spoiled child.

How long had it been going on – her and the man on the phone? How long had she been lying to him? Sneaking around behind his back. Janette's fictional break-up, the rehearsal on Sunday that wasn't: lies.

What was it Ronald Berwick – champion house-breaker – had said? *'Never trust a woman, they'll fuck you over every time.'*

LIES

28

Last night's snow hadn't come to much, just a thin veneer of white that melted away as soon as the sun touched it, making the roads steam. Logan stood at the window of DI Steel's office, not really watching the people marching by on the streets below – enjoying the brief respite from winter – he was too busy brooding. When he'd punched 1471 into the phone to find out who Jackie had been speaking to last night it was Rennie's number that came back. He should have known: the two of them had always been close. Simon Bloody Rennie. Two-faced, backstabbing—

'. . . or am I just being a vindictive old cow? Hoy, Earth to Lazarus, come in Lazarus!'

'Sorry,' he said, 'miles away.'

'I said the wee shite's lookin' at eight to twelve years before he gets out. The PF'll try for more, but you know what judges're like when it comes to sentencing wee kids. Soft bastards.'

'Oh, Sean Morrison . . .' he turned back to the

window. 'You ever wonder what happened to him? You know, to make him that way.'

'Nope. Don't know, don't care. We caught the wee bastard and he's going away for a long time. That's all I need to know.'

'Hmm . . .' A patrol car turned into Queen Street, the sunshine glinting off the windscreen as it stopped to let an old lady cross the road. 'Six months ago he was a normal little eight-year-old boy, and now he's a murderer. Big step for a small kid.'

'You sound like a bloody social worker. He's a spoilt wee shite and that's all there is to it.' The noise of a petrol station lighter scritch-scritch-scritching, and a curl of white smoke snaked its way towards the window.

'You don't kill an old man just because mummy and daddy won't buy you a pony.' He looked back over his shoulder – Steel was stretched out happily in her chair, heels dug deep into the carpet, arms up over her head, like a dishevelled cat, puffing away happily to herself. 'Something must have happened.'

She pulled the fag from her mouth, peering at him through tendrils of smoke. 'Gonnae do me a favour an no' piss on my parade? We won: enjoy it.' She dragged her sleeve back and squinted at her watch. 'Come on, just time for a pee break before the PF gets here. And cheer up for God's sake, you're starting to make Doc Misery-Guts look cheery by comparison.'

*   *   *

The Procurator Fiscal sat in the least manky of the inspector's chairs, looking tanned and golden, but her deputy – the one she'd left in charge while she was off basking on a beach somewhere – had taken on the typical Aberdeen mid-winter pallor. Rachael Tulloch: skin so pale it was almost white, her long, curly auburn hair held back in a loose ponytail that she fiddled with while the PF and Steel talked through the list of offences they were going charge Sean Morrison with.

She was pretty; Logan couldn't believe he hadn't noticed before. Not beautiful, but wholesome, Celtic, girl-next-door pretty. She looked up, caught him staring at her, and smiled.

Feeling like a naughty teenager he blushed and looked away.

When they were finished, Rachael hung back, letting Steel and the PF march on ahead. 'So,' she said, undoing her hair, letting the curls fall across her shoulders and down her back, 'I hear you caught Sean pretty much single handed.' Logan demurred, but she was having none of it. 'Not to mention solving all those burglaries.' A smile played across her lips, then she rolled her eyes, putting on a cheesy American accent, 'Is there *anything* you can't do?'

'I . . . well . . .' Suddenly Logan was having difficulty stringing two words together.

'You know,' taking a deep breath, 'I'm sure I still owe you a drink. From before.' Resting her fingertips against his arm.

'Ah, well . . .' and then he thought of Jackie and Rennie – *he doesn't suspect a thing* – 'Now you come to mention it, I do remember something about a large gin and tonic.'

'When?'

'Er . . . tonight?'

'Tonight. Seven o'clock, Ferry Hill House Hotel, the bar, not the lounge. Don't be late.' Rachael grinned, turned, and hurried after the Procurator Fiscal. She only looked back twice.

Logan bumped into Big Gary on the way down the stairs. The big man took one look at him and groaned. 'What are you doing in? Thought I told you to stay off till Saturday.'

'DI Steel.'

'Why do we even bother having a shift rota?' He dug his notebook out and scribbled something in it. 'Any idea when Her Holiness will let you back to normal duties?'

'No. You seen Rennie about?' Logan didn't know what he was going to do to the constable, but it wasn't going to be pretty.

'Court. All day,' Gary said, putting his notebook back where he'd found it, 'two unlawful removals, three shoplifters and an indecent exposure. He's in tomorrow though.'

Logan thanked him and stomped down the stairs to his commandeered incident cupboard, sitting in the windowless little room, thinking about marching over to the court building, grabbing

Rennie by the throat and beating the shit out of him. He was stamping on the little bastard's testicles when his phone started to ring.

It was Mr Skate Or Die from the IB's tech team, wanting him to know he'd tried those servers from the Garthdee house.

Logan frowned. 'Garvie, not Garthdee. Frank Garvie.'

'*Aye, whatever. Plugged them in this morning – everything's encrypted.*'

'Can you crack it?'

There was a pause and then some derisive laughter. '*No.*'

'I'll be right up.'

The servers they'd confiscated from Garvie's flat lay in the middle of a landfill site of empty Diet Coke cans and bits of wire. Both machines were hooked up to flat-screen monitors – reams of letters and numbers glowing pale green on black. 'What you're looking at,' said the techie, ball-point pen sticking out of his mouth, 'is two-five-six bit asymmetric encryption. Everything is wide open on the box, no security at all, but you can't make any sense out of it without the matching keys.'

'There has to be something you can—'

'Not a sodding chance.' He tapped one of the boxes with his pretend cigarette, 'the military use hundred and twenty-eight bit for secret documents. Two-five-six is like, three hundred and forty billion, billion, *billion* times more secure.

That's your super top, top secret NSA, MI6 kind of thing. We won't be able to crack stuff like this for *at least* another twenty-five years. And before you ask: you can buy encryption software off the internet for less than the price of a football ticket.' The pen went back in his mouth. 'Without the key we haven't got a chance in hell of finding out what's on these machines.'

'Nope, not in.' The voice of Alpha Thirteen. *'We went round a couple of the neighbours, but they've no' seen him since last night. Apparently he was pissed – standin' in the stairwell, shoutin' about how they was all a bunch of bastards and he'd never done nothing.'*

Logan clamped a hand over the telephone's mouthpiece and passed on the message to DI Insch. 'Not in.'

The fat man glowered. 'Tell them to keep going back. Every hour, on the hour. Soon as Garvie's home I want the encryption key to those bloody files.'

By eleven o'clock Logan was back in his gloomy little incident room, with the lights switched off, brooding about Jackie and Rennie, unable to work up any enthusiasm for the piles of paperwork he was supposed to be catching up on. How the hell could she *do* that to him? And with *RENNIE*! Simon Bloody Bastarding Rennie. Simon Bloody Bastarding Arse-Features Thick As Pig Shit Rennie Bastard—

The sound of the door opening. Someone said, 'Eh?' and suddenly the room was full of light, leaving Logan blinking and cursing. Big Gary stood on the threshold, one hand on the light switch. 'What you doing in here in the dark?'

'What do you want Gary?'

'Jesus, you sound cheery . . . That Glaswegian git's been on the phone.'

Logan waited for the rest of it, but nothing else was forthcoming. 'And?'

'The hell should I know – I look like your bloody secretary? If you switched your phone on every now and then you'd know, wouldn't you?'

'Fine.' He went back to staring at the wall. 'Anything else?'

There was a sigh, Gary muttered, 'I give up,' switched off the light and closed the door behind him.

Logan pulled out his phone and called Colin Miller back. It seemed to ring forever before the reporter's voice came on, deeper and more gravelly than normal.

'What you want?'

'Morning, Colin. Feeling better?'

'Like a cat's pissed in my mouth.'

'You phoned.'

'Did I?' There was a loud, rattling cough. *'Urgh . . . Did I do anythin' stupit yesterday?'*

'Yes. Isobel speaking to you yet?'

'She shouted a bit.' Logan got the feeling that was something of an understatement – Dr Isobel

MacAlister wasn't the kind to suffer in silence. Colin groaned. *'Said I was an irresponsible bastard for disappearin'. That anything could've happened. Aye, like last time, remember? When you fucked me over and—'*

'We went through this yesterday: you forgave me! Said I was your best mate.'

'Must've been really pished . . .'

'Doesn't matter, you can't un-forgive someone.'

There was a long pause – enough to make Logan think Miller had hung up – and then the reporter said, *'Izzy says I have to make nice.'*

'That mean no more kicking the crap out of us all over the front page of the P&J then?'

'I'll think about it.' Another cough. *'Oh God.'*

'Well, if we're all friends again . . .' Logan hesitated, this was a perfect opportunity to get Rennie back – ask Miller to screw him over in the press. 'Any chance you could dig up some dirt on someone for me?'

'Depends: who?'

Rennie, Rennie, Rennie . . . Logan closed his eyes, bottling out at the last minute. He just couldn't do it. Not even to Rennie.

'You there? C'mon – who?'

Yes he could. 'Detective Constable Simon Rennie.'

There was silence from the other end of the phone, and when Miller's finally spoke, his voice had its professional edge back. *'Been up to somethin' has he?'*

'Depends what you find out, doesn't it?'

'And I get to publish what I dig up?'

'No skin off my nose. Just as long as you tell me first.'

'See what I can do.' And then Miller hung up.

That was it: no turning back now. If there was dirt to be had, Miller would find it and Rennie would be splattered all over the *Press and Journal*. Ruined. It took nearly five minutes for Logan to start feeling guilty. Sitting on his own, in the dark, he covered his face with his hands and swore and swore and swore.

29

By the time he got back to the flat that evening
– having spent most of the day sulking and
brooding in his little room at FHQ – Jackie was
just heading out, dressed up in her black cat-
burglar outfit again. She paused at the front door.
Scowled. 'You hear about the rape?'

'Dundee last night? Yeah.' The worst one yet:
Wendy Nichol, twenty-six, computer programmer
with a games company, bringing up her five-year-
old daughter on her own. If a taxi driver hadn't
seen her leg sticking out of a bush she'd have bled
to death. Insch had gone through the roof when
the call came from Tayside Police: DCI Cameron
blaming the whole thing on the fat man's inability
to put Rob Macintyre behind bars.

'Unbe-fucking-lievable, how the hell . . .' Jackie
stopped. 'I'm going to have to go out again tonight.'

'Really.' Not a question. Trying to keep the anger
out of his voice.

'Aye. You know what it's like.'

Logan nodded. He did indeed. He knew exactly what it was like. 'I'm going out too. You going to see Cathy again?' Trying to catch her off guard by using a random name.

'No: Janette.' The same name she'd given him earlier. Clever.

'Right. Janette.'

Jackie looked as if she was about to say something, then gave him a quick peck on the cheek instead. 'Don't wait up.' She banged out through the main door and Logan stood where he was for a moment, before turning round and following her. Sneaking out onto Marischal Street in the rain, watching her march up the road with her mobile phone clamped to her ear. Jackie got to the top and made a right onto Union Street, coming to a halt in the bus shelter opposite the Tolbooth. She stuffed the phone back into her pocket and stood there, breath streaming in the cold night air.

He hung back, loitering at the door to The Tilted Wig – where she couldn't see him, but he could see her – cold rain plastering his hair to his head, seeping through his jacket. Three bendy buses had come and gone by the time an anonymous Citroën pulled into the stop, windscreen wipers going full tilt. Jackie threw her hands in the air, shouting, 'About bloody time!' then opened the passenger door. The interior light flickered on and Logan got a good look at the driver before Jackie climbed in and the door slammed shut. The Bastard Simon Rennie.

The car indicated, then drew out into the steady stream of traffic. Joining the rush hour. Soaking wet, Logan stood and watched until the car disappeared.

The Ferryhill House Hotel was one of the few places in Aberdeen optimistic enough to boast a beer garden – a collection of picnic benches sulking, unused, in the steady downpour. Logan marched through into the bar, looking like a drowned rat. Shivering, he peeled off his jacket and scanned the crowd. Not quite seven o'clock yet. No sign of Rachael.

All the tables around the open fire were taken, so he made do with the next best thing, hanging his dripping jacket over the back of a chair. Then went up for a pint of Stella, taking it back to the table and staring at it; wondering if it wasn't too late to chicken out. Maybe he should just go home? This was—

'You came!' He looked up to see Rachael Tulloch taking off a bright orange waterproof. Too late to back out now. She pulled out the seat opposite and sank into it, little droplets of water falling from her hair to sparkle on the tabletop. 'Oh, you've got a drink, I'll . . .' she went to stand, but Logan shooed her back into her chair.

'It's OK, I'll get it. Gin and tonic?'

She blushed. 'Please.'

By the time Logan got back to the table Rachael was putting a lipstick back in her bag. 'Thanks,' she said, accepting the drink, 'you wouldn't *believe* the day I've had. Cheers,' Holding up her glass for Logan to clink his off.

They drank in silence. 'Er . . .' she said, coughed, and tried again. 'We got someone in court today for those unlawful removals. In Tillydrone?'

'Yeah? That's great.'

'Yeah . . .' More silence. 'I didn't think you'd come.' She played with the glass in her hands, not looking at him. 'Thought you'd make some excuse, or say no, or something . . .'

Logan tried for a laugh, but it came out sounding slightly strangled. 'Sorry.' He took a gulp of lager. 'I'm glad you asked.' Not sure if he was lying or not.

She smiled. It made her eyes shine.

The Indian restaurant on Crown Street was only a five-minute walk away, but they were both soaked to the skin by the time they hurried in through the door. At least eating would give them something to do in the awkward silences. Which were getting fewer. Mostly they talked about work: Logan told her about Zander Clark's stash of Victorian porn, then launched into an anecdote about DI Steel chasing a prostitute who'd been shoplifting from Ann Summers, leaving a trail of vibrators, crotchless knickers and lubricant as she tried to get away. So Rachael told him about a man she'd prosecuted for trying to abort his girl-friend's pregnancy with a bottle of bleach.

As the night wore on, Logan tried hard not to think about what Jackie was up to. It didn't matter anyway, she was sleeping with Rennie: it was over. First thing tomorrow morning he'd ask her to move out. And that would be that. So he told jokes and stories, and tried to convince himself he didn't care.

Outside afterwards, standing on the restaurant steps, waiting for the taxi. 'You know,' said Rachael, her voice coming out in a plume of steam, lightly scented with cardamom, cumin and garlic, 'I'm really glad you came.' She stared down at her woolly gloves, cheeks flushed and shiny pink.

'So am I.' And this time he meant it.

'Would you . . .' Deep breath. 'Ah sod it.' She grabbed him by the lapels and kissed him, her lips soft and warm and slightly spicy . . . And that's when Logan's phone rang.

'Bloody hell,' he mumbled, and she backed off laughing as he checked the number. It was FHQ. 'Sorry.' He hit the call button and Sergeant Mitchell's voice burst into his ear, *'. . . No I do not, now get your backside in gear . . .'*

'What can I do for you, Eric?'

'What? Oh halleluiah, it's got its phone switched on for once! You sober?'

'Yes.' He'd been on pints of water since they arrived at the restaurant, not wanting to make a complete tit of himself. 'Why?'

'DI Insch isn't. You've had Alpha Thirteen wasting time all day checking on an address in Danestone – a

Frank Garvie – ring any bells?' Logan admitted that it did. *'Right,'* said Mitchell, *'we've got reports of a disturbance at that address.'*

Logan didn't see what that had to do with him. 'And?'

'And Insch says you've got to go—'

'But—' Rachael was making 'cup of coffee' motions at him.

'Hey, if you want to tell Insch to sod off, you're on your own. I'm staying well out of it.'

Logan screwed up his eyes and wished a painful and embarrassing death on Detective Inspector Bloody Insch. 'OK, OK, I'll need a car.'

'Fine, Oscar Foxtrot Two's going that way. You can cadge a lift.'

He hung up. 'Sorry—'

'You've got to go, haven't you?' she said, as the taxi pulled up behind her.

'Yes. You know what DI Insch's like these days.'

'I've heard.' She opened the taxi door. 'Come on, I'll give you a lift to the station.'

Logan lurched out onto the rain-swept forecourt of FHQ, hoping he didn't look like a drag queen, clarted in lipstick. He hurried through into the reception area as the taxi drove off into the night. Oscar Foxtrot Two – a small, grubby van with wire mesh over the rear windows – was sitting out back, waiting for him with the engine running, the sound of opera seeping out into the downpour. Logan jumped into the passenger seat, and immediately started coughing and spluttering. The whole thing *stank* of wet dog.

'You'll get used tae it in a bit,' said the woman sitting behind the steering wheel. 'Gonnae give them a bath when we get hame, aren't we, babies?' Logan turned to see a pair of enormous Alsatians with their damp liquorice noses pressed up against the grille separating the back of the tiny van from the driver and passenger seats. The bigger of the two began to snarl and the dog handler laughed, telling the dog, 'It's OK, baby he'll no' hurt you.' Then patted Logan on the knee. 'Dinna make eye-contact, for God's sake.'

Logan faced the front. Quickly.

She drove him out to Garvie's flat in Danestone, keeping up a three-way conversation with Logan and her dogs about the documentary she'd seen last night on BBC2 about Bonny Prince Charlie sharing his bed with two Italian courtesans and a bloke from Ireland when he was over for the Jacobite rebellion. 'Of course,' she said, as she turned into Garvie's cul-de-sac, 'I've got a cousin who's gay and he *loves* Drambuie. But he's from Elgin.'

The lights of Alpha Thirteen swept bars of blue through the rain, making it sparkle, as if it'd been electrified. Logan thanked the dog handler and scrambled out of the van and over to the patrol car. 'What's the story?'

The PC pointed up at Garvie's building. 'Neighbour called in about half an hour ago complaining about the noise. They've been on the bloody phone every five minutes since, wanting to know why we've not done anything about it.'

'When did Garvie get home?'

The constable shrugged and Logan cursed. 'You were supposed to be keeping an eye on the place!'

'Don't look at me – I only came on at ten.'

'Oh for God's sake . . .' Logan turned his collar up and dashed through the rain, up the short path, and in through the building's front door. Angry voices echoed down from the floors above, shouting over a continuous loop of blaring music. He climbed the stairs, the noise getting louder with every step.

BOOM! BOOM! BOOM! 'TURN THAT FUCKING THING DOWN!' A man's voice.

'SIR, I'M NOT GOING TO ASK YOU AGAIN—'

'YOU SEE WHAT WE HAVE TO LIVE WITH?' A high-pitched woman.

'OPEN UP, YOU PERVERT BASTARD!' The man again.

They were on the second floor: five angry residents and an annoyed-looking policewoman. The noise from Garvie's flat was deafening, whooshing and booming and roaring, violins and keyboards building to a teeth-rattling crescendo. Then silence. Then round it went once more, in an infinite loop. No wonder the neighbours were spitting nails; an hour of this and the Pope would have been rampaging down Union Street with a baseball bat.

Garvie's front door had been given another paint-job, obscenities covering the woodwork, spreading out over the walls like an angry infection. Logan tapped the constable on the shoulder. 'Anything?'

'WHAT?'

'I SAID: HAVE YOU GOT ANYTHING?'

She looked confused for a moment, then shouted back, 'NO. IT'S BEEN LIKE THIS SINCE WE GOT HERE. HOUSEHOLDER'S NOT ANSWERING—'

'OK.' Logan stepped up to the front door and squatted down, nose wrinkling at the smell of human urine. He pulled on a single latex glove and prised open the letterbox. The hallway lay in darkness, just a ripple of light seeping through from the lounge where that God-awful, repetitive racket was coming from.

'I'VE TRIED THAT!' the constable shouted. 'NO SIGN OF HIM.'

Logan motioned for her to join him downstairs. As soon as they were out of sight the neighbours started hammering on the door again. 'It's their own fault,' said Logan. 'They've been terrorizing the poor sod: graffiti, piss through the letterbox, dog shit in a burning paper bag. He's probably got the most annoying bit of music he has, put it on a short loop, cranked up the volume and sodded off to a hotel for the night. Getting his own back.'

The constable nodded. 'So what we going to do?'

Logan stared back up the stairs as another cycle began. 'We're going to have to break in. If we don't they'll lynch him when he gets back. You—'

'WHY THE HELL AREN'T YOU DOING ANYTHING?' A balding, middle-aged man stormed down from the floor above, bright scarlet with apoplectic rage.

'Do you know anything about the vandalism to Mr Garvie's flat, sir?'

The man stopped. Going pale, then bright red again. 'Are you accusing me of something?'

'Thought so.' Logan turned to the policewoman. 'Did you get this gentleman's name and address, Constable?'

'Yes, sir.'

'Good.' They stood and stared at the man as he backed away up the stairs. He disappeared from sight as the loop started again. 'Come on then,' said Logan, 'if I listen to that any longer, I'm going to end up thumping someone.'

The constable asked to be excused for a minute, hurrying out into the rainy night and the lazy blue sweep of the patrol car's lights. She came back, shaking the water off her police waterproofs, grinning, holding up what looked like a little gun. 'Got it off the internet,' she explained as they climbed the stairs into the deafening noise. 'Been dying for a chance to try it out.'

'Hold on,' said Logan as they got to the first-floor landing, digging out his mobile phone and calling Control, telling them he was concerned for the safety of the householder and that they were going to force entry. There was no sign of the angry mob on the second-floor landing – Mr Middle-Aged had probably warned them the police were more interested in persecuting *them* for vandalism than doing something about Frank Garvie's serenade of eternal damnation. 'KICK IT IN.'

'NO NEED.' The PC swaggered up to the door and slid the pointy end of her 'gun' into the keyhole, twisting it slightly and pulling the trigger. If anything happened it was inaudible beneath the racket. 'HA-HA! LOOK AT THAT!'

The door swung open and the noise got even worse. Logan slapped his hands over his ears and picked his way into the flat. The welcome mat stank of piss so he stuck to the wall, not wanting to tread in anything as he picked his way down to the end of the short hallway. The home cinema system in the lounge was pumping out an incredible amount of sound, making the floorboards thrum beneath his feet as the loop built to yet another crescendo. Logan stepped into the living room just as everything went quiet.

Frank Garvie was hanging from the stainless steel hook in the ceiling. Twitching.

The loop started up again.

30

It took the IB 'team' twenty minutes to turn up: a lone woman in white SOC coveralls, clutching her sample case and trying not to yawn. 'Is this it?' asked Logan as she looked around the now-silent flat.

She shrugged. 'Iain's retirement bash. I'm the only one on call.' She stopped at the living room door and had a good long stare at the body. It was dressed from head to toe in dark red rubber, the material stretched nearly to bursting point, polished and glittering, a zipped mask obscuring the face. Thin black wires trailed from the crotch and backside to a small case sitting on the floor. The body didn't dangle from the ceiling, but hung slack, legs bent, toes resting on the floor. White silk rope, pulled taut by the body's weight, reached from the hook in Garvie's ceiling to the slipknot at the back of his neck – the cord buried so deeply in the shiny rubber around the throat it was nearly invisible.

'Death been declared?' she asked scanning the carpet for footprints.

'Got the ambulance men to do it.' But Logan had checked first. Garvie wasn't just dead, he was cold – he'd been dead for hours. The deafening racket had come from a DVD – *Buffy the Vampire Slayer*, season four. He must have had the disk on 'play all' and when the episodes were over, and Garvie was gone, it jumped back to the main menu, and the never-ending loop of music.

The IB tech nodded. 'OK, well, you go wait outside and I'll let you know when it's OK to come back in. I'll need—'

'Shoes and suit. I know.'

'Good, now bugger off, I've got about three people's jobs to do.'

Logan was sitting in the back of Alpha Thirteen, three hours later, eating a sandwich from the twenty-four-hour supermarket up the road, when the pathologist finally appeared. 'Look out,' said the PC as Isobel's familiar silver Mercedes parked behind their patrol car, 'the Wicked Witch of the West's here.'

Colin Miller emerged from the Mercedes's driver seat, and hurried round to the passenger side, helping Isobel out into the faint drizzle. Fussing over her till she slapped his hands away and glowered at him. Then apologized.

She stood for a moment, breathing heavily, one hand pressed into the small of her back, the other cupping her bulging stomach. Then waddled towards the flats.

Logan stuffed the rest of his sandwich back in the carrier bag and climbed out to join her, hesitated halfway down the path, then turned back to the Mercedes and opened the passenger door. 'You look rough.'

Miller tried to give Logan the finger, but the effect was ruined by the prosthetics in his gloves, making it look as if he was trying for a deformed shadow puppet instead. He gave up. 'This the same Garvie you arrested for the Fettes kid's death?'

'You know I can't tell you any—'

'Thought we was supposed to be friends again. What? I'm good enough to go diggin' up dirt on your polis buddies, but you'll no' tell me about your suicides?'

'Touché. Frank Garvie: used to work in adult films with Jason Fettes.'

The reporter stared past Logan's shoulder at the block of flats. 'Did he now . . .'

'You can't print anything about this, OK? We're—'

'DS McRae?' It was the PC from Alpha Thirteen, waving an Airwave handset at him. 'Control.'

Logan turned back to Miller, 'Look, no printing stuff without my OK!'

'Aye, aye. Nothin' wrong with havin' a poke about though, is there?'

'DS McRae?' the PC again.

'Yes, fine, I heard you the first time! And you,'

He looked at the reporter, thinking about giving him a lecture on social responsibility and the victim's right to privacy . . . 'Try not to get me fired.'

Control was a chief inspector with a clipped Aberdonian accent, wanting an update on the Garvie suicide and how long Alpha Thirteen was going to be tied up for: after all, there was a whole city out there to patrol, even if it was quarter to three on a dreich Friday morning. Logan passed on what they knew and hurried into the flats after Isobel, catching up with her before she'd got as far as the first landing. She was leaning against the wall halfway up the stairs, breathing heavily.

'Are you OK?'

Isobel grimaced, running a hand back and forth across the top of her bump. 'I've got heartburn, swollen ankles, a foot in my bladder, the little sod does gymnastics at two in the morning, I'm boiling the whole time, and I'm the size of a bouncy castle. And I'm *really* not looking forward to tomorrow.'

'Why don't you just go home, it's only a suicide after all, we can always—'

'You actually think I'm going to miss the last crime scene I'll see for six months? No chance.'

Up at the top of the stairs he helped her clamber into the biggest white paper oversuit they had, the zip barely making it over her bump. 'Erm, Isobel . . .' He handed her a pair of latex gloves. 'When we were together . . .' This was stupid.

'What?'

'Nothing.'

She scowled at him. 'What?'

He took a deep breath, looked her in the eye, and said: 'When we were together, did you ever see anyone else?' Watching closely for a reaction, not expecting the one that he got. Her bottom lip trembled, her eyes filled with tears and she started to cry. 'Look, I'm sorry, I didn't mean anything. It wasn't—' She hit him, a stinging slap on the chest. 'Ow!'

'How could you ask me that?' Advancing on him as he backed away. 'How the hell can you – ' she hit him again, 'ask – ' and again, 'me –' and once more for luck, 'that?'

'I'm sorry!' His back bumped into the wall. 'I . . .' He came within a hair's breadth of telling her about Jackie and Rennie, but the words wouldn't come. Logan closed his eyes and hung his head. 'I'm sorry.'

She must have heard something in his voice, because she laid a gentle hand on his arm and told him not to worry, some day he and PC Watson would have a baby of their own. He would have laughed, but got the feeling it would come out strangled and frightening, so he opened the door to Garvie's flat instead.

The IB tech was standing halfway down the hall, fiddling about with a laptop, cables snaking back into the lounge. She saw them stepping over the threshold and waved them back. 'Give us a minute, I'm doing the last three-sixty . . .' a pause, then an electronic bleep. 'OK, you can go in. I've done fibre, prints, body fluids, video and photos. No sign of forced entry, all the windows are locked, curtains drawn. Got some good prints off the gimp suit . . .' She yawned, not bothering to cover her mouth, showing off a vast array of good, old-fashioned Scottish fillings. 'Phhhhh . . . What time is it?' Logan told her and she swore, rubbed a hand over her face then started packing the spherical picture kit away, sticking the goldfish-bowl-on-a-tripod back in its case, muttering about having to be up this late when everyone else was out on the pish.

Isobel circled the body, peering at it, gently poking the musculature through the fingerprint-powdered suit. She stopped, sniffed, then prodded the rubber where it bulged over the silk rope. Frowning.

'Something wrong?' Logan asked.

'Perhaps . . .' she peeled back the hood, exposing Garvie's neck, her latex gloves squeaking on the dark rubber, then sank her fingers into the exposed, waxy skin. 'Cold . . . I'd expect the body to be stiffer than this.'

'Well, he was twitching when we got here—'

She looked appalled. 'Then why the hell didn't you cut him down?'

'Already dead. I checked.'

'Don't be ridiculous. Dead bodies don't twitch.'

Logan pointed at the small transformer lying on the Persian rug. Two thin wires stretched from there to the little flap in the crotch of the suit, a third disappearing into a similar hole in the back-side. 'You want to see?'

Isobel nodded so Logan picked up the plug and stuck it back in the wall socket where he'd found it. Immediately the body began to twitch. 'It's an electrostim set,' he said, as Frank Garvie's corpse danced for them, 'it's supposed to heighten orgasm.'

'Turn it off.'

FHQ was almost deserted, just the wub-wub-wub of a floor polisher somewhere down the corridor breaking the silence as Logan made himself a cup of coffee at the small kettle in the corner of the CID offices. The milk in the fridge looked like an unexploded bomb, the plastic carton swollen and well past its sell-by date. He had it black.

It had taken him two hours to get all the paper-work done for their visit to the house and the discovery of Garvie's body. He slumped back in his seat and stared at the computer screen, scrolling through the transcribed door-to-door interviews they'd done while the one-woman IB team worked the flat. He wasn't really reading them, just killing time. Putting off going home and the inevitable confrontation with Jackie. The accusa-tions, the lies, the shouting . . . The betrayal. And the worst part, the very, very worst part, was that beneath all the anger and resentment and desire to ram his fist down Rennie's fucking throat – he still loved her.

But that didn't mean it wasn't over.

So he went back to the witness statements, reading *their* lies instead. No, they hadn't done anything to the man in flat four. Graffiti, Officer, me? Piss through someone's letter box? Never!

A familiar shape lumbered into the CID office, carrying a huge steaming mug: Big Gary. He stopped when he saw Logan. 'Er . . .'

'Don't bother,' Logan told him, 'there's no milk left to steal.'

'Bugger.' Big Gary peered into his mug. 'Anyway, I wasn't going to steal it . . .'

'You're a dreadful liar.'

Gary shrugged. 'That's why I never made the move into CID: too honest. What you still doing here?'

'Making sure everything's done before Insch comes in.'

'Aye, well . . . Don't forget to tell him he's got till noon if he wants to put in for the Ice Queen's leaving present.' A sad look slid onto Gary's fat features. 'Been a hard sell: at this rate we'll be giving her something nicked from the lost and found and a homemade card.'

Logan blushed and dug out his wallet. 'Put me in for a . . .' Five? Ten? They did sleep together for six months and at least *she'd* never cheated on him. He pulled a dog-eared twenty out and handed it over.

Gary took the note with an impressed whistle, then held it up to the light. 'God, it's a real one too! Come down to the front desk when you get a minute, you can sign the card.' He turned and lumbered off, calling back when he got to the door, 'And take some bloody time off, you're screwing up the overtime bill.'

'Hoy, Rip Van Winkle.' The smell of coffee, smoky bacon, and stale cigarettes. 'We're no' paying you to sleep on the job.' Logan peeled open an eye to see DI Steel looming over him.

Groaning, he swung his legs off the blue, plastic-coated mattress and onto the cold brown floor, searching blearily for his shoes.

'Jesus,' said Steel, 'you look rough.'

'What time is it?' Yawning and stretching. The lining of his brain seemed hotter and rougher than normal, as if someone had pebble-dashed the inside of his skull with warm gravel while he'd been asleep.

'Here,' she handed over her mug of milky coffee, 'I'm no' needing this as much as you.'

Logan hesitated for a second . . . then accepted it, taking a deep gulp before putting it down on the floor so he could struggle into his suit jacket. It took two goes to get his watch in focus enough to read the hands. Eight seventeen. He'd managed a whole two hours' sleep.

Steel sat down on the cell mattress next to him and finished off her bacon buttie while Logan got his shoes on. 'Least they let you keep your laces.' She sooked the tomato sauce from her fingers. 'Let me guess: trouble in paradise?'

'Has Insch been in?'

'Nope. Detective Inspector Fat-and-Grumpy is stuck on the road in from Oldmeldrum. Some idiot tried overtaking a tractor and got smeared all over the front of a dirty-big truck. So he'll be in a right crappy mood when he finally gets here. Same as usual, eh?' She smiled, looked him up and down, then patted him gently on the shoulder. 'Go home.'

'Can't,' he said, levering himself to his feet, 'got to hand over the Frank Garvie case, and the post mortem's at ten.' And Jackie was supposed to be on a day off today, so he didn't want to go back to the flat.

'Aye . . . Well, have a shower then. You smell like day-old curry.'

His hair was still wet when Insch arrived, already three shades redder in the face than normal. The inspector bellowed, 'McRae, my office!' and stomped past, PCs scurrying to get out of his way.

Insch's office was filled with ominous muttering as he skimmed the pile of paperwork Logan had left on his desk the night before. The fat man pulled the last sheet from the case file: Garvie's suicide note, wrapped in a clear plastic evidence bag. '"I'm sorry" – is that it?'

Logan stifled a yawn. 'There's a poem on the back.'

'I'll bet there is.' Insch flipped the evidence bag over and read it, his lips moving as he went. 'Actually,' he said at the end, 'that's quite good.'

He went back to the front. '"I'm sorry" . . . Well, it would've been better if he hadn't left off the whole "for killing Jason Fettes" part, but I suppose it'll have to do.' Insch slipped the note back into the folder. 'What about that encryption key?'

Logan held up a small evidence bag, the bottom littered with shattered bits of plastic and slivers of twisted metal. 'We found it in his kitchen.'

The inspector snatched it out of his hands, frowning at the contents. 'Can we—'

'IB says it's been repeatedly smashed with a hammer. Anything on there is gone.'

'Hmph.' Insch dumped it on his desk and stared thoughtfully at his big *Mikado* poster. 'Did we get anything back from Computer Forensics on that email address for Fettes?'

'Not yet.'

'Oh for crying out loud! You had Fettes's hotmail address days ago!'

'I've been chasing them up,' he lied. 'I was planning on trying again after I'd seen you.'

'Well tell them to get their finger out. Just because Garvie's dead doesn't mean we're not going to finish this investigation properly. I do *not* want them slipping it to the bottom of the pile. Understand?'

'Yes, sir.'

'Post mortem?'

'Ten.'

Insch glanced at his watch. 'Then what are you

hanging around here for? Get those lazy IT morons onto it! And tell Rennie I want to see him.'

Logan nodded, feeling something catch fire in his head. Just because he was avoiding Jackie didn't mean he wouldn't 'have words' with DC Simon Fucking Rennie.

31

'*DC Rennie – what's up?*'

'Where are you?'

'*Eh? Downstairs. Getting the teas in again. Do you—*' Logan hung up on him and marched down to the second floor.

The constable was slouched against the wall, yawning his head off as a kettle rumbled to the boil. He looked up as Logan approached and pulled on a smile. 'Never guess what,' he said in a theatrical whisper, 'Beattie's missus was up for one of those High Street Honeys things! Look . . .' He rummaged around in his pockets, coming out with a small, shiny, dog-eared booklet from one of the more risqué lad's mags, holding it up so Logan could see the picture. 'I mean, we always suspected she was a bit—'

'A word, Constable.' Logan marched straight past.

'Eh? Oh, OK . . . sure.' Rennie stuffed Beattie's wife back in his pocket and scurried after him, down the corridor and into the tiny room Logan had appropriated for the break-in investigation. It was slowly turning back into a cupboard, piled high with files and junk. 'What can I—'

'I know.' He kicked the door shut. Ever since he'd found out about them – Jackie and DC Halfwit here – he'd been wondering how he'd feel when it finally came to this. And the answer was surprisingly fucking angry.

Rennie backed up, banging into the little desk, sending a pile of forms skittering to the carpet tiles. 'Hey, I don't know what—'

Logan grabbed him and shoved him up against the wall. 'I trusted you!'

The constable's eyes went wide, words falling out of him, 'Look, it wasn't my idea, we—'

'Don't you bloody—' He curled his right hand into a fist.

'It was Insch! He made us do it!'

For a moment Logan forgot to breathe. 'Insch? What the hell does—'

'We're supposed to take turns—'

'TAKE TURNS?' That was it: Logan was going to smack him one.

'But . . . but I had rehearsals Monday and Wednesday and Jackie was at that party and I couldn't get to Macintyre's house in time and—'

'Macintyre?' Logan let go of him.

'Watching his house. I couldn't get there till after rehearsal and I watched the house all night, but he could've been out already and I didn't mean to let him get away and that girl got raped and—'

'Oh God.' He sat down on the creaky office chair, feeling sick – they'd just been keeping tabs on the footballer . . . And he'd kissed the Deputy PF! Logan covered his face with his hands and groaned; he was supposed to be seeing Rachael again tonight! Jackie was going to kill him.

Rennie was still babbling, 'I wanted to tell you, but Insch didn't want to get you involved. He . . . Are you OK?'

Logan said, 'No,' and went back to banging his head off the desk.

The morgue was surprisingly empty for Dr Isobel MacAlister's farewell performance: just Logan, DI Insch, and Brian – her floppy-haired assistant. Thank God this wasn't a suspicious death, or the PF would be here and so would Rachael. And Logan was dreading having to speak to her . . . A nervous-looking man with a shaven head and a bad case of the fidgets bumbled through from the storage room. 'This,' said Isobel, her voice even more disapproving than usual, 'is Dr Milne. He'll be standing in for me while I'm on maternity leave.'

The man raised a twitchy hand and said, 'Hi. Call me Graeme, I'm sure we're all going to—'

Isobel cut him off. 'Shall we get started?'

Frank Garvie's rubber-clad body nearly filled

the stainless-steel cutting table. Normally he would have been stripped, his clothes sent up to the IB for examination, but Isobel had insisted that she was going to be the one to peel Garvie's remains; arguing that the gimp suit was so tight it needed to be seen in context with the corpse. But Logan got the feeling she was just doing it to spin the whole thing out for as long as possible. Making the most of her last post mortem. Never wanting the fun to end.

First the mask came off, the rubber squeaking as Isobel rolled it back, revealing Garvie's sallow face. The jaws were slightly open, something red and shiny just visible between the pale lips. 'A ball-gag,' said Isobel, getting her assistant to photograph the thing in situ, before extracting it. Next the rope around the man's throat came off, was dropped into an evidence bag, documented and logged. And then she ran a scalpel along the suit's seams, the rubber suddenly contracting back to its original size, letting Garvie's waxy skin bulge out onto the cold metal table.

Four and a half hours later they were done, and everything Isobel had taken out of the ex-porn star was stuffed back inside, except for his brain – which now hung upside down in a white plastic bucket of formalin – and the six-and-a-half-inch bipolar probe she'd removed from his rectum: the other half of the electrostim set he'd been wired up to. 'Well,' she said, while her assistant and the new pathologist manhandled Frank

Garvie's violated body onto a gurney, 'I'd say it's almost certainly self-inflicted. The groin area of the suit was covered in seminal fluid: the electrical pads strapped to his penis and perineum would have milked the prostate. That, the rope round the throat, and the gag make it look like autoerotic asphyxiation taken to its logical conclusion. Bruising of the neck indicates he's probably tried it before . . .' She turned and gazed at her beloved morgue, the water gurgling in the cutting table, sluicing away the last traces of Frank Garvie. 'I'm . . .' a small catch in her voice, 'I'm going to miss this place.' Her eyes sparkled, and she wiped them with the heel of her hands. 'Excuse me.'

Logan and Insch watched her go.

'Right,' said the inspector clapping his hands together as the morgue door closed behind the departing pathologist, 'lunch.'

'Well, you should have got here earlier then, shouldn't you?' said the man clattering two plates of microwaved moussaka down on their table. 'There's no chips.' He saw the look on Insch's face. 'It's not my fault! We're cleaning the fryers for the next meal. I shouldn't even be serving!'

'So,' said Logan as the man went back to his dirty deep-fat fryers and Insch went mad with the salt and pepper, 'how's the Rob Macintyre case coming?'

The huge man froze for a moment, then started eating. 'There *is* no case, remember?'

Logan just sat there and stared at him, not saying a word. Giving him a taste of his own medicine.

'What?' Insch shovelled in another mouthful, chewing. Then another. Before finally coming out with, 'Who the hell told you? It was Watson wasn't it? I *knew* I shouldn't have—'

'It was Rennie. And I didn't give him any option.' Which was almost true. 'Why didn't you tell me you were keeping tabs on Macintyre?'

'You didn't need to know. And neither does anyone else, so if you breathe a word of this I will personally see to it that both your testicles end up hanging on my office wall. Clear?'

'Crystal.'

Insch nodded and polished off the last forkful. 'We've got one car out the front of Macintyre's house – Rennie and Watson alternating. Not perfect, but it's all I've got.'

'But,' said Logan as the inspector started wiping the plate clean with a podgy finger, sweeping up the sauce and grease then sooking it clean, 'you can't just—'

'I made a promise! Those women deserve justice! Robert Macintyre raped them and I'm going to put him behind bars if it kills me!'

The head of CID was waiting for them in the Fettes incident room, leaning back against the wall with his arms folded, a smile on his face, and very little hair on his head. 'Inspector,' he said as Insch froze on the threshold of the nearly empty room.

The handful of uniform and CID were gone, leaving just the skeletally thin admin officer and a pile of file-boxes.

'Where are all my—'

'I've got some good news for you.' The Detective Chief Superintendent picked a sheaf of paperwork from a folder on the table next to him. 'Garvie was your prime suspect and he's committed suicide, yes?'

'Yes . . .' Insch sounded cautious, as if he wasn't sure where this was going.

'And you're certain he was the one involved in . . .' he checked the sheets in his hand, 'Jason Fettes's death?'

'Positive. We're just looking for corroborating evidence, and—'

'Excellent. In that case we're going to de-prioritise this one. Your men have been reassigned to other active cases; finish up the paperwork and we'll consider it done.'

The inspector opened his mouth to say something, but the DCS held up a hand. 'No, don't thank me yet,' he reached into his inside pocket, pulled out a crime report and passed it over, 'soon as this came in I knew you'd appreciate it.'

Insch unfolded the form, eyes scanning the details, his face slowly splitting into a wide grin.

'Thought so.' The DCS winked. 'Just try not to piss him off too much, OK? If I get more than three complaints about your behaviour I'm giving it to someone else. Understand?'

'Yes, sir, thank you, sir.'

'Very good. Carry on, Inspector.' The DCS picked up his folder, gave them both a jaunty wave and left.

Logan waited for Insch to explain, but the huge fat man was too busy dancing a happy little jig. It wasn't a pretty sight.

'You'll never guess what,' he said at last, face flushed and sweaty. 'Hissing Sid's in hospital. Someone's kicked the living shit out of him.' He threw his arms open to the heavens and burst into song, 'Zipidee doo dah . . .'

Jackie wasn't having an affair, and Sandy Moir-Farquharson had been given a good hiding. Logan smiled. Maybe the inspector was right. Maybe it wasn't such a bad day after all.

32

Aberdeen Royal Infirmary. It was a private room, the blinds drawn against the weak winter sunshine, while Sandy Moir-Farquharson seethed. The lawyer's face was a mess – split lip, swollen cheek, black eye, his nose bridged with plastic and tape, a wad of sterile bandage strapped to his forehead. A morphine drip snaked into his left arm, the right resting on top of the sheets, swathed in a cast from elbow to fingertip. 'You thee thomething funny inthpector?' He was missing at least two teeth.

Insch closed his eyes for a second, then said, 'I was just thinking of an amusing anecdote I heard last week, sir.' Fighting to keep a straight face.

'I don't . . .' The lawyer coughed, eye screwed up in pain. 'Aaggg . . .' Taking shallow, hissing breaths. And Logan began to feel sorry for the man. They'd treated it like a joke all the way up here in the car, laughing about someone being beaten up badly enough to require hospitaliza-tion. Moir-Farquharson slumped back in his bed, a faint sheen of sweat making his forehead glisten. 'I don't want you.'

'I beg your pardon, sir?'

'I don't want you here. I want thomeone else.'

DI Insch shook his head sadly. 'I'm sorry, sir, but this isn't a dating agency. Now what can you tell us about your accident?'

'I wath athaulted!'

'Really?' Insch pulled out an immaculate-looking black notepad and flicked through it. 'Ah, yes, my apologies. Assaulted last night as you left your office. Now, do you have any idea who might have some reason to hate you? Any enemies? Anyone you've screwed over, or annoyed? Neighbours, acquaintances, passersby, members of the general public perhaps? Outraged at your putting paedophiles, muggers, burglars and rapists back on the streets?' He got a scowl in return.

'How dare you thtand there and—'

Logan jumped in before things got any worse. 'I can assure you that we take assaults like this very seriously, sir.'

The lawyer turned his baleful, one-eyed gaze on Logan. 'I don't want you either! Thith ith nothing more than a joke to the pair of you!'

'Well, you're welcome to make a complaint about that if you want to—'

'Don't you worry, I will! I'm—'

'—but you *know* DI Insch and I will do everything we can to find those responsible.' Silence settled in, leaving just the sound of someone screaming for the nurse from further down the corridor. 'Now,' said Logan, 'can you take us through the events leading up to the attack?'

'Well?' said Insch, as they drove back to FHQ, 'what do you think?'

'Wallet missing, watch, briefcase . . . could just be a mugging.' Logan frowned. 'But it's a bit OTT, isn't it? More like a punishment beating. I mean it's not like he's short of enemies.'

'Lucky to still be alive. If that cleaner woman hadn't come out when she did the world would be a happier place right now . . . What? Don't give me that look. I'm only kidding.'

'Forensics?'

Insch dug in his pockets, coming out with a packet of chocolate-covered raisins. 'Too rainy last night. Couple of bloodstains under the car, but fibre's a washout. They're running some prints from the driver's door.'

The traffic grew heavier the closer they got to the centre of town, slowing to a crawl. 'We should start with victims, witnesses, people he's belittled in court.'

'Aye,' said Insch, fighting his way into the packet, tipping a small pile of little brown pellets into his hand and throwing them into his mouth, mumbling as he chewed. 'Better check with Watson first then. She holds a grudge like nobody's business.'

That was what Logan was afraid of.

* * *

Back at the station the day shift was winding down. Five to five. Time to grab one last cup of tea before signing out. Logan sat in what was laughingly known as the 'Review Suite' – little more than a cupboard with a filing cabinet, a unit full of removable hard drives from the police vans' surveillance cameras, and the MUX desk wedged into it. Once upon a time the MUX had been cutting-edge technology, but now it felt like a steam-powered torture device. Feeling more than a little nauseous Logan ejected the current CCTV tape and slotted in the next one. If you were running the cameras you had some say over where they pointed. The picture moved because *you moved it*. Watching the tapes afterwards was an impotent exercise in motion sickness as the operators panned and zoomed about as if they were playing a video game. It didn't help that it was roasting in here: the ancient oscillating fan sitting lifeless on the carpet, beyond all hope of resurrection. Not even kicking it had helped. So Logan had wedged open the door in a vain attempt to get some air into the place.

He twisted the big circular control on the MUX and sent the tape reeling into fast-forward, looking for someone running away from Golden Square – where Hissing Sid had his offices – around the time the lawyer was attacked. The middle of Aberdeen was like a wildlife preserve for CCTV cameras, and Logan had last night's tapes for all of them stacked up on the floor beside him.

Insert tape: whirrrrrrr forward till the time-stamp said nine pm; watch people lurch past at one frame a second; look for anything suspicious; feel guilty for not trusting Jackie; feel even guiltier for not telling Rachael it was all a big mistake; watch until the timestamp said nine thirty; eject tape and repeat.

The only highlight came when he was going through the Union Terrace tape – the camera tilted at a funny angle, picture partially obscured by a fat-arsed pigeon clinging onto a window ledge. Behind the grey feathers was the little alleyway that linked the Terrace with Diamond Street. Half past nine: cars swept by, headlights reflecting back off the rain-slicked tarmac. People wandered into shot, drunks, more cars, a bus, more people – Logan scrutinizing each and every face to see if they were on the 'Who Hates Hissing Sid' list he'd compiled with DI Insch – and then it happened.

A pair of girlies, staggering up towards Union Street, arms round each other for balance as much as camaraderie, ignoring the rain. The one on the left was wearing what could almost be called a skirt – even though it must have been freezing that night – her companion a skimpy top and a pair of trousers that looked painted on. But they'd have needed a *lot* of paint – she was huge. They looked up and spotted the camera, laughed, then the big girl hoicked up her top and jiggled.

'Oh dear Jesus . . .' Logan didn't know whether to laugh or cry – it was like watching someone swinging a pair of watermelons about in a duvet. A figure emerged from Diamond Place, hands in pockets, did a double take and limped past, trying not to look at the woman's naked boobs. She put them away fast, then she and her friend roared with laughter and carried on up the road and out of sight. Logan ejected the tape, wrote FLASHER on a Post-it note and stuck it to the label. With any luck it would make it onto the Christmas blooper reel, along with all the other idiots who thought it was a good idea to expose their breasts, willies and arses to the surveillance cameras.

He dumped the videos back in the CCTV control room and went home.

Eight o'clock. Logan sat bolt upright, blinking, trying to figure out where the hell he was . . . In the lounge, on the sofa, something awful on the television, his mobile phone's shrill squeal competing with the lumpy-looking 'celebrity' singing away on the screen. He grabbed the remote and put her out of his misery, then picked up the phone.

'Hello?' Trying not to sound as if he'd just woken up.

'Logan? It's Rachael,'

Oh shit. Shit, shit, shit, shit, 'Rachael, hi. I—'

'Thought we had a date?'

Logan checked his watch: eight o'clock, he was supposed to be at the cinema half an hour ago. Which probably meant she was bloody furious.

'I'm really sorry.' Why the hell didn't he call and cancel? 'I got caught up in an assault case. Didn't get back . . .' he sighed. 'I fell asleep.'

'I see.'

'Look, I'm really sorry. I was at that call all last night, only got two hours sleep, then it was non-stop all day. Hissing Sid got attacked . . .' He sagged back into the sofa cushions, running a hand over his face, trying to figure out how on earth he was going to tell her it was all one big mistake.

'Believe it or not I understand. The number of men I've left standing outside things, or sitting in restaurants on their own . . .' an embarrassed cough. *'Well, it's not been hundreds, or anything like that. Maybe one or two. I mean I'm not . . . ehm . . .'* Silence. No doubt waiting for him to make the next move.

'I'm *really* sorry,' he said, stalling for time, 'look, we need to—'

'Damn: hold on, I've got someone else trying to get through . . .' and the line went silent. She'd put him on hold.

'—talk.' Logan swore, pulled himself to his feet and wandered over to the window, peering out into the dark night. A thin dusting of white clung to the sill, small flecks of snow drifting through streetlamp haloes. The sound of singing, muffled by the double glazing, came from somewhere down the street. He'd just have to come out with it: he'd made a mistake. He was seeing someone, and he'd thought Jackie was having an affair and . . . no, that would just make Rachael sound like

327

a rebound. Even if it was true, she wouldn't want to hear it. He—

'Sorry, I've got to go: suspicious death in Tillydrone. I'll call you later, OK?'

'Wait, Rachael—' But she'd already hung up.

The street was quiet. Expensive cars lined the road, chinks of light shone out between drawn curtains onto snow-whitened gardens while more flakes slowly floated down from the orange-black sky, melting where they hit wet tarmac, clinging to skeletal trees and the cold metal of parked cars. There was only one vehicle the snow wouldn't cling to: an anonymous silver Vauxhall, on the opposite side of the road and two doors down from Rob Macintyre's house.

Logan jumped into the passenger seat.

Jackie didn't even look round. 'Wondered how long it'd take you.' She was dressed in her cat burglar outfit again, the plastic mug from the top of a tartan thermos clutched in her gloved hands.

'Why didn't you tell me you were watching Macintyre?'

'Insch didn't want you blabbing to Steel.'

'Yeah, because *that's* going to happen.'

She shrugged. 'Not my call.'

He sat, frowning out the window. 'You could have told me.' No response. 'You know what's going to happen when it gets out you've been doing an unauthorized surveillance—'

'You're in *no* position to talk about unauthorized surveillance ops!'

'And look what happened!'

Jackie turned to look at him for the first time since he'd got in the car. 'I spoke to Rennie. So don't talk to me about trusting you – you didn't bloody trust me!'

Logan hoped to God she couldn't see him blushing in the dark car. 'Don't be ridiculous—'

'Rennie might be thick as two shorts, but I'm not, OK? I know what you were doing!' She turned in her seat and slapped him on the shoulder, face creased and angry. 'How could you think I was having an affair? And with Rennie!' She hit him again. 'What's wrong with you?'

'I—'

'No! You don't trust me and—'

'What was I supposed to think?' Not quite shouting, but getting close to it. 'You're never in, you're having sneaky get-togethers, I heard you on the phone – talking to him, telling him how I didn't suspect a thing, like I'm some arsehole to be—'

'Macintyre! How Macintyre didn't suspect I was bloody watching him. For fuck's sake! Eight months we've been living together, why didn't you just ask?'

Silence settled into the car.

'You could have told me.'

'Yeah, well I didn't, OK?' She turned back and glowered out of the window at Macintyre's house, while Logan sat beside her, wishing he'd never come.

A sharp elbow dug into his ribs, bringing him snorking back to the land of the living. 'Whh?' Logan blinked blearily in the thin streetlight.

'You're snoring.' Jackie, still scowling at him.

'I'm awake.' Logan sat up in his seat and stretched as best he could in the cramped car. Ending with a shudder. 'Cold . . .'

'Yeah, well, you should have worn something warmer then, shouldn't you?'

Logan bit back his reply, and checked the car clock instead. Just after one in the morning. 'Sandy the Snake got the crap beaten out of him,' he said, going for neutral territory.

'I heard.' Silence.

'Look, if you don't want me here, just say so, OK? I'm sick of being growled at.' He opened the passenger door and climbed out into the frosty night. For a moment Jackie looked as if she was going to say something, but it passed, and she went back to watching Macintyre's house. 'Fine,' Logan closed the car door, turned up his collar and . . . There was a man standing in the shadows, just up the street, three or four cars behind Jackie's. Shortish, heavy build. Staring across the road at the footballer's place.

He didn't know he was being watched.

Logan reached down and gently tapped on the passenger window. Nothing. He tried again. The driver's door opened and Jackie stuck her head out. 'Bloody hell, what now?'

The man in the shadows' head snapped up, staring wide-eyed at them. And then he was off, running as fast as his little legs would carry him. Cursing, Logan ran after him, shoes slithering on the frost-coated paving slabs. Behind him he could hear Jackie starting the car, pulling out into the road for the three-point turn she'd need to get the car facing the right way.

The lurker was moving fast, his shoes more suited to the slippery pavement than Logan's, as he turned the corner and sprinted onto Great Western Road. Heading back towards the centre of town. But by the time Logan skidded out onto the road, there was no sign of him.

Jackie's pool car screeched to a halt at the junction, both windows wound down so she could shout, 'Which way?' Logan pointed in the vague direction of the traffic lights, and the car roared off.

33

Bent double, panting like an old lady at a Tom Jones concert, Logan was halfway down Burns Road. He'd checked as many of the neighbouring streets as he could, but there was no sign of Mr Lurks-in-Darkness. It was ten minutes since the man had run and Jackie still wasn't back yet, her parking space hollow and empty among the snow-crusted cars like a missing tooth.

Logan stamped his feet and buried his hands in his armpits, hoping she'd give up and come back soon. It was bloody freezing. Snow spiralled lazily down all around, making his ears sting, his breath coming out in thick clouds of white. He marched up and down for a while, trying to keep the circulation going. Far too cold to be hanging about in the middle of the night . . . He stopped pacing, staring down at a shimmering trickle of frozen urine on the pavement, solidified on its way from a tall box hedge to the kerb. Right about where he'd first spotted their mystery lurker.

'Bloody hell . . .' The man had stopped for a pee: that was why he'd run when Logan saw him – he didn't want to get attacked by an irate householder for poisoning his hedge. Swearing, Logan went back to pacing. It was so stupid – who'd hang about on the street when the weather was like this? You'd have to be a complete idiot. Trying to ignore the irony in that thought as his toes slowly went numb.

No, you wanted a vehicle to sit in. Somewhere warm, out of the bloody snow. He should have stayed in the car with Jackie. At least he'd be warm now, even if she was giving him the cold shoulder.

Logan's eyes followed the trail of frozen piss to where it disappeared under a foosty-looking Renault Clio. Not the sort of car you expected to see in a place like this. Well, unless it belonged to someone's kid, but even then, he'd expect it to be newer. He stepped closer, peering in through the passenger window. Discarded chocolate wrappers, empty packets of crisps, a bag of sherbet lemons, two Marks & Spencer sandwiches, three tins of Red Bull, and a hot-water bottle with faint curls of steam rising from it. Logan pulled a handkerchief from his pocket, using it as a makeshift glove as he tried the car door. It wasn't locked.

So the Phantom Piddler *had* been watching Macintyre's house. A quick call to Control got him a name and address for the Clio's owner – a Mr Russell McGillivray, living in a flat on George

Street. Logan stood, contemplating the car, the junk food and the hot-water bottle. OK, so it was *possible* this was just a coincidence, that Mr McGillivray was up to something else, but he doubted it.

Taking one last look up and down the street, Logan folded the passenger seat forward and hopped into the back. He grabbed the hot-water bottle and stuck it under his jacket, before pulling the door closed, enjoying the warmth as it slowly spread across his chest.

A quick rummage in the back turned up a couple of old copies of the *Daily Mail*, and for a moment Logan toyed with the idea that McGillivray might be a journalist, but then why would he run? Logan settled back in the seat, shoogling down, keeping himself as hidden as possible.

A car slid past outside – the engine noise dying, not fading, soon afterwards. That would be Jackie, returning to her surveillance parking spot. Logan pulled out his mobile and called her.

'Jackie?'

'Where the hell have you been? I—'

'Listen, I found the guy's car, it's about twenty yards behind you. He'll be back for it. I need you to keep out of sight, OK? If he sees you he'll do another runner.'

'I'm not going anywhere! Insch would kill me. And that wee fuck Macintyre might get out again!'

'You don't have to—'

'You know what happened last time I wasn't here,

don't you? Your bloody mother's birthday party, and some poor cow—'

'For God's sake! I'm not asking you to abandon your bloody post, OK? Just keep your head down!' Snapping at her. There was an ominous silence from the other end of the phone.

'I know you don't think this is important, but—'

'When? When did I ever say it wasn't important?'

'You said—'

'I didn't say anything! How could I? You never bloody told me what you were up to. Instead of acting like a spoilt brat at the party you could have told me! I would have made an excuse for you. Hell, I'd've come round after with a doggy bag of cake and fucking ice cream! You—'

She hung up on him.

Swearing quietly to himself, Logan reached over into the front of the car and helped himself to one of the sandwiches and a tin of Red Bull. Then he settled back to eat and brood.

It was nearly forty-five minutes before a ceasefire was declared – Jackie phoning to tell him there was a 'suspicious-looking wanker' hanging about at the far end of the road. Logan shifted round till he was peering out the rear window, between the UP THE DONS!!! stickers. A short, stocky figure stood beneath a streetlight, watching the road, breathing plumes of pale fog into the cold morning air.

Logan reached under his jacket and pulled out

the now cold-water bottle, letting it fall into the footwell.

Whoever it was surveyed the street one last time, then started towards the manky Clio. Logan scooted further down, keeping out of sight, listening to the crunch, crunch, crunch of footsteps on crisp snow. A shadow fell across the car's interior, then a jingle of keys, a clunk, and the driver's door was hauled open. The man shivered in behind the steering wheel, filling the car with stale BO, turned the engine over and cranked the heater up to full.

He rubbed his hands together, stared up at the Macintyre place for a moment, then put the car into gear. Logan waited until the man was going for the hand break, before leaning forward and saying, 'Going somewhere?'

The whole car reverberated with a terrified scream. The car lurched, the engine stalled, the driver fumbled frantically for the door handle, but Logan reached out and pressed the central locking button, before clambering into the passenger seat.

The man stared at him, terrified, sweat pricking out on his sloping forehead. 'I've no' got any money!' He was young – no more than mid-twenties, twitchy, surprisingly pale, even allowing for the jaundiced streetlighting.

Logan held out his warrant card. 'Police. Are you Russell McGillivray?'

'I . . . I've no' done nothin'! You scared the crap out of me! I'm makin' a complaint! I—'

'Name. I'm not going to ask you again.'

The young man coughed. 'Don. Don Macbeth . . . er . . . but people call me Hamish, you know, because of the telly, I—'

'You do know it's an offence to give a false name and address to the police, don't you?'

'I'm no' lyin'!'

Logan stared at him, letting the silence grow.

'Seriously! I'm no' lyin'!'

'This your car Mr Macbeth?'

'No . . . Yes . . . I mean it belongs to a mate.'

'I see . . .' Logan nodded. 'Well, Don "Hamish" Macbeth I'm detaining you on suspicion of trying to pervert the cause of justice by giving false details—'

'Oh come on! I'm no' lying! I'm no'!' He made a bid for freedom, stabbing the central locking off with his thumb, then wrenching open the driver's-side door. He scrabbled out into the road, only to find himself face to face with PC Jackie 'Ball Breaker' Watson.

'Don't even think about it!'

He wasn't bright enough to take a telling.

'So then,' said Logan, walking back into interview room one, carrying the results from the finger-print department, 'there seems to be some mistake, "Mr Macbeth". We sent your prints off to the main database and they came back belonging to a Russell McGillivray. Isn't that strange?

Don Macbeth, AKA Russell McGillivray, fidgeted

337

in his seat, one hand going to the crotch of his trousers, making sure everything was still there after his abortive attempt to get past Jackie. 'It's . . . aye . . .' His skin shone with sweat, his body twitching and twisting on its own, while he gnawed away on his fingers. Twitch, chew, twitch, fidget, twitch . . .'Any chance of a fag? I'm gaspin'.' Voice trembling, breath smelling stale and rancid, adding to the general stink of unwashed armpits.

'So, Russell, you want to tell me why you were sat outside Rob Macintyre's house at one in the morning?'

'Aye . . . well . . . it's . . .' he coughed, bit the inside of his cheek for a bit, then said, 'Go on, give us a fag . . . I'm fuckin' dying here!'

'Maybe. But only if you tell me everything. What were you doing there?'

More fidgeting. 'I . . . I'm a big fan, like. Wanted tae get his autograph.'

Logan stared at him. 'Yeah, and I'm Harry Potter.' He pulled out McGillivray's file, flicking through it until he got to, 'Three counts for possession with intent, two for breaking and entering, one for possession of stolen property, one for driving under the influence . . .' He looked up from the sheet and smiled. 'Well, look at that, we're going to have to do you for driving while disqualified as well. That's on top of giving a false name and resisting arrest. *And* I see you're on bail.' Logan gave a low whistle. 'Wow, sucks to be you.'

'Aw fuck . . .' McGillivray folded up, sweaty head on the tabletop, arms piled over the top.

'So, come on then, Russell, before we cart you off to prison for violating your parole, what were you doing lurking about outside Rob Macintyre's house?'

McGillivray peered out between his arms. 'I'm no' well, man, no' well . . .'

Logan pulled a rumpled packet of Benson & Hedges from his pocket – filched from DI Steel's office – and placed it on the table, drawing McGillivray's eyes like a magnet, making him lick his lips in anticipation as Logan placed a cheap plastic lighter beside the cigarettes. 'Now then, how about I start you off?' The sweaty, shivering man sat up and nodded, never taking his eyes off Steel's stolen fags. 'While I was running your prints through the computer, guess what else I found? They match a set of partials we took from a Mr Moir-Farquharson's car. He was assaulted yesterday evening at around nine fifteen, just before you got a free glimpse of some woman's boobs, remember?'

'I . . . no, I was at home with—'

'I've got you on CCTV, Russell. So let's try again, shall we? We caught you lurking outside Robert Macintyre's house, and yesterday you were hanging round where his lawyer was beaten up. Want to explain why?'

Twitch, judder. 'I . . . I was . . . Come on, just one ciggie . . .'

Logan shook his head and picked up the lighter, twirling it between his fingers, before sticking it back in his pocket. Then reached for the cigarettes—

'Oh, come on! I'm beggin' here . . .'

'Must've been sweet,' Logan pulled on an 'all chums together' smile, 'kicking the living daylights out of some slimy lawyer, eh? Who'd blame you?'

'One puff! Just a wee one. Come on . . .'

'Talk first, cigarette later.'

It took nearly an hour, but in the end McGillivray came clean, and all for the price of a smoke. 'I needed the money, OK? I need the money for, you know . . . for somethin'.' Rubbing away at the crook of his arm, reliving the memory. 'He's a lawyer, right? Knew he'd be loaded. Cash and that . . . Thought the footballer would be good for a bob or two, too. You know?' Whimpering like a puppy. 'Come on, you said, eh? If I told you, you said!'

Logan let him help himself to Steel's cigarettes.

34

'Ungrateful bastard.' Insch, stood with his back to the window in his office. Saturday lurked over the city behind him – slate-grey skies threatening a proper fall of snow to coat the thin crust of frozen slush that lined the pavements, street lights glowing like amber fires in the dark, dreary morning. 'Hissing Sid gets him off with nicking some pensioner's life savings four years ago, and McGillivray still goes and beats the living crap out of him.' He chewed thoughtfully. 'Not that I'm complaining, but honour among nasty wee bastards and all that.' He unwrapped another chocolate toffee éclair and popped it in his mouth. 'But it's a result, so I suppose I shouldn't complain.'

'I've got Moir-Farquharson coming in at eight to get photographed,' said Logan, checking the paperwork. 'You wouldn't believe how many people have been asking for an extra set of prints . . .'

'Aye? Put me down for a couple too. If you can

get a good one of his ugly mug all battered and bruised, it's going on my Christmas cards.' Insch levered himself off the desk and stretched, groaning his way into a yawn. 'These late nights are killing me. I tell you: never, *ever* volunteer to direct a bunch of talentless half-wits doing Gilbert and Sullivan. Christ knows what it's doing to my blood pressure . . .' Two fingers going to side of his neck to check. 'Don't fancy coming along to prompt do you?'

'I think I'm busy that night, sir.'

Insch just stared at him.

'Ehm . . .' Logan checked his watch. 'Ah, well, I've got to go get the paperwork done for . . . that thing.' Backing towards the door. 'I'll just . . .' pointing over his shoulder, and out into the corridor. He almost made it.

'Half-six, Baptist church hall on Summer Street. And wear your thermals: it'll be freezing.'

A last-minute phone call from DI Steel – whinging on about how someone had stolen a whole packet of Benson & Hedges from her desk and what was the world coming to/police station her sharny arse – meant that Logan was running behind schedule. By the time he made it downstairs Sandy Moir-Farquharson had been sitting in the lobby of Force Headquarters for nearly fifteen minutes, while a procession of Grampian's finest manufactured excuses to walk past and have a bit of an ogle at his battered face and black eye. 'Are you quite finished?' Logan asked as Big Gary marched through the coded entry door from reception into the corridor again with a big grin on his face.

'Gets better every time I do it!' he said, 'Here, what do you call a lawyer with the shit kicked out of him?'

'Gary—'

'No, wait a minute, it's what do you *get* if you kick the shit out of a lawyer?'

'I'm taking him up to get his photo taken before he files another complaint.' Logan went through into reception, trying not to listen as the desk sergeant shouted out, 'A medal!'

It wasn't much of a photo studio, just the corner of a room on the third floor with a rumpled roll of grey backing paper, a bare seat and a couple of fill-in flashes on tripods.

Sandy the Snake demanded the door be closed before he'd take off his shirt, disappointing the crowd in the corridor. The photographer clicked a huge Nikon digital camera onto a tripod and wired the flashes up while the lawyer struggled to get the sleeve over the cast on his broken arm.

It had only been a day and a half since the attack, but already the bruises were spectacular – a web of purple, black, green and blue that stretched nearly all the way around Sandy's torso.

'Trousers too, please,' said the photographer, firing off a couple of shots, then checking them on the little screen.

'I don't see why I should—'

'Relax, it's just for evidence, we need—'

'Don't think I don't know what you're doing! You and that bunch of jackals out there – you just want to humiliate me!'

Logan sighed. 'Mr Moir-Farquharson, we do this with all victims of serious assault. You know that. The more evidence we have, the longer your attacker's sentence is going to be. You want him put away for as long as possible, don't you?'

He could see Sandy thinking about it, probably struggling with the idea of putting someone behind bars, rather than helping them get away with it, for a change. The lawyer scowled. 'If I see, or hear of, any of these images being used for non-evidential purposes I'm going to sue.' And then he reluctantly stripped. Standing there in his socks and pants, embarrassed and semi-naked, the lawyer looked like a very different man. Thin legs, slight pot belly, grey hairs dusting his chest. He was bruised all over – Russell McGillivray had *really* gone to town on him.

The photographer was quick and efficient, documenting the lawyer's injuries, especially the one on his left shoulder: a boot-print-shaped mass of dark purple, clear enough that you could see the individual treads where his attacker had stamped on him. When it was all over, and Sandy Moir-Farquharson had climbed gingerly back into his clothes, Logan pulled out the identity booklet he'd printed out earlier: a dozen faces from the force database, including one Russell McGillivray. He handed it over, but the lawyer refused to pick anyone out, saying only, 'It was dark.'

'Are you sure?'

The lawyer scowled at him, one eye clear and blue, the other vampire-red, the iris floating on a whorl of blood. 'Of course I'm sure! It was dark. If I saw the person I'd identify them.' He took another glance at the collection of faces. 'I'll not help you fit up an innocent man, just because you can't be bothered to find who actually did it! I knew this would happen if—'

'We've got a fingerprint and a confession.' Logan went to take the booklet back, but the lawyer held it firm, bloodshot and good eye locked on the row of little faces. 'The ungrateful bastard!'

'Surprisingly enough, sir, that's what DI Insch said.'

He escorted Hissing Sid back out the front door and told him he'd be in touch as soon as a trial date had been set. Much to Logan's surprise, the lawyer had shaken his hand and told him he was doing a good job – sounding as if he was grudging every syllable, but saying it nonetheless – before limping out into the chilly morning, just as the first flakes of snow began to fall. Logan stood beneath the canopy, in the cold, and watched him go. Wondering how it was possible to despise someone and feel sorry for them at the same time.

* * *

A night in the cells had done nothing to improve Russell McGillivray's BO. Stale sweat mixed with the sour smell of someone rapidly plummeting through the nightmare world of the DTs. Needing his next fix like a suffocating man needs air. Twitching one minute, still as the grave the next, sweat making his face shine like the pale belly of a toad, eyes bloodshot and ringed with dark purple. Every mother-in-law's nightmare.

Logan sat one of the two coffees he'd brought in with him on the off-green terrazzo floor and shut the door. 'Well, Russell,' he said, taking out what was left of DI Steel's stolen cigarettes and rattling the packet, 'you looking forward to your fifteen minutes of fame?'

Painful smile, wheedling voice: 'Gie's a . . . gie's a ciggie. Go on, gie's a fag, eh?'

'Shouldn't take long: into court, bish-bash-bosh, back to Craiginches for a couple of years on the parole violation. Not to mention all that extra time for driving while disqualified, without insurance, resisting arrest, perverting the course of justice, attempted murder—'

'WHAT?' McGillivray was up on his feet like a shot, twisting his fingers round and round, making the joints pop and crack. 'I didnae murder no one!'

'Oh, did I not mention that last night?' Logan shrugged, 'Must've slipped my mind. You think—'

'I didnae murder nobody!'

Logan dug out a cigarette and the lighter. 'One last smoke for the condemned man.'

'I DIDNAE MURDER ANYONE!'

'No, but you had a bloody good crack at it, didn't you? That cleaner hadn't come out when she did, you'd've beaten him to death.'

'OhJesusfuck . . .'

'Here.' Logan lit one then passed it across, the long-forgotten burn of inhaled smoke making his scarred lungs twitch. 'Might as well enjoy it while you can.'

McGillivray wrapped himself around the burning cigarette, puffing frantically, as if it could make this all go away. 'Wasnae murder . . . I . . . wis just supposed to teach them a wee lesson.'

'The lawyer and . . . ?' leaving a gap for McGillivray to fill, even though he knew the answer already.

'An the fuckin' footballer. Both of them for three hundred.'

'Three hundred's *way* too cheap, Russell: you'll devalue the market.'

'It's no' my fault! I need my medicine . . .'

'Who? Who gave you the three hundred?'

He shrugged, eyes on the floor, cigarette held in a cupped hand, as if he was trying to hide it. 'Dunno, some bloke in a pub.'

Logan treated him to an uncomfortable silence. The kind of silence Insch would have used, if he hadn't sodded off for an early lunch to go shout at the woman doing the 'Gentlemen of Japan' costumes.

'I dunno! OK, I dunno . . . didn't ask, three hundred for two fuckers.'

'Cash in advance?'

McGillivray sooked the last gasping breath from the orange filtered stub, then ground it out beneath his foot. 'Gie's another fag, eh?'

'Did you get paid in advance?'

He licked his lips, staring at Logan's pocket, where the cigarettes were hiding. 'Hunnerd up front. Hunnerd after the lawyer. Hunnerd after the footballer . . .' More fidgeting. 'He's a fuckin rapist, isn't he? No *my* fault! You—'

Logan pulled out another cigarette and McGillivray's junkie eyes lit up. 'Which pub, Russell?'

'Can't remember.'

Logan shook his head, then snapped the fag in half. 'Which pub?'

'Ah fuck! Come oan! I'm no—'

Crack and the cigarette was half the size again.

'Garthdee Arms!'

'I want a name.'

'He didnae gie's his name! He didnae!' Panicking, eyes on the tiny smokable stub. 'Tall bloke, looked like shite, beard, glasses . . . for fucksake . . .'

Logan gave him what was left.

It took less than twenty minutes with the e-fit software to come up with a likeness – thin face, bags under the eyes, round glasses, high forehead, beard. Logan sighed and printed it out, not needing to post the picture on the force intranet to find out who it was. Macintyre's third victim – Gail Dunbar – this was her husband, the man who'd accosted Insch outside the court when the footballer was released. The man Insch had promised justice.

They picked him up from work, taking him away in an unmarked CID car to be fingerprinted, DNA-sampled and photographed. Listening as he went from sullen silence to shouted complaints: the lawyer got that little fucker off with what he'd done to Gail. He deserved all he fucking got! His only regret was that McGillivray had started with Moir-Farquharson instead of that footballing little fuck. Far as he was concerned it was two hundred pounds well spent.

Insch was just coming back from lunch, passing through the rear doors as Rennie and Rickards manhandled Gail Dunbar's husband down to the cells. The man took one look at the inspector and exploded. 'YOU! YOU PROMISED ME! YOU PROMISED YOU'D PUT HIM AWAY! YOU PROMISED, YOU FAT FUCK!' And then he got violent.

'Bloody hell,' said Logan, slumped back against the wall while Dunbar was dragged away, shouting, swearing and screaming.

'He's right,' said Insch as the racket was muffled by a slamming cell door, '*we* can't touch Macintyre.

Someone rapes my wife: you better believe I'm going to do something about it.' He sighed, staring off into the distance for a moment. 'Only I wouldn't use a junkie toe-rag like McGillivray. I'd do the bastard myself.'

35

Half past two and Logan was getting ready to shut down his computer when DC Rennie swore his way into the room, holding a wodge of damp paper towels against his cheek. 'Bastard fucking shite bastard fuck . . .'

'What happened to you?'

'Your bloody beardy-weirdie took a swing at me! Took three of us to get him in a bloody cell.'

'He's a primary school teacher.'

'He's a bastard!' Pulling away the damp towels and fingering the angry red welt beneath. 'I was on a promise tonight as well . . .' Rennie stopped and glowered at the tissue, then hurled it into the bin. 'Insch wants to know if you need a lift tonight. To the rehearsal?'

Logan shook his head. 'I'm going home. Anyway, thought you lot only met on a Monday, Wednesday and Friday.'

'Two weeks till we're on, so it's pretty much every night from now till—'

'So who's supposed to watch Macintyre then?'

Rennie blushed. 'I can come back later if—'

'It's Jackie, isn't it? For God's sake!' If she was supposed to watch the footballer's house every night for the next two weeks she'd be in a permanent foul mood. 'What if she's supposed to be on nights, or the back shift?'

Rennie shrugged. 'I'm just doing what I'm told.'

'This is stupid.' Logan stood. 'We know Macintyre's not hunting in Aberdeen any more; all we have to do is stick his number plates into the ANPR system and call Tayside if he leaves the city.'

'Er . . . the inspector doesn't want anyone else knowing about—'

'Yeah? Well guess what? I don't care.' He grabbed his coat and headed downstairs, Rennie trailing along behind him like some sort of bloody puppy, yapping away about how Insch wouldn't like it and wouldn't it be better to just keep their heads down . . .

The windowless CCTV room was quiet, lit by a wall of little fourteen-inch television screens: seventy-one of them flickering away, showing different views of Aberdeen. Three operators sat at the central desk, headphones on, working the cameras by remote control and drinking mugs of tea. Logan grabbed the inspector in charge and asked if he could have a word in the review suite across the corridor. 'Can you do me a favour?' he asked when the door was shut, leaving Rennie standing outside, looking anxious. 'I need these number plates in the ANPR.' Scribbling down the registrations for all of Rob Macintyre's vehicles. Being personalized vanity plates, they were easy enough to remember.

The inspector took the list, holding the thing as if it was poisonous. 'Why?'

'Because you owe me.'

He thought about it. 'We can't just stick number plates in the system willy-nilly. I mean there's an audit trail and—'

'If any of those cars leave town – you give me a call. Day or night. Pretend Insch said to watch them a couple of weeks ago.'

'Insch?' The inspector looked down at the list, frowned, then said, 'These Rob Macintyre's cars? Coz if they are, they're already in the system. They were set up ages ago. No one told us to stop monitoring them, so we didn't.'

In Aberdeen, the Automatic Number Plate Recognition system monitored every car entering or leaving the city by a major road, recording the licence plate and searching for it in the local and national databases. If the car was on the 'watch' list, it got pinged. Rob Macintyre's cars were *all* on the watch list. None of them had been ID'd leaving Aberdeen. Logan read through the log files again and swore. 'What about Dundee?'

The inspector shook his head. 'Nothing. If they'd

clocked his car they'd have called us. It's all the same database.'

'Damn . . .' Logan sat back on the desk in the small room. 'Do us a favour and give them a call, OK?'

'It won't do any good. They—'

'Get them to pull their CCTV for the road into Dundee – maybe he's obscured his number plate? He could have got one of those special ones off the internet—'

'Believe it or not, we've already done it. Insch was in here shouting the odds when the first copycat rape happened. Same again with the second. *We* checked. *Tayside* checked. Macintyre just wasn't there.'

Out in the corridor Rennie was trying, and failing, to chat up one of the admin assistants. Logan marched right past, through the door and down the stairs. Rennie scurried after him. 'Er . . . he's not going to tell anyone, is he? Insch'll kill me if he—'

'It can't be Macintyre – his car would've set off the ANPR. It has to be a copycat. That, or it was never Macintyre in the first place.'

Rennie groaned. 'The Inspector isn't going to like that.'

'Tough.' He passed through the back door and out into the snow-shrouded car park.

'So,' said Rennie, sliding in the icy slush, 'you coming, then? To the rehearsal?'

'No.'

354

'Aw, come on! Please, Insch thinks—'

'I don't care! I'm not spending my evening watching you lot ponce about on stage forgetting your lines. So you can stop pouting: I'm not going.'

36

The Baptist church hall was every bit as cold and depressing as Logan had expected: dark wooden floorboards, stained by years of dirty shoes, pockmarked with tiny high-heel dimples; someone had given the room a coat of magnolia a long time ago, but it had been ignored ever since, the paintwork flaking and peeling as if the place had a nasty dose of eczema. The inspector sat at a small, collapsible desk, watching as his gentlemen from Japan and schoolgirls lurched through the operetta.

Insch's cast were . . . *challenged* was probably the polite way to put it. They didn't know their lines, forgot where they were supposed to be and when they were supposed to be there, sending the inspector into regular, purple-faced fits about timing, places, and learning the bloody words. The only person he didn't yell at was Debbie Kerr: AKA Debs – the woman playing Katisha – and Logan could see why. She was the only one of them who seemed to have any clue what she was doing. Rennie certainly didn't – Logan had seen more coordinated jellyfish.

He lasted two whole hours before making his excuses, picking his moment carefully, when the inspector was too busy shouting to notice.

There wasn't much of a queue in the Ashvale chip shop that night, just a couple of tweedy-looking women peering at the menu, arguing over whose turn it was to pay. Logan got two haddock suppers with pickled onions, Irn-Bru, and a polystyrene cup of mushy peas to go, stuffing the plastic bag of fish and chips down the front of his jacket, vinegar-scented steam rising up around his face as he hurried along Great Western Road.

The snow had kept up a slow, relentless pace: fat, wet flakes of white that stuck to his hair and jacket, piled up in the gardens, or turned to turd-brown slush in the gutters. When he was young, the snow and the rain had hit long before Christmas, making the school holidays a time for sledging, pornographic snowmen, and being pelted with snowballs, but as the years went by the season for snow had become erratic. Now it came any-time between December and April, the blizzards howling in to turn the world all Dr Zhivago. The north-east of Scotland, twinned with Siberia.

By the time he reached Macintyre's road his hands, feet and face were frozen, but sweat trickled down the small of his back. The result of marching along in a thick padded jacket with a bag of fish suppers stuffed up his simmit.

Jackie was parked in the same space as before, where she could watch the footballer's house without sitting right in front of it. She looked surprised to see him as he climbed in beside her. 'I didn't—'

'Fish and chips.' Logan, dug the bags out from under his jacket. 'Thought you'd be tired of cold sandwiches and cups of thermos coffee.' She accepted a paper parcel and unfolded it, filling the car with warm, tasty smells.

'Thanks.' They ate in silence.

Sunday morning should have involved nothing more strenuous than a lie-in and a late breakfast. Instead it creaked and groaned after a night spent in the passenger seat of a manky Vauxhall Vectra. Predawn had turned the sky purple, slowly lightening between the silent grey buildings, making the snow glow pink in the gloom. Jackie was fast asleep in the driver's seat, legs splayed out like a frog, snoring gently with her mouth open. Very feminine. But at least they were on speaking terms again.

Logan tried to stretch, yawned, shook his head, then checked his watch. Six twenty-two. He knew this was a complete waste of time – the ANPR would have picked Macintyre up if he really *was* driving to Dundee to attack women – but if it meant an end to the fighting and angry silences, he was prepared to put up with an uncomfortable night in a filthy car. Even if it was his day off.

There was a light on in one of Macintyre's upper rooms and had been for nearly fifteen minutes. The front door opened and Macintyre stepped out into the early morning cold, a heavy holdall in one hand, a mobile phone clamped to his ear with the other. Logan leant over and shook Jackie's shoulder.

She surfaced with a, 'Phff, emem, neghe . . .' blinking and yawning, as Macintyre locked up then climbed into his brand-new silver Audi with the personalised number plates.

She didn't pull out until Macintyre was down at the end of the street, indicating left onto Great Western Road. Right would have taken him to the junction with South Anderson Drive and the road to Dundee. Left went towards the town centre.

They followed him at a safe distance, joining a convoy of cars crawling along behind a council gritter, its yellow flashing lights reflecting back from dark and lifeless shop windows all the way down Union Street, then along King Street too . . . Macintyre took a right halfway down, and so did Jackie, leaving the main road for a snow-covered side street, hanging back as far as possible.

The footballer pulled into the car park opposite Pittodrie Football Stadium, but Jackie kept on going, drifting past, then stopping at the end of the road, where they could watch Macintyre climb out of his car, march round the back, take out the large holdall, then swagger off towards the players' entrance. Giving some slope-foreheaded troglodyte a high five on the way.

'Sod it,' said Logan, 'he's just going to morning practice.'

But just before the footballer disappeared into the ground, Logan could have sworn he looked directly at them and winked.

The Inversnecky Café was something of an institution in Aberdeen: a dark green, single-storey building, lurking on the seafront along with half a dozen other ice cream places and restaurants, facing out towards the grey, wintry North Sea. The amusement arcade on the corner was open, but it was unlikely to be doing a lot of business on a freezing cold Sunday morning: There was no one about to see the bright flashing lights but bulldog-sized seagulls who waddled grumpily along the cold pavement, tearing into discarded chip papers and burger cartons.

Surprisingly, Colin Miller was already waiting for Logan as he pulled into one of the parking spots opposite. The reporter was huddled round the side of the building, puffing away on a cigarette, looking out over the sea, oblivious to everything but the crashing waves and screeching gulls.

'Didn't know you smoked.'

Miller cringed, dragged back from the middle distance. 'I don't. And if you tell Izzy any different

I'll fuckin' do you. She's mad enough at me as it is.' He looked better than he had outside Garvie's flat the other night. The stubble was gone, but the bags under his eyes were as dark as the clouds lowering over the water. At least he was dressed more like his old self: an expensive suit with scarlet woollen scarf and heavy black overcoat. He pulled the cigarette from his lips with black leather fingers and coughed long and hard, then flicked the butt out into the road.

It was warm inside the café, the hiss and gurgle of an espresso machine sounding over a radio tuned to Northsound Two: the weather report predicting doom and gloom for the week ahead. It was busier than Logan had been expecting, couples and families down for the full fried Scottish heart attack experience. No one went to the Inversnecky for a bowl of muesli and half a grapefruit. A tall, gangly man, with a hairline that wasn't so much receding as running hell for leather, took their order and left them to find their own table. Miller picked the one closest to the heater, complaining the whole time about how come they couldn't get any decent weather in this shit-hole town for a change.

'It's March,' said Logan settling in opposite, 'what did you expect – a heat wave? Not exactly the Costa Del Sol, is it?'

The reporter scowled, rubbing his gloved hands in the heater's warm glow. 'No, Aberdeen's the Costa Del Shite.' He looked up to see the man from the counter standing over him with two coffees and a raised eyebrow. 'Aye, no offence like.'

'You're going to get spit in your breakfast, you know that, don't you?' said Logan when he'd gone.

'Nah, Martin's all right, I come here often enough. He knows what I'm like.'

And so did Logan. 'Come on then – why all the secrecy?' There had been a mysterious message waiting on Logan's answering machine when he'd got back to the flat after the unofficial stakeout: *'Meet me at the Inversnecky, nine o'clock, you're buying.'*

'Eh? Oh . . .' Miller shrugged and stirred an extra packet of sugar into his mug. 'Wanted to get out the house, you know? Only been a day and a bit and she's already goin' stir crazy. Next six months are goin' tae be a soddin' nightmare.'

'Try the next eighteen years. Maybe longer – my brother didn't leave home till he was thirty-two.' Logan grinned. 'And if it's a girl, you've got boyfriends to worry about, teenage pregnancy, drugs, tattoos, piercings—'

'Gonnae no dae that?'

'Why?'

'Just gonnae no! Bad enough as it is without you stirring.'

The door jingled open and a red-nosed couple stomped in from the wintry outdoors, bringing a blast of cold air with them. Miller shivered, even though they were practically sitting on top of the heater. 'And get this,' he said, pulling a disgusted face, 'They want me to do a "Baby Diary". Fuckin' investigative journalist and they want me to do puff pieces on changing shitey nappies . . .' He went off on a whinge, complaining about how he wasn't appreciated, and how *The Scotsman* had offered him a huge chunk of money to move down to Edinburgh and work for them. And how he was seriously considering it, even though Logan knew there was no way in hell Miller would ever return to the central belt. Not if he wanted to keep the fingers he had left. He finally stopped whinging when their breakfasts arrived.

Logan grabbed the tomato sauce. 'You know I asked you to dig up some dirt on—'

'DC Simon Allan Rennie, twenty-five, five foot eleven, went to Powis Academy – suspended six days for getting into a fight with his maths teacher. Lives in a flat on Dee Street . . .'

Logan listened to Miller detailing the minutiae of Rennie's life between bites of sausage, bacon, mushroom and egg. The reporter knew everything: from who the DC's first girlfriend was, to the number of complaints made against him by members of the public in the last three years. But the upshot was that the Bastard Simon Rennie was clean. 'How the hell do you know all this?'

Miller smiled, piling beans up on a corner of toast. 'Findin' stuff out is what I do.' Not like him to be so modest. He stuck the forkful in his mouth and chewed smugly. 'Now, you goin' tae ask me about your boy Garvie?'

'What about him?' Logan put down his cutlery.

'Up to his ears in debt. See all that shite he had in his house – computers and home cinema and gadgets and that – owed a fortune. So he rents some stuff out on the side.'

Logan scooted forward in his seat, lowering his voice to a whisper. 'Let me guess: hardcore bondage pornography?'

'Fuck's sake, man, it's no' the bloody Dark Ages!' A sudden silence hit the dining room and all eyes turned to the reporter as he laughed. 'You can get as much of that crap you want off the internet for free – no, he was rentin' out server space. Encrypted server space. The kind you use for data you *really* don't want people findin' out about.'

And Logan thought about the memory stick they'd found smashed to smithereens in Garvie's flat. 'What was it?'

That was where Colin Miller's encyclopaedic knowledge ground to a halt. 'No idea. *Yet*. But you can bet it's gonna be splashed all over the front page soon as I find out.'

37

It took nearly an hour to round up all the dirty washing and stuff it in the machine. The flat was a pigsty – it always was whenever they were both up to their ears, working too much overtime – so Logan spent most of the afternoon grumbling around the place, trying to make it habitable again. He was in the middle of hoovering the lounge when the doorbell went: a long, insistent buzzing that finally managed to filter through the vacuum cleaner's drone. It was PC Rickards, standing outside the main door, hands rammed deep into his pockets, shivering. Logan let him in. 'Let me guess, DI Steel's suddenly remembered—'

'Sorry, sir. It's the DCS – he wants you up at the station, now.'

'What? I haven't had a whole day off for weeks! Can't it—'

'He was really, really insistent.'

Logan didn't like the sound of that.

*   *   *

The Chief Constable's office looked like something out of a horror movie – DI Insch, the DCS in charge of CID, Big Gary, and that ginger-haired bastard Inspector Napier, all looking very unhappy. The CC sat behind his desk wearing a face like thunder, staring at Jackie as she stood to attention in the middle of the room.

'. . . think so, don't you?' Sandy Moir-Farquharson stopped talking as Logan walked in, then pulled his bruised and battered features into a smug smile. 'Well, well, well, if it isn't the great PC Watson's partner in crime.'

Logan ignored him, staring at Insch instead. 'Sir?'

But it was the Chief Constable who answered: 'What the *hell* were you thinking? Didn't you stop to consider the repercussions? Grampian Police does *not* need maverick officers bringing the force into disrepute!'

Nope, going to need more of a clue than that. 'Sorry, sir?'

Hissing Sid leant forward in his visitors' chair, cradling his broken arm. 'You and Watson have been carrying out an illegal, *unauthorized* surveillance on Rob Macintyre's property, even though I have a court order requiring you to stay away from my client.' He smiled like a shark – the missing teeth filled with bright white, temporary dentures. 'This is blatant harassment and we will not stand for it.'

So Logan had been right: the little footballing

bastard *had* winked at them. Maybe it wasn't too late to bluff his way out? After all it'd just be Macintyre's word against theirs. 'I don't—'

'And don't even bother trying to deny it.' The lawyer held up a hand-held camcorder and pressed a button on the shiny silver plastic. Tinny sound bristled in the crowded room, a man with a pronounced Aberdonian accent talking to himself while the picture on the little built-in screen jostled from a close-up of an expensive watch – three fifteen in the morning – round until it was pointing straight back at the person holding the camera. Rob Macintyre grinned and waved, then swung the thing back again, pointing it at a darkened window. It took a moment for the autofocus and light balance to catch up, but eventually the picture showed a dark street, lines of parked cars beneath drifting flakes of snow. A wobble, then the camera zoomed in on a depressingly familiar Vauxhall and its occupants: Logan and Jackie, watching the foot-baller's house.

Hissing Sid was right, there was no point denying it, so Logan didn't.

The CC slammed a palm down on his desk, making everything shudder. 'How could you be so stupid? You knew we'd been ordered to stay away from Macintyre!'

Logan sneaked a quick glance at Jackie, standing boot-faced beside him. She'd obviously not told anyone it'd all been Insch's idea in the first place, or the fat man would be up here getting his arse chewed off with them. And given the satisfied look of righteous indignation on Inspector Napier's face, Logan had a shrewd idea what was coming next: gross misconduct, suspension and demotion. If they were lucky. And all because that fat bastard Insch was obsessed with pinning everything on Rob Bloody Macintyre.

Logan took a deep breath and asked what day the tape had been recorded.

'What?' The CC looked shocked, 'You were there more than once?'

'You see!' Hissing Sid snapped the camcorder screen shut. 'I told you they've been running an illegal surveillance operation. We—'

'Was this last night, or the night before?' Logan asked again.

'Last night.'

Logan nodded. 'Yes, we were watching Rob Macintyre's house.'

Inspector Napier levered himself to his feet, like a praying mantis in a black uniform. 'Detective Sergeant McRae, I'm suspending you immediately pending a formal review by Professional Standards. You've shown a remarkable lapse in judgment and—'

'We were protecting him: Macintyre.'

Napier was about to say something, but the Chief Constable cut him off. 'You what?'

'After the attack on Mr Moir-Farquharson I made a list of possible enemies.' Which was true: it was everything else that was a barefaced lie.

'Top of the list were those allegedly raped by Mr Macintyre, who might be looking for revenge on one or both men. Knowing that Grampian Police had been formally warned not to approach Mr Macintyre directly, I persuaded Constable Watson to accompany me on an un-authorized surveillance operation of his property, in case he was targeted for attack.' It sounded like a prepared statement for court. Logan was rather pleased with himself.

There was a moment's silence, then Moir-Farquharson said, 'You don't seriously expect us to believe—'

'It's how we caught Russell McGillivray. If we hadn't been there watching the house, he'd have attacked Macintyre. And maybe this time he'd have gone all the way. We'd have been looking at a murder.'

The angry red was slowly draining from the Chief Constable's face, to be replaced by a cheery pink glow and a big smile. 'And you went back last night . . . ?'

'Because we couldn't be sure McGillivray was working alone.'

The CC looked from Logan, to Jackie, to the lawyer, then back again. 'I see. So you were only watching Mr Macintyre's house—'

'For his safety. Yes, sir.'

'On your own time.' He nodded, smiled, then said, 'In which case I apologize, Sergeant. Good work.'

Moir-Farquharson lurched to his feet, wincing all the way. 'But—'

'There's going to be a letter of commendation for you and Constable Watson.'

'But—'

'Well then, now that's all settled we can get back to work. If you'll all excuse me, I have other matters to attend to.' He picked up his phone and started dialling. The interview was over.

Out in the corridor the lawyer stared at Logan as the CC's door swung shut behind them. 'But . . .' He cleared his throat and tried again. 'Given the circumstances, I think it's no longer appropriate for you to watch my client's house.'

'You remember what you said to me when I showed you Russell McGillivray's photo?'

The lawyer frowned, 'I . . . I called him an ungrateful bastard.'

'You can see yourself out.'

38

Sitting with Jackie in DI Insch's office afterwards, watching the inspector swearing his way into a jumbo bag of fizzy dinosaurs, Logan had to admit that he'd been expecting more of a celebration. Instead Insch picked up a manila folder from his in-tray and tossed it across the desk.

The contents had been emailed up by Tayside Police: another rape. 'Bastard . . .' Jessica Stirling, attacked just off the Kingsway – a huge dual carriageway that stretched across Dundee. She was only nineteen. Logan couldn't even look at the victim photographs.

'She was in town for a friend's birthday last night.' Insch picked up a purple brachiosaur and stared at it. 'Studying musical theatre at RADA. Going to be a star . . .' He stuffed the dinosaur back in the bag, uneaten. 'Check the time.'

Logan skimmed through the report – the attack took place between twenty to and twenty past three. The exact same time they were being videoed watching Macintyre's house.

Insch turned his back on the room, gazing out into the wintry afternoon. 'It wasn't him. All this time I've been dicking about chasing the little bastard and it wasn't even him.' There was a short humourless laugh. 'If I hadn't been so bloody convinced, we might have actually looked for someone else. And those girls wouldn't . . .' He stopped and ran a hand over his fat features, shoulders slumped. It was as if he'd aged a decade in as many seconds, his voice flat and listless. 'Why don't you two go home? Forget about this evening. It's not him.'

'But, sir—' Jackie, not looking happy, '—the wee fuck attacked me! He *has* to be—'

'IT'S NOT HIM!' Insch spun round, face bright purple. 'Understand? It was all crap! All of it!' He snatched a pile of files from his desk and hurled them at the far wall. 'It was *never* him!'

'But—'

'It's over, Constable. *Finished*.' Turning back to the window. 'I screwed up. Go home.'

Thankfully Jackie didn't say anything else, just grabbed her coat and stormed out, slamming the door behind her.

Logan caught up with her on the stairs as she stomped down towards the basement locker rooms. 'Look,' Logan made a grab for her arm, 'I know it looks bad but—'

'Don't you *dare* patronize me!'

'What am I supposed to say? He can't have done the Dundee rape! We were watching him, *you were there*! He didn't go anywhere, he—'

'Bloody Russell McGillivray had the right idea.' She shoved through into the female changing room, closing the door in Logan's face.

'You OK?'

'What? Logan looked up from his cup of tea to find Rickards and Rennie settling down on the other side of the canteen table. The bruise on Rennie's face had taken on a bluish five-o'clock-shadow tinge. 'Oh, yes. Great. Never better.'

'Tell you what,' Rennie threw an arm round his companion's shoulders, 'why don't we have a lads' night out tonight, after rehearsals? Beer, balti, and talking bollocks.'

'I can't.' Rickards blushed then mumbled about a prior engagement he couldn't get out of.

'Ah,' Rennie leered at him, 'going to see your bondage buddies, eh? On a promise are we? Oh, spank me Mr Mainwaring!'

'You can f—'

'What are they like?' Logan asked. 'People in the scene?' Thinking about Frank Garvie and his encrypted data.

'Well . . . they're all . . . different.'

Rennie laughed. 'I should bloody think so!'

'No – I mean there's no real "type"! Everyone's different.'

373

'Oh.' That's what Logan had been afraid of.

'You know what,' said Rennie, unwrapping a Tunnocks teacake, 'you should totally go with him!'

Rickards scowled. 'They're *people*, OK? Not a freak show. You can't just go play "laugh at the perverts"!'

'Hey,' Rennie held up his hands, 'I was only saying.'

'Well don't! It's—'

'Actually,' said Logan, finishing his tea, 'that's not a bad idea.' It would give him a chance to ask around, see if anyone knew what Garvie had been up to with his dodgy rented servers. And it wouldn't hurt to have an excuse to avoid the flat for a while: let Jackie and her foul temper calm down a bit. 'I'd like to go.'

Rickards blanched. 'But . . . but . . .'

'It's all right, Constable, I promise not to embarrass you.'

'But . . .'

'Then it's settled!' Rennie slapped him on the back. 'Play your cards right and *I'll* come next time. As the actress said to the bishop.'

The upstairs balcony bar in Café Ici had changed since Logan was in there last. In the old days it'd been covered in black and white tiles like a Victorian urinal; now it was all magnolia walls and projected lighting effects. The downstairs bar was virtually empty – not too surprising for six forty-five on a Sunday night, but upstairs seemed to be hosting some sort of reading group. As Logan cleared the top of the stairs he could see about a dozen people at various tables with well-thumbed paperbacks of Ian Rankin's *Black and Blue*. The talk was low and animated.

Logan was about to ask Rickards if they'd come to the right place when the constable marched up to the nearest table and asked a heavily built woman in a suit if she wanted the same as usual. A number of the others turned and waved hello, then stopped to stare at Logan, before losing interest and going back to their conversations. He joined Rickards at the bar. 'I thought you said this was—'

'You want a pint, or a pint and a nip?'

'Please.' Logan turned and scanned the assembled book-lovers. They looked like lawyers, bankers, insurance brokers, accountants, middle managers . . . they looked . . . they looked normal. A couple could have been described as 'a bit bohemian', but he'd been expecting outrageous piercings, shaved heads and tattoos. It was all a bit disappointing.

'Here you go.' A pint of Stella and a tiny glass full to the brim with something very cold and clear. Rickards had the same.

'You know,' said Logan, taking an experimental sniff, trying to figure out what it was he'd just been given a shot of: vodka? 'I have to admit, I wasn't expecting this.' He pointed at the people Rickards had come here to meet.

'Told you it wasn't a freak show.'

That was true. 'What's with the books?'

'It's how you tell someone's in the Aberdeen scene. You all meet up in a certain place, and if they've got a copy of *Black and Blue*, you go say hello.'

'I didn't know Ian Rankin was—'

'No: bits of the book are set up here and it's called *Black and Blue*. Eh? *Black and Blue*!' Really labouring the point. 'Thought it was pretty obvious actually . . .'

Logan looked at him.

'Sorry, sir.'

'"Sir", eh?' A shortish, chunky woman with green eyes and a hazel ponytail, expensive-looking casual clothes and an empty glass. 'You got yourself a new top, John?'

Rickards went the same colour as a baboon's arse. 'We're not . . . he's not . . . we . . .'

Logan stepped in and helped out. 'I'm his boss. We work together. I'm not "in the scene".'

'Yeah?' She rested her weight on one leg, the other stuck out at a jaunty angle, hands on hips – like the principal boy in a pantomime – and looked him up and down. 'Well, it takes all sorts I suppose.' She poked Rickards in the chest. 'Buy a girl a drink, Sailor?'

The constable did the honours.

Less than an hour later and Logan had discovered there was very little difference between Rickards' bondage buddies and Insch's theatre troupe. Both sets spoke their own language of acronyms and euphemisms, both told anecdotes about people Logan didn't know, and both – if he was being one hundred per cent honest – got a bit boring after the first thirty minutes. And no one seemed to know anything about Frank Garvie. Apparently the north-east hosted about a half dozen different munches, where the various bondage communities got together to socialize, and not everyone mingled. If Garvie was active in the Ellon scene he wouldn't necessarily be meeting with the Aberdeen crowd. And some people didn't like to be known in their local communities – which explained why most of those he spoke to had names like 'Mistress Maureen' and 'Kinky Dave'. God knew what Garvie called himself.

The similarities between the constable's friends and Insch's became even more obvious when the woman who'd thought Logan was Rickards' new top cornered him at the bar and told him all about the time she'd played the lead in *Jack and the Beanstalk*. Going on about the feeling of freedom that comes with becoming someone you're not, someone with no limits, willing to open themselves up to new experiences. If you only ever eat vanilla, how will you ever discover double chocolate caramel fudge?

Logan smiled and nodded and wondered what the hell he'd been thinking coming here in the first place. She gave him another look up and down, as if she was measuring him up for a leather harness. 'You've never tried it, have you?'

'No.'

'What do you think I am: top, bottom, dom, or sub?'

'Er . . .' he didn't have a clue what the difference was between a bottom and a sub; weren't they the same thing? But whatever this woman was, it wasn't submissive. 'Top?'

She beamed at him. 'Wrong! Because that's not where the power is.'

'Right, right . . .' downing the last of his pint with a gulp, eyeing the exit.

'Think about it: who wields the power, the person whipping, or the person being whipped?'

'Well, I—'

'If I'm being whipped it's for *my* pleasure. It's being done to arouse *me*, the guy on the end of the whip is just a prop – it isn't about him, it just looks like it. You see—'

'Ahh.' Logan leapt upright, then fumbled in his pocket. 'Sorry, got the phone on vibrate; scares the hell out of me when it goes off.' He pushed a button and the screen lit up. 'Damn, excuse me: I've got to take this . . . Hello? . . . Yes . . . OK, hold on . . .' Mobile clamped to his ear, Logan grabbed his jacket, hurried down the staircase and out into the cold night air.

Union Street glowed like a Christmas tree with the constant swoosh of yellow headlights and scarlet brakes beneath a plum-coloured sky.

Sunday night in early March and about fifty per cent of the people wandering about didn't even have a jacket on, not caring that it was below freezing. Half-naked teenagers rubbed shoulders with people old enough to know better, all out to get absolutely rat-arsed and cop a feel in some darkened corner of a pub or club.

Logan stopped pretending there was someone on the other end of the phone and checked his messages instead. Still nothing from Jackie. He called the flat again. Ring, ring. Ring, ring. Ring, ring. Ring, ring: answer phone. He hung up and tried her mobile instead. 'Jackie? You want to go grab a bite, or a pint or something?'

The reception wasn't wonderful, but it was good enough to hear her turning him down. She wasn't in the mood – still furious about the whole Macintyre thing. Knowing her, she'd come lurching back to the flat at three in the morning, smelling of booze and kebab. Well fine, she could sulk if she wanted, *he* was going to go home, order a pizza, find a decent movie on Sky, and spend the rest of the evening on the sofa. Not exactly a mad, whirlwind existence, but it was better than moping about like a spoilt brat. Sooner or later she'd just have to come to terms with the fact that Rob Macintyre wasn't guilty.

The gate creaks beneath his hands as he vaults over it in the dark, sending a small flurry of icy water droplets sparkling in the gloom. Everything is shrouded in night, shapes and features indistinct, even to his eyes – and he has excellent night vision – but he's not worried. He knows there's no one there to see him. There never is. The police are so fucking stupid it's unbelievable! He grins, jogging lightly along the small lane hidden between the back gardens, making for the cluster of garages and parking spaces at the end. Did they *really* think he didn't know they were there? That he needed that slimy lawyer bastard to tell him he was being watched?

But it'd been the lawyer's idea to get it all on video. He'd have loved to have seen their faces when they watched that.

Grinning, he unlocks the door of the anonymous small red hatchback, throws his kit bag in the back and climbs in behind the wheel. Number Nine is in for a treat tonight. He's celebrating. No more police. No more accusations. Just him and a long line of tasty bitches, all dying for him to show them what happens when you play with fire. Lucky Number Nine.

He wonders what she'll look like.

39

Aberdeen had done its usual bipolar trick – after the weekend's freezing temperatures, snow, sleet and wind, Monday morning was surprisingly warm. Lulling everyone into a false sense of security with its blue skies, wispy clouds and snowdrops. It would have been pleasant, standing in a little suntrap in Cults, shielded from the wind by a row of granite shops, if it wasn't for the blaring alarm bolted to the off-licence wall. 'I STILL DON'T UNDERSTAND WHAT WE'RE DOING HERE!'

'WHAT?' Steel cupped a hand over her ear and Logan repeated himself. 'OH,' she yelled, 'I'VE GOT A SOCIAL WORK REVIEW FOR THAT BLOODY SEAN MORRISON CASE AND I CAN'T BE ARSED—' the alarm fell silent, '—LISTENING TO ALL THAT SHITE ABOUT . . . Oh. Right.' The small crowd of onlookers were staring at her as if she was some sort of dancing monkey. 'Ahem, yes, well, as I said, carry on, Sergeant.'

The key-holder bolted from the off-licence door,

hands over his head, screaming for help as an empty bottle of whisky soared past his ear and shattered against the pavement. 'He tried to kill me!' He was closely followed by PC Rickards and a volley of gin bottles. They screeched to a halt behind the patrol car parked at the kerb.

'Well, Spanky?' asked Steel, sauntering over with her hands in her pockets. 'You talk him down like I asked you to?'

A full bottle of brandy spun end over end from the doorway, exploding in a shower of sparkling glass and amber liquid. The key-holder looked as if he was about to faint. 'That stuff's ninety quid a bottle!'

Rickards pulled on a sickly smile and shrugged. 'Sorry, ma'am.'

She shook her head. 'Never send a bondage freak to do a lesbian's job.' Steel hooked a finger in Logan's direction. 'Come on Lazarus, you go first: he might get frisky.'

Logan edged along the wall and peered through the shop window. The place was a mess, bottles littering the wooden floorboards, some full, some empty, some smashed. No sign of the intruder. He— A bottle crashed into the window by his head, turning the safety glass into a cracked spider's web as advocaat oozed down the inside. Logan stared at Steel who shrugged back at him.

'Soon as you're ready.'

Logan poked his head round the open door and shouted, 'We only want to talk!' That got him four tins of Tennants and a bottle of Merlot. The wine smashed, but the cans just dented, then fizzed out spumes of lager all over the place. Taking a deep breath he dashed inside. The shop was a long rectangle, stretching away from the front window – shelves on all walls, counter and glass-fronted fridges on the right, display stands of wine on the left – and a limp leg being dragged behind a stack of Australian sparkling. Logan charged for the counter, vaulting it as a Drambuie hand grenade exploded on the shelves beside him. He dived to the floor, scrabbling forwards on his hands and knees as more glass burst above, showering him in gin, whisky and vodka.

DI Steel shouted in from outside: 'You got him yet?'

Swearing quietly, Logan eased himself to the edge of the counter and peeked round. The intruder was slumped back against a stack of Italian wine, swigging from a bottle of Talisker, his left leg bent back at a *very* funny angle. He pulled the bottle from his mouth and belched, and that was when Logan recognised him. 'Tony?' The man turned a bleary, bloodshot eye in his direction, the other squinted shut, presumably to help him focus. 'Jesus, Tony, what the hell have you done to yourself?'

'Fffff . . .' He waved the bottle at Logan. 'Fffffuckin' fell, did . . . didn't I?' He pointed at the unnaturally bent leg and Logan realized what the lump sticking out of the side of Tony's calf was.

'We need to get you an ambulance Tony, OK? You've fractured your leg.'

The man wobbled a bit. 'Does . . . doesn't hurt . . . at all!' And took another swig. 'Ffffffukin' skylight *bastards*!' He grabbed a bottle of rioja and sent it flying out the front door. Even drunk on his arse the man's aim was impressive.

'Come on, Tony, let me help you. I'm drowning in booze here . . .'

'Iss, isss . . .' He belched, winced, and rubbed at his chest. 'Iss too late. Only wannnned some money. Couple of hunnerd, tops. Juss . . . juss enough. Eh?' More Talisker disappeared. 'Passssport. Gonnae take mother on . . . on . . . Florida! See Mickey Mouse! Big . . . big fuckin' mouse.'

Logan pulled out his phone and called for an ambulance.

'Cannnn go see Mickey Mouse withow . . . withow passport.'

'Ambulance is on it's way Tony. You'll be OK. You going to come outside with me? Sit in the sun? Much nicer out there.'

'Fffffff . . . no – can't get passssport back. Have . . . have to . . . you like horses?' Tony giggled and helped himself to more whisky. 'I like horses! But . . . but money . . . too much money . . .' He leant forward, tapping his nose conspiratorially, his voice a wet, loud whisper as he keeled over onto his face, 'Ma woan . . . woan let me . . .' THUD! 'Passssssport. Big fuckin' mouse . . .' He was snoring long before the ambulance got there.

* * *

384

'You smell like a brewery.' Steel was sitting on a low granite wall, rewarding herself for her inspirational leadership with a cigarette.

'Thanks for your help.' Logan peeled off his coat and tried wringing the alcohol from the sodden sleeves, already starting to feel a little light-headed from the fumes. 'He breaks in about three in the morning, bypasses the alarm with a set of crocodile clips, only the rope he's using to lower himself in through the skylight breaks. He falls about eighteen feet, smashes his mobile phone, breaks his leg and lies there in agony. Then realizes he's surrounded by bottles of DIY anaesthetic—'

Steel laughed, bellowing out a cloud of second-hand smoke that ended in a coughing fit. 'Christ,' she said when it had all settled down again, 'think I weed myself a little bit . . .'

'Owner turns up at half eight to open up and do a stock take, only before he can enter the alarm code he's being pelted with pinot grigio and sweet sherry.'

The inspector doubled up, slapping her thigh and hooting with laughter as Logan told her how Tony Burnett had only done it to get back his passport – security against a loan from Ma Stewart to cover his losses on the Hennessy Gold Cup.

'Brilliant,' she said, wiping a tear from her eye. 'Silly bugger could have just gone got himself a replacement passport, but he goes and does a

Mission Impossible in Oddbins instead!' And she was off again.

It didn't look like much from the outside, which just went to show: sometimes you *could* judge a bookies by its cover. J Stewart & Son – Bookmakers est. 1974 – was the sort of place that gave old men and their phlegm somewhere to hang out drinking tins of special till the last race was run and it was time to go home for their tea. The betting shop's name was purely ornamental: J Stewart Snr was long dead, and the '& Son' had run off to London with a marine biologist called Marcus. So now it was just Donna 'Ma' Stewart: sole proprietor, widow, and one of Logan's first-ever arrests.

The place wasn't quite empty: there was a handful of auld mannies in bunnets and anoraks, fidgeting uncomfortably under the No SMOKING signs as the horses for the Sparrows Offshore Handicap Hurdle from Ayr jerked and pirouetted to the starting line on half a dozen widescreen televisions bolted to the wall.

Ma Stewart was behind the counter, draped over some shiny celebrity gossip magazine, one fat cheek supported by a beringed hand as she flicked through the pages, giving Logan and Rickards a perfect view of pasty, wobbling cleavage. Ma's ratty grey hair was swept up on top in a bun, the chain for her glasses glittering against a violently colourful blouse. She didn't look up till they were standing at the counter. 'Afternoon, what . . .' and then she recognized Logan and beamed at him. 'Sergeant McRae! How lovely! You don't come round nearly often enough! Have you eaten?' Turning to bellow through the back, 'Denise! Get the kettle on, and see if we've still got any pizza left.'

A muffled, 'A'm busy!' came from the open doorway behind the desk.

'Get the bloody kettle on, or I'll make your Michael look like a bloody pacifist!'

'A' right, a' right . . .'

And the matronly smile was unleashed on Logan again. 'There we go. What can we do for you? You're looking lovely by the way; you got some sun, didn't you? Hasn't the weather been dreadful!'

Logan knew Ma Stewart wasn't a day over sixty, but she looked anything between fifty and a hundred and three in that strange, ambiguous way fat old ladies have. The wrinkles smoothed out from the inside by layers of subcutaneous lard. He tried not to cringe as she lent across the desk and pinched his cheek. 'Honestly,' she tutted, 'you're nothing but skin and bone. That woman of yours isn't feeding you properly! Marcus is just the same with our Norman, it's all tai chi and no tatties.'

'I need to speak to you about Tony Burnett, Ma.'

'And who's your little friend?' She turned the smile on Rickards who stammered and stuttered.

'Oh, a shy one! We like *him*! Denise! Where's that bloody tea?'

'Coming! Fuck's sake . . .'

'Anyway, I was just saying the other day that we don't get enough policemen in these day. Oh it's not like it was when my Jamesy was alive, we—'

'We've asked you not to confiscate passports as collateral, Ma.'

'Especially with the Cheltenham Gold Cup coming up; you could have a sweepstake down the station!'

'The passports, Ma . . .'

A short woman with a black eye pushed through from the back room, carrying a tray with four teas on it and what looked like reheated pizza slices. 'I've no milk, so it's that evaporated stuff from a tin or nothin'.'

They took their tea and microwaved spicy American in Ma's office: a small room out back, the walls and ceiling lined with varnished tongue-and-groove wooden floorboards like a homemade sauna. Ma Stewart had a thing for little porcelain figurines of Scottie dogs, and photos of her grand-children: the whole place was festooned with them. A little old-fashioned transistor radio sat on a high shelf, dribbling music into the potpourri-scented room as they ate. 'Have you been watching that *Celebrity Pop Idol*?' said Ma, taking a big bite of reheated pizza. 'I never would have thought that coloured man off the news had such a lovely voice.'

Logan tuned her out. She was always a nightmare to deal with. Not obstreperous, just . . . nice. And completely bloody oblivious. And how on earth did she find enough time to dust all these nasty wee china dogs? He looked around the room. Maybe they should just . . . There was a plain brown box sitting the floor by Ma Stewart's desk, right next to Logan's feet; the top open just far enough for him to make out the words *Lesbo Nurses*. He picked it up, and emptied it out onto the desk. It was a pick-and-mix of hardcore porn, and right at the bottom a copy of *In Deep Sheep: Five* and other 'animal husbandry' titles.

'Oh Ma, not again!'

'What?' She dabbed at her scarlet lips with a pristine hanky. Logan settled back in his seat and stared at her, his bit of pizza solidifying on its paper plate. 'Oh, all right!' she said at last. 'So sometimes I sell a few naughty movies to people who can't get out on their own. Where's the harm in that? Half these poor old dears can't even get it up, never mind do anything else!' She leaned forward, exposing her cleavage again, tapping on the desk with a bright-red nail. 'If I can help spark the flames of their wrinkly ardour, I will. It's my public duty. Not like it's illegal or anything.'

Logan groaned. 'Yes it is! You have to be a licensed sex shop to sell R-eighteen movies! And this stuff . . .' he poked the cover of *Farmyard Frolics*, 'isn't legal *anywhere*.'

'You're not eating your pizza . . . You want some cake? We've got some Battenburg – Denise's other half works in a baker's and we get all sorts in here—'

'Ma: the DVDs. Where did you get them?'

An exasperated breath sent the pale cleavage heaving. 'Can we not come to some sort of arrangement? I mean, I didn't know it was against the law! I would never—'

'Where!'

She pouted. 'You used to be such a nice young man . . . Are you sure you don't want some cake?'

The search team Logan had called in from FHQ made bulls in china shops look like ballet dancers, much to the distress of Ma Stewart, who stood at the epicentre of destruction shouting, 'Be careful with that! It's a family heirloom!'

'Everything's a family bloody heirloom,' muttered a PC, sticking one of the millions of china dogs in a cardboard box.

Ma turned pleading eyes on Logan. 'Oh, *do* make them be careful!'

'Find anything yet?'

Rickards pointed at a pair of cardboard boxes sitting on top of a cleared desk. 'Movies. Nothing too filthy, just the latest blockbusters, all stuff still in the cinema.'

Logan gave Ma Stewart a chance to explain

herself and she puffed up like a prize pigeon. 'It's for my old folks,' she said with her nose in the air. 'They can't get out to the pictures, so I bring the magic of Hollywood to them. There's nothing wrong with that!'

'You know how long you can get for pirating movies? Kill someone you'd be out sooner. The Federation for Copyright Protection are like the Gestapo, only without the winning sense of humour.'

'I didn't pirate anything. I'm providing a service to the community—'

'Have you checked the computers?'

Rickards nodded. 'Nothing,'

'What about the basement?'

'Isn't one: I checked. But we . . .' Rickards trailed off, following the invisible line between Logan's pointing finger and one of the desks: a scuffed Formica-and-chipboard job, the sort of thing you could pick up cheap from B&Q or Argos. It sat on a big red, brown and pink rug with elephants round the edge. The constable stared at it for a minute, then admitted he didn't have a clue what Logan was on about.

'Desk's been moved. Look at the rug: you see the dark red bit with the dimples round it? That's where it normally sits. And the wall behind it: you can't see half the calendar – it's hidden behind the edge of the desk.'

'Ah,' said Ma, 'we had a book on feng shui and they said—'

Rickards grabbed a policewoman and got her to help shift the desk off to one side.

'—bad luck to move it! It destroys the energy flow of the whole room! It—'

The edge of the rug was rolled back, exposing the dark border between trapdoor and floorboard. 'Of course,' said Logan, as an embarrassed Rickards apologized, 'it probably helps that I've raided this place before.'

The basement didn't quite stretch the length of Ma's office. It was a claustrophobic space in white-painted concrete blocks, one end stacked floor to ceiling with cardboard boxes – cigarettes, whisky, wine, and for some unfathomable reason, nappies. The other side had been given over to a mini pirating empire – four PCs and a stack of DVD burners. It wasn't even automatic: someone would have to manually change the disks. A small colour laser printer sat in the corner, a stack of labels sitting next to it, and a couple of boxes of blank DVDs.

'I'm really just storing these things for someone else,' said Ma with her best harmless-little-old-lady smile. 'Now, would anyone like a nice cup of tea? We've got Eccles cakes.'

Logan arrested her.

40

'You know,' said Rickards when Ma had been processed and stuck in a cell, 'I thought she'd be more . . . upset.'

Logan snorted. 'She's used to it. We've been doing her for peddling porn for years. We arrest her, she won't tell us who her suppliers are because, "naebody likes a clype", goes up before the Sheriff and does her, "I'm just a confused old woman" routine, he takes pity on her, she gets a small fine, some community service – which she actually *enjoys* – and about a year later we'll catch her doing the same thing, and it all goes round again.' He shook his head. 'The circle of porn.'

'Do we—'

'Sorry to interrupt,' DC Rennie, looking flustered and out of breath, 'but DI Insch wants to see you in his office.'

'Can it wait?'

Rennie shifted uncomfortably. 'Well, you see . . . there's been another rape . . .'

Logan closed his eyes. 'Fuck.'

'That's not the worst part.'

By the time Logan pushed through into the inspector's office most of the shouting seemed to be over, but the air still crackled with pent-up fury. Insch's face was a furious shade of purple, glowering at Jackie as she stood with her hands behind her back in front of his desk, flexing her fingers. The room's other occupant was a uniformed PC, slumped in one of the visitor chairs, holding a big wodge of toilet paper to his nose and making groaning noises.

'I was just—' was as far as Jackie got, before Insch held up a fat finger.

'Not another word!' There was some mumbling from Mr Blood and Toilet Paper, but Insch wasn't in the mood. 'That goes for you too!' Silence.

Logan's heart sank. It didn't take a genius to work out what had happened. 'You wanted to see me, sir?'

'About bloody time. Take *this*,' pointing at Jackie, 'and have a word with it. Tell it that it's this bloody close to getting suspended and if it doesn't pull its bloody socks up I WILL KICK ITS ARSE FROM HERE TO BALMORAL!' Flashes of spittle arced through the stuffy office. He turned a baleful eye on Jackie. 'Get out of my bloody sight!'

She stood there, staring furiously at the carpet for a moment, then turned on her heel and pushed past Logan and out into the hall. Logan froze, looking from the inspector's thunderous expression to PC Nosebleed, thought better of asking, and hurried out after Jackie, closing the door behind him as another tirade of abuse began.

She was almost at the stairs by the time he caught up with her. 'You want to fill me in?'

'What the hell is wrong with everyone?'

'What happened?'

'I don't want to talk about it.' Then she started marching off again. 'A woman's been raped and he's making jokes!'

'So you clobbered him? Jackie, if he makes a complaint you're going to get carpeted.'

'One fucking night we're not watching Macintyre . . .'

Logan grabbed her. 'Where, what happened?'

She yanked her arm free of his grip. 'Wendy Smith. Student nurse. She was eighteen. Finished her shift and Macintyre jumped her. Only this time the bastard beats and cuts her so badly she's lost the sight in one eye. Her face looks like fucking strips of liver! Three hundred stitches! *Three hundred!* The people she worked with in A&E couldn't even recognize her, and he gets a seven-figure book deal!'

'Where? Where did it happen?'

'Dun-fucking-dee. Same as usual. The little shite—'

'Then it's not him.'

'Of course it's him!'

'IT CAN'T BE HIM!' Losing it. Clenching his teeth to try and calm down. 'We were there last time – remember? All night! He was at home when the last girl was raped: it's on the video!'

'It was him.' She turned and made for the stairs.

'How? How can it be him?'

'It's him!'

This was pointless – like arguing with his mother – she was never going to admit she was wrong. Logan let her go.

There was no way he was going straight home – not if she was in that kind of mood – so when the shift was over Logan asked if anyone wanted to go to the pub. No takers, not even Rennie.

'Rehearsals. Come along, it'll be fun. John's coming, aren't you?'

Rickards nodded happily. 'I'm prompting.'

'Oh, well . . . Don't worry about it. I'll go see a film or something.'

'No, come!' Rennie made various theatrical gestures. 'And then we can go get that curry we were talking about – lads' night out!'

Logan shrugged: why not?

They marched up Union Street, with Rennie babbling on about how some plot in *EastEnders* was a parable for *Othello*.

'So,' said Rickards when Rennie managed to shut up for thirty seconds, 'you got cornered by Tina last night.'

'Tina?' It took Logan a moment to figure out

who he meant – Mrs Bottoms Wield The Power. 'Yeah . . . she's a little . . . *intense.*'

'Yup, that's our Tina. They're not all that bad you know. She's just a bit evangelical about the whole thing. Husband left her for a dental hygienist and she's been on this self-empowerment trip ever since. Last year we got dragged along to see her in some bloody awful pantomime.'

'Yeah, she said.' They stopped at the lights on Union Terrace and watched the traffic grumble past. The day's warmth was long gone and a cold wind whistled up Bridge Street, sending an old newspaper flapping drunkenly into the air like a dying seagull.

'Be surprised how many people do both, you know: the scene and performing. Always thought about giving it a try myself. That's how come I'm prompting. Next year—'

'Hang on a second . . .' Logan's phone was ringing. According to the caller ID it was R TULLOCH – DPF. He stood, staring at the illuminated display as it rang, debating whether to take the call or pretend to be busy. Not really wanting to do either.

Rennie: 'You going to answer that then?'

He'd speak to her. It wasn't fair not to. He . . . the ringing stopped – it'd gone through to voice-mail.

Now he'd have to ring her back. 'Shite.' He dialled in and checked his messages. There was some hissing and clicking, then one from his mother he'd been avoiding for nearly a week –

he skipped it; one from DI Steel about some stolen office equipment; and last but not least:

'Hi, Logan? It's me . . . er . . . Rachael. Look, I had a good time the other night and I wanted to know if . . .' the volume dropped, as if she was muttering to herself. *'Bloody hell, this was easier when I thought about it in the car . . . Look: dinner, tomorrow night. I'm making something scary out of an old Delia Smith book. Make it half-six, and you can keep me going with wine while I cook.'* A pause, then she remembered to leave him the address and hung up.

Logan's thumb hovered over the 'delete' button; now he *had* to call her back. 'Fuck, fuck . . . fuck.'

Rennie smiled at him. 'Good news?'

'Shut up.' Logan stuck the phone back in his pocket, message intact, and trudged away to Insch's rehearsal. Maybe a bit of very amateur dramatics would make returning Rachael's call a bit easier. Or maybe he was just being a spineless bastard.

He knew which one his money was on.

41

... and his eyes flickered open in the darkness, the dream coming to a sudden halt. Logan screwed up his face and peered out blearily from beneath the duvet – according to the clock radio it was nineteen minutes past four. No wonder it was cold: the heating had been off since half eleven.

He stuck a hand out, feeling along the mattress for Jackie, finding nothing but a deep-frozen expanse of bed. Still not home yet. No change there then, she was never . . . A noise from the hall – probably the same one that had woken him – someone fiddling with the flat's front door. Cursing quietly, he shivered out of bed, grabbed his trousers off the chair in the corner and pulled them on, followed by what felt like a sweatshirt, and padded barefoot out into the hall just in time to see the door swing open and a familiar figure bundle in from the stairwell. Jackie, wearing her cat burglar outfit.

She clunked the door closed behind her, trembling as she peeled off her coat and gloves and headed for the kitchen.

'Jackie?'

She froze for a moment, not looking round, then carried on, stripping in front of the washing machine, throwing everything in – hat, scarf, jacket, gloves, shirt, trainers, trousers, underwear – then added a couple of detergent pouches and switched the thing on. The hiss of rushing water sounded in the kitchen. Arms wrapped round her pale, shivering body, she marched through to the bathroom without a word. Her knuckles were swollen and red.

'Jackie? What's going on?'

Click: the shower power cord was pulled, then another click and the blow heater filled the bathroom with a deep whubwhubwhoooo and the faint smell of burning dust. The light came on, and Jackie's pale skin fluoresced white as she clambered into the bath, goosepimples disappearing behind the blue plastic shower curtain. Wafts of steam billowed out into the cold room.

Logan closed the door. 'Jackie, what the hell happened? What's going on?'

'Nothing.' Her was voice muffled by the water, curtain and noisy heater, but he could still hear the tremor in it. 'Nothing's happened. If anyone asks, I was here all night.'

Oh fuck . . .'Jackie?'

'All night, OK? We spent the night here. You and me.'

'Jackie what happened?'

'Nothing happened. I was here all night: remember?'

'Jackie?'

No answer. He hung around but she wouldn't say anything else. As far as PC Jackie Watson was concerned, the matter was closed.

DARKNESS

42

Logan was up and out as soon as the alarm went off. They'd spent the night back to back, Jackie smelling of the large whisky she'd poured herself after her shower, Logan staring at the alarm clock's glowing numerals. Waiting for the night to be over.

He was half an hour early for the start of his shift, sat in the CID office with a big waxed-paper cup of fancy coffee from the canteen and two buttered rowies, hoping the caffeine would kick in soon and make the world a better place. Knowing it was too much to hope for.

'Right,' said Steel when the morning briefing was over and they'd all done their best rendition of *We Are Not At Home To Mr Fuck-Up*, 'what you got on just now?'

Logan didn't have to think about it for long. 'Nothing much, all the big stuff's with the PF's office. Just wee things to tidy up . . .' He finished off with a huge yawn.

'Good. You can take a couple of days off – you look like shite and the DCS's been nagging me about the overtime bill. Like I *care*!' Which was fair enough; he'd spent most of his three days off in the office anyway, so as far as Logan was concerned he was due some time in lieu. Steel got her cigarettes out, one winding its way into her gob where it bobbed and wove unlit while she talked. 'When you come back we'll take a look at some hate-mail wee Sean Morrison's parents been getting.'

'Hate-mail?'

'Aye, well, nothing special. "Your kid's a murderin' wee shite", that kind of thing. Just some arsehole blowin' off steam. Meantime, finish up anything you've not done and fuck off out of it.'

There was a box of DVDs in the corner of the CID office – seized from Ma Stewart's shop then signed in and out of evidence so people could borrow a couple of films for the evening. Not surprisingly all the hardcore ones had been first to go. Logan pawed through the remainder, looking for anything that might fill the awkward silence permeating the flat, unable to face another night of Insch's *Mikado*.

A policewoman sauntered over, carrying a handful of Hollywood blockbusters – most of which weren't even in the cinema yet – and dumped them back in the box, saying, 'That new one with Tom Cruise is OK, but a couple of the others were well dodgy copies.'

'Mmm?' said Logan, not really paying attention.

'Yeah. Is it OK if I borrow this one?' Holding up a case for something animated with a penguin on the cover. 'Got my niece coming to stay tonight.'

'Just make sure you get it back by lunchtime – they're shifting this lot to central storage tomorrow afternoon.'

'Will do.'

Nine o'clock and he was all set to go home, hoping that Jackie wasn't there. He grabbed a handful of DVDs from the top of the pile, stuffed them into his heavy overcoat, and headed out of the door.

The whole flat sparkled. It was weird: the carpets had been hoovered, the surfaces dusted, and Logan got the sneaking suspicion that even the bathroom had been given a once over. And from the kitchen came the smell of baking. A sudden, very nasty thought occurred, but when he risked a peek in through the kitchen door, it wasn't his mother standing in a blue-and-white-striped apron, it was Jackie. Which, if anything, was slightly more scary.

'Did you fall on your head last night?' he asked.

Jackie didn't even turn around. 'Don't be daft, I was *here* all last night, remember? Now you go get changed and I'll put the kettle on.'

Whatever she'd been up to she wasn't going to

talk about it without a fight. And Logan couldn't face that right now. 'I got some films from the raid yesterday.'

Jackie peered out of the kitchen window, watching the thick blobs of rain join together and run down the glass. 'Good, it's a shite day anyway. We'll watch something, have lunch, go get a couple bottles of wine, something for tea, nice lazy afternoon. How does that sound?'

It sounded eerily like Jackie used to be before her obsession with Rob Macintyre. 'Er . . . good. That'd be good.' He hooked a thumb over his shoulder at the front door. 'They're in my coat – big pocket at the back.' He went through to the bedroom and swapped his damp work suit for jeans and a casual shirt, wondering how long this small bout of normality was going to last. How long it would be before she started—

'What the hell's this?' Amusement and surprise sounded from the hall and then Jackie appeared, carrying a small stack of DVDs.

'I told you: we raided Ma Stewart's yesterday. I—'

'You dropping a hint or something?' She held up the DVD on top of the pile, showing him the cover: *Crocodildo Dundee*. 'Think our love life needs spicing up with a bit of hardcore porn?'

'What? No . . .' He went to take the DVD from her, but she danced back into the hall, laughing.

'You're such a pervert McRae!'

'It's . . . No: the guy who made it – the film –

he gave me and Rickards a copy for getting back some stolen goods. Insch got one too!'

'Join Michelle "Crocodildo" Dundee, as she struggles to find her feet, and other bits, in the big city,' she read, putting on an appallingly over-the-top Australian accent. 'She's a filthy girl who can't wait to have adventures "Down Under"!'

'I'd forgotten all about it! Look, I didn't ask for it, OK? It's not—'

'Oh we are *so* going to watch this!'

'Jackie . . .' But she was already running into the lounge to close the curtains and fire up the DVD player.

'Come on then! And put the heating on, just in case we get all carried away and naked.'

It was one of the most embarrassing things Logan had ever done in his life. Jackie roared with laughter the whole way through as the actors did a reasonable pastiche of the original film. He'd only ever seen the thing on fast forward before, looking for suspects that would match the e-fit of Frank Garvie, but to be fair it wasn't as awful as it could have been. The jokes were actually funny, there was a plot, and enough sex to keep Jackie in hysterics as people from the north-east of Scotland pretended to be antipodeans. But it was excruciating sitting here watching it with her, not wanting to seem too turned on by the whole 'other people having sex' thing.

The heroine stood in a dark alleyway and a

woman with a skimpy outfit and *huge* hair stepped out of the shadows, demanding, *'Give me all your money!'* as she brandished an eight-inch rubber willy then twisted the end, setting it vibrating.

'That's not a dildo,' said Michelle Dundee, hauling a massive eighteen-inch job from the holster on her back, *'THIS is a dildo!'*

Jackie could barely sit on the couch, she was laughing so much. 'Oh, yeah!' she yelled, in a better Australian accent than any of the actors, 'Dan't knaw about you, Cobber, but oim randier than a snake on a barbie! Show us yer didgeridoo!' And then she jumped on him.

'I don't—'

'Ooh, it's all excited! Rippa!' as she burrowed into his trousers.

Then Jason Fettes appeared onscreen – making his porn debut, not knowing that it would only be a couple of years before he'd be lying face-down on a slab in the morgue with a police photographer taking stills of his cold, dead body. The thought didn't do a lot for Logan's ardour.

'Ah naw, Blue!' Jackie pulled a startled face. 'We're losin' it! Quick – mouth to mouth!'

And Logan suddenly found it very easy to forget all about Jason Fettes and his ruptured innards.

The happy, post-coital glow lasted a whole two hours, the pair of them lounging about in bed, laughing and joking, enjoying each other's company for the first time in what felt like years.

Ignoring the phone; letting the answering machine take care of it.

It wasn't until some bloody-minded sod kept ringing, hanging up and ringing again and again and again that Logan grumbled his way through to the lounge – stark naked – and picked up. 'What?'

DI Steel. *'That's no' very friendly.'*

'We're . . . busy.'

'Aye, well, you can put it away for five minutes. Telly: ITV news.'

Logan sighed, picked up the remote and clicked the television on, getting the lunchtime news – something about the latest balls-up in the war against terror. 'So what? It's . . .' and the picture switched to a stock photo of Rob Macintyre's ugly mug. He cranked up the volume.

'—missing from his home late last night. The twenty-one-year-old signed a seven-figure deal for three volumes of his autobiography this week—'

'Maybe he's just off getting drunk somewhere?'

Macintyre's face was replaced by his fiancée at a press conference, looking distraught in a cleavage-revealing top and perfectly-styled hair, sniffing and crying away as she told the world that her husband-to-be hadn't come home last night. That he'd missed practice this morning. That they were worried for his safety.

Someone from the media office appeared beside her and made an appeal to camera. Logan hit the mute button. Oh fuck. Oh fuck, oh fuck, oh fuck,

oh fuck, oh fuck, oh fuck, oh fuck, oh fuck, oh
fuck—

'You still there?'

'Er . . . yes. Yes.' Eyes darting towards the bedroom where Jackie had started singing.

*'Right, get your arse back to the station – Hissing
Sid's shooting his mouth off, the press are all over us
and the CC's having kittens.'*

'I . . . You said I could have a day off and—'

'Now, Sergeant!'

Cursing, Logan hung up. 'Jackie?' He found
her in the kitchen, drinking orange juice from the
carton. 'Macintyre's gone missing.'

'Yeah?' She shrugged, wiped her mouth and
put the juice back in the fridge. 'You want Thai
or Italian for tea?'

'Jackie, what happened last night?'

'Nothing happened. I was here with you,
remember?'

'Jackie—'

'I fancy noodles. If you're going out, pick some
up, eh?'

'But—'

'Dinner's at seven.' She planted a kiss on the
end of his nose. 'Don't be late.'

43

The sky had taken on an ominous grey-blue tinge, spears of low, golden light sparking off the granite buildings, making them glow as if they were on fire as the sun sank towards the horizon. It was cold, leaching into Logan's bones as they walked the search perimeter, checking in with the teams. 'I still don't see why we're going to all this trouble,' he said. 'Macintyre's a grown man, only been missing what, thirteen, fourteen hours?' Just because the footballer had disappeared, it didn't mean he was lying dead in a ditch somewhere . . . Please don't let Jackie have killed him!

'Because,' said Steel, face creased up against the chilly wind, nose and ears bright red as she tramped along beside him, 'he's a missing *celebrity*, and they're much more important than low-life nobodies like you and me. Famous people aren't allowed to disappear while the media are watching.' She stopped, looking up and down the line of skeletal trees and porcupine bushes. 'Nobody looking?'

'No, you're safe.'

'Thank God for that . . .' She pulled out a packet of cigarettes with trembling fingers and stuck one in her mouth, lighting it and puffing frantically, shuddering with pleasure, then coughing violently. 'Ohhhhhh, I needed that! Whose bloody idea was it to give people points for clypin' on folk?'

Logan just shrugged. So far he'd made twenty quid by telling the DCS running the 'Fit Like' programme when Steel was smoking. 'Watch out – incoming.' He pointed at a uniformed constable labouring her way up the hill. The park was a wedge of yellowed grass, snow and frost-bitten trees, sweeping downhill from Bonaccord Crescent to Willowbank Road. It wasn't huge, but it was the closest patch of open ground to where Rob Macintyre was last spotted, and there were plenty of places to hide a body.

Steel took one last puff and hid the cigarette behind her back, waving a hand in front of her face as if that would actually get rid of the smell. 'Well?'

The PC clambered up the last bit of slippery path and shook her head. 'Nothing. Any chance of a fag? I'm gasping.'

Steel handed one over. 'Bugger all here and bugger all in any of the gardens. The little sod's probably coked up in the arms of some daft tart, but I suppose we'd better widen the search area. Who knows, we might . . . Oh bugger.' She squinted off into the distance at a large grey van with a satellite dish on top of it, pulling up on the other side of the park. 'The bloody media's here. Tell everyone to look busy!' She started down the hill, dragging the constable with her, shouting back to Logan, 'Chase up that useless bugger Rennie!'

Langstane Place and Justice Mill Lane were one long parade of trendy nightclubs and bars. Just the sort of places a local 'celebrity' like Macintyre would want to be seen. The sort of place he could pick up some impressionable, star-struck girlie, go back to her place and practise the offside rule.

Please, dear God, let Macintyre have gone home with someone! The alternative was too worrying to think about.

Logan found Rennie in a huge, fancy-looking nightclub, the drone of vacuum cleaners fighting with a portable radio tuned to Northsound Two. The constable was sitting at the bar, drinking cappuccino and making eyes at the manageress. At least he had the decency to look guilty when he saw Logan. 'Er . . . thank you, Miss,' he said, putting his cup down next to a half-eaten muffin, 'you've been very helpful.' Then marched over to report in. 'Bingo.' He flipped through his note-book. 'Taxi drops Macintyre here at half-eleven after some charity bash. He's a bit pished, but they let him in anyway because he's famous. Security cameras show him leaving with a group of people – mostly fit birds, lucky bastard – at one twenty-three, but he didn't go to any of the other clubs on the street.'

Logan breathed a sigh of relief: so it probably *was* just a late night of booze, boobs and bonking. Thank God for that. 'Get onto the Media Office, we want anyone who remembers leaving the club with Macintyre, etc. etc.'

'Already done it, sir.'

'Then there's hope for you yet. We—'

A crash as the front door was thrown open; DI Steel stood silhouetted against the last rays of the dying sun. 'Don't just stand there! They've found a body!'

Cromwell Road: the ambulance slithered its way in through the chainlink gates, digging muddy trenches into the playing-field grass as Rennie made a dog's ear of parking outside on the street. Two patrol cars had got there first, their lights spinning lazily in the growing gloom, while their occupants cordoned off the area with blue-and-white POLICE tape. With all the media interest it wouldn't be long before someone got down here and started taking photos or shooting video, demanding sound-bite comments, or just making shite up.

Logan hurried under the fresh cordon of tape, following Steel and the twin trails of churned-up grass. The ambulance slid to a halt and the crew jumped out, dragging equipment from the back before hurrying over to where a uniformed officer was waving her arms about as if she was drowning, shouting, 'Over here!'

Logan ran after them, fingers crossed. 'Please don't let him be dead, please don't let him be dead!'

The lead paramedic took one look at whatever the female PC was standing over, turned on his heel and sprinted back the way he'd come.

Logan's heart sank. He was dead. Macintyre was dead. And Jackie had come home last night and thrown every scrap of clothing she had on into the washing machine to boil . . .

'Out the bloody way!' It was the paramedic, running back from the ambulance with a neck brace in one hand, a silvery blanket under his arm, and a bottle of oxygen over his shoulder. He crashed into the bushes and disappeared from sight.

Logan crept forwards.

Macintyre was lying on his side, arms and legs splayed out like a broken swastika on the cold, damp, blood-soaked ground. His face was swollen almost beyond recognition, eyes closed, mouth open, a trail of spittle and dark red trailing across the ambulance men's gloved hands as they strapped the neck brace into position and slipped the oxygen mask over his smashed nose and mouth. 'Oh Jesus . . .' Logan's voice was little more than a whisper. 'Jackie, what the hell did you do?'

She'd been thorough: every visible inch of flesh

was speckled with livid, purple bruises, the skin in between pale and waxy. Rob Macintyre had been beaten to death. He just hadn't got around to dying yet.

44

Logan stood at the back of the room feeling sick as the Chief Constable read out the prepared statement, cameras flashing away as he told the world the *official* version of events. Rob Macintyre had been the victim of a particularly violent robbery. The podium was crowded – DI Steel, Macintyre's fiancée and mother, Hissing Sid, someone from Aberdeen Football Club, and the woman from the press office, all there to appeal for any information on Rob Macintyre's movements last night. Wanting whoever had attacked him to come forward and hand themselves in.

Logan almost laughed. There wasn't a chance in hell Jackie was going to stick her hand up for what she'd done to Macintyre. Unless someone had seen her, or they found some forensic evidence, this was one case that was going to go unsolved because Logan wasn't going to say a word. Keep his head down. Pretend it never happened. Be an accessory after the fact and pervert the course of justice. Even though the guilt was killing him. But what else was he supposed to do?

Colin Miller sidled up as the Media Officer unveiled replicas of the items believed to be missing from Macintyre's body when he was discovered: a thick leather wallet; a Rolex watch; three gold rings; a thick gold chain-bracelet; and the footballer's trademark ruby earstud. Anyone offered any of these items was to contact the police immediately.

'Course,' said Miller, nodding at the display, 'this is all shite, isn't it? No *way* this wiz a muggin'.' He waited for Logan to reply, got nothing, then said, 'Come on – I been up the hospital. Fractured legs, broken arms, ribs . . . it wiz professional. Doctor I spoke to said eighty per cent chance of extensive brain damage. Aye, and that's if he ever wakes up! Between you an' me,' Colin lowered his voice to a whisper, 'both his nuts wiz ruptured. No' just battered either, totally crushed. If it wasnae for the hypothermia he'd be deid by now.'

When the CC threw the conference open to questions it took all of three seconds before someone else made the same connection that Miller had. It was difficult not to, with Hissing Sid sitting up there covered in bruises. And as soon as the lawyer let slip that protective surveillance had been withdrawn from Macintyre the night before last, the knives came out. The guy from AFC insisted that the police could, and *should* have done more, Hissing Sid claimed that a number of significant errors of judgment had been made, Macintyre's fiancée sat there and cried asking how she could bring up a baby without its father, while his mother stared out at the cameras demanding justice. Someone had to pay for her wee boy being in a coma.

It didn't take long before the Chief Constable brought the whole thing to an unceremonious halt.

Logan watched Moir-Farquharson limp from the room, handing out soundbites to anyone who'd listen, demanding an official enquiry.

'Two-faced slimy bastard!'

'Mmm?' Miller had switched his mobile back on and was peering at it, holding the thing at various bizarre angles in his black-gloved hands. 'Come on ya wee . . .' A sudden smile, and Miller punched a button then held the phone to his ear, listening in silence for a moment, before hanging up. He gave Logan a nervous smile. 'Izzy wiz gettin' twinges this mornin'. Reception here's shite byraway. What if the contractions start?' He poked his phone again. 'Think I'm runnin' low on battery . . .'

'How'd you like an exclusive?'

'I mean it's no' an exact science is it? They say forty-two weeks, but it could be more or less. And how do they *know* it's been forty-two weeks? It's no' like—'

'An *exclusive*, Colin.'

'What? Oh, right, aye, that'd be grand.' He swung his phone about a bit more. 'Can we do it somewhere I can get a signal, but?'

Steel was in her office, pacing back and forth in front of the window, looking down at the knot of journalists outside. 'Bloody hell – it's a disaster! Why could they no' give this one to Insch? What did I do to deserve it?'

Logan let her moan as he pretended to read the interview notes. Since they'd found Rob Macintyre's battered body all the women he was supposed to have raped had been questioned, along with their partners and families. Not surprisingly none of them expressed any sympathy for the footballer's condition. And they all had alibis. Tayside police had been asked to do the same thing with their victims, but Logan knew it was pointless. How the hell was he supposed to investigate Macintyre's getting beaten half to death, when he lived with the person who'd done it? And there was no way he was going to fit anyone else up.

He joined Steel at the window, watching as the television camera lights winked off one by one, and the crews dispersed, leaving three figures standing together in the car park: the familiar brassy blonde of Macintyre's fiancée, his horrible, blue-rinsed mother, and his battered lawyer. 'Doesn't matter what we do,' said Steel, as Sandy Moir-Farquharson shook the women's hands and

422

limped off towards his Jaguar, 'we're going to get screwed on this one.'

Logan watched the two women march across to a small red hatchback, climb in and reverse out of their parking space. Steel was right – this whole thing was a complete and utter disaster.

45

He was poring over the preliminary forensic report on Rob Macintyre's clothes, praying they hadn't found anything, when the PC collared him. 'I've got a bone to pick with you!' she said, pointing at the collection of seized DVDs in the corner of the CID office. 'That bloody film – put it in expecting to see some Disney pish with my six-year-old niece and what do we get? Hardcore homemade bondage! What was I supposed to say when her mum got back?'

'Not my fault, you knew Ma Stewart was peddling porn when you borrowed it.'

'Shagging I could have coped with, but this was fucking foul!' And just to prove it, she marched over to the box of pirated films, rummaged around, pulled out the offending DVD and handed it to him. 'Go on, try it!'

Sighing, Logan dragged himself away from his desk and slipped the disk into the player set up by the fridge. It was hooked up to an old twelve-inch

TV set and the picture fizzed and crackled into a low-definition image of a man strapped face-down on a table with his legs open wide as someone hammered the living hell out of his thighs, back and arse with what looked like a leather ping-pong paddle.

'Look, you borrow stuff from the evidence box, you get what you . . .' Logan trailed off into silence, standing with his head on one side, watching the people on the screen. There was a full-length, gilt-edged mirror on the wall at the end of the spanking table, showing the whole scene from the opposite angle. The figure strapped to the table was blond, wearing a gag. And he looked a hell of a lot like Jason Fettes.

'See? You imagine trying to explain that to a six-year-old? I tell you, I was—'

'Get Insch. Get him here *now*!' Logan sank down into the seat, watching the last dirty movie Jason Fettes ever made. 'Move it!'

The image stuttered then froze into place: Fettes lying flat on his face, the person in the black bondage suit and strap-on fully visible in the mirror. Logan tapped the screen. 'You see? Garvie was a big man, overweight, large belly. Look at the shape of the thighs and upper torso – yes the chest's squashed flat, but I'm pretty sure this is a woman.'

Insch harrumphed. 'But these suits distort—'

'And Garvie's suit is dark red, this one's black. He didn't have a spare.'

The inspector stared at the screen. 'You know what this means, don't you?'

Logan nodded. 'We pretty much hounded an innocent man till he killed himself.'

'The Chief Constable's going to have my balls.'

The street was dark and silent, just the sound of the windscreen wipers to keep them company as Logan pulled up outside Ma Stewart's house. All the lights were out. 'Bloody hell.' DI Insch closed his mobile phone and stuffed it back in his pocket. 'I miss one sodding rehearsal and it all goes to hell in a handbasket.'

Logan knew better than to ask. Instead he picked the case file off the back seat, and climbed out of the car. It was cold: that penetrating, drizzly kind of rain Aberdeen did so well melting away the last remnants of snow, leaving the city grey and bleak. Insch had been in a foul mood ever since Logan dragged him in to watch the video – he never liked being proved wrong.

The inspector gave the nod and Logan leaned on Ma's bell: a metallic *prringgg* sounded from somewhere inside. They waited and waited, but nothing happened, so Logan tried again – *prrrrrringggggggggggg* – keeping his finger on the button until a light blossomed on in the hall. But still no one came to answer the door.

'Mrs Stewart!' Insch hammered on the door with the palm of his hand, making the whole thing boom and rattle. 'We know you're in there!' BOOM, BOOM, BOOM!

A light came on next door. The curtains twitched as Insch did it again. BOOM, BOOM, BOOM! 'Police! Open up!'

'Hoy! Keep it down!' An irate-looking man in his late sixties, complete with walking stick.

'Police, Mrs Stewart: Open up!' BOOM, BOOM, BOOM!

'You leave her alone!'

Logan tried for the nice-cop approach. 'Please go back inside, sir.'

'Don't you bloody tell me what to do! I pay your wages!'

BOOM, BOOM, BOOM! 'Come on, Mrs Stewart!'

'Bugger off out of it: she's done nothing wrong!'

'We know you're in there!' BOOM, BOOM, BOOM!

Logan tapped the inspector on the shoulder. 'That's probably not helping, sir.'

'Did I *ask* for your opinion?' BOOM, BOOM, BOOM! 'Open up!'

By the time a rumpled Ma Stewart appeared at the front door, half the street was up: auld mannies and wifies in their dressing gowns and corduroys telling Logan and Insch they should be ashamed of themselves for hounding an old lady! Ma stood on the top step, blinking as if she was having difficulty getting them into focus. She looked terrible: heavy bags under her eyes, the folds of fat pulling her face out of shape. She just wasn't the same without all the make-up and permanent beatific smile. She was old.

'Mmmmph . . .' she said, rearranging her features with a podgy hand. 'Tea. I'll make tea . . .' A stifled yawn, then, 'And cake. Everyone likes cake . . .'

They convened in the kitchen.

'Tea, tea, tea, tea . . .' Ma bumbled around, opening cupboards and closing them again. Logan steered her into one of the kitchen chairs and told her not to worry about it: he'd do the honours.

'Do you know why we're here?' said Insch, while Logan was playing hunt the teabag. 'One of the DVDs we seized from your shop turned out to be some sort of home-video footage.' He paused, leaving a gap for her to jump in and fill. She just yawned. 'It shows someone being strapped to a table and killed. It's a snuff film.' Which wasn't strictly speaking true: Jason Fettes didn't actually die on camera, but going by the date/time stamp in the bottom right-hand corner of the picture, he was dead less than an hour later.

'Cake . . .' she lurched to her feet, and squatted down in front of one of the kitchen cabinets, struggling with the cupboard door, and then a collection of Tupperware boxes, peering into each, then stacking them on the floor, one by one, like building bricks.

'Mrs Stewart, the video?'

'Can't have our brave boys in blue starving to death now, can we?'

Insch slammed a fat hand on the worktop – it sounded like a gunshot. 'Where did you get the video?' He was already starting to turn scarlet.

'You know,' she said, taking hold of the inspector's hand, 'my Jamesy, God bless him, took a stroke when he was about your age; fell down stone dead. Just like that. You should try relaxing a bit more.'

And that was when DI Insch went off the deep end.

'I think she'll be OK now,' said Logan, slouching back through to the lounge. The room was tidy, covered in flock wallpaper, china dogs, plates and photos of smiling grandchildren – just like the betting shop. A collection of crude watercolours depicting Benachie had been framed and given pride of place above the fireplace. The only thing that didn't look like it belonged in an old lady's house was DI Insch, sitting on the settee practising his breathing technique, eyes screwed shut, two fingers pressed against the side of his neck. Logan closed the door quietly and sank down into one of the armchairs, keeping his mouth shut until the fat man had finished. He was beginning to wonder how long it would take before something inside the inspector burst. There was no way this was healthy for a man that size.

'We might be better off appealing to her sense

of decency,' said Logan, when Insch had returned to a more normal, human colour. 'We could—'

'Decency? You've got to be kidding me: she sells porn to schoolchildren!'

'Yes, but she thinks that's fair game. If she doesn't do it, how will they learn about sex?' He held up a hand before Insch could do more than open his mouth. 'I know, but it makes sense to her. I think if we show her the video and maybe some PM photos she'll come over all community spirited.'

The inspector snorted, but Logan ignored him. 'She helps out with jumble sales for the old folks, she raises money for the local scout troop. She sees herself as a bastion of the community.'

'She's a bloody nightmare more like!' He was starting to go purple again.

'Er . . .' he was probably going to regret this. 'Are you OK, sir? You seem a bit . . .' there was no good way to finish that sentence.

Insch glowered at him. 'Thirteen stone, OK? You happy? That's how much they told me to lose.'

'Oh.'

'How the hell are you supposed to lose half your body weight? Nothing like setting realistic bloody goals, is there? Bloody Fit Bloody Like – if I ever find the bright spark—'

'I've made tea.' Ma Stewart marched into the room looking a lot more like her normal self, wearing a floral skirt and blouse, pastel cardigan, beaming smile and far too much make-up. You'd never have known she'd just spent fifteen minutes bawling her eyes out because Insch had yelled at her. She even gave him the biggest slice of cake. And thirteen stone or not, the inspector ate it.

Logan waited until Insch had a mouthful before saying, 'Ma, I've got a film I want you to watch.' He pulled out the DVD case with cartoon penguins on it. 'It's the one we found in your shop.'

She clapped her hands. 'I'll get the sherry!'

She watched the home movie unfold in silence, impassive as Jason Fettes screamed and struggled against his leather restraints. 'It's not very good,' she said at last. 'I mean the special effects are all right, but who'd want all that whinging? It's not very sexy.'

'It's real.' Logan opened the case file and pulled out the glossy shots of Jason Fettes' post mortem. 'Jason was twenty-one.' He put a photo on the coffee table. 'He wanted to be an actor. He was writing a screenplay. He died in agony. His mother and father came back from holiday to find out he was dead.' Laying out one picture for every sentence, until the coffee table was covered in stomach-churning Technicolor.

'I . . .' She ran a dry tongue over her scarlet lips. 'I'd like a glass of water please.' Closing her eyes so she wouldn't have to look at the photos.

'Who did you get the film from?'

'I'm feeling a bit sick . . .'

'A young man's dead, Ma. He was in the Scouts when he was wee. Just like your grandsons.'

'I don't . . . Oh God . . .' She scrambled out of her seat, rushing through to the kitchen. They could hear her retching from the lounge. Logan picked up the photographs and put them back in the folder.

It didn't take long before she was back in her chair again, looking decidedly unwell, clutching a glass of water.

'So,' said Insch, 'do you want to tell us where you got the film from?'

Ma shuddered. 'I never knew. I thought it was just . . . you know. Someone messing around. If I'd known . . .'

'So who was it?'

'I get most of my stuff from this bloke from Dundee. Comes round once a month with DVDs and . . .' She suddenly stopped talking, as if realizing she was about to say something she *really* shouldn't and cleared her throat instead. 'Anyway, he wasn't well – poor soul's got sciatica and it's a long drive up from Dundee if you've got a bad back. My Jamesy was just the same, God rest his soul. When we went to Prestwick for our holidays—'

'Ma,' Logan leant across the table and took one of her cold, flabby hands, 'the film. It's important.'

She took a deep breath, stared at her hand in Logan's and said, 'Sometimes people are stretched a bit, and maybe they've been unlucky on the horses. They give us things to look after . . . or sell for them.' Which was the most genteel description of seizing property for non-payment Logan had ever heard. 'The . . .' She pointed at the television and shuddered. 'That film was in a DVD player someone handed in.'

Insch leaned forward in his seat. 'Who?'

'I don't know, I'll have to check.' She got up and rummaged in an old sideboard, coming out with a tatty blue exercise book, flipping through the pages, talking to herself. 'Derek MacDonald.' She scribbled the details down on a piece of pink notepaper with roses round the edge and handed it over.

Insch accepted it with a grunt then passed it to Logan.

'Recognize the name?'

'Derek MacDonald?' Logan shrugged. 'Could be anyone. Hundreds of them living round here. Assuming it's even the guy's real name. The address rings a bell though . . .'

'Call it in.'

So Logan did, standing out in the hallway with the lounge door closed, listening as Control came back to him with details on half a dozen Derek MacDonalds with police records in the north-east. Only three of them lived in Aberdeen: one with a drink driving conviction, one with a couple of assaults to his name, and one unlawful removal – nicking cars in Tillydrone. None of them lived at the address Ma had given them. But according to Control the building *was* under surveillance by the drug squad – part of an ongoing operation to pick up some likely lads from Newcastle who were having a serious go at moving into the Aberdeen market. Which meant Insch would have to clear it with the Detective Chief Superintendent in charge of CID before he went barging in there like a bear with piles.

'Address is flagged,' said Logan, back in the lounge. 'DI Finnie. But there's no Derek MacDonald at that address.'

Ma tutted, arms folded under her enormous, pasty bosom. 'Trust me, there is. We're very careful about that kind of thing. When people owe you money, it always pays to know where they live.'

46

Reggae music. Logan *hated* reggae music, but it was coming out of the alarm clock radio anyway, dragging him back from dark dream. Groaning, he mashed the snooze button and retreated beneath the duvet. There was some indistinct muttering from the other side of the bed, and Jackie rolled over and wrapped herself around his torso, burying her head into the crook of his neck. All warm and cosy . . . It wasn't until the alarm went off again that Logan woke up enough to remember he wasn't speaking to her, and why.

DI Insch's Range Rover slid into the kerb, the engine pinging and ticking in the cold morning air. 'This it?'

Ma Stewart peered out of the window, then down at the piece of paper in her hand. 'Have you ever tried those Magic Tree things? They work wonders for doggy smells.' Which was her polite way of saying the inspector's car stank.

'Is – this – the – bloody – house?'

'Yes. Honestly, there's no need to be like that. I was only saying.' She sniffed. 'They come in all sorts of different flavours these days, not just pine.'

Sitting in the back with Ma, Logan tried not to groan. The pair of them had been at it since they'd picked her up at half-eight. She'd do her usual rambling non sequitur thing, Insch would snap at her, she'd sulk for a bit, and then it would all start up again.

The address she'd given them was deep in darkest Mastrick, part of a long line of grey granite tenements that looked even drearier than normal under the blue-grey clouds. Muttering darkly about old ladies, blunt objects and shallow graves, the inspector called into Control and told them the Drug Squad could take a running jump at themselves: he was going in. 'I don't care,' he said to whoever it was on the other end of the phone. 'I'm investigating a murder: it takes precedence. Finnie can—'

Someone knocked on the window, a jowly, middle-aged man with wide, rubbery lips, floppy hair, leather jacket and a pained expression. Insch hung up on Control and buzzed the window down.

'Not wanting to be funny,' said the man, 'but what the fuck do you think you're playing at?'

'Derek MacDonald.'

'This is an ongoing surveillance operation you idiot! Get out of here!'

'I'm going nowhere without Derek MacDonald.'

'That's it.' DI Finnie pulled an Airwave handset from his jacket pocket. 'I'm calling the DCS.'

'Fine,' said Insch, with a nasty smile, 'you tell him I'm after a murderer, but you're busy playing cops and junkies. I'm sure he'll be dead impressed.'

'Oh, for God's sake . . .' The man glanced back over his shoulder at the house. 'Who did you say you were looking for?'

'Derek MacDonald.'

'No, can't help you. Now if you wouldn't mind fucking off before someone sees you, I've got a surveillance operation to—'

'I don't give a toss about your operation.'

'You're such an arsehole.'

'I'm investigating a murder.'

'Fine. Be like that. Fuck over six weeks' worth of work. Way to be a team player, Insch.'

'All I want is Derek MacDonald.'

'HE – DOESN'T – LIVE – HERE!'

'Tall chap,' said Ma, beaming at him out of the window, 'brown hair, sideburns, mid-twenties, squint nose, little round glasses like Harry Potter?'

Finnie marched round to the Range Rover's passenger side and climbed in the front. 'Go down to the end of the street and take a left.'

'Are you deaf? I'm not—'

'I'm trying to help, OK? Now go down to the end of the bloody street and take a left!'

Left and left again took them up a small side street running parallel to the one they were just on.

'Pull in here.' Finnie pointed at a space next to a suspiciously familiar-looking scabby Vauxhall. 'Five minutes.' He climbed out into the cold morning, let himself through a wrought iron gate into the garden of a boarded-up house, and disappeared round the side of the building.

'You see the paper this morning?' said Insch when Finnie was gone, pulling a copy of the *Press and Journal* from underneath his seat. Front page headline: LAWYER BLOCKED MACINTYRE'S POLICE PROTECTION! and a big photo of Hissing Sid's bruised and battered face. 'You know,' said the inspector, grinning, 'I'm starting to like that soap-dodging Weegie bastard of yours.'

Logan skimmed the article while Insch started in on a packet of Refreshers. Colin Miller had done a proper hatchet job on Sandy Moir-Farquharson, contradicting half of what the lawyer had told the other papers, making him look like a self-serving, arsehole. No wonder Insch was happy.

'I'm getting that framed.' The inspector took the paper back, laying it out on the dashboard and smoothing it flat. 'Nice photo too, don't you think? Really shows up the bruises.'

'Well I think it's a terrible shame!' said Ma, arms crossed, face set. 'That poor wee lad had his whole life ahead of him and a baby on the way. Whoever beat him up should be ashamed of himself. Whatever happened to National Service? You know, I was just telling Denise the other day—'

Insch told her to shut up.

Ma was still sulking when Finnie returned, clutching a brown A4 envelope. He pulled out a glossy photo. 'This him?'

Ma squinted at it for a second. 'Oh, yes. He's got lovely hair, don't you think? Like our Norman's boyfriend. I'm sure he uses a full-bodied shampoo.'

'Jimmy Duff. Local lad. Small-time dealer.'

'We want him,' said Insch, staring at the photo, then opening negotiations with DI Finnie to get the guy picked up.

Logan was the only one to see the expression on Ma's face when she found out 'Derek MacDonald' wasn't who he'd said he was. It wasn't pretty.

Back at FHQ the computer forensics people had finally got around to forwarding on the contents of Jason Fettes' hotmail account. Logan worked his way through the emails, ignoring the spam and day-to-day dross, concentrating on the messages from people in the BDSM scene instead: offers of money for sex, and personal appointments.

From the look of things Fettes had a number of regulars, none of whom gave their real name. The email addresses weren't much help either, they were all things like 'nastydombitch69@yahoo.com' and 'kittymisspainslut@hotmail.co.uk'. From the look of things the usual practice was to meet Fettes at the regular Aberdeen munch first, and after that it was, 'My place: six, Thursday. Bring your lube.' No names and no addresses. And no bloody use.

He put them all in date order, then took the lot up to DI Insch.

'No, I don't . . . no . . . Look, just because you think you're . . . yes . . . just pick the bastard up, OK? Because if you don't, I bloody well will!' The inspector slammed the phone down and scowled at it, then dug about in his desk, coming out with a Sherbet Fountain. 'I'd offer you one,' he said, ripping the orange and yellow paper off the top, 'but you know how it is.'

Logan dumped the pile of emails on the inspector's desk, watching in hypnotic fascination as Insch sooked the end of the liquorice straw, dibbed it into the white sherbet, and transferred it back to his mouth. Then repeated the whole process: dib, sook, dib, sook . . .

'Yes, anyway,' he said at last, snapping out of it, 'Fettes's emails: I've been through them. Nothing on the night he died, but I highlighted any BDSM appointments for the fortnight before he got dumped outside A&E.'

'Names?' asked the inspector, white powder dusting his top lip like cocaine.

'No real ones, it's all, "Mistress Nicky" and "Jenny Spank Me", that kind of thing.'

Insch nodded and went back to the dibbing and sooking. 'Not a lot of bloody help then.'

'We can forget about anyone who's a bottom, sub, or masochist,' said Logan, sorting through the file. 'They'd be the ones strapped to the table, not Fettes. So it's got to be a top, a dom, or a switch.'

The inspector looked at him, one eyebrow raised, the liquorice straw sticking out of his mouth like a thermometer. 'You're getting a bit . . . *familiar* with this whole bondage thing, aren't you?'

'Point is these people are probably local. And if they're active in the Aberdeen scene we can find out who they are from their bondage names. Hell, Rickards might even know them!'

Insch tipped the last of the sherbet into his mouth, tapping the empty paper tube to get every last milligram of powder out. 'Well? Go get him then!'

'Yes, sir.'

According to Control, Rickards was out on a shout with DI McPherson, so Insch would have to wait. In the meantime Logan had paperwork to catch up on. That DVD of Fettes was causing no end of grief – Garvie was dead because they'd screwed up and jumped to conclusions, and as if Logan didn't feel guilty enough about that, the Chief Constable was on the rampage. Insch was determined to keep Garvie in the frame: the person in the bondage suit might be female, but there was still the driver with the Irish accent – Garvie fitted the description perfectly . . . but Logan was beginning to have doubts about the whole thing.

He was heading downstairs to watch the CCTV

footage from the hospital again, when shouting and swearing echoed up the stairwell from the custody suite. Crash, bang and wallop. More swearing. Whatever it was, Logan wanted nothing to do with it. He'd got as far as the ground floor when half a dozen constables charged past, heading for the disturbance. Another loud crash and more shouting.

Logan left them to it.

'Fucking hell . . .' DI Steel lurched over to Logan's table in the canteen, clutching a blue icepack against the side of her head, and nearly collapsed into the chair opposite. 'Don't ask. And go get us a coffee: three sugars. And a doughnut or something.'

Logan opened his mouth, but Steel cut him off: 'I said: don't ask.' He shrugged and went up to the servery.

'They've no doughnuts, so I got you a KitKat.'

The inspector didn't seem to mind, just slurped and munched and winced. 'Fucking McPherson's a bloody disaster magnet,' she said at last. 'You know how many days the bastard's had off sick in the last four years?' Logan didn't and said so. Steel frowned. 'Me neither, but I bet it's heaps. Probably has more days off than he works.'

'What happened?'

'Which part of "don't bloody ask" do you no' understand? And how come you're in? Did I no' tell you to take a couple of days off?'

'We got a last-minute lead on the Jason Fettes

killing.' He stood, stacking his empties back onto a tatty plastic tray.

'Yeah?' She polished off the last chocolate finger and scrunched the silver paper up into a little ball. 'I thought Insch the Amazing Fatty already solved that one.'

'Yes, well . . . we unsolved it.'

The inspector pointed at Logan's vacated seat. 'Sit. This I want to hear.'

'Not much to tell. We found a film of Fettes strapped to a table, getting spanked and fisted. He pretty much bleeds to death on camera.'

Steel grabbed her coffee and stood, 'Well, come on then, let's see it.'

'But—'

'Fettes is my case remember? DI Fatboy is just helping me out. So get your finger out and make with the film.'

She watched it all the way through in silence. 'Let's see it again.'

Logan set the DVD playing once more. There was a knock on the door as the mystery woman started dripping hot candle wax onto Jason Fettes' back. PC Rickards stuck his head in and said, 'Sergeant Mitchell said you wanted to see me, sir?'

'I've got a list of pseudonyms I want you to go through and . . .' he trailed off, realizing there was something wrong with Rickards' face. Or more wrong than normal. His left cheek was all swollen. 'What happened to you?'

'DI McPherson.' As if that was explanation enough.

Steel didn't take her eyes off the screen, 'What was the verdict?'

'Broken arm, two cracked ribs and a concussion, ma'am. They're keeping him in overnight.'

'Wonderful. Of course you know who's going to get stuck with his caseload, don't you? *Again*.'

Logan waited for someone to elaborate, but they didn't. So he pulled out the list he'd made of Jason Fettes' BDSM contacts and gave it to the constable. 'I need real names and addresses for all of them.'

Rickards blanched. 'Ah, yes . . . er, sir, I can't . . . I mean it wouldn't be ethical of me to . . . they . . .'

'Come here,' said Logan, pointing towards the screen where the hot wax had given way to the leather ping-pong paddle. 'See that? That's our victim, the guy who's backside got turned the wrong way out. You think it's more important for your bondage mates to remain anonymous, or for us to catch whoever killed him?'

'Well . . . I . . . it's just . . .' The sound of spanking grew louder, mingling with muffled grunts from the shackled and gagged Fettes. And then the strap-on came out. 'Look,' said Rickards, blushing, 'we can probably eliminate half the names, get rid of anyone not into penetration . . .' he took out his pen and started scoring his way through the list. 'Sometimes a top will change their MO to accommodate a bottom's new fantasy, but most just like what they like.'

He watched until things got serious, then his blush went nuclear. 'Er . . . that kind of fisting isn't all that common . . .' More names disappeared. There were only three left after Rickards had finished: 'Big Dunk', 'Dirty Nicky' and 'Mistress Barclay'.

Insch was in his office, grinding his teeth as Logan handed the shortlist over. The fact that DI Steel was slouched in the inspector's visitors' chair, fiddling about with her bra strap, *supervising*, probably didn't help. And Logan knew it would somehow end up being his fault. 'We can forget about "Big Dunk",' he said as Insch scowled at the list, 'I've watched that DVD a dozen times now and it's definitely a woman in the rubber suit. Rickards says the other two are into the kind of stuff being done to Fettes, but they're not likely to have screwed up like that. They're experienced.'

'Bring them in anyway. Big Dunk too. If we lean on them they'll . . .' The inspector ground to a halt and stared at DI Steel. 'What?'

She shrugged. 'Oh, nothing. I just think you'd have more luck playing this one a bit more softly, softly.'

Insch scowled at her. 'Thank you for your valuable input, *inspector*, but I've no intention of pussyfooting around with a bunch of rubber-clad—'

'Look, I'm only saying, OK? I've met a few of

the spanking crowd and they'll clam up like a virgin's legs if you come on all rough and ready. They're no' wee scroats you can just push about: they're accountants and lawyers and bloody business analysts.'

Logan had to agree with her. 'It's a pretty middle-class thing, BDSM.'

'Oh for God's . . . fine. OK, bring them in and we'll give them tea and bloody biscuits.'

'In the meantime,' said Steel, giving up on her bra, 'you should get a lookout request going for Jimmy Duff. Watch him though, he's a slippery wee shite.'

Insch was rapidly heading from pink to purple. 'Yes, *inspector*, anything else, *inspector*?'

'Oh, aye: I'm going to have to borrow Laz here for a wee while.'

'But we—'

'You let me know how you get on, OK? Be nice to see a proper result on this one. No' like last time.' She was out of the office door before the fat man started swearing, with Logan hurrying after her, not wanting to get caught in the crossfire.

'Where are we going?' he asked, looking back over his shoulder at Insch's door, almost expecting to see the inspector come crashing out into the hallway and go on the rampage like an angry pink Godzilla.

'Sean Morrison's: hate mail, threats, remember?'

'But, Jason Fettes—'

'You and I both know Insch is going to get bugger all done till they pick up Jimmy Duff. So what's the point hanging about watching him screw up them BDSM interviews?' She slapped Logan on the back. 'Come on, think how much more fun you'll have without his fat ugly face looming over you.'

But all Logan could think of was what Insch would do to him when he got back.

47

There was a Bon Accord Glass van sitting outside the Morrison house, a couple of guys struggling with a large sheet of plywood, trying to keep it from sailing off in the blustery wind. Hesitant raindrops made polka-dot patterns on the pale wood as they heaved it up against the shattered window frame and started fixing it into place. The view was stormy today: dark clouds, dark sea, and gloomy buildings, but Logan barely glanced at it as he hurried after DI Steel into the house.

Mr Morrison wasn't coping well: the bags under his eyes were deep purple, his cheeks sunken and speckled with stubble, hair sticking out all over the place. He let them in without a word, slouched through into the living room, fell into an armchair and stared at the big sheet of plywood that blocked out half the light. A radio on the sideboard burbled out local news into the darkened room: something about floral tributes flooding in for Rob Macintyre, then on to a piece about some local band who'd just been signed to a major record label.

A large lump of granite was sitting in a splash-pattern of broken glass. It must have taken two or three people to heft something that heavy through the double glazing – the thing was huge.

'Indoor rockery. Classy.' Steel scratched away at her shoulder, then dug out a packet of nicotine gum, offering it round as if it were cigarettes. 'Any more hate mail, or was it just the dirty big stone?'

Mr Morrison didn't even look at her. 'Someone could have been hurt. Gwen's not well . . .'

'Aye, you're right. Sorry.' Much to Logan's surprise, she actually sounded genuine. 'You still getting the phone calls?'

He shook his head. 'We went ex-directory when Sean was . . . found.'

'Well, that's something at least.' She picked her way across the carpet, glittering shards crunching beneath her boots, and peered out of the one remaining pane of glass. 'What happened to all the journalists?'

Morrison shrugged. 'We just want our son home.'

'Uh-huh. Got any idea who'd chuck a lump of granite through your window?'

'They'll let him home to visit his mother, won't they? She's not well . . .'

Steel closed her eyes, rubbing at the bridge of her nose with nicotine-stained fingers as if she were trying to shift a headache. 'Sergeant McRae, maybe you should go make us all some tea, eh?' she said at last. 'And see if you can find any biscuits.'

The Morrisons' kitchen was a mess: unwashed dishes piled in the sink; overflowing laundry basket; a black, oily crust of burnt-on food like scabs on the hob; stuffed black bags sitting next to the bucket, as if Sean's dad was scared to go outside and put them in the wheely bin for collection. Feeling nosy, Logan had a good rummage through the kitchen, pretending he was looking for tea bags. The cupboards were bare, not so much as a tin of soup. Like it or not, Mr Morrison was going to have to go outside soon, or they'd starve to death in here. Logan wondered if the man would be safe enough ordering takeaway, or if it would come delivered with a free side order of sputum and dog shit. Nothing like being the parents of an infamous child.

There was a small container on the work surface marked TEA, but it was as empty as the food cupboards. In fact, other than plates, gadgets and cutlery, the only thing Logan could find in the kitchen was a drawer full of envelopes. Some opened, most not. He slipped on a pair of latex gloves and pulled one out: YOUR SON IS AN ABOMINATION! THAT OLD MAN DESERVES BLOOD! It went on for a page and a half, but the basic message was that they should bring back the death penalty and give it to Sean Morrison. Even if he was only eight. And hanging was too good for him.

Logan picked them all out of the drawer and carried everything through to the lounge. 'Sorry,' he said, setting them down on the coffee table, 'there's no biscuits. Or milk. Or tea.'

'Oh.' The inspector looked disappointed, but she perked up again when she saw the stack of letters.

'I found them when I was looking for the teabags.'

Morrison shuddered. 'We've been keeping them, like you said. I don't open them any more . . .'

Steel nodded, borrowing Logan's gloves so she could poke through the pile, pulling sheets from the open ones and squinting at them in the dim light. 'Aye, nasty wee shites one and all.' She flicked through another couple then asked if Logan had an evidence bag on him. 'We're going to take these away and see if we can get anything off them. And I'll get someone from fingerprints to come down and give your rock the CSI treatment. OK?'

Morrison didn't reply, just went on staring at his boarded-up window.

'I was wondering,' said Logan as they stood to leave, 'Sean's friend: Ewan. Has his dad been in touch with you at all?'

The man looked puzzled, as if trying to remember why they were there. Logan got the feeling he probably hadn't slept in a week. 'No. Not since Sean stopped going round there. Not since we came back from Guildford.'

'So he hasn't said anything to you about his house getting vandalized?'

'Look, I'm sorry but Gwen needs her medication.' He levered himself out of the armchair. 'She's not been well.'

They let themselves out, scurrying through the rain to the car. 'Can you no' keep your mind on one thing at a time?' asked Steel as Logan cranked the blowers up to full. 'Vandalism, my sharny arse.'

'You never wondered about Sean—'

'Oh for Christ's sake, no' this again: I get enough grief from the bloody social workers. He's a wee shite. That's all there is to it.'

Logan pulled out from the kerb, heading downhill back towards FHQ. 'I don't buy it: you don't go from being a well-balanced wee boy to a thieving little thug who knives old men and policewomen for no reason. Something happened.'

Steel sighed. 'Look, and I want you to pay attention this time: I – don't – care! OK?'

'Oh, come on, you've got think it's a bit—'

'I – don't – care! Bloody hell. In the good old days you caught the bad guy, you banged them up, and you forgot about them for seven, eight years. Nowadays it's all "community-fucking-service" and "addressing offender behaviour". That social work department needs a stiff kick up the arse with a pointy boot!'

'Why was he vandalizing his ex-best-friend's house?'

'We speakin' the same language here? Hello? I couldn't give a rat's arse!'

'How come the family never reported him for all the damage he did to their house? They *knew* it was him. We—'

'OK! OK, FOR GOD'S SAKE!' She sat and seethed. 'Ten minutes. We go round there for ten minutes, and if we don't find anything you never, *ever* get to mention that wee shite again? Understand? Like a bloody broken record . . .'

Ewan Whyte – Sean's ex-best friend – was still at school and his dad was at work, but his mother and little sisters were in: the girls finger-painting in the kitchen while Mrs Whyte made sure they didn't do anything stupid, like eat the paint, or start colouring in the walls. DI Steel begged a cup of coffee and a custard cream while Logan went outside to talk to the grandfather.

The old man was in the shed at the bottom of the garden, the little wooden hut smelling of engine oil and hand-rolled cigarettes as he cleaned the blades of an old-fashioned lawnmower. Rain drummed on the roof. He smiled and waved when Logan shouted, 'Hello?'

'Here, hold this bit, will you?' Mr Whyte Senior tipped the mower up on its side.

'You remember when I was here before,' said Logan, as the old man started in with the WD40, 'we talked about Sean Morrison?'

Whyte nodded. 'I read all about his arrest in

the paper – can you believe they used pepper spray on the poor wee soul? He's only eight . . . Thanks, you can let go now.'

'I wonder why your son didn't report Sean – for all the vandalism.'

The old man smiled sadly. 'Oh, he wanted to, but there was never any proof, and I thought Sean had enough to deal with without all that. What with his granddad being at death's door and problems at school. It wouldn't have been right.' He levered the mower down from the worktop with a grunt. 'Old sporting injury. Always gives me gyp when it's wet out. Now, would you like a cup of tea? It's no bother.'

They were walking back across the lawn when Mr Whyte stopped at the koi pond. A large orange and white fish broached the rippled surface, then disappeared back into the shadowy depths. 'My son's a good man, Sergeant. A better father than I was in many ways. He just gets a bit stressed from time to time. I'm sure he'll forgive Sean eventually. His brother's death hit him hard, and Sean looks so much like Craig.' He shivered. 'Anyway, what about that tea?'

In the rain FHQ looked even more miserable than normal, the lobby slick with dirty grey water walked in off the streets. Sergeant Mitchell collared Logan as soon as he was back in the building. 'Hoy, what the hell is it with you and mobile bloody phones? Do I look like your secretary?' Moustache bristling.

Logan pulled out his phone and peered at it. The battery was dead, but he wasn't about to admit it. 'You sure you're calling the right number? I—'

'We give everyone a sodding Airwave handset for a reason!'

'What's the message?'

'That Weegie reporter of yours has been on half a dozen times – call him back for God's sake. I have to listen to his soap-dodging nonsense once more I'm going to kill someone. The rest are in your bloody email.' He wagged his finger under Logan's nose like an irate schoolteacher. 'And switch your bloody phone on, or I'm going to report you. Got better things to do than sod about after you all day!'

There was always a big mess of phone chargers in the CID office, so Logan helped himself to one that fit and plugged his mobile in, then rummaged through his desk until he found his Airwave handset. It was about four times the size of his normal phone, but it would have to do. The battery was nearly fully charged, which wasn't surprising: he'd barely used the thing; it had spent most of its life switched off in a drawer. He tried calling Miller, but it went straight through to voicemail so he left a message and contact number. If it was anything important the reporter would call him back soon enough. Until then Logan had some digging to do.

* * *

Over an hour later he was no further forward. As far as the various police databases were concerned, Sean's ex-best-friend's family were clean. Not so much as a parking ticket. In fact, the only blemish on the Whytes' family tree was Craig, the dead brother. He'd got into a fight when he was sixteen and ended up crippling a lorry driver with a snooker cue. The man had accused him of being gay. There was a spell at Her Majesty's pleasure, followed by a battered girlfriend, therapy, then an overdose of sleeping pills. Daniel had no reason to be jealous of his younger brother – he'd not even made it to twenty-four.

When the Airwave handset started ringing it was such an unfamiliar noise that Logan nearly didn't answer it. 'Hello?'

'Where the hell you been, man? I been callin' you for ages!' Colin Miller sounding agitated, which was pretty much par for the course these days.

'Afternoon.' Logan tried for one last mouthful of coffee, only to find it stone cold. He spat it back out into the mug. 'Urgh, Jesus . . .'

'She's done it!'

He peered at the marbled liquid then tipped it into the nearest pot plant. 'Done what? Who's done it?'

'It's a wee boy! Seven pounds! He's fuckin' brilliant! Wee fingers an' toes an' everythin'!'

'Oh . . .' There were things you were supposed to say to new fathers: 'Congratulations. How's Isobel?'

'Knackered. Says if I come near her again she's going to chop ma dick off!' He laughed. 'Can you believe it: six days early?'

'Well, I suppose it's—'

'You gotta come see him!'

'Thing is, Colin . . .' Logan looked at his desk. It wasn't exactly overflowing with urgent actions, just DI Steel's paperwork – all the things she was supposed to do, but never did. And the sooner he reported back to Insch, the sooner the grumpy sod would shout at him for being dragged away in the first place. As if Logan had any say in the matter. 'No, sounds good. See you soon.'

He abandoned his CID pool car as close to the maternity ward as he could and hurried in out of the rain. A nurse gave him directions and after a brief shopping spree in the Women's Royal Voluntary Service shop, he was marching down the corridor, clutching a cat-shaped helium balloon, a box of chocolates and a Hallmark card with IT's A Boy! on it. As if the parents didn't already know.

The reporter was waiting for him at the maternity ward door. 'Laz, my man! Come see the bairn!'

The next twenty minutes passed in something of a blur. The baby, no matter what his proud father said, looked like a shaved monkey, but Logan kept quiet about it and pretended not to notice. Isobel looked dreadful: pale, tired and sweaty, with dark purple bags under her eyes. She clearly wasn't up to a prolonged visit, so Logan made his excuses, promising to meet up with Colin when the fathers were kicked out at nine, to wet the baby's head with some thirty-five-year-old single malt whisky the reporter had bought specially.

Outside, the rain had stopped, late-afternoon sunlight cutting through the low clouds, painting everything gold and ochre, casting long blue shadows as it sank towards the horizon. Logan climbed into the pool car and switched his handset back on, trying to remember how to check for any messages and failing abysmally. So he called Control and asked Sergeant Mitchell.

'For God's sake! I'm not your—'

'Bloody secretary, yeah, I know. Look, I'm using the damn thing, what more do you want?'

'Will wonders never cease? Insch is looking for you.'

'Any idea what—'

'No. So don't ask.'

Logan hung up. It was just on the cusp of five: if he could stay out of the inspector's clutches for another ten minutes he could sign out and slope off home, putting off the inevitable shouting at till tomorrow. But that would mean going back to the flat and dealing with Jackie . . . He dialled Insch's mobile.

'Where are you?'

Logan thought about lying, but it probably wasn't worth the aggravation. 'Up at the hospital.'

'What?' There was a moment's pause, then the

inspector said, *'How did you get . . . ? No, never mind. Is that slimy bastard there yet?'*

'Er . . .' He looked up and down the car park, trying to figure out what Insch meant. 'Which one?'

'Hissing Bloody Sid – who do you think? Soon as the TV cameras turn up he's all over the place like a foul smell.'

'Ah, right, not seen him yet.' Which was true.

'I've got a rehearsal at half-six, so I'm relying on you: don't let the wee shite say anything stupid, OK? Last thing we need is more grief.'

Logan didn't have a clue what the inspector was on about, but it would probably be bad. It usually was.

48

They were gathered outside the main entrance, holding up placards with things like WE LOVE YOU ROB!, GET WELL SOON! and AFC CHAMPIONS! scrawled on them. Floral tributes were piled up to either side of the hospital doors, with the occasional teddy bear dressed up in Aberdeen Football Club colours thrown in for good measure. Half the crowd had their replica shirts on under their thick jackets, and all of them were tearfully singing football songs.

'Oh for God's sake . . .' Logan stood next to one of the uniformed constables stationed at the hospital, staring out at this public display of grief. 'They been at this long?'

The constable nodded, her face puckered up like a chicken's bum. 'Aye, ever since it was in the papers this morning. One bugger drops off a bunch of manky carnations from a petrol station, and suddenly everyone's at it. Like he's Lady Fucking Di or something.' She pointed off into the middle distance where a group of TV journalists were hanging about drinking tea and coffee from polystyrene cups. 'And those bastards aren't helping.'

It was nearly half an hour before things kicked off: Rob Macintyre's mum and her grieving daughter-in-law-elect emerging from the hospital blubbering bravely for the fans and cameras. The sun had long since disappeared, but it'd been replaced by the harsh white glare of television lights. Macintyre's mother shuffled forwards and dabbed at her eyes. 'I want to thank you all for coming to wish my wee boy well,' she said, launching into a speech about how her little darling was the best son in the world, who didn't deserve this, and if anyone knew who was responsible . . . pretty much the same thing she'd said at the press conference, only this time Sandy Moir-Farquharson was nowhere to be seen.

'Good wee boy, my arse,' said the constable, keeping her voice down, in case anyone overheard. 'Little rapist fucker got what he bloody deserved. Whoever did him wants a medal.'

Then the questions started from the press, most of which were variations on the theme of, 'How does it feel to have your son in a coma?' as if his mum and fiancée were going to say it was great. Then it was onto Macintyre's medical condition and what it meant for the wedding plans. Ashley struck a determined pose, one hand over her tiny pregnant bulge. 'We're still getting married! Robert *will* get better – his baby needs a daddy and I'll always stand by him!'

'Aye,' hissed the constable, 'and his seven-figure book deal. How much you think she's in for, fifty per cent with the mother? They'll be rolling in it.'

'Well,' said Logan, 'the guy *is* in a coma—'

'Best place for him.'

The questions kept coming. Up till now, Hissing Sid had handled the media side of things, manipulating, spinning, lying, but without him Macintyre's mother was forced to take centre stage, and she was doing a surprisingly good job of it too, only wheeling Ashley out for the emotional bits.

The footballer's fiancée was in the middle of telling everyone how her Robert wouldn't hurt a fly when a man lurched drunkenly up from the road, shouting, 'Fucker deserves to die!' As soon as he opened his mouth Logan recognized him: Brian something, boyfriend of Macintyre's sixth victim: Christine Forrester. The one before he'd tried it on with Jackie and got himself kneed in the balls and arrested.

'Here we go . . .'

The man wasn't just drunk, he was pickled: tears rolling down his face, slurring as he shouted the odds about how Macintyre was a raping scumbag who deserved to die for what he'd done. How a coma was too good for him. How he'd ruined Christine's life. Killed her. The cameras were on him in a flash, capturing his pain for the next news bulletin.

Logan pushed through the ring of journalists and took hold of the man's arm. 'Come on, Brian, you don't want to do this. Let's you and me—'

But Brian was stronger than he looked, breaking free and hurling a barrage of foul language at Macintyre's family. Logan waved the constable over and told her to take Brian inside. But he had no intention of coming quietly; lunging at Ashley, shouting: 'You gave him a fucking alibi! You lying *bitch*! They could've stopped him!' Taking a wild swing and missing. 'It's your fault!'

'Come on, sir.' The constable grabbed his wrist, twisting it up behind his back before he could do any real damage, and frogmarching him away, the TV cameras hurrying after them.

With the spotlight off Macintyre's nearest and dearest, Logan suggested it might be best if they went home now. 'Before anything else happens.'

Macintyre's mum glared after Brian – watching him struggle as he was forced through the doors into the hospital. 'I want to press charges! He's got no right talking to us like that when my boy's in a coma!'

'Why don't we talk about that tomorrow, when everyone's calmed down?' said Logan, escorting them through the throng of well-wishers, across the road and up into the ranks of parked cars. Macintyre's mum pulled out a key fob and pointed it at a silver Audi – one of the footballer's collection of expensive motors – setting the hazard lights flashing as it unlocked. Obviously the little red hatchback wasn't good enough for her any more. 'Nice car. New?' She ignored him and climbed in behind the steering wheel. Logan held onto the door frame, preventing her from closing it. 'What happened to your lawyer: Moir-Farquharson?'

She gave him a withering stare. 'If it wasn't for him my wee boy would be fine! I saw the papers – he made them stop protecting Rob.' Her face was an ugly, hard line. 'He won't see another penny!' She pulled on her seatbelt as Ashley got into the passenger seat, looking shaken by Brian's outburst. Logan let go of the door and it was slammed shut.

The driver's window buzzed down and Mrs Macintyre's angry face glowered up at him. 'My wee boy's been half killed: you should be out there catching whoever did it, no' going on about lawyers and cars! Call yourselves policemen? You should be ashamed!' And then they drove off, leaving Logan to think that yes, he probably should.

'Well that was stupid.' Logan leant back against the wall, looking down at Brian as he cried quietly to himself. 'Look,' he said, 'they want to press charges. I'll try to talk them out of it, but even if they *do* make a complaint it's not going to go further than a warning. So it's not the end of the world: OK?'

Christine's boyfriend didn't answer, just cried harder. The man was a wreck.

Logan sighed. 'Come on, I'll take you home.'

Brian had settled down to a gentle, near-silent sob by the time they pulled up outside the house. It lay in darkness, curtains open, lights off, like all the life had been sucked out of the place. Logan waited, but Brian didn't budge from the passenger seat. 'Christine will be waiting for you.'

No response. Logan climbed out of the car. He really didn't need this tonight – he had more than enough on his plate without having to spend the evening babysitting someone's drunken, crying boyfriend.

Brian just sat there, not looking at the house. The front door was lying open. He'd probably forgotten to close it when he staggered out to shout at Macintyre's family, too pissed to notice. Nothing to worry about. But Logan still felt something cold crawling about in his innards.

'Are you . . .' He stared up at the dead-looking house. 'Why don't you wait here and I'll just—'

'She's in the bathroom.'

And the cold thing inside Logan grew claws.

The ambulance crew declared Christine Forrester dead at nineteen minutes past six. She was in the bath; the water would have been hot once, but now it was cold and deep pink. This wasn't a cry for help: Christine had done a thorough job. Two long, pale-edged scars stretched from the crook of her arms all the way down to her wrists, several horizontal slashes opening the veins up even further. Just to be on the safe side there were two empty packets lying on the bathroom floor: one of heavy-duty painkillers, the other sleeping tablets.

It would have been nice to say she looked serene in death, but she didn't. Her once-pretty eyes stared lifelessly at the ceiling, mouth hanging open as if she was about to say something. Like blame Logan for not stopping Macintyre before he raped her. Even the scar that twisted its way down her face seemed to stand out more than it had when she was alive. A trail of pain etched in broken skin.

'You want us to get her out of there?' asked one of the ambulance men, peeling off a pair of latex gloves.

'No . . . thanks, if you can just leave her where she is.' He'd have to call Insch and probably the Procurator Fiscal too, even if it was obviously a suicide. Christine had left a note – apologizing for not being stronger. For not being able to cope. For letting everyone down. As if it had all been *her* fault.

Logan couldn't look at her any more. He closed the bathroom door and showed the ambulance crew out.

It took three goes before the inspector would answer his phone, an angry, *'What now?'* blaring out into Logan's ear.

'Christine Forrester's dead. Slit her wrists and took a pile of pills.'

Silence, then swearing and then the sound became muffled, as if Insch had clamped his hand over the mouthpiece. But Logan could still hear him shouting that they should do the finale again, and this time try not to screw it up. Then some crackling, and finally what sounded like a heavy door closing. *'When?'*

'About three or four hours ago. Boyfriend came home and found her in the bath. He drinks all the whisky in the house, then goes up to the hospital for revenge. I think if he could have got into Macintyre's room he'd have killed him.'

'Bloody hell . . .'

'You want me to tell the PF?'

Insch thought about it for a moment. *'No, I'll do it . . . Why the hell did she have to go do something stupid?'*

But they both knew why – because they'd let Rob Macintyre get away with it.

49

The funeral directors took Christine Forrester away in a stainless steel coffin. The IB had been in and photographed her body in situ, but it wasn't the usual bells and whistles job, just the recording of a life ended. Without suspicious circumstances the PF didn't need to turn up, and neither did the rest of the travelling circus, which made it all the more sad. As if Christine's life wasn't worth as much as some junkie knifed in an alleyway for the price of a burger.

Logan left her boyfriend with a Family Liaison officer and followed the undertakers' grey van back to headquarters. The day shift was already two and a half hours over by the time he got there, but he had a heap of paperwork to do.

The CID room was dead, just the repetitive, hungry bleep of the fax machine wanting more paper, spoiling the silence. Logan settled down at his computer and began to type.

* * *

'Oh for God's sake – not you again!' Big Gary looked up from his copy of the *Evening Express*: Tributes Pour In For Brave Macintyre and watched Logan signing out. 'I'm going to start charging you rent!'

'One of Macintyre's victims killed herself.'

The big man's face fell. 'Aw shite . . .'

'Yeah. So you can stop giving me a hard time. Got enough of that from bloody Eric today.'

'Aye well,' Gary smiled, 'don't take it too personally: his daughter borrowed the family car and wrapped it round a bollard yesterday. She's OK, but the car's buggered. Mind you,' said Gary, leaning over the desk to whisper theatrically, 'it's his own fault for letting her have the keys in the first place. I wouldn't trust her to blow her nose, never mind drive to the shops. Still, that's kids for you . . . What?'

Logan had turned on his heel and was already hurrying back the way he'd come, ignoring the shouts of, 'Hoy! You've got to sign back in!'

The CCTV team were in the process of following a group of teenagers down Union Street, tracking them from camera to camera as they sung and shouted and staggered their way past the closed shops. Logan accosted the inspector in charge. 'Can you run an ANPR check on old tapes?'

'How old are we talking?'

'Sunday and Monday.'

He thought about it for a bit. 'Don't see why not, but it'll take a while.'

Logan frowned. 'Any way to speed it up? I only need from about . . .' taking a rough guess, 'call it ten pm onwards?'

'You got the number?'

'It's a red hatchback, probably registered to Rob Macintyre's mother.'

'Be quicker to just run the tapes on the MUX and fast forward till you see a red car, then. Soon as we've finished with these wee buggers,' he said, pointing at the teenagers on the screen, 'I'll give you a hand.'

'You've got to be bloody kidding me!' said Insch, mouth hanging open, bits of half-chewed jelly babies stuck to his teeth, while the chorus launched into the entrance of the Mikado for the second time since Logan had pushed through the church hall doors. 'He borrowed his *mum's* car?'

'Technically it's his aunt's car. Took us a while to track down the registration, but it was caught on camera taking the road south last Sunday *and* Monday. I've got the team going back through the tapes for all the other nights there was a rape – the ones we've still got anyway. Tayside are doing the same.'

'And you're sure it's him driving?'

Logan helped himself to a green baby, biting its head off with a grin. 'Perfect shot of him going down the Drive, and one more coming back about four hours later. More than enough time.'

The inspector looked confused. 'But he had that video – the one with you and Watson—'

'All he had to do was change the time on his watch before he shot it. Half three in the morning: I was keeping watch and Jackie was asleep. On the video we're both awake. I didn't twig till we traced the car.'

The singing came to a halt, but it took Insch a couple of moments to realize the chorus were all staring at him. He stood and glowered back. 'Did I tell you to stop? Keep going! Right,' he said when they were up and running again, 'we wait for Dundee to get back to us. Soon as they do: we go to the Fiscal.'

Tayside Police had promised to call Logan back as soon as they found anything, so he settled down to watch the rehearsal. He had to admit Insch's cast was getting better, even Rennie, but the star of the show was Debbie – the one everyone said was brilliant. Two steps on stage and she shone – changing from a wavy-haired woman in her late thirties into a bitter, twisted old battleaxe, cheated out of love. What she was doing with the rest of Insch's performing monkeys was anyone's guess.

The call from Dundee didn't come for nearly an hour. 'Well?' said Insch as Logan thanked the woman on the other end and hung up.

He tried to keep a straight face, but it was impossible. 'We've got him.'

*   *   *

The drinks just kept on coming. After rehearsal they decamped to the Noose and Monkey, where Insch was in such a good mood he bought a round for the entire cast. Logan found himself sitting next to Rennie and his groupies, while Rickards sat at the far end of the table, deep in conversation with Debbie. Logan wasn't really listening to Rennie telling his 'When I Met Billy Connolly' story, he was watching Rickards laughing and joking with the only decent thespian the production had. Logan smiled, remembering that night in the Illicit Still when he'd seen the contents of her handbag, and wondering if the Rankin paperback she'd been carrying around was *Black and Blue* or something else. Maybe she and Rickards had a lot more in common than anyone knew? It would certainly explain the fur-lined handcuffs.

The guy who played Poo-Bah sauntered over and cajoled Debbie into doing her party piece – an impersonation of their beloved director. She put her wine down, puffed up her cheeks, lumbered to her feet and harangued them all in a pretty good facsimile of the inspector's bass rumble for not knowing their bloody words. All the time eating invisible sweeties from an invisible bag. Everyone laughed, even Insch.

'So,' said Logan, catching Insch after the applause had died down, 'what's the plan with Macintyre?'

'Haul his mother and skanky girlfriend in. Charge them with perverting the course of justice, giving false alibis, lean on them. Impound the car, get the IB to go through it with a fine-toothed comb. The bastard may be in a coma, but we're going to nail him anyway!' The inspector stood, towering over Logan, 'Time for more drinks!'

A bleary face peered out from beneath the duvet as Logan lurched in, clicked on the bedroom light and started to fight his way out of his octopus-like clothes. The socks were the worst. 'You'll never guess,' he said. 'Go on: guess.'

'Oh for God's sake.' Jackie buried her head under a pillow with a muffled, 'Switch the bloody light off!'

'Come on, have a guess . . .' He threw the last sock at the light switch, but it didn't work, so he had to turn it off by hand. 'We got him!'

'It's after one!'

'Everyone was . . . was . . .' Logan collapsed on the bed and tried to figure out what he wanted to say. 'He . . .' a small belch. 'You shouldn't have done it though.' Having a bit of difficulty with the words. 'But it was him, so no one cares.' He lent over and patted her leg through the duvet. 'You shouldn't have done it though.'

'You're drunk. Go to sleep.'

'I didn't tell anyone,' he said, then shooshed her, then giggled. 'I'm a fucking awful policeman.' And suddenly it stopped being funny. But he was asleep before the guilt could really take hold.

* * *

'Well, isn't this *nice*,' said Insch, sipping from his delicate china cup, a Tunnocks caramel wafer balanced on his knee. Macintyre's house was gloomy, icy rain rattling the windows as Ashley, her mother-in-law to be, Logan and Insch took morning tea in the front room.

The footballer's mum sniffed and scowled at him over the top of her glasses. 'I resent your accusations, Inspector: My Robby was home.'

'No he wasn't.'

'I just said he was! You've no right to call me a liar in my own home! How dare you!'

Insch let her rant for a bit, before cutting her off in mid flow. 'Well, if you're telling the truth, why do we have CCTV footage of him driving your sister's car from Aberdeen to Dundee every night there was a rape down there?'

The inspector had his eyes fixed on the old woman, but Logan was watching Ashley – she'd dressed all in black today, the ruby pendant joined by a matching bracelet and pair of earrings, her make-up perfect – and as soon as Insch mentioned the rapes she flinched as if she'd been slapped. But she kept her mouth shut.

Macintyre's mum put her cup down and poked a finger at the fat man. 'You're the one who's lying.'

'Tayside police have identified your son from their cameras. He was there.'

'I don't speak to ugly, fat liars. I'm making a complaint.' She stood, and glowered down at the

474

inspector. 'You can't speak to me like this: my son's in a coma!'

'Let me just get this crystal clear,' said Insch, settling back into the couch with a smile, 'you're telling me Robert Macintyre was here all night, every time. Never went out.'

'I want you out of my house!'

'Is that what you're saying? That your son never took your sister's car to Dundee to rape women?'

'What's wrong with you? YES: my Robby's a good boy!'

'What about you, Ashley?'

'Tell him Ashley! You tell him Robby was here!'

Macintyre's fiancée stared Insch in the eye, but Logan could see her left leg trembling. 'Robert was here. With me. All night.'

'Excellent.' The inspector lurched to his feet. 'Then I'm arresting you both for conspiracy to pervert the course of justice. We'll continue this down the station.'

The swearing started when Insch pulled out the handcuffs.

'Christ,' Sergeant Eric Mitchell winced, standing in the corridor outside the women's cells, 'is she ever going to shut up?'

Logan shrugged, 'Who knows?' Macintyre's mum had kept it up all the way through her interview, shouting at them for being corrupt and incompetent and out to get her poor wee boy. 'Think she'll upset the muggers and shoplifters?'

'Fucking upsetting me.'

Back up in interview room number two, Rob Macintyre's fiancée was fidgeting in the suspect's chair. 'This thing's bolted to the floor . . .' she said, as Logan returned from the canteen bearing three big, wax-paper cups of fancy coffee. 'Did you know this chair's bolted to the floor?'

'It's for the junkies and murderers,' explained Insch, accepting his latte with extra cinnamon, nutmeg, chocolate and vanilla without so much as a thank you. 'In case they hurt themselves.'

'Oh . . .' She stared at the coffee Logan placed in front of her. 'I . . .'

The inspector gave her a chance to get the rest of the sentence out, but nothing came. 'OK, Ashley,' he said at last, 'we know you're lying about Macintyre's whereabouts. We've got proof. That means when you give him an alibi you're trying to pervert the course of justice. You can get seven, eight years for that. You're a pretty girl,' he said, taking a sip from his coffee, 'probably do well in prison. Some butch lesbian makes you her bitch and you won't have to worry about getting stabbed in the showers. The years will just fly by.' All said in a quiet, matter-of-fact voice.

'I . . . I've . . . Robert's a good man. He's done nothing wrong.' Wiping tears from her eye with the heel of her hand, smearing her mascara. 'I . . . I don't want to talk to you any more. I want to go home.' Breaking down completely on the last word.

Insch reached out and took her hand, but she jerked it back as if she'd been scalded, hiding it under the table, letting the tears fall unchecked on the tabletop. The inspector nodded sadly. 'It's OK, Ashley, I understand. It's hard. But if you talk to us, tell us where the car is, we can maybe do something about your sentence. We've got search teams out there already, we'll find it sooner or later, but if you help us we can help you.'

But all Ashley wanted to do was cry.

The dynamic duo – Rennie and Rickards – were in full flow, joking and laughing about last night's rehearsal, when Logan got back to the incident room. 'Of course,' said Rennie, checking his reflection in a lifeless computer monitor, 'Liz was all over me.'

Rickards grinned. 'In your dreams. She's married!'

'They're the best kind. Anyway, you were getting very pally with Debs.'

The constable shrugged, but Rennie slapped him on the back and called him a leather-clad studmuffin. Rickards blushed. 'She's very talented.'

'Only one of us who is. Don't break her heart for God's sake, we'd be buggered if she took the hump and left.'

'So . . .' said Logan, choosing his words carefully, 'Debs: she's a Rankin fan.'

Rickards froze, and that was all Logan needed

to know he'd been right: she was part of the BDSM scene.

'I saw the book in her handbag.'

'Oh.' The constable shifted uncomfortably in his seat. 'Not a problem, is it?'

'Not with me.'

'Good.'

He supposed it wasn't that surprising Insch's top star was into bondage – that Tina woman in Café Ici kept banging on about performing being like pulling on a second skin. Being something and someone you weren't. Just like wearing a full-body rubber suit. Which probably explained why Rickards was attracted to her. Logan wondered if that made her a top, or a bottom. Looking at the constable it was easy to see him as the spankee rather than the spanker, but you never knew.

He frowned, feeling the little wheels going round in his brain. 'Shite.' It was obvious when you thought about it.

'Sir?'

Logan grabbed the DVD of Jason's final performance and hurried from the room. There were a couple of things he needed to check, but he had a sinking feeling he knew what he'd find.

And DI Insch was *not* going to be happy about it.

50

'No.' The inspector scowled at the printouts Logan had spread across his desk. 'This is just a load of—'

'But if you look at the—'

'No: it's not her!'

'Look at the pictures! She's the same body shape as the woman in the bondage suit, she's in the scene – ask Rickards – and she's a switch, *exactly* what Fettes was advertising for. Plus she's new, inexperienced, likely to make mistakes.' It had taken some doing to get all that out of the constable without letting him know why, but eventually Rickards had spilled the beans.

'It's not her! You should be out there chasing up that search team, not in here wasting my bloody time!'

Logan shuffled through the images. 'Here – the e-fit of the driver, if you lose the moustache, glasses and goatee it looks just like her.' He'd cheated a bit on the second image, using the various *Mikado* posters Insch had stuck up all over the station for reference, making sure the new e-fit had Debbie Kerr's eyes and mouth: the resemblance was uncanny. 'There never was a second person, it was all her.'

Insch picked up both pictures and held them side by side. 'Her face is more heart-shaped. This isn't—'

'Remember the impersonation she does of you? She's a brilliant mimic, how hard would it be for her to slap on a fake moustache and Irish accent?'

'Don't be bloody . . .' Insch went silent, staring at the printout. 'It's a coincidence.'

'She even moves the same way – watch the video again and you'll see! You know she's a good enough actor to carry it off. They say BDSM lets people be someone else – someone without boundaries. That's what she does on stage, isn't it? Be someone else?'

The inspector sighed, screwed up his face and swore. Logan knew it seemed like a stretch, but he could feel it in his gut, between the scars: the amazing Debbie killed Jason Fettes. All he had to do now was prove it.

Logan grabbed a couple of uniforms and sent them off to do a background search on Deborah Kerr, hoping it would turn up some sort of history: drugs, violence, parking tickets – he wasn't fussy. And if they could find out where she might have taken Fettes that would be a bonus – friends' or relatives' houses, rented accommodation, holiday home, secret bondage dungeon – exactly the same thing they'd done with Frank Garvie before he killed himself.

And then he went to check up on Insch's search team.

The wind whistled through the granite streets, stealing the warmth from bundled-up bodies as they picked their way through Holburn, Ruthrieston and Mannofield, looking for the little red hatchback Rob Macintyre had taken on his jaunts south. 'Anything?' asked Logan, collar turned up, hands deep in his pockets as a large, shivering policeman slowly succumbed to hypothermia.

'Bugger all.' The sergeant cupped his hands and blew into them, ears and nose neon red. 'Bloody thing could be anywhere. If it was me, it'd be a burnt-out wreck somewhere out Ballater way by now, or at the bottom of a loch. We'd never find it.'

Which was pretty much what Logan was starting to think. And without the car they had no forensic evidence.

Four o'clock and they still hadn't found the hatchback, so he and Insch were back in interview room two with Rob Macintyre's fiancée. A day in the cells hadn't done her any favours – her make-up was smudged, mascara all down her face, her eyes red and watery, nose raw from wiping it on the sleeve of her black blouse, leaving little, glittering silver trails. Logan doubted she'd stopped crying since they'd questioned her that morning.

Insch didn't beat about the bush: 'Where's the car?'

Ashley shrugged, eyes down, picking the red varnish off her nails. 'Think Rob's auntie might have picked it up again'

'She lives in a nursing home in Ellon. She's in a wheelchair.' They'd checked.

Another shrug. 'Not my car.'

'Let's try something else then.' Logan opened the case file and started pulling photographs out, laying them one by one in front of Ashley. 'Christine, Gail, Sarah, Jennifer, Joanne, Sandra, Nikki, Jessica, Wendy. These are the before shots.' All smiling young women, making nice for the camera with their whole lives ahead of them and no idea what was coming. Looking at them all together like this, it was obvious that Macintyre was a predator of opportunity. None of his victims had anything in common, other than being young, attractive, and in the wrong place at the wrong time. 'Would you like to see what they looked like after your fiancé got hold of them?'

Ashley stared at him. 'My Robert didn't do anything.'

'Sarah Calder.' Logan laid the photograph taken when she'd got out of hospital on top of the smiling 'before' image. Dark hair, frightened eyes, bruised chin, her left cheek held together with black stitches: an inch and a half of raw, puckered flesh. 'She's twenty-three. Was getting married in April, but now she can't stand for her boyfriend to touch her.' He took the next pic out and placed it over another happy face. 'Jennifer Shepherd, she was second.' A deep-purple bruise stretched across her forehead, her nose swollen and misshapen where it had been rammed into the pavement, the mark of the knife curling from her left ear to the side of her mouth. 'She works with disabled children. On tranquillizers now, too scared to leave the house.' Then it was numbers three, and four, and five, and six, the violence and scarring getting worse every time. 'Christine killed herself: swallowed a pile of sleeping pills and painkillers, climbed into the bath and slit her wrists from here to here,' Logan took hold of Ashley's arm and demonstrated with the tip of his finger.

She yanked it back out of his grasp, rubbing at the skin as if it were infected. 'He didn't! I . . .'

'You gave him an alibi, Ashley: you lied for him. And he went out and he did *that*.' Pointing at the women. 'Every time you lied, another one got added to the list.'

He pulled out the first photo from the Dundee attacks. 'Nikki Bruce.' And as Logan went through the list Ashley got paler and paler, crying quietly, eyes wide and bloodshot. Rocking back and forth with an arm wrapped around herself, as if that would hold her world together.

He almost felt sorry for her.

Logan placed the last photo down, completing Rob Macintyre's mosaic of pain. Insch leant forward. 'What did it cost?' he asked, tapping the table with a fat finger. 'What did he give you to lie for him? New car? Jewellery? Don't tell me: you did it for love!' Logan's money was on jewellery, like that fancy gold and ruby necklace she'd been wearing the day they went round to interview Macintyre after the first Dundee rape. The one she played with whenever the attack was mentioned. Then there were the earrings and the bracelet. A brand-new, blood-red ruby for every woman her fiancé attacked.

Bottom lip trembling, she wiped the tears from her eyes with the heel of her hand. More welled up in their place. 'Why?'

'Why what?'

'Why are you doing this? He's in a coma, for God's sake!'

Insch's voice was like a dark rumble in the silence that followed. 'Can you not *see* the photographs? Do you think your boyfriend being in hospital makes it all better? That they don't wake up screaming in the dark, because of him? They deserve more than that.'

She jumped to her feet, eyes full of fire and tears. 'WHAT ABOUT ME? WHAT DO I DESERVE?'

Insch stood, looming over her. 'Right now you deserve five to eight years. You covered up for him and he ruined nine women's lives. You'll get out on parole in three, maybe four years, but they'll *never* stop suffering. And it's all your fault.'

By the time Logan finished off everything he needed to do, the day shift had been over for more than an hour. There was still no sign of the little red hatchback and no confession from Macintyre's mum or fiancée. And to make things worse, the team Logan had sent off to look into Debbie Kerr had come back with nothing more exciting than two outstanding parking tickets and a drunk and disorderly when she was eighteen. All in all it had been a crap day.

Logan switched off his computer, leant back in his chair and scowled at the ceiling tiles. Now he had to go home and deal with Jackie. Why the hell couldn't he have got involved with someone more *stable*? Someone like . . .'Fuck.' Rachael – the dinner invitation, something scary from Delia and wine. What was it, last night? The night before? He'd not even called her back to cancel, and now he couldn't even find his mobile to check the message again. 'Bloody, sodding, bastarding *fuck*.'

DI Insch thundered into the CID office, his voice making the walls shake, 'Where the hell have you been? I've been calling you for the last half hour.'

Logan pulled out his handset and checked it. 'It's not—'

'I've been calling you on your bloody mobile.' Insch turned and marched back towards the door.

'Well, come on then, get your backside in gear or we're going to be late for rehearsal.'

Oh Christ: not another night of Gilbert and bloody Sullivan. 'Actually, I'm going to give it a miss tonight, I—'

'No you bloody don't! This is all your stupid idea. And if I've got to question the only person in my entire cast with any talent, you're sodding well going to be there too!'

It might have been Logan's imagination but Insch's driving seemed to be getting worse the further they got from the station. Roaring out at junctions, leaning on the horn every two minutes to berate some motorist or pedestrian. Swearing a blue streak when an old lady dared to use the zebra crossing. So Logan kept his mouth shut and tried to remember what he'd done with his mobile phone. The damn thing had to be *somewhere*!

'Can you believe they've still not picked the bastard up?' said Insch, swinging onto Summer Street, 'Oh, they *say* they can't find Duff, but we all know the truth, don't we? They don't want to do any sodding work, so— LEARN TO BLOODY DRIVE!' The Range Rover's horn blared at a wee blue Mini Metro trying to turn right from Crimon Place. 'That bastard Finnie's asking for a punch in the teeth. Bloody drugs squad think they own the place . . .' The tirade dried up as Insch fought his huge car into a tiny parking space just up from the church hall. He clambered out into the chilly evening.

'You,' said Insch, poking Logan in the chest with a fat finger, 'are going to light a fire under uniform tomorrow – I want Jimmy Duff picked up. If Finnie isn't going to do his bloody job, we will!'

Inside the church hall it was chaos. Half of the inspector's acting crowd were in costume, the other half struggling to get dressed, everyone talking at once.

'Can we not just get the DCS to pull rank on him?' asked Logan as Insch settled his huge frame into a creaky plastic chair. 'Tell Finnie to get his finger out?'

'Bloody DCS wants the drug bust. According to him it takes precedence over some wee pervert who rented himself out to bondage freaks.' He turned to face his cast, pulled on a smile that reeked of false bonhomie, and said, 'Places everyone please – we're going all the way through tonight.'

The men scurried into position, freezing into oriental poses, holding paper fans and jars and plastic samurai swords. The ladies hung back against the hall's dingy walls, waiting for the chorus of schoolgirls and their chance to shine. Logan scanned their faces, trying to pick Debbie Kerr out. 'What about the CC?'

The piano lurched into the overture and Insch nodded. 'Got a meeting with him: half-eleven tomorrow morning.' The piano changed tune and suddenly all the posing figures came to life, chasing one another around the masking tape stage in shuffling steps.

And then they started to sing.

Logan watched a look of pain crawl across the inspector's face. It was going to be a long, long night.

51

Logan never wanted to see another Gilbert and Sullivan operetta as long as he lived. He'd not been a big fan to start with, but having to sit through Insch's production *yet again* was torture. Afterwards, when it was all over and the inspector had conducted his ritual post mortem, the gentlemen and ladies of Japan clambered out of their costumes and back into their heavy, winter jackets. Insch called his star performer over. 'Debs, you were brilliant. Loved *Bellow of the Blast*, gets better every time.' She flushed slightly, enjoying the compliment while she untangled her wavy brown hair from the severe bun she'd put it into to play the part. The inspector paused, shifted uncomfortably, cleared his throat. 'I need to ask you a couple of questions . . .' A gaggle of middle-aged women chattered by and Insch smiled at them, told them they'd all been great tonight, then led his star off into the corner and out of earshot.

Logan stayed where he was, watching as Insch

ejected Rickards from the prompting desk so he could settle one huge buttock on top of it while he talked to her. It didn't matter how obvious it was that Debbie Kerr had been involved in Fettes' death, the inspector refused point blank to do anything more formal than have a quick chat at rehearsal. Now that his best actor was a suspect, the fat man was a lot more inclined towards the 'unfortunate sexual adventure gone wrong' way of thinking. So much for 'Jason Fettes died in agony,' and 'we're going to treat this as a murder enquiry'. Hypocrite.

Rickards wandered over, hands in his pockets, looking back over his shoulder as the cast slowly drifted out through the door, heading for the pub. 'Wish I'd got here a couple of months sooner. I'd love to be on stage . . .'

'Uh huh.' Logan wasn't really listening, he was watching to see how Debbie Kerr reacted to Insch's questions. Right now she was shaking her head, arms folded across her chest, wearing a frown.

'I mean I know all the words and all that. I could probably pick up the moves easy enough.'

Insch was holding up his hands, making calming, placatory gestures.

'You think the DI would let me? Bit late in the day, I know, but—'

An angry: 'NO!' rang out across the hall and everyone froze, turning to stare at Insch and Debbie. 'What, just because I'm in the scene you think I'm guilty? You're questioning me because of my *sexuality*?'

The only person not watching the floorshow was Rickards, he was staring at Logan instead. 'Oh Jesus . . . oh, you didn't, did you?' His face went deathly pale. 'Please tell me you didn't!'

Logan shushed him.

The inspector said something, his voice too low to be heard from where they were, but Debbie's carried loud and clear. 'Who's next? You going to arrest all the homosexuals? Jews? Why not round up all the ethnic minorities while you're at it? You narrow-minded, pig-ignorant, fat *bastard*!' She turned and stormed off with the inspector hurrying after her. Pleading.

'Debs! I had to ask! It wasn't my idea; we just needed to eliminate you from our enquiries, we—'

'And you!' She marched straight up to Rickards and gave him a huge ringing slap across the face, nearly knocking him off his feet. 'I *trusted* you! Don't think I won't tell everyone what a shit you are, 'cos I will! You won't be able to put foot in a munch ever again!'

'But—' Rickards.

'Debs, if we can all just calm down—' Insch.

'Fuck the lot of you!' And she was on the go once more, the inspector trying to convince her he hadn't meant anything by it, all the way out of the hall.

He was back two minutes later, looking more

shocked than angry. 'She's quit the show . . .' He looked around at the remaining members of his cast. 'We . . .' he cleared his throat and tried again. 'Just a small misunderstanding. Nothing to worry about. It'll be fine.'

Rickards stood with one hand covering his cheek, a red weal already starting to bloom. 'She'll tell everyone! Oh God . . .'

'What about Fettes?'

Insch turned back to Logan, 'She wasn't even in the country that day – away at an IT conference in Bristol. With about half a dozen people from work . . .'

'I'll check it out tomorrow morning. She could still be—'

The inspector buried his face in his hands. 'Why the hell did I ever listen to you?'

Under the circumstances Logan decided to give the pub a miss. Insch's shock would wear off soon enough: then there would be recriminations and shouting. All directed at him.

The sound of something dreadful on television filtered out into the hall as he unlocked the flat's front door. That meant Jackie was home. Sighing, he peeled off his work clothes in the bathroom, then climbed into the shower without saying hello. She was through five minutes later, talking to him over the drone of the blow heater. 'Are you still sulking?'

'I'm not sulking.' Standing under the hot water and lying.

'Then what? You want a divorce? You're just trying to piss me off? Aliens stole your balls? What?'

He hung his head and closed his eyes. Trying to keep his voice neutral. 'Just had a bad day, OK?'

'You've been ignoring me all week! I left God knows how many messages on your bloody phone!'

And that's when Logan remembered where he'd left his mobile: charging in the CID offices. 'It's not working. I've been on an Airwave thing since yesterday.'

'That's not the point. You've not been around for days – you've been avoiding the flat, and don't bloody tell me you've not, because you have!'

'Jackie, I—'

'It's because of Macintyre isn't it?'

'I—'

'Not bad enough the little raping fuck attacks all those women, now he's—'

'Enough!' Logan stuck his head round the side of the shower curtain, water dripping onto the bathroom floor. 'OK? Enough. Leave it. I don't want to talk about—'

'No? Well I do! I'm not putting up with you dragging your pitiful arse round the whole time! Get—'

'YOU PUT HIM IN A COMA!' There was silence, just the dull drone of the heater and the spluttering shower. Logan sat on the edge of the bath, with his back against the cool tiles. 'You could have killed him. You made me an accessory after the fact and I'm on the bloody investigation! What am I supposed to do?'

She stared back at him through the cloud of steam. 'Did it ever occur to you that I didn't actually do it?'

'Oh come off it. You hated him. You come back, throw everything in the washing machine, ask me to lie and say you were here all night, and next morning he turns up battered so badly they don't know if he'll ever wake up. Look at your knuckles for God's sake, they're still bruised.'

Jackie held up her hands, turning them so Logan could see the dark purple patches. 'I got into a fight, OK? I was in a pub and some arsehole started going on about how the police should leave Macintyre alone 'cos he was a hero and we're all corrupt fuckwits and those women were asking for it. He threw something, it got nasty. I think I broke his chin . . .' Flexing her hands and wincing. 'I'm not proud of it, but I didn't want to get caught. They'd suspend me, or worse, and he started it! I'm not getting chucked off the force 'cos some slope-headed fuckwit wants to pick a fight.'

Logan looked at her, trying to work out if she was telling the truth or not, searching for the telltale signs, but there weren't any. If it was a lie it was a good one. 'So you never laid a hand on Macintyre?'

'I kicked him in the ribs when I arrested him,

yeah, kneed him in the balls, but I didn't put him in a bloody coma, OK? How could you think I would *do* something like that? I'm a police officer!'

'I . . .' Logan put his head in his hands. 'It's been a shite week.'

She nodded, slipped off her shoes and clambered into the bathtub with him, fully dressed, her shirt going transparent in the shower, revealing a hideous grey bra. 'Well,' she said, pulling him to his feet and stepping close, 'if you think I'm a dirty cop, you'd better give me a damn good wash.' And then there was kissing, full frontal nudity, and soap-on-a-rope.

Seven am Friday and there was no sign of Insch at the morning briefing, so Logan handed out the assignments, hurrying through them, hoping he could be done and out of there before the inspector arrived. Not believing his luck when he managed it.

It was too early to try breaking Deborah Kerr's alibi – the IT company she worked for didn't open its doors till nine according to their website – so that left Rob Macintyre's mother and fiancée.

Logan opted for the lesser of two evils.

It was strangely silent downstairs in the custody wing, just the muffled band-saw sound of someone snoring in one of the male cells, echoing down the short flight of concrete steps to where the women were kept. Ashley was looking rough, hair all skewed, dark bags under her pink eyes, grey face, scarlet nose. She'd obviously had a bad night, done a lot of soul searching and crying. She'd suffered. Which was exactly what Logan was hoping for. She sat upright on her blue plastic mattress, back ramrod straight, not looking at him as he stepped into the sour-smelling cell.

'So,' he said, settling down next to her, 'you had a think about what you saw yesterday?'

She wouldn't look at him. 'When I met Robert he was the coolest guy ever. Twenty years old and rolling in cash. The house, the cars, the clothes, foreign holidays . . .' She sniffed. 'Course he had his mum with him the whole time, wouldn't let him out of her sight. Strong woman. You know, emotionally? His dad died, and this is like six months after I started seeing Robert, and she didn't cry once. Like a rock. *And she liked me.* Said I wasn't like all those gold-digging bitches who tried to get their claws into him before. She hated them, but she was good to me. *He* was good to me.'

'But he changed, didn't he? Something happened.'

'We were going to have a family. Two boys and a girl.' She lifted her gaze from the wall to the thin window running along just beneath the roof. It was still dark outside, the etched glass milky grey. She sighed, one hand going to her tiny pregnant bump. 'Don't suppose that'll happen now.'

'Ashley, you don't have to lie for him any more. He can't hurt you.'

She turned and frowned at him. 'He *never* hurt

me. I'd've broken his bloody nose for him if he'd tried. And his mum would've had his balls!'

Logan took her hand and stared into her bloodshot eyes. Trying again: 'Think about what you saw yesterday. All those women. You—'

'Oh I've been thinking a lot.' And she smiled. It was like watching a wound tear open. 'I'm going to court at four today for this perverting justice crap you're trying to pin on me. I'm going to tell them how Robert was a perfect gentleman and you're all bastards. Then I'm going to talk to that lawyer who got Robert off and sue you fuckers for every penny you've got.'

He let go of her hand and stood. 'You do that. It'll be something to keep you busy when you're in prison.' And she actually laughed.

'I'm pregnant, you idiot. They don't send pregnant women to jail. You've got nothing – no evidence, no witnesses, nothing. Because my Robert's innocent!'

Mrs Macintyre had fared a lot better than her son's fiancée. They'd put the old woman in a cell on the floor above, at the far end of the corridor, one of two that could be segregated from the rest of the detention area by a set of black, metal bars. She was lying flat on her back, fully dressed, staring up at the advert for Crimestoppers painted on the ceiling. 'Shame,' said Logan, leaning back against the wall, 'you'd've thought she'd be tougher than that.'

Macintyre's mum didn't bother getting up. 'What do you want now?'

'Ashley: one night in the cells and she's telling me all sorts of interesting things about Wee Robby Macintyre.'

'Your mother never wash your mouth out for tellin' lies? She peeled open an eye and glowered at him. 'Our Ashley's a good quine. She's no' said a thing, 'cos there's nothin' to say.'

'Coma or not, we're going to prosecute him. Everyone's going to know what your boy did. She's given us more than enough to—'

'I will not stand for lies!'

'—make sure that if he ever wakes up, he'll be going straight to jail for thirty years to life—'

'You're nothing but filth!' Macintyre's mum bustled to her feet and marched across the dark green terrazzo floor till she was standing right in front of him.

'—with all the other perverts and rapists and paedophiles—'

She spat in his face.

52

There was still no sign of Insch, but it didn't make Logan feel any better: whatever the inspector was up to, it just postponed the bollocking he was going to get for last night's fiasco. So when Colin Miller called it was all the excuse he needed to get the hell out of FHQ.

A cold wind whipped through the streets, the sky opaque and milky-grey as Logan drove up Schoolhill, making for the maternity hospital. A crowd of nervous fathers-to-be and knackered fathers-already-been clustered just around the corner from the hospital doors, smoking. Miller was on the outskirts, yawning his head off, a cigarette cupped in his hand as if he was trying to hide it. He barely looked at Logan, took one last drag and dropped the butt, grinding it into the concrete with his foot. 'Here.' The reporter pulled a thick envelope from his pocket and handed it over.

'What's this?'

'Read it.'

Inside were about two dozen bank statements belonging to Frank Garvie. 'How did you—'

'I didn't. Whoever you got them from it wasnae me.'

Logan flicked through the sheets. Most of Garvie's purchases were online, bits of electronic equipment and gadgets. 'What am I supposed to be looking . . .' He frowned – there was a payment into Garvie's account every month marked BACS, that would be his salary, but there were others, cheques coming in at regular intervals.

Miller unwrapped a packet of extra strong mints and stuffed three in his mouth: crunching. 'Bloke rents out encrypted server space.'

'Did you—'

'No idea what you're talkin' about.' And the reporter marched back through the doors into the maternity hospital.

Logan called Force Headquarters, looking for Insch, even though he *really* didn't want to speak to him. Voicemail. He left a vague message and tried DI Steel instead. *'Don't care.'* Then there was a chest-rattling cough and some swearing. *'Better off when I was bloody smoking . . . Garvie's no' getting any less dead, is he? And I've got whoever battered Rob Bastarding Macintyre to worry about: search teams are a waste of bloody time, door-to-doors are useless and everyone who says they left the nightclub with the wee footballing shite can't remember a thing. Blootered out their faces. And the CC's getting right up my . . .'* she went on for a bit, but Logan had stopped listening. He was scribbling down the cheque numbers paid into Garvie's account. When she finally hung up, he crossed his fingers and dialled the PF's office, hoping to get anyone other than Rachael.

He wasn't lucky. There was an awkward pause, then she said, *'You didn't call.'*

Bollocks. He wandered away from the maternity ward, heading back to where he'd parked as the first spits of rain put a dull sheen on the ranks of cars. 'I'm sorry. It's been . . . Macintyre and Fettes and . . .' And he was a spineless bastard who should have phoned up and cancelled.

'Boeuf bourguignon. I had to throw half of it out.'

Idiot, idiot, idiot, idiot. 'I'm really, really sorry.'

Another pause. Then a sigh. *'I've never gone out with a policeman before. Is this what it's like? Never knowing if you'll be there or not?'*

Logan closed his eyes and tried not to think about where this was leading. 'Pretty much, yeah.' Tell her. 'I—'

'What do—' She stopped. *'You first.'*

'I . . .' TELL HER! 'I need to ID some people from their cheque numbers.'

He drove back to FHQ, cursing himself all the way. Rachael had forgiven him for not turning up and promised to get back to him as soon as she'd got a warrant together, so now he felt doubly guilty . . .

The incident room was quiet, just a single uniformed constable, dribbling information into HOLMES as it came in. Apparently the hunt for Rob Macintyre's little red hatchback was running out of steam, they'd searched every street in a two-mile radius from the footballer's house and come up empty. The question was: how did Macintyre's mum know to get rid of the damn thing? His fiancée had given a pretty convincing performance this morning, as if she *genuinely* didn't know what her beloved was up to – or didn't want to believe it – that left the boot-faced old cow who'd been lying for Robert since the day he was born. It wasn't hard to see her brow-beating Ashley until she toed the party line: *'Yes officer, Robert was with me all night.'*

Ashley was the weak link. There had to be a way to break her.

He was still trying to figure out how when Insch stormed into the incident room looking about ready to burst – scarlet, puffy face, gritted teeth, angry, piggy eyes. Logan scrambled to his feet. Here it came.

'Well, don't just stand there: get your coat!'

'But . . . Garvie: I'm waiting on—'

'NOW!'

Logan grabbed his jacket and followed in the huge man's wake as he thundered out of the room and down the stairs. Sergeant Eric Mitchell was halfway out of his seat as they marched past, then he caught the expression on Insch's face and sat right down again, keeping his mouth shut.

All the way through the building and out to the rear podium car park, constables, sergeants, ancillary staff and inspectors got the hell out of the huge man's way. He marched up to his filthy Range Rover, plipped the locks, then threw the keys to Logan. 'You're driving.'

There was a brand new Magic Tree air freshener hanging from the rear-view mirror. 'Where to?'

'Can you believe that bastard Finnie? How the hell he *ever* got to be a bloody DI . . .' Insch went hunting in the glove compartment, coming out with a tiny packet of Jelly Tots, shoving them in his mouth one at a time. 'You'd think we were all supposed to be on the same side: solve crime, keep the streets safe, put bloody crooks away. But not Finnie, *no* he has to be the *big* man.'

Logan knew better than to ask. Instead he started the inspector's car and pointed it in the direction of Mastrick, already having a pretty shrewd idea where the fat man's rant was heading.

'Where does he get off telling the DCS to cancel my lookout request? Not in the interests of his ongoing investigation, my arse!' Insch threw the last little disk in his mouth and crushed the packet in his huge fist. 'When I get my hands on him I'll . . .' The words stopped coming, but the inspector went on trembling with rage, breathing in and out through his nose, doing his calming-down exercises again. It was getting more alarming every time Logan saw it. Never mind thirteen stone, at this rate Insch would be dead long before he lost any of it. 'Right,' said the fat man, when he was finally back to a nearly normal shade of pink, 'we're looking for Jimmy Duff, so get your backside . . .' he trailed off as Logan pulled up to the kerb, directly opposite the address Ma Stewart had taken them to last time. Where Jimmy Duff was supposed to live. 'Oh . . . right.'

Logan went to unclip his seatbelt, but Insch's huge hand covered his own. Holding it in place. 'Well?'

Here it came. 'I called her work this morning, then I checked with the hotel and convention centre in Bristol, and the airport, and—'

'*Today*, Sergeant!'

'Her alibi looks sound, sir. Sorry.'

Insch nodded, but didn't let go of Logan's hand. Instead he increased the pressure slightly, until Logan's bones started to groan. 'You mean to tell me I pissed off the only person in my entire cast who was any bloody good because you got it *wrong*?' The pressure increased again. Now it was actively painful.

'Ah . . . yes, sir, sorry, sir!' Logan tried to make his hand go limp, before Insch squeezed the life out of it. 'Do you think you could—'

'If I can't get her back, Sergeant, I'm going to have your bollocks on a plate. Are we crystal clear on that?' And all the time the inspector's voice never rose above a polite conversational level, his face didn't even go red as he threatened Logan. Which somehow made it even worse.

'Yes, sir!'

'Good.' He let go, then clambered out into the sunny morning, leaving Logan to lock the car. As soon as the fat man's feet hit the pavement his phone started to ring – *Behold the Lord High Executioner* sounding in the cold morning air. He switched it off.

Then the Airwave handset in Logan's pocket started bleeping at him. 'McRae.' He flexed his fingers, trying to get some life back into them as he followed Insch up the path to the front door.

'What the fuck is wrong *with you?'*

Logan pulled the thing away from his ear and frowned at the illuminated display, looking to see if he recognized the caller's badge number, as the voice on the other end went into a full-blown rant about teamwork and loyalty and what would happen to them if they didn't turn round and get the hell away from that bloody house!

'Sir,' he said, tapping Insch on the shoulder before the big man could start pounding on the front door, 'I think it's for you.'

Insch took the handset and mashed the off button with a huge thumb, passed it back, then started knocking so hard it felt as if the whole front of the house was vibrating. 'OPEN UP!'

Logan closed his eyes and swore quietly to himself – the inspector might not give a toss about his own career, but Logan *really* didn't want to get hauled up in front of Professional Standards yet again.

Finally the door opened a crack and a sliver of face peered out at them. 'What?' Not a local accent, somewhere between Manchester and Liverpool.

'Jimmy Duff.'

'Do I look like a fucking haggis-muncher?'

'Where is he?'

'How should I know?'

Insch pulled a sheet of paper from his inside pocket. 'I've got a warrant here for his arrest. You can hand him over, or I can force entry and have a good look round. Up to you.'

'Hold on.' The face disappeared and the door closed. Two minutes later it opened again, and a battered and dazed figure was unceremoniously thrust out into the sunshine: tall, brown hair, side-burns, but the nose wasn't just squint any more: it'd been flattened. Dried blood outlined the nostrils in crumbling black; mouth and cheeks swollen; bruises hiding the man's natural pallor. Duff's right leg was encased in fresh plaster, and so was his left arm, all the fingers splinted together on that hand. Someone had given him a proper going over, but Jimmy Duff felt no pain.

He stood, wobbling on the top step, pupils constricted to tiny black pinpricks. Insch grabbed him by the collar, dragged him back to the Range Rover, and climbed in after him, shouting at Logan to get a bloody move on.

Sighing, Logan climbed in behind the wheel. This would all end in tears, he just knew it.

* * *

DI Steel was standing outside interview room one when Logan came back from the canteen with a tray of black coffees. 'You know the DCS is going mental, don't you?'

Logan groaned. 'Don't look at me, I'm—'

'You've got about half an hour before it all hits the fan.' She sniffed, then nodded her head at the interview-room door. 'Going to get a confession by then?'

'Doubt it: Duff's smacked off his tits.'

The inspector nodded sagely. 'Right, well, let me know when he's back *on* his tits again. If we're lucky they'll have suspended DI Fat And Grumpy by then and we can all get on with our lives.' She tipped him a wink, then helped herself to one of his coffees, said, 'Cheers,' and wandered off.

Through in the interview room, Insch was wasting his time. There was no way Jimmy Duff was going to say anything coherent in the state he was in, and whatever he *did* say wasn't going to be admissible in court.

Duff rocked back and forth in his seat, clutching his broken arm to his chest, trembling and sweating, mumbling about the walls being too loud while the inspector kept hammering on about Jason Fettes. Not surprisingly, four black coffees did nothing to straighten Duff out, they just made him twitch faster.

Steel had underestimated the Detective Chief Superintendent – it was only twelve minutes before the knock came on the interview-room door and the DCS barged in without waiting for a reply. 'DI Insch,' he said, voice like a sharpened knife, hooking his thumb over his shoulder at the corridor outside, 'suspend your interview and join me out here, please. *Now.*'

When the door was closed, Logan sat back in his seat and swore. Insch had really done it this time. The head of CID had looked apoplectic. DI Finnie would be screaming blue murder about his operation being ruined, and all so they could drag a doped-up halfwit in to drink coffee, twitch, and complain about the décor trying to kill him.

Jimmy Duff leaned across the table, his one good hand scratching at the Formica, as if it was itchy, and stared Logan straight in the eye. 'I wanted to be a fireman.'

Yesterday it had been Macintyre's mother shouting the odds in the cell block: today it was Jimmy Duff, screaming about snakes and policemen made of broken glass. Logan left him to it. There was some sort of 'who can tell the filthiest anecdote' competition going on in the CID office, with DI Steel adjudicating: giving points for originality, creativity, and pure smut. Which probably meant she was avoiding paperwork and Logan would be lumbered with it instead.

DS Beattie was in the middle of his 'two pokes of chips for a blowjob' story when a familiar poly-phonic ring tone sounded in the room. Groans of 'Not a-bloody-gain!' and everyone patted their pockets, pulling out various phones and declaring it not to be them. It took Logan nearly eight rings to find his mobile, buried in the nest of wires, plugs and rechargers piled up on the desk by the window. 'McRae.'

'*Logan, hi.*' It was Rachel. '*I've been onto the bank's legal people. Took some doing, but they've come back with names. I can email them?*'

'Please.' He wandered over to the window, looking down on the rear podium car park, watching a pair of seagulls fighting over what looked like a discarded sandwich as she read out a list of names. A large, familiar figure burst out of the rear door, stormed across to a filth-encrusted Range Rover and threw itself in behind the steering wheel. Logan could actually hear the squeal of tyres through the double glazing as DI Insch put his foot down and roared out of the parking lot, nearly flattening a couple of uniforms enjoying a cigarette in the small square of sunlight at the top of the ramp down to Queen Street. The pair stood in the middle of the road, watching the inspector's car long after it had disappeared from Logan's line of sight. Then, shaking their heads, they went back to their fags.

'*. . . OK?*'

'Mmm? Oh, yes, sure.' He'd not been able to see from this distance, but Logan was pretty sure Insch's face would have been a bright, scary purple.

'*Good. Oh buggering hell, that's my other line. Don't forget: seven sharp!*'

Fuck! 'Wait – seven? What's . . .' But she was already gone. Logan pulled the dead phone from his ear and stared at it, horrified.

'You look like someone's hidden a jobbie in your sock.' DI Steel stood right behind him, one hand hauling her trousers up, nearly under her armpits. 'Better watch that: the wind might change and you'll end up with a face like Fat Boy Insch.' She nodded her head in the direction of the corridor. 'Speaking of whom: my office, five minutes. Bring tea and bacon butties. I'm wasting away here.'

53

Logan sat in the inspector's spare chair fidgeting, distracted, wondering what the hell he'd just agreed to do at seven tonight with the Deputy Procurator Fiscal. Steel's news was . . . mixed. DI Insch might be a huge pain in the neck right now, but you couldn't deny that he put a lot of people behind bars.

'Two weeks?' asked Logan as Steel wiped a blob of tomato sauce from her chin.

'Yup. CC didn't think a slap on the wrist covered it this time. Who knows: maybe he'll come back a better person? But my money's on an even grumpier fuck than usual. And in the meantime, guess who has to carry his bloody caseload?' She stuck a hand up, just in case Logan had lost all grasp of irony. 'And guess who gets to help me?'

Logan groaned and Steel snorted, cramming the last chunk of buttie into her mouth and chewing round the words, 'Don't know what you're whinging about: I've got all Jinx McPherson's cases too.' She dug about in her in-tray, retrieving a manila folder and throwing it across the desk to Logan, then went hunting through her drawers. 'You read. I want to know what I've been stuck with.'

So Logan opened the folder and read through a summary of Insch's caseload, with Steel stopping him every now and then to ask questions. But most of the time she just said, 'Nope, you can have that one too,' while she fought her way into a new packet of nicotine patches. The only investigations she seemed even remotely interested in were Jason Fettes and Rob Macintyre.

'If we can get Macintyre on the rapes,' she said, rolling up her sleeve, exposing a length of pasty-white skin, 'maybe the press'll forget all about him being in a coma and the CC will get off my back for not catching whatever public-spirited citizen kicked the crap out the wee shite.' She slapped another patch in place, then peered at the packet. 'Meantime you better go poke the IB – got to be something we can use from those bushes we found him in: fibre, fingerprints, DNA, ouija boards, I'm no' fussy . . . Fuck, can you believe I've got to wait another four hours before the next one?'

'Jason Fettes.' Logan held up the report. 'Duff's still out of his face, but I—'

'Still?' Steel checked her watch. 'Jesus, that's no' bad goin'. Better get on to the court: slide him back to last call tomorrow, or he'll be out before he's straight enough to interview.'

'I've also got a lead on Frank Garvie, he was the one who—'

'Ex-porn star, dodgy secret computer stuff, hung himself. Believe it or not I *was* actually paying attention. You deal with it, I'm up to my ears as it is and I'm no' needing any more shite shovelled on the top.' She waved a hand at the pile of case notes. 'Palm as much off as you can: got a whole CID department to choose from, but Rennie'll do in a pinch. Do him good to get the hell away from me before I kill him.'

Logan gathered up DI Insch's cases and slid them back in the folder, trying not to sigh. 'Yes, ma'am.'

'And don't sulk. We're two DIs down: this could be your chance to shine, sparkle, stand out from the crowd. Long as you don't fuck things up . . .'

His fellow CID officers whinged and complained but eventually Logan managed to palm off all the cases Steel didn't want, then printed off the email from Rachael, hoping there would be some clue about seven o'clock tonight. There wasn't. Instead he had a list of names of people who'd paid money into Frank Garvie's bank account on a regular basis. He was willing to bet this was only the tip of the iceberg – anyone with an ounce of sense would have paid Garvie in cash, making sure there was nothing leading back to them if anything went wrong.

But some people just weren't that bright. Like Kevin Massie: forty-five, tall, hair like a loo brush and hands like a child molester. Which was why he was on Grampian Police's register of Sex Offenders.

The house was immaculate, not a speck of dust to be seen in the two-bedroom semi-detached in Northfield. According to his social workers Kevin Massie had been a good boy ever since he'd been let out of Peterhead Prison three and a half years ago. He'd done all the S.T.O.P. courses, was in therapy, didn't associate with anyone dodgy, and followed his supervisory order to the letter. He was about as cured as anyone convicted for molesting their seven-year-old nephew could be.

Logan sent Rickards off to make the tea while he, Kevin Massie and his social worker sat in the lounge, listening to the pop-click of the gas fire. Kevin sat on the couch, knees clamped firmly together, wringing those small, sweaty hands of his, smiling. 'So,' he said, filling the silence, pointing at the grey-haired woman sitting opposite. 'Laura said you wanted to speak to me?' Logan didn't even nod. Kevin cleared his throat, looked up at the framed print above his fireplace, then down at his hands. Coughed. 'I . . . yes, well, I've been doing good. I got a job with a little accountancy firm in Dyce, it's nice . . .' More silence. 'Er . . . do you fancy our chances this weekend? It's only Dundee, but with Rob Macintyre gone we—'

'Frank Garvie.'

Kevin licked his lips, and the hand-rubbing intensified, squeezing all colour from the pink knuckles. 'I was saying to Laura that the Dons really have to pull their socks up if we're going to get to the finals—'

'You rented encrypted server space from him.'

'I . . . we . . .' He looked at his social worker, pulling on a sickly smile. 'We like the football, don't we?'

Her face didn't move. 'You need to tell Sergeant McRae what happened, Kevin.'

'Ah, well . . . it was . . .'

Logan leant forward. 'Garvie was in receipt of stolen goods: that makes him a criminal and you've been associating with him. That's against your supervision order.'

'I . . .' Kevin jumped to his feet as Rickards came in, carrying four mugs of tea. 'I . . . biscuits! I'm sure I've got biscuits somewhere.'

His social worker sighed, and covered her face with her hands. 'God, Kevin, we talked about this! You can't hang out with people who break the law, or you'll end up back inside. Do you *want* to go back to Peterhead?'

The little hands fluttered. 'I'm sorry.' He stared at the carpet. 'I didn't mean . . . it wasn't . . . I didn't want to do anything, I didn't! I wanted to . . .' he trailed off and wiped at his face. 'It's hot in here, isn't it? I'll turn down the fire.'

'KEVIN!'

He flinched, wrapped his pink, shiny fingers

into a knot and led them through into the spare bedroom. It had been turned into a small study: a cheap-looking flat-pack computer desk against the wall beneath the window, the walls covered in pink wallpaper with a silver stripe and little red roses. A laptop sat in the middle of the desk, perfectly aligned with the edges. 'I . . . I didn't want to touch anyone.' He shuddered. 'I want to be better. I don't want . . .'

The social worker pulled on a professional smile: understanding, sympathetic and brittle. 'It's OK, Kevin. You can just show us if you don't want to talk about it.'

And so Kevin did, booting up his laptop and navigating to a folder on his desktop. Clicking on a file and getting a screed of gibberish. He pulled a memory stick from the desk – a shiny red USB thing no bigger than Logan's little finger – and plugged it into the side, before calling up the decryption programme.

It was a movie file. A little blond boy, no more than eight years old, standing with his back to the camera, stripped down to his underwear. The social worker sighed again. 'Kevin . . .'

'I'm sorry. I'm sorry. I didn't touch anyone! I didn't . . . but I *need* . . .'

A hand fell on the boy's shoulder, he turned to look back at the camera, eyes full of tears. And Logan said, 'Oh fuck.' It was Sean Morrison. The hand turned the boy round till he was facing sideways, then the man stepped forwards, visible and naked from the waist down, a puckered line of scar tissue running from his thigh to his knee, between the grey hairs. Murmured, soothing noises echoed out from the laptop's tinny speakers. *'Shhh, shhh, there's a good boy . . .'* Sean stared at the camera, terrified, and then . . . Logan turned away. He'd seen enough.

It took a lot of effort not to smash his fist into Kevin Massie's throat as he burbled on about how he'd never touched anyone, he only watched the video, and it was all his uncle's fault he'd turned out this way, and he didn't want to go back to prison.

'Good boy, such a good boy . . . Oh what a good boy . . .'

Logan told Rickards to turn it off.

'My good boy . . . Oh Craig . . .' Click. Silence.

Mid-afternoon and the rain was drumming down from a lead-grey sky. The road glistened, reflecting back the rotating blue and white lights from Alpha Two Seven as Logan climbed out of his pool car and into the downpour. Hamilton Place was quiet – there was no sign of the Whytes' people carrier.

'You bring the warrant?' he asked and Rennie nodded, digging it out of his jacket pocket and handing it over. Logan checked to make sure it was all signed in the right places before marching up to the front door and pounding on it like DI Insch. No response.

'Maybe they're not in?'

Logan tried again, waited, then marched round to the back of the house, Rennie and Rickards trotting along behind him. A small radio was playing in the shed at the bottom of the garden, the Rolling Stones' (*I Can't Get No*) *Satisfaction* mingling with the rain. Someone sang along, slightly off key. Mr Whyte Senior had a hand-rolled cigarette sticking out of the side of his mouth as he worked a chisel back and forth on an oil stone, pausing every now and then to check for sharpness. He looked up and smiled as Logan stopped just outside the shed. 'Sergeant McRae, how are you? Anything I can do to help?'

'I want to see your leg.'

The old man raised an eyebrow and ground his cigarette out on a china saucer. 'On a first date? What kind of—'

'This isn't a joke.' Logan held up the warrant. 'I'm detaining you on suspicion of child abuse.'

'Surely there's been some mistake. I would never touch a child. It's repulsive—'

'You remember Sean Morrison, Mr Whyte? Remember how much he looks like Craig? Your wee boy? The one who ended up killing himself? Because of what you did?'

Whyte looked down at the chisel in his hand, then back up at Logan. 'I'm not listening to this any longer.' He tightened his grip on the handle. 'I want you off our property.'

'What did you do, play the surrogate granddad?

You're about the same age. He's worried about his grandfather and you took advantage—'

'If you don't leave, I won't be held responsible for my actions.' He stepped forwards, the chisel weaving back and forth like the head of a snake. 'Get out of my garden. Now.'

'And you were stupid enough to video it!'

'Lies!' Whyte's face darkened. 'You've no business being here!'

'We found it this morning. You abused an eight-year-old boy and you videotaped yourself doing it, you moron. The old sporting injury.' Logan pointed at the man's leg. 'We're going to match your scar to the one in the film and then I'm going to lock you up where you can't—'

'I've done nothing wrong!' The words came out in a small shower of brown spittle. 'You get out of here, NOW!' Another step forward, weak sunlight glinting on the chisel's freshly sharpened edge.

Logan pulled out a canister of pepper spray and levelled it at Whyte's face. 'Put the weapon down and step out of the shed.'

Whyte's eyes darted over Logan's shoulder, to where Rennie and Rickards stood. No way out. He looked at the canister in Logan's hand, then dropped the chisel. It fell end over end, landing point down and burying itself in the sodden grass. 'I want a lawyer, I—'

Logan sprayed the old man in the eyes. He screamed even louder than Sean Morrison had.

54

'Fuck's sake.' DI Steel sat at her desk reading Logan's report. 'And he'd no idea Garvie was floggin' the video to other kiddie fiddlin' bastards?'

'We don't even know if he was. Kevin Massie's come over all repentant now he's looking at another stretch in Peterhead – says there were five or six of them, sharing homemade videos and pictures, and stuff they got off the internet. They encrypt it, so only they can see it, and upload it to Garvie's server. Massie *claims* he never knew who the other members were: no one ever used their real names, so he can't finger them.'

'That's convenient.'

'Whyte's not saying anything, but the scar on his leg matches the one in the video. So he's screwed anyway.'

Steel nodded sagely. 'See! I told you there was more to this Sean Morrison thing than met the eye.'

Logan didn't bother answering that – DI Steel's selective memory strikes again – instead he slouched in his chair and stared out of the nicotine-filmed window. 'The IB've tried the encryption key we found at Daniel Whyte's place on Garvie's servers.'

The inspector's face lit up, all the wrinkles looking excited. 'Aye?'

'Twenty video clips, that's it. It won't decrypt any of the other files. There's still thousands and thousands we can't get into.'

'Oh . . .' The excitement evaporated and Steel's face fell back into its usual leathery sag. 'Ah well, win some, lose some. Get all the other fuckwits who paid Garvie by cheque hauled in and we'll give them a hard time. Meantime,' she leant back in her chair, swivelling back and forth, 'I had to cancel the search for Macintyre's rapemobile. Fuckin' thing's nowhere to be seen and the DCS's been banging his gums about the overtime bill. Apparently,' she put on a Banff and Buchan Teuchter drawl, 'DI Finnee's operation taks precedence.' She scowled. 'Glory-hogging bastard. And see if you can get us some tea, eh? I'm gaspin' here.'

Twenty past four and Logan was staring at the phone, debating the merits of calling Rachael Tulloch back and making up some excuse to cancel whatever he was supposed to be doing with her tonight. A large shadow loomed over him and he flinched, expecting to see DI Insch's furious purple face. But it was just Big Gary with a pile of incident reports in one hand and a mug of tea in the other, a rowie clamped between his teeth. 'Mmmwow, gowfffmmm mounnsmmmph.'

Logan just stared at him, so Gary took the cowpat-shaped roll out of his mouth and tried again. 'Don't tell Watson, but your girlfriend's outside.'

'What?' How the hell did Gary find out about Rachael? And if Gary knew, it would be all over the station in a matter of minutes. Jackie would have his balls for earrings!

'Ashley is it? Macintyre's bint – she's out front telling everyone what a bunch of shites we are. Only got out of court five minutes ago and she's already giving bloody press conferences.'

Thank God for that. 'Oh.'

'Here,' Gary said, dumping half of the incident reports on Logan's desk, 'Steel says you're in charge of these.' He took a big bite of rowie, and lumbered off.

Logan took one look at the pile of paperwork and decided he really couldn't be bothered. He grabbed his coat and left the building instead: he had a sudden masochistic urge to hear what lies Macintyre's fiancée was coming out with now.

The camera crews were packing up as he pushed through the front doors. Rickards was standing on the top step, watching the woman from Sky News doing a piece to camera. The welt on his cheek where Debbie slapped him had faded overnight, leaving nothing more than a pitiful, skelped-arse look. He gave a big puppy-dog sigh as Logan stopped beside him.

'Well, what did Macintyre's fiancée say?'

Rickards shrugged. 'The usual.'

Logan scanned the dispersing crowds, looking for Ashley's telltale brassy blonde hair. She was climbing into a taxi with Macintyre's mother. 'If you were . . .' he frowned, watching as it pulled away. All that time they'd spent searching the city for the missing little red hatchback, when everyone knew the car would be a burnt-out hulk by now, dumped in the middle of nowhere, miles from civilization. But what if everyone was wrong? He grabbed Rickards. 'Go: get a pool car, now!'

As the constable scurried off, Logan pulled out his mobile and called the inspector in charge of the CCTV room, telling him to get his cameras tracking the Rainbow taxi currently turning right onto Broad Street. 'And I need backup – a couple of—'

'Aye, right, Finnie's got a big drug bust going on; every bugger's off playing Miami Vice. They've no one spare. Tell you, I had a gang of shoplifters . . .' He was still moaning two minutes later when Rickards puttered up in front of the station in a fusty old Vauxhall that smelled of armpits.

Logan jumped in the passenger seat. 'What the hell took you so long?'

'It was—'

'Well, get a shift on! Out, left on Broad Street . . .' he held the phone to his ear again, 'School-hill . . .'

Rickards put his foot down and the scabby car lurched out onto the road, pausing at the junction to let a huge bendy bus hiss and judder past. The constable strained forward in his seat, looking for a gap in the traffic. 'I don't get it: why are we—'

'They've just got out of court, they're charged with perverting the course of justice, they know the only way we're going to prove Rob Bloody Macintyre's guilty is if we find that little red hatchback. No car: no forensic. No forensic: no conviction. If you were them, what would you do?'

'Oh.'

'Exactly.' They followed the trail of CCTV cameras, Logan relaying instructions as Rickards did his best to catch up with Macintyre's nearest and dearest.

'There!' Logan jabbed a finger at the windscreen – the taxi was at the head of a queue of traffic, waiting for the lights to turn green and let them out onto Union Street. Red, amber . . . and they were off, trailing more than a dozen cars behind. A taxi ahead of them jerked to a halt as a pissed teenager lurched out on to the road, swinging her arms and singing incoherently for the benefit of her equally drunk friends. A sudden braying of horns, some swearing, threats and the vomit-spattered girl staggered back to the kerb, giggling.

The traffic started moving again, just in time for the lights to do their slow parade back to red.

Rickards snapped on the siren, the noise wailing out into the rain-speckled afternoon, but nothing happened. The cars were too tightly packed on Chapel Street to get out of their way. By the time the lights were green again the taxi was nowhere to be seen. Logan got an update from the CCTV team and Rickards floored it, siren blaring, nipping between cars and buses as they pulled over to let them past, traumatizing an old lady with a shopping trolley halfway across a pelican crossing on Union Grove.

Logan grabbed the dashboard as the constable slammed on the brakes, trying not to make OAP pâté. 'Switch it off!'

'Eh?'

'The siren, you idiot – switch it off! If they hear us coming they're not going to lead us to the car, are they?'

Rickards did as he was told.

The pasty-faced old woman hobbled out of the way, clutching her chest as Logan checked in with the CCTV team again. They were screwed: the taxi had disappeared off the network. Wherever the car was, they'd run out of camera coverage. 'Fuck!' Logan slammed his hand off the dashboard.

Rickards cringed. 'It wasn't my fault!'

Ignoring him, Logan punched the number for Rainbow Taxis into his mobile and listened to it ring. 'Come on, come on—' Someone picked up at the other end. He cut them off before they could get into the whole introductory spiel. 'You had a pick-up from Queen Street – the police station – ten minutes ago. Where's it going?'

'I'm sorry, I can't give out that kind of information over the phone—'

'Fine: you call Grampian Police and you tell them where that taxi's going. OK? You tell them that DS McRae needs to know urgently.'

'Well . . . we—'

'Urgently!'

The woman on the other end said she'd do her best.

His phone went not long after – Control with the address from the taxi firm. It was Rob Macintyre's house. Logan swore. So much for that theory. *'Aye, they say the driver dropped the mother off, then took the younger one to another address.'*

'Where? Where did he take her?'

'You're sure it was here?' said Logan, looking around the flat, featureless car park, sitting in the shadow of a tower block on the outskirts of Kittybrewster. The wind was picking up again, sending an empty polystyrene carton bouncing across the damp concrete.

'Aye.' The taxi driver pointed a stubby finger at the far corner, where a ragged opening punctured the chain-link fence. 'Dropped her right here an' she tottered off ower there wie her box.' He sniffed, looked up at the cold, blue sky, and said, 'Nae bad weather for a change, eh?'

'Box? What box?'

A shrug. 'No idea. The mother goes intae the house and comes out with this cardboard box and gives it to the blonde bit in the back. Tells me to drive her here.'

The box – Macintyre's trophies, the ones the search team couldn't find – they were getting rid of the evidence. Logan thanked him and hurried off towards the hole in the fence, trying not to listen to Rickards moaning on about how Debbie Kerr would tell everyone in the Aberdeen scene he was a rotten wee shite and not to be trusted as he slouched along behind.

A churned mud path reached through the grass from the fence towards another tower block. Logan ducked through. Four o'clock on a Friday afternoon and the parking spaces in front of the tower block were empty. There were another two eighteen-storey blocks in the development – bland concrete towers that dominated the skyline – but their car parks were virtually empty too. No sign of a little red hatchback.

According to the taxi driver he'd dropped Ashley off only a couple of minutes earlier: so where the hell was she?

'I mean it's not as if I did it on purpose! Why did Debs have to—'

'Look, would you shut up about your bloody bondage buddies for two fucking minutes and help me find Macintyre's car?'

Rickards blushed and mumbled an apology, but five minutes later he was whinging again.

There was a small road lined with lock-up garages, tucked down the side of a cluster of shops. Puddles shone with oily rainbows, glittering in the sunlight as Logan picked his way between the potholes. The garage doors were peeling and chipped, bare metal showing through ancient paintwork; only one was open, down at the far end, the sound of someone talking to themselves just audible over the chattering of a single magpie and Rickards' incessant whining.

'What am I supposed to do? I mean it's not as if—'

Logan hit him. 'Shhh!' pointing at the open garage door. 'Down there.'

They crept forward, the voice becoming clearer with every step. It was Ashley, swearing away to herself. 'Fucking bastards with their fucking fuck . . . shit . . .' Something clanged.

Logan peered inside: Ashley was on her hands and knees fishing about beneath a little red hatch-back, her pert, rounded backside wiggling in the air. Logan resisted the urge to take a running kick at it. 'Lost something?'

She froze. Swore. Then slowly turned to stare at him, eyes wide, mouth hanging open. 'This . . . you . . . private property, you can't—'

'Step away from the vehicle please, Miss.' It was hard to keep the grin from his face, so Logan didn't even try. They finally had . . . He frowned, beneath the smell of dirt and oil was something a lot more worrying: bleach. The box – the one she'd collected from Macintyre's house – was full of cleaning products and a tiny, handheld vacuum cleaner.

'I was . . .' She looked over Logan's shoulder, eyes wide: 'What the hell?'

Logan didn't even bother looking round. 'Nice try. On your feet.'

She swore again, and stood. 'Bastards.'

'Rickards, do the honours, will you?'

The constable pulled out his cuffs and started reciting Ashley's rights, getting as far as, 'anything you *do* say will be—' before she kneed him in the balls. 'Aya, fuck!' She was fast, slamming an elbow down on the back of Rickard's head as he crumpled, sending him crashing to the dirty garage floor, then snatching something out of the cardboard box – a squeezy bottle of bleach – spraying it in Logan's face.

He got his arms up just in time, his head surrounded with fumes as she barged past, bouncing him off the hatchback's passenger door. He stumbled, tripped, and landed on his backside as Ashley ran for it.

He clambered to his feet. Rickards was groaning, coiled up around his battered testicles. He'd live, but he'd be bugger-all help. Swearing, Logan burst out of the garage, skidding to a halt on the pock-marked tarmac.

She was running for the main road, shouting, 'HELP! RAPE!' at the top of her lungs, going as fast as her high heels would carry her.

Logan caught up with Ashley outside a small newsagents, grabbing the back of her jacket and spinning her round. She swung at him, her fist whistling past his nose as he dodged back. He returned the favour, only he didn't miss – there was a soft crack and she went down, landing flat on that pert backside of hers, blood dribbling out between her fingers as she clutched her broken nose and moaned.

Logan hauled Ashley to her feet, shoved her up against the newsagents' window and hand-cuffed her wrists behind her back. She left a smear of bright red on the glass. 'You fuck! You fucking fuck! I'm pregnant! I'm fucking suing you! POLICE BRUTALITY!'

The newsagent's door sneaked open a crack and a wee mannie peered out into the street, shaking his fist, staying well back. 'You leave her alone!'

Blood streaming down her face, Ashley glared at the not-so-have-a-go hero still hiding behind his shop door. 'You saw! You saw him attack me! Police fucking brutality!'

'Police? Oh, er . . . I . . .' He blanched, gripping the edge of his door, inching it closed again.

Ashley spat a mouthful of scarlet at him.

Logan frogmarched her back to the garage.

55

DI Steel fiddled with a packet of cigarettes as the IB crawled all over Macintyre's little red hatchback. She kept glancing back towards the ambulance and the woman sitting on the tailgate glowering out into the drizzle: squint nose still leaking bright red blood, eyes already beginning to blacken. 'Jesus Laz, could you no' just ask her to come quietly? How's it going to look – "Police Beat The Shite Out O' Pregnant Bint"? You're a walking PR disaster. I've . . .' She frowned. 'What happened to your jacket?'

Logan looked down, saw nothing, then twisted his arms round: blotches on the sleeves were slowly going pale blue/brown where the bleach had hit. 'Bastard . . .' Now he'd have to get a new suit. 'She just about castrated Rickards.'

'Aye?' Steel shrugged and put her fags away. 'Best thing for him. Stop the wee fucker breeding.' She shifted uncomfortably from foot to foot, then took the cigarettes out again. 'Fuck's sake, what's taking them so *long*?' pointing at the IB team in their white coveralls. One team was going through the interior, another guddling about in the boot, pulling out all manner of junk, photographing it, and sticking it into labelled evidence bags. 'Got to be something . . . Shite, can you imagine what would happen if this was all just some big fuck-up?'

One of the IB team hefted the spare tyre out of the boot with a grunt. There was a pause, then: 'Bloody hell!'

'What?' Steel lurched forward to the cordon of blue and white POLICE tape, standing on her tiptoes, trying to see past the sudden clump of white oversuits. 'What is it? If it's a pile of cash I call first dibs!'

The video operator filmed, the photographer flashed and the IB poked about. Steel took a deep breath and bellowed, 'What the fuck is going on?'

There was a sudden silence and the head technician turned round, an Aberdeen Football Club holdall in his hands – the sort you could buy at any sports shop in the city. He reached in and pulled out a knife. 'There's bits of jewellery and all sorts of shite in here!'

'Oh thank *fuck* for that.' DI Steel closed her eyes, sighed, then turned to Logan and grinned. 'See, I keep tellin' people you're no' just an ugly face.'

The rear podium was crowded by the time they got back to FHQ – vans and patrol cars double-parked by the rear doors as half a dozen struggling, swearing men were dragged through into the custody area. Two support officers were unloading what looked like bricks wrapped in black plastic and brown packing tape, stacking them up on a wheeled trolley. And right there in the middle, directing things like a taller, uglier version of Napoleon was DI Finnie. He held up an imperious hand as Logan and Steel manhandled Ashley out of the back of their pool car.

'Well, well, well, if it's not DS McRae.' Finnie grabbed one of the blocks from the trolley, shaking it at them. 'Half a million in uncut heroin! You can thank your lucky stars all this was still there when we raided the place. After that crap you and Fat Boy Insch pulled this morning they could have moved the lot, and next time we saw it it'd be getting sold on the streets! You're not a police officer, you're a bloody disgrace.' And with that he barged past, bumping Logan with his shoulder on the way.

'Ach,' said Steel, 'don't listen to him. Wanker probably hasn't had a shag for years.'

The Procurator Fiscal was a hair's breadth away from doing cartwheels – the jewellery in the holdall was a perfect match for each of the victims, the ones from Aberdeen *and* the ones from Dundee. If he ever woke up from his coma, Macintyre was going to prison for a long, long time. Steel let Logan phone Tayside Police with the good news, getting little more than a grunt and *'About bloody time!'* from that craggy-faced tosspot DCS Cameron.

'Well?' said Steel as Logan hung up. 'He overcome with gratitude?'

'No.' He checked his watch: six thirty-one. 'What about Jimmy Duff?'

The inspector slouched back in her chair and stared at him. 'Jesus, can you no' enjoy the moment for once? We just caught The Granite City Rapist! Fuckin' balloons, jelly and ice-cream time.' She shook her head. 'Kids today . . . Fine, go, play with Duff, but you better get your arse back here by seven o'clock sharp: press conference. Then you, me and Spanky are having a booze up.'

She was right of course, he should have been celebrating, but he really wasn't in the mood; Finnie's little outburst had managed to take the shine off things. Because much though he couldn't stand the abusive bastard, the man had a point – they'd compromised an ongoing drugs operation just so Insch could get his hands on a junkie who *might* have something to do with an accidental death. It wasn't as if Jason Fettes had been murdered: he was into rough sex, it went too far, he died. End of story. But accident or not, it still needed tidying up, and it gave Logan something to focus on, other than how badly he'd fucked up. How he'd nearly ruined Finnie's drug bust. How he'd thought Insch was blinded by his need to pin everything on Rob Macintyre. But mostly how he'd doubted Jackie. She wasn't obsessed, she was right.

He phoned down to the cells to see if Jimmy Duff had come back from orbit yet. The custody assistant said, *'Hud oan, I'll check,'* then disappeared for a bit. He was back a couple of minutes later. *'Nope, still boldly going where millions of other buggers have been before. He's due in court at . . .'* another pause and some rustling, *'aye, half three the morn. Bags of time. You want me to get someone to interview him tonight?'*

Logan thought about it. 'No. I'll do him when I get in tomorrow.' After all, it wasn't as if there was a rush. Jason Fettes wasn't going to get any more dead.

The press conference went surprisingly well: all the newspapers and TV crews seemed to have conveniently forgotten that this time yesterday they'd been smearing the front pages and national news with, GRAMPIAN POLICE'S SHAMEFUL CAMPAIGN OF HATE AGAINST BRAVE ROBBY MACINTYRE! Suddenly the footballer was a monster and it was a good job he was in a coma and couldn't hurt anyone else.

Afterwards they hit the pub: Logan, Steel and Rickards, with Rennie bringing up the rear – anything for a free drink.

'So,' said Steel, watching Rickards scamper off

to the bar for another round, 'where's Watson then? Thought she'd be gagging for a celebratory pint or three.'

Logan shrugged, still feeling guilty about the whole thing. 'Day off. I left her a message.' Wherever she was she didn't have her phone switched on, but Insch did. Suspended or not, he was on his way in to join the party.

'Course,' said Steel, helping herself to another large whisky when Rickards got back from the bar, 'now every bugger says they always knew Macintyre was guilty. But they didn't catch him, did they? No: Spanky and Lazarus did!' She held up her glass, proposed a toast to the pair of them – sending Rickards into a bright-red blushing fit – then downed her drink in one and sent Rennie off to the bar with her wallet.

She was halfway through a filthy joke about two nurses and a shipment of cucumbers when someone tapped Logan on the shoulder and asked if the seat next to him was taken. He got as far as, 'No, help yourself, we—' before he realized who it was: Rachael Tulloch, still wearing her work suit. He'd never got around to calling her back.

'Thought I'd find you here,' she said, sitting down next to him, then addressing the table, 'the PF says, "bloody well, done and the next round's on her".' That got a cheer.

The inspector went back to her joke as more people drifted in from FHQ – off-duty constables, sergeants, inspectors, all of them telling Steel how they knew she'd get to the bottom of it. Rachael laid a hand on Logan's thigh when she was sure no one was watching. He tried not to flinch and she smiled at him. 'I sort of thought you'd be stuck here tonight, what with Macintyre and everything.'

'I . . . yes, about that, we—'

'Come over tomorrow instead. It'll be fun, I've got the weekend off, as long as nothing major happens.' She gave his thigh a squeeze.

Oh God. 'We . . . I'm . . .' TELL HER! 'I'm living with someone.'

Rachael smiled at him. 'I know.'

Logan didn't know what to say to that, so he drank half his pint in one and announced he had to go to the toilet, scurrying away before she could say anything else. Round the corner, through the doors, up the stairs . . . He stopped on the landing and leant back against the wall with his eyes closed. Fuck. What the hell was he supposed to do now? He'd done the hard bit: he'd told her he was living with Jackie and it didn't make any difference! Fuck, fuck, fuckity, fuck. It wasn't as if he didn't like Rachael – he'd kissed her for God's sake! And it'd been nice. And she was probably a lot less volatile than Jackie, who wasn't exactly easy to live with. And . . . and he didn't know what to do.

'Fuck.' The fact he was even debating it probably said a lot.

Marching back downstairs to the bar Logan saw

DI Insch, hulking over the small table where Steel and the rest of them sat, clapping people on the back and telling them how he'd always said it was Robert Bloody Macintyre. The only person missing now was . . . Talk of the devil: Jackie Watson, coming in from the rain, hair plastered down to her head, jacket dripping on the blue-and-yellow carpet.

Logan froze, just out of earshot, watching as Jackie beamed, paused, then hugged DI Insch. The large man looked momentarily taken aback, then shouted, 'Drinks!' And all the way through, Rachael just smiled.

Oh God . . . Taking a deep breath, Logan joined them.

56

Saturday morning hurt. Not as much as it could have done, but enough to make Logan regret staying up till two in the morning, drinking. He rolled out of bed, groaned, and scrubbed his face with his hands. Some grumbling from under the duvet next to him and he hit the off switch on the alarm, then slouched through to the shower.

FHQ was busy. Ten past seven and the day shift were catching up on all the arrests from a standard Aberdeen Friday night on the piss. Logan signed in and grabbed a big cup of coffee from the canteen before checking with the front desk to see who was about. Sergeant Eric Mitchell frowned at him. 'You're supposed to be on the back shift.'

Logan shrugged. 'Jimmy Duff – he's off to court at half three.'

'Bloody hell . . . Take some sodding time off! You know how much of a pain in the arse it is to balance the books with buggers like you screwing up the overtime bill?'

'Steel in?'

'Nope. And neither's Insch . . .' He leant forward and put on a dramatic whisper: 'Been suspended!' Then a sniff. 'Finnie's about, if you're desperate.'

'Never mind.' Logan would never be *that* desperate. 'I'll manage.'

The cell block stank of disinfectant, urine and vomit, the custody assistant pushing a mop back and forth on the filthy green floor and muttering away to himself. 'Dirty fuckers . . .'

Logan took a quick look at the clipboard hanging on the wall. 'Anything interesting?'

'Fights, drunk and disorderlies, pissing in shop doorways, the usual.' He slopped another mopful of grey water on the floor. 'How come I'm always the one lumbered with the—'

'Jimmy Duff straight again?'

'Eh?' He made dirty, swirly patterns on the green terrazzo floor. 'Oh, aye. He's whinging about that kicking he got though. Little bugger hasn't shut up since I came on. "Oh I'm in pain! Oh I'm dying. Oh I need some medication. Blah, blah, blah."' He scrubbed at a blob of gritty pink chewing gum. 'I've got a bad back, and you don't hear me—'

'Do me a favour and get someone to stick him in an interview room.'

'What did your last bloody slave die of? . . . OK, fine. Not like I've got anything *better* to do.' He sighed and stuck his mop back in the bucket. 'Room one?'

Logan thought about it. 'The heater working in there?'

'Aye, three's still buggered though.'

'Stick him in three then.'

There was an overwhelming air of doom and gloom in what used to be DI McPherson's incident room, and it was all coming from a hungover-looking PC Rickards, *still* complaining about Debbie Kerr, and how his life was ruined. He was sharing a desk in the middle of the room with Rennie, who looked as if he was doing his best to ignore all the moaning and get some work done; fighting through the paperwork Logan had lumbered him with yesterday. 'Right,' said Logan, looking round the room, 'anyone free?'

Rennie's hand shot out, pointing at Rickards. 'John's free, aren't you John? Yeah, take John. Do him good to get out of the office!'

Logan looked at the dejected figure and got as far as, 'Ah . . .' when Rickards looked up, sighed and dragged himself to his feet. 'Actually,' said Logan, backing away from the desk, trying to play it cool, 'don't worry about it: you're busy. It was just questioning a prisoner, I can always . . .' But Rickards was already retrieving his jacket from the back of his chair and pulling it on over his wrinkled white uniform shirt.

He stood there, looking as if the world had just

caved in, saying: 'You want me to get coffees.' Not a question.

'Well . . . I . . .'

'Fine.' And he slouched off.

Rennie sank down in his seat till his head was resting on the desktop. 'Oh, dear God – *please* don't bring him back!'

Interview room three was like a sauna. The sun blazed in through a crack in the blinds, striking the back of Jimmy Duff's head, making his rumpled hair glow like a halo. Which was probably about as close to divinity as he was ever likely to get. Yesterday the bruising had been bad, but today it was even worse: purple, dark blue, green and yellow covering most of his face, like a gaudy, camouflage tattoo. The custody sergeant had confiscated Duff's broken glasses, so he had to squint, screwing up his blackened eyes, complaining about only being given paracetamol for his aches. 'I need morphine! Or you know somethin' a bit . . . You've got gear here, right?'

'For the last time: no, OK? We're the police not your dealer.' Logan settled back in his chair and pointed the remote control at the TV set Rickards had set up in the corner. The picture fizzed and crackled until the DVD player came online. 'Recognize this?'

Duff squinted at the screen, watching Jason Fettes being strapped to a table and spanked. 'Look, I'm really in pain here. I need some medication.'

'Do you recognize it?'

A shrug that ended in a wince. 'Never seen it before.'

'No? Well, how come Ma Stewart says you gave it to her: security on a loan?'

At the mention of Ma's name Duff flinched. 'Ah,' he said, licking his broken, swollen lips, 'if Ma says it, then yeah. I recognize it. Gave it to her. Yeah.' Jimmy's unbroken hand stroked the plaster covering his left arm. 'If Ma says it.'

'Uh huh. She the one did this to you Jimmy? You gave her a fake name, didn't you?'

'No! Nothing to do with her. I . . . I . . . A couple of guys in a pub. Spilt their pints, they . . . you know.'

'Sure.' The second 'it was a pub fight' story Logan had heard this week. At least Jackie's had sounded a lot more convincing. 'The DVD. Where'd you get it?'

'You sure I can't get somethin' for the pain, eh? It's really—'

'The DVD Jimmy! Where – did – you – get – it?'

'—couple of diffs, some jellies . . . you know, make it stop hurtin' for a bit.'

Logan slammed his hand down on the tabletop, and Duff flinched again, trembling into silence as Logan said, 'If you don't tell me where you got that bloody DVD from, Jimmy, I'm going to see Ma Stewart and tell her how you're pressing charges for assault. And loan-sharking.'

A look of terror leapt onto Duff's bruised face. 'No! I didnae! I didnae say anything!'

'*She* doesn't know that.'

Jimmy shivered in his seat, scratching away at his cast. 'I . . .' He looked from the screen to Logan, to Rickards, then to the camera bolted up on the wall. 'It was this bird, er . . . woman, you know? I needed the cash. I mean, you know, I'm no' into it, or nothing, I just needed the cash . . ."

Logan listened to DI Steel giving someone a hard time on the other end of the phone, threatening them with all manner of horrible repercussions if they didn't come round and fix her toilet. The inspector slammed the handset down and stuck her middle finger up at it. 'Well, what did Duff say?' she asked. 'He cop to Fettes's backside?'

'Thought you weren't coming in today?'

'Aye well,' she shrugged and unwrapped a stick of nicotine gum, 'Susan's mum's up from bloody Dundee and she's getting on my wick. Told them I had an urgent case on. So: Duff?'

'We got an address – says he lifted the movie with Fettes in it by accident. Disk was in the DVD player he nicked, along with some jewellery, CDs, and electrical stuff. Said it was compensation for what the householder had done to him.'

'Yeah?' She popped the gum in her mouth and chewed. 'Let me guess—'

'Strapped him to a table and spanked him.'

'Same as Fettes.'

'Identical. She showed him the DVD and told him it was all an act: special effects. Wanted him to scream and struggle, just like Fettes.'

'Freak.' Steel tried to blow a bubble, and ended up spitting the gum onto her desk. 'Fuck . . .' She picked it up and stuck it back in her mouth. 'So? Did he let her fist him?'

'Couldn't sit down for days afterwards. So he went back, broke in and helped himself to her stuff. Said it was only fair.'

'Probably right.' She stood, worked a crick out of her neck and grabbed her jacket. 'Come on then, backside in gear. You can grab Spanky while I go to the bog. Christ knows what was in that kebab last night, but it's no' agreeing with me.'

'Ah . . . maybe we should take Rennie instead, he—'

'Spanky. Not Rennie: bastard's on the shit list after that crap he pulled last night with the pork scratchings. And let the PF know we've got a suspect.' She pushed past him, pausing to grab a copy of that morning's *Press and Journal* from her in-tray: OLD AGE PERVERT MADE MY WEE BOY KILL! Exclusive.

She was probably going to be a while.

As soon as the door swung shut, Logan groaned. Closed his eyes. Counted to ten. Then pulled out his phone and called the Procurator Fiscal's office. It rang twice then diverted, probably to the mobile of whoever was on duty this weekend. 'Please not

Rachael, please not Rachael, please not . . .'
Rachael answered the phone. 'Bollocks.'

'What?'

'Er . . . no, not you, something here. Erm.
Look—'

'I knew you'd call. I had a good time last night.'

Logan hadn't, he'd spent the whole evening on
tenterhooks, waiting for her to lean across the
table and tell Jackie about their curry and snog.
'We—'

*'So tonight, I'm thinking lasagne, red wine and a
movie. You can bring a bag of salad and something for
dessert.'*

'I can't I . . . I'm . . . Look, Rachael, I like you,
you're smart and pretty and fun—'

'If you're about to say "but" you can stop right there.'

'I'm living with someone. I can't do this.'

Silence. *'I see . . . So what: I was just a fling?'*

Oh bloody hell. 'No, it's not like that, it's . . .
well . . .' Silence. Bloody fucking hell. 'I'm sorry.'

*'You need to sit down and figure out what you actu-
ally want, Logan. And don't take too long – I'm not
going to hang around like an idiot forever while you
make up your mind.'*

Bloody, fucking, sodding hell. This was just
getting worse, so Logan told her about Jimmy Duff
and the woman he'd got the DVD from. Asking
for an arrest and search warrant.

'You've got to be kidding me!' said Rachael when
he'd finished going through all the details. *'All
you've got is Jimmy Duff's word this woman's involved:*

*and he's a known drug user, pusher and thief. Not exactly
a credible witness.'*

'He . . . look, he says he was spanked, buggered
and fisted by the householder. It's not exactly the
kind of thing you lie about to make yourself look
good, is it?'

She admitted he had a point, but she still wasn't
going to give him a warrant. Not unless he could
come up with something better than the word of
some junkie scumbag. And that was the end of
the discussion. *'Don't forget,'* she said, before he
could hang up, *'I'm not going to wait forever.'*

'Where the hell you been?' asked Steel, shivering
at the back door, hands jammed deep in her
armpits, still chewing away on her nicotine gum.

Logan stepped out into the cold, grey morning.
'We're not getting a warrant.'

'Didn't think so. Still, worth a try, eh?' She
turned and bellowed out into the rear podium car
park, 'Come on Spanky, get a bloody shift on!'

A grumbling PC Rickards appeared from a filthy,
battered pool car, carrying armfuls of chips papers
and old burger boxes. He'd changed into his 'going
out' clothes – the crumpled shirt and tie replaced
by a black T-shirt and stab-proof vest. With the
fluorescent yellow waterproof jacket on over the
top, he looked like a short, grumpy lollypop man.
He dumped the rubbish in the wire-mesh bin at
the back of the building. Then went back for
another load.

'Honestly,' the inspector pulled the gum from her mouth and squeeged it into the brickwork by the door, 'some people treat this place like a tip.' She grabbed Rickards as he deposited his load of rubbish in the bin. 'Right, that'll do. Fun though this is, I'm freezing my tits off here.'

The address Jimmy Duff had given them was for a small, bland, two-up, two-down on the outskirts of Blackburn. It sat in the middle of a row of identical houses, all sulking away beneath the featureless grey sky. A wee blue mini was parked at the kerb, in front of a neglected garden decorated with gnomes.

'You know,' said Steel, as Rickards pulled up opposite and killed the engine, 'I'm thinking of going blonde.'

Logan checked the details he'd printed off back at the station. 'Vicky Peterson . . . You sure you don't recognize the name?'

'They say blondes have more fun. But they also say two's company and three's a crowd, and we know that's shite, don't we, Spanky? Three's a very fine number in the bed department.'

'Er . . .' Rickards coughed, then looked back between the seats at Logan. 'It doesn't ring any bells, but she might not go by her real name at munches.' And then his face fell. 'Not that I'll ever be able to set foot in one again. I'm—'

'Blah, blah, blah.' Steel clambered out into the cold morning. 'We've put up with your whinging all the way from the bloody station: OK, we get it. Your life's ruined. Everyone hates you. It's no' fair. Etcetera, etcetera, etcetera. Now shut up about it.' She slammed the car door and Rickards sagged even further into his seat.

'She doesn't understand! Nobody understands . . . they were my family. The only people who understood what it's like.' He sighed. 'How would you feel if you could never speak to your family ever again?'

Logan didn't even have to think about it, 'Fucking delighted.' It wasn't the answer the constable was expecting, but at least it shut him up.

Steel was waiting for them at the front door, stomping her feet and blowing into her cupped hands, making little clouds of steam. 'About time.' She hoicked a thumb at the bell. 'Spanky, you're on point.'

A long-suffering sigh, and Rickards leant on the bell. Brrrrrrrrrrrringgggggg.

'What d'you think?' Steel asked as they waited.

'Well,' Logan looked up at the building, 'I checked with records – no one reported a break-in at this address. Wouldn't be the first time Duff's sold us a line. He's not exactly the font of all honesty.'

Steel slapped him on the arm. 'Not bloody Duff! Me: blonde or auburn?'

'Oh, er . . .' Saved by the answer to the bell. The door creaked open revealing a familiar-looking woman: slightly shorter than Rickards, green eyes,

549

shiny brown ponytail, overweight, expensive casual clothes, shocked expression—

'Tina?' The constable waved and Logan groaned. Tina. The intense one from Rickard's bondage group, the one who wouldn't shut up about *Jack and his Bloody Beanstalk*. 'Er . . . can we come in?'

Tina, AKA Vicky Peterson, looked Rickards up and down. 'You never said you were a policeman.'

'Er . . . sorry about that.'

There was an awkward silence. 'Do they let you take your handcuffs home?'

The constable got as far as another, 'Er . . .' when Steel poked him in the back and said, 'Get a shift on, Spanky: we're freezing out here!'

Rickards went bright red. 'Can we . . . er . . .'

Tina rolled her eyes, gave a big, dramatic sigh, then turned and marched into the house. 'Sure, why not. Wipe your feet though.'

Logan hung back, cursing Jimmy Duff's name.

'What's up with your face?' hissed Steel as they followed Tina and Rickards through the rubber-scented hall and into a tidy lounge.

'It's not her. She's a bottom. Whoever fisted Jason Fettes was a top, or a dom. And look at her: she's too short and heavy to be the woman on the video. That bastard Duff lied to us.'

Steel swore. 'Just what I need, another wild bloody goose chase.'

'So,' said Tina, striking her pantomime pose again, fist on hips, legs spread wide, 'to what do I owe the pleasure?'

Rickards cast a panicked look at the inspector who just shrugged and passed the buck on to Logan. 'Ah . . .' he said, 'we're . . . Burglaries.'

'Burglaries?'

'Burglaries. We've had a number of break-ins reported in the area, and we're going door to door to see if anyone saw anything. And, you know, if their properties are secure.'

'Oh.' Tina stood with her head to one side, like a cat. 'I know Mrs Ross had her car nicked, but I thought that was in town.'

'So you haven't seen anything?' Brazening it out.

'Nope.'

Logan nodded, as if he'd feared as much. 'Right, well, we'd probably better take a quick look round. Make sure everything's secure before we go next door.' And if they were lucky she'd never even know she was under suspicion. After the fiasco with Insch's star performer, the last thing Logan needed was someone else shouting about sexual bias and making official complaints.

They started the 'security inspection' in the kitchen, then through to the tiny dining room, then the lounge, then up the stairs. The master bedroom was nothing out of the ordinary: pile of books on the bedside cabinet – Marian Keyes, a couple of those true-crime serial killer things, and a psychology textbook – towelling dressing gown draped over the back of a chair, one rogue sock poking out from under the bed. Bathroom: the window was open, so Logan got to do his 'crime prevention' talk about giving burglars an inch and them taking everything you've got. And last up was another small bedroom, completely empty except for a flat-pack wardrobe and that rubbery/fabric odour again, fighting against the smell of fresh paint and one of those plug-in air fresheners. He scuffed his shoe across the carpet beneath his feet, back and forth and back and forth, making a little lozenge of blue fuzz.

Steel grimaced and clutched at her stomach. 'Any chance I could use your loo?'

'Oh . . . yes. Down the hall.' Tina pointed at it, even though they'd just come from there. 'Watch the lock though, it's a bit temperamental. What about you two?' she asked as the inspector hurried off. 'Would you like a cup of tea? That's what you're supposed to offer policemen, isn't it? They always do on the telly.'

Logan nodded. 'Please.' Not really paying attention as Tina and Rickards headed back down to the kitchen. Back and forth and back and forth . . . 'New carpet?'

The answer was shouted back up the stairs. 'Yeah, I'm doing the spare room up, spilt a whole tin of barley white. Ruined the carpet in there *and* the one in the hall too.' The sound of a kettle starting to boil. 'Bloody insurance said I wasn't covered for DIY, can you believe that?' Some clanking. 'What do you both take?'

Rickards: 'Just black for me, he's milk, no sugar. The inspector's milk and two. You want a hand?'

Logan stepped back into the spare room. No wonder the carpets looked so clean. He reached for the wardrobe door and pulled it open: one full-body rubber suit; a collection of paddles, buckles and straps; a corset; ball gags, and masks with strange inflatable bits; thigh-high black high-heeled boots; the box for an electrastim set; and a large collection of sex toys. All neatly hung on their own little hooks, or placed on shelves. And there, stuffed in beside the suit, was a full-length, gilt-edged mirror.

He slid it out and propped it up against the wall, stepping back until . . . perfect. All the room needed was Jason Fettes and a table to strap him to. It wasn't spilt paint that had ruined the carpets, it was Fettes haemorrhaging to death.

The corset would change her body shape, make her thinner, the high-heeled boots would make her taller, just like on the video. And she'd played the lead in *Jack and the Beanstalk* – give her a stick-on beard and an Irish accent and she'd be a dead ringer for the driver that dropped Fettes off at the hospital.

It looked as if Jimmy Duff was right after all.

57

He sighed and closed the wardrobe door. Insch would have been over the moon that they'd finally caught someone, but as far as *Logan* was concerned, this wasn't going to end well for anybody. Tina hadn't killed Jason on purpose. It was just a case of kinky sex gone tragically wrong, but she'd get dragged up on charges anyway, the trial would be splashed all over the papers, her life would be ruined. And it wouldn't make Jason Fettes any less dead.

He headed back downstairs, trying not to hear the Battle of the Somme noises coming from the bathroom as he passed. He could hear Rickards moaning in the kitchen, complaining about being blackballed from the Aberdeen scene, Tina telling him he could always try the Ellon lot instead.

She looked up, saw Logan standing in the doorway, smiled, and asked him if he'd like a chocolate biscuit. He asked her where she was the night Jason Fettes died.

The kettle gave a click and fell silent while she stared at him, face going pale. And then it all went wrong. She wrenched open a cutlery drawer, pulled out a huge, serrated bread knife and grabbed Rickards by the collar. He got as far as, 'What the f—' before she spun him round. Now she was directly behind him, putting his body between Logan and herself; using Rickards as a shield. She grabbed a handful of hair and yanked the constable's head back, pressing the blade against his throat. He squealed. 'Argh, Jesus, Tina!'

'Whoa!' Logan held his hands up, not moving. 'You don't need to do this. Fettes was just an accident. We—'

'I . . . I'd like you to leave, please,' she said as Rickards' terrified eyes locked onto his.

'It's OK, you're not in any trouble.'

She almost laughed. 'Not in any trouble? I KILLED A MAN!'

'Sir, I—' Rickards made a strangled noise and stopped talking, a thin trickle of blood running down to soak into his black T-shirt.

'I fantasize about it all the time. All the time! You understand? I watched that film of Jason dying over and over again, till I knew every word off by heart. All the sounds, the screams. Again and again and again.'

'Come on Tina, let . . .' Logan had to wrack his brains for Rickards' first name, 'John. Let John go. You don't want to hurt him.'

'No?' She let go of Rickard's hair and ran her

hand down the front of his stabproof vest, across his belt, until she was cupping him through his trousers. 'John wants me to hurt him, don't you John?' She squeezed and the constable whimpered, closing his eyes. 'Yes he does . . .'

'Tina, you're a bottom, remember? You only did what Fettes asked you – it's not your fault.'

Steel's voice, muffled from upstairs. 'Hello? The lock's stuck. Hello?' The sound of a door being rattled.

Tina looked Logan in the eye. 'It *is* my fault.' The tears started. 'I'm a serial killer.'

'Oh for fuck's sake. You're not a serial killer, OK? Fettes was into rough sex and it went too far. It was an accident, that's all. End of story.'

'Hello?' The rattling got louder. 'Where the hell is everyone?'

'I *am* a serial killer! I fucking am! I got the books off the internet – I *read* them. It's me! I tried to make it happen again, with the other one, the bastard who stole my bloody stuff, but he wouldn't die!'

'You're not a serial killer!'

Steel had obviously run out of patience. She was hammering on the door, yelling, 'WHAT THE FUCK IS GOING ON OUT THERE?'

Tina stared at him, shaking her head softly. Telling him to keep his mouth shut.

Logan shouted over his shoulder: 'Ms Peterson's taken Rickards hostage. She's got a knife to his throat.'

Tina's eyes went wide. 'You bastard!' She clutched tighter at the constable's crotch and he whimpered. Then groaned.

'WHAT? Fuck . . .' The rattling turned to booming. From the sound of things Steel was trying to kick the door down. And then it went silent, followed by a one-sided, muffled conversation.

'You're not a serial killer, Tina. It was an accident. Yes you fantasize about it, but it's a long way from there to holding a police officer at knifepoint! You know what she's doing right now?' pointing up the stairs to where Steel was still talking to herself. 'She's calling for an armed response unit. They've got guns.'

Tina let go of Rickards groin and fumbled her way round his belt till she got to the handcuffs in their leather holster and pulled them out, keeping the knife against his throat. 'Wrists together, behind your back.' The constable did as he was told. There was a metallic click, then another. Her hand worked its way back to the front and tugged at the belt buckle.

Rickards said, 'Please don't!' but she shushed him, and undid it anyway, then unbuttoned the top of his trousers.

'Come on, Tina, they're on their way here now. It's not too late to let John go before this gets out of hand.'

She put her lips against the constable's ears as she slid his zip down and his trousers fell round his ankles. 'They don't understand, do they?' She worked a hand into the waistband of his underpants and tugged them down as far as she could reach. Rickards' erection sprang free and she smiled. 'But we do.'

'Please—' Tears sparked at the side of his eyes.

'Shhh,' she grabbed him and started stroking, 'you need to be silent unless I say so.'

'But— Aaargh!'

She dug her nails into his penis. Then went back to stroking it.

'Oh, Jesus.' Logan really didn't need to see that.

A loud bang from upstairs, a pause, and then Steel limped down the stairs. 'Now what the hell is everyone . . .' she drifted to a halt as she saw a shivering Rickards with his trousers round his ankles, his pants round his thighs, and his dick in Tina's hand. The one not holding the knife. 'There's a sight you don't see every day.'

No one laughed.

'Firearms team's on its way, five, ten minutes tops.' Steel said, digging a brand-new packet of cigarettes out of her pocket and tearing the cellophane off with her teeth, adding, 'You don't mind?' as she winkled a fag out and stuck it in her mouth.

'I'd rather you didn't smoke in my house!'

'Aye?' The inspector shrugged and pulled out a cheap, petrol-station lighter, her hand trembling as she lit up and sooked in the first lungful of smoke. 'Well, I'd rather you didn't wank off my constables with a bread knife. So we're even.'

They stared at each other as the silence stretched, then Tina said, 'I . . . I was so sorry when I found out Jason was dead. He was . . . special. I'd never been a top before . . .' She shivered. 'I felt him scream and wriggle and bleed all up my arm. It was so warm . . .'

Rickards whimpered again and she speeded up her stroke. Then slowed right down. Keeping him hanging while the blood from his throat soaked dark-red into his T-shirt, making the black material glisten. 'I didn't realize till afterwards how special it was.' She smiled. 'The power of life over death.'

58

The phone rang in the living room and everyone jumped. Steel took the latest cigarette from her mouth, and lit the next one in the chain before dropping the dog end onto the carpet with its friends. 'That'll be them now.' So much for five or ten minutes, it'd taken the response team nearly twenty to get here.

Tina nodded. 'What will they do? The firearms people?'

'Well,' Steel blew a long column of smoke at the ceiling, 'first they'll try to negotiate. Then they'll try negotiating some more. And if that fails, they'll go in for a bit of the old negotiation.'

'They won't shoot me?'

'Only if they have to. It makes a shite heap of paperwork.'

Tina bit her bottom lip, still working away at Rickards' erection, keeping him on the brink without ever letting him fall over. 'What if I kill him?'

'You really, really don't want to do that. Seriously, it's a crap idea.'

Ring, ring. Ring, ring . . .

'You might want to get that.'

'You,' she took her hand off Rickard's cock long enough to point at Logan, 'answer it. Tell them I'm not coming out.'

'You've got to some time, Tina. You can't stay in here forever.'

'Answer the fucking phone!' She twisted the knife and Rickards yelped, the slow dribble of blood from his neck turning into a steady trickle.

'OK! OK, I'm going!' Logan hurried through into the lounge and grabbed the phone out of its cradle – it was one of those little cordless ones so he carried it back to the kitchen, listening as the negotiator launched into his opening speech about how he was just here to help and nobody needed to get hurt. 'Yeah, hang on a second, Jim,' said Logan, stopping the man before he got too far into the whole empathising thing, 'she's right here.' He held the phone out to Tina. She'd have to put the knife down, or stop playing with Rickards. Either would be a result in Logan's book.

'I look stupid?' She asked. 'You talk to him.'

'OK. What you want me to say?'

'I don't fucking know, do I?'

'Well . . . how about we start with what you want? Your demands? What do you want to get out of . . .' Logan paused, watching as a single red dot of light blossomed on Tina's knife arm, then jittered up to the middle of her forehead. Another one joined it, then a third, like tiny neon lady-birds.

'What?'

'I . . .' He turned to look at the inspector who sighed, took a deep drag on her cigarette, then blew a cloud of smoke into the air between them. Red laser-sight lines glowed like sparkling threads.

'Time to put the knife down.'

Tina put her lips to Rickards ear, whispered something, opened her mouth wide and sank her teeth into the cartilage, tearing her head back and forth till a chunk came free in a spurt of blood. The constable screamed. Someone yelled on the other end of the phone in Logan's hand. Tina spat out the mouthful of Rickards' ear, pounding away on his erection. Steel yelled, 'NO!' and lunged forwards. Something sizzled past Logan and a small black dot appeared above Tina's left eye. Perfectly round. Dark.

And then the back of her head exploded.

BLOOD

59

Opening night and DI Insch's band of merry troubadours were doing their best to murder Gilbert and Sullivan in front of a crowd of friends and relatives. Logan sat on his own in the darkness of the Arts Centre, surrounded by strangers. Brooding. He reached into his pocket and pulled out the thing he'd found in Jackie's bedside cabinet, twisting it back and forth between his fingers for the umpteenth time that evening. Even in the muted light it glittered. He'd been hunting for the spare set of flat keys – the ones Jackie always borrowed because she kept losing her own – and there it was . . .

The noise coming from the front of the theatre grew to a crescendo, dragging him back to the land of the living. They'd finally made it to the finale. Two curtain calls, one encore, a short speech from DI Insch about how hard everyone had worked, flowers for the leading ladies, round of applause, and off to the bar.

The little space was crowded, thespians spilling in from the changing rooms, beaming with pride as their nearest and dearest told them how wonderful they'd been. Even the crap ones.

Logan jostled his way through to a small clearing, clutching a bottle of Newcastle Brown and wishing he hadn't said he'd go out for a curry after the show. He really wasn't in the mood.

Someone slapped him on the back and he turned to find Rennie beaming at him: face all polished and shiny, traces of stage makeup still hiding in his hairline. 'Well, was we brilliant or what?'

Logan lied and said he'd enjoyed it.

'Can you believe we got Debs back? Insch had to do some *serious* grovelling, but—'

'You heard anything from Rickards?'

'Not a peep. Went up there this afternoon, nurse said he wasn't having visitors. Oh, ta . . .' he accepted a bottle of beer from one of the three little maids from school – Logan couldn't remember which one – and took a hearty swig. 'Mind you, don't blame him, poor bastard. Breakdown is what I heard.'

Logan wasn't surprised: if he closed his eyes he could still see the back of Tina's head splattering all over the kitchen window in slow motion. Scarlet drops and grey chunks as she falls lifeless to the floor, still clutching Rickards, showering him with blood and brain and little shards of bone as he screams and screams and screams . . . And she'd been his friend. No wonder he couldn't cope.

'Just between you and me,' said Rennie, leaning in to whisper over the hubbub, 'I think he'll be going off on the stress. A dead woman clutching your dick can't be good for you. You know: mentally. I think . . .' he stopped, staring off through the crowd. DI Insch was glad-handing his way towards them, accepting compliments left, right, and centre. 'Whatever you do, don't mention Finnie, OK? He's got a right bee in his— Inspector: look who I found!'

Insch looked like a vast, overstuffed penguin in his dinner jacket and bow tie. 'Can you believe that bastard Finnie?' he asked, then took a swig from his Guinness. 'What the hell did they think they were doing, making a tit like that Detective Chief Inspector?'

Rennie groaned, rolling his eyes when Insch wasn't looking.

Logan ignored him. 'Well, he did bring in half a million quid's worth of cocaine, they probably—'

The inspector's face darkened. 'Four hundred thousand. Not half a million.' He cast an eye over the assembled crowd. 'Where's Watson?'

'Back shift.' And then Logan changed the subject, steering them round to the *Mikado* again, listening to them bang on about what a great show it was. Not wanting to talk about Jackie, or think about the thing in his pocket. And then Insch had to go be congratulated by someone else, Rennie was dragged off for a photograph, and Logan was alone again. He finished off his beer and wandered out into the cold night, standing on the top step of the Arts Centre, watching the slow-fire blink of tail lights the length of King Street.

He pulled the thing from his pocket once more – the thing he'd found in Jackie's bedside cabinet – holding it up so it sparkled in the city's sodium glow. A large ruby stud earring, just like the one stolen from Rob Macintyre when he was battered into a coma.

Red, the colour of Aberdeen Football Club.

The colour of fresh blood.

Logan McRae is back in

FLESH HOUSE

Out in hardback, May 2008

Turn the page to read an exclusive sneak preview

the world is shaped by fear

30 October 1987

'No, you listen to me: if my six-year-old son isn't back here in ten minutes I'm going to come round there and rip you a new arsehole, are we clear?' Ian McLaughlin slapped a hand over the phone's mouthpiece and shouted at his wife to turn that bloody racket down. Then back to the idiot on the other end of the phone: 'Where the hell is he?'

'When I got back from the pub they were gone, OK? Catherine's not here either . . . maybe she took the boys for a walk?'

'A WALK? It's pissing down, pitch black, freezing cold—'

'What? What's wrong?' – Sharon stood at the door to the living room, wearing the witch costume she'd bought from Woolworths, the one that hid her pregnant bulge and made her breasts look enormous.

Ian grunted, not bothering to cover the phone this time. 'It's that moron Davidson: he's lost Jamie.'

'Jamie's missing?' Sharon clapped a hand to her mouth, stifling the shriek. Always overreacting, just like her bloody mother.

'*I never said that! I didn't say he was lost, I just—*'

'If we're late for this bloody party, I'm personally going to see to it that—'

The doorbell: loud and insistent.

'—*your life is going to be—*'

The doorbell again.

'For God's sake, Sharon, answer the bloody door! I'm on the phone . . .'

There was a clunk and a rattle as Sharon finally did what she was told, and then she shrieked again. 'Jamie! Oh Jamie, we were so *worried*!'

Ian stopped mid-rant, staring at the soggy little tableau on the top step: Jamie and his best friend Richard Davidson, holding hands with some idiot in a Halloween costume. 'About bloody time, I told you to be home by five!' The two small boys looked wide eyed and frightened. And so they bloody should be. 'Where the hell have you two been?'

No reply. Typical. And look at the time . . . 'Jamie!' Ian hooked his thumb in the direction of the stairs. 'Get your backside up there and get changed. If you're not a Viking in three minutes you're going to the party as a kid in his vest and pants.'

Jamie cast a worried look at his partner in crime, then up at the stranger on the doorstep – the one wearing the blood-stained butcher's apron and

Margaret Thatcher fright mask – before slinking up to his room, taking Richard with him. Great, now they'd have to drop the little brat off at his parents' house.

Today was turning into a *complete* nightmare.

'House of Blood' parents missing

EXCLUSIVE
by Martin Leslie

A MAJOR police operation was launched last night to try to locate Ian McLaughlin (27) and his wife Sharon (22) who disappeared from their house on Seafield Drive in the late hours of Friday.

In a statement issued to the press Detective Chief Inspector Brooks claimed that the police were 'significantly worried' for the McLaughlins' safety.

The alarm was raised when friend of the family Christopher Davidson became concerned after his six-year-old son failed to return home after visiting the McLaughlins.

"I went round to check if

the lounge and the kitchen was covered in blood."

Speaking from outside the Children's Hospital, where both his son and Jamie McLaughlin (6) are being treated for shock, Mr Davidson was clearly distressed.

"My wife was with the children when they left our house. Something terrible must have happened – she would never have left them unattended!"

Police refused to comment on rumours that the two boys could have witnessed the assault, but stressed the need to locate Mr and Mrs McLaughlin, and Catherine Davidson, as soon as possible.

DCI Brooks said, "We are concerned that one or all three of

The McLaugh

McLaughlin
giant BP, is
Table, helpi
pounds for
year. His wi

Flesher arrested

Aberdeen killer caught
Police suspect more deaths

IN A DAWN RAID yesterday Grampian Police arrested the man chillingly known as 'the Flesher'.

It was the night before Halloween, but little did Ian and Sharon McLaughlin know that something more terrifying than

discovered in a disused butch shop, leading detectives to fo their enquiries on Aberde meat trade.

missing body parts

DCI Brooks, who led the 50 strong taskforce said tha arrest "represents a signi

congratulations to you both

2 - Deaths

MCLAUGHLIN
Tragically, as the result of vicious attack, on October 3 1987, Ian John McLaugh and his beloved wife Shar McLaughlin. Devoted paren to Jamie, who misses h mummy and daddy. Both a deeply mourned. Funera arrangements to follow.

PARKER
(Aboyne)
Peacefully, at Aberdeen Roya Infirmary, on November 06

Fears for mother's safety

EXCLUSIVE
by Martin Leslie

Catherine Davidson walked home with Jamie McLaughlin and her son

THE HUSBAND of Catherine Davidson spoke last night of his fears that his wife will never be found.

Speaking exclusively to the *Aberdeen Examiner*, Christopher Davidson (27) shared his thoughts on his wife's disappearance: "I am very worried about her. She is a devoted mother and our son, Richard (6) has had nightmares ever since she disappeared."

"All we know is that she walked Richard and his friend Jamie home the night before Halloween. I can't believe she's gone."

"Whatever happened that night," he said, "has left its mark on my family. The police have done their best, b[...] find Ca[...]

A s[...] Police, [...] witnes[...] Octob[...] nothin[...] invest[...] said th[...] not v[...] extrem[...]

Remains Found

POLICE have confirmed that the remains found in a derelict shop on Palmerston Road are human.

Sources within Grampian Police have hinted that the remains may belong to Ian and Sharon McLaughlin, missing since the 30th of October, but they will be unable to confirm this until further tests are carried out.

A nationwide manhunt was sparked when the McLaughlins disappeared from their Mannofield home on the night before Halloween.

The McLaughlins' son, Jamie (6) was discovered hiding in his bedroom closet with his friend Richard Davidson (6). Neither boy was able to clearly recall what had happened that night, but Richard's mother, Catherine Davidson (24) went missing at the same time.

Despite a UK-wide search effort no sign of the missing adults was found. Although initially questioned as a suspect, Mr Davidson was released without charge.

Speaking from his Porthlethen home Mr Davidson said, "We're devastated by this discovery. But in my heart of hearts I know that Catherine is still alive. She's a [sur]vivor!"

When birds

RESIDENTS of a small North East community have been stunned by the sudden increase in the seagull population. "It's like something out of a Hitchcock film," said Rose Murray (63), "you can't sit in your back garden for fear of being dive bombed."

The p[...] coun[...] backl[...] Rose [...] had [...] but t[...] It's a[...]

THREE DEAD IN [T]ENEMENT HORROR

[GL]ASGOW police issued [an] urgent plea for infor[mat]ion last night, follow[ing a]n anonymous tip-off that [led t]hem to a tenement flat [cover]ed in blood. "We can't [...]

similarities to a recent case in Aberdeen. The killer, dubbed, 'The Flesher' (the old Scots term for Butcher) is believed to be responsible for up to a dozen murders all over the [...]

W[...] k[...]

THE N[...] differe[...] someti[...] until to[...]

Spea[...] institut[...] of impr[...] vital. "[...] the dif[...] your h[...] applica[...]

This [...] when th[...] post-na[...] "Some[...] but afte[...]

20 Years Later

1

Detective Sergeant Logan McRae winced his way across the dark quayside trying not to scald his fingers, making for a scarred offshore container bathed in the harsh glow of police spotlights. The thing was about the size of a domestic bathroom – dented and battered from years of being shipped out to oilrigs in the middle of the North Sea and back again – the blue paint sprinkled with orange rust. A pool of dark red glittered in the Investigation Bureau's lights: blood mingling with oily puddles on the cold concrete, while figures in white oversuits buggered about with cameras and sticky tape and evidence bags.

Four o'clock in the morning, what a *great* start to the day.

The refrigerated container was little more than a metal box, lined with insulating material. A wooden pallet took up most of the floor, loaded up with boxes of frozen peas, chicken bits and other assorted chunks of meat, the brown-grey cardboard going black and saggy as the contents slowly defrosted.

Logan ducked under the cordon of blue and white POLICE tape.

It was impossible to miss Detective Inspector Insch: the man was huge, his SOC coveralls strained to nearly bursting. He had the suit's hood thrown back, exposing a big bald head that glinted in the spotlights. But even he was dwarfed by the looming bulk of the *Brae Explorer*, a massive orange offshore supply vessel parked alongside the quay, all its lights blazing in the purple-black night.

Logan handed one of the Styrofoam cups of tea to Insch. 'They were out of sugar.' That got him some rumbled swearing. He ignored it. 'SKY News have turned up. That makes three television crews, four newspapers and a handful of gawkers.

'Wonderful.' Insch's voice was a dark rumble. 'That's all we need.' He pointed up at the *Brae Explorer*. 'Those idiots found anything yet?'

'Search team's nearly finished. Other than some incredibly dodgy pornography it's clean. Ship's Captain says the container was only onboard for a couple of hours; someone noticed it was leaking all over the deck, so they got onto the cash and carry it came from. Shut. Apparently the rigs go mad if they don't get their containers on time, so the Captain got someone to try fixing the thing's refrigerator motor.'

Logan took a sip at his still scalding hot tea. 'That's when they found the bits. Mechanic had to shift a couple of boxes of defrosting meat to get at the wiring. Soggy cardboard gave way on one of them, and the contents went everywhere.' He pointed at a small pile of clear plastic evidence pouches, each one full of a chunk of red. 'Soon as he saw what was in there, he called us.'

Insch nodded. 'What about the cash and carry?'

'Firm called Stephenson's in Altens: they supply a couple of offshore catering companies. Frozen meat, veg, toilet paper, tins of beans . . . the usual. They don't open till seven am, so it'll be a while before—'

The large man turned a baleful eye in Logan's direction. 'No it won't. Find out who's in charge over there and get the bastard out of his bed. I want a search team up there now.'

'But it—'

'NOW, Sergeant!'

'Yes, sir.' Arguing with Insch wasn't going to get him anywhere. Grumpy bastard. Logan pulled out his mobile phone and wandered off to call Control, getting a search team and warrant organized between mouthfuls of tea. Doing his best to ignore the cameraman circling him like a short, balding shark.

Logan finished the call, then scrunched his polystyrene cup up and . . . there was nowhere to get rid of the thing, unless he just chucked it down on the dockside, or over into the water. Neither was going to look good on the television. Embarrassed, he hid it behind his back.

The shark lowered its HDV TV camera – no bigger than a shoebox, with the BBC Scotland logo stencilled on the side – and grinned. 'Perfect. Thought the sound was going to be a bit ropey there, but it's not bad. This is dynamite stuff! Dismembered bodies, boats, tension, mystery. Ooh,' he pointed at the crumpled-up cup in Logan's hand, 'where'd you get the tea: I'm gasping.'

'Thought you were meant to be a fly on the wall, Andy, not a pain in the arse.'

'Aye, well, we all have our—'

Insch's voice bellowed out from the far side of the quay: 'SERGEANT!'

Swear. Count to ten. Sigh. 'If this programme's a success, can I come work for you guys at the BBC instead?'

'See what I can do.' And Andy was off, hurrying to get a good angle on whatever bollocking the inspector was about to dish out.

Logan followed on behind, wishing he'd been assigned to someone, anyone else. Especially as the news from Control wasn't exactly good. These days, talking to Insch was like trying to do an eightsome reel in a minefield. Blindfold. Still, might as well get it over with, 'Sorry, sir, they don't have any bodies spare – everyone's down here and—'

'Bloody hell!' The fat man ran a hand over his big, pink face. 'Why can no one do what they're bloody well told?'

'Another hour or so and we can free up some of the search team here and—'

'I told you, I want it done now. Not in an hour: now.'

'But it's going to take that long to get a search warrant. Surely we should be concentrating on doing a thorough job here—'

The inspector loomed over him: six foot three of angry fat. 'Don't make me tell you twice, Sergeant.'

Logan tried to sound reasonable. 'Even if we pull every uniform off the boat and the docks, they're going to have to sit twiddling their thumbs till the search warrant comes through.'

Insch got as far as 'we don't have time to bugger about with—' before he was tapped on the shoulder by someone dressed in the familiar white SOC oversuit. Someone who didn't look particularly happy.

'I've been waiting for you for fifteen minutes!' Doctor Isobel McAllister, Aberdeen's chief pathologist, wearing an expression that would freeze the balls off a brass gorilla at twenty paces. 'You may not have anything better to do, but I can assure you that I have. Now are you going to listen to my preliminary findings, or shall I just go home and leave you to whatever it is you feel is more *important*?'

Logan groaned. That was all they needed, Isobel winding Insch up even further. As if the grumpy fat sod wasn't bad enough as it was. The inspector turned on her, his face flushing angry-scarlet in the IB spotlights. 'Thank you so much for waiting for me, Doctor, I'm sorry if my *organizing a murder inquiry* has inconvenienced you. I'll try not to let something as trivial get in the way again.'

They stared at each other in silence for a moment. Then Isobel pulled on a cold, unfriendly smile. 'Remains are human: male. Dismemberment looks like it occurred some time after death with a long, sharp blade and a hacksaw, but I won't be able to confirm that until I've performed the post mortem.' She checked her watch. 'Which will take place at eleven am precisely.'

Insch bristled. 'Oh no it won't! I need those remains analysed now—'

'They're *frozen*, Inspector. They – need – to – defrost.' Emphasizing each word as if she were talking to a naughty child, rather than a huge, bad-tempered Detective Inspector. 'If you want, I suppose I *could* stick them in the canteen microwave for half an hour. But that might not be very professional. What do you think?'

Insch just ground his teeth at her. Face rapidly shifting from angry-red to furious-purple. 'Fine,' he said at last, the word coming out strangled, 'then you can help by accompanying DS McRae to a cash and carry in Altens.'

'And what makes you think I—'

'Of course, if you're too busy, I can always ask one of the other pathologists to take over this case.' It was Insch's turn with the nasty smile. 'I understand the pressure you must be under: working mother, small child, can't really expect the same level of commitment to the job as—'

Isobel looked as if she was about to slap him. 'Don't you *dare* finish that sentence!' She flung an imperious gesture in Logan's direction. 'Get the car, Sergeant, we've got work to do.'

Insch nodded, pulled out his mobile and started dialling. 'Now if you'll excuse me, I've got a call to make . . . Hello? . . . That West Midlands Police? . . . Yes, DI Insch: Grampian CID, I need to speak to Chief Constable Mark Faulds . . . Yes, of course I know what time it is!' He turned his back on them and wandered away out of the spotlights.

Isobel scowled after him, then turned and snapped at Logan, 'Well? We haven't got all night.'

They were halfway to the car when a loud, 'Will you FUCK OFF with that bloody camera!' exploded behind them. Logan looked over his shoulder to see Andy scurrying in their direction while the inspector went back to his telephone call.

'Er . . .' said the cameraman, catching up to them by Logan's grubby, unmarked CID pool car, 'I wondered if I could tag along with you for a while. Insch is a bit . . .' He shrugged. 'You know.'

Logan did. 'Get in. I'll be back in a minute.' It didn't take long to pass the word along: he just grabbed the nearest sergeant and asked her to give it forty-five minutes, then tell everyone to finish up and get their backsides over to Altens.

Andy was in full whinge when Logan got back to the car, 'I mean,' the cameraman said, leaning forward from the back seat – knee-deep in discarded chip papers and fast-food cartons – 'If he didn't want to be in the bloody series, why'd he volunteer? Always seemed really keen till now. He shouted at me – I had my headphones on, nearly blew my eardrums out.'

Logan shrugged, threading the car through the barricade of press cameras, microphones and spotlights. 'You're lucky. He shouts at me every bloody day.'

Isobel just sat there in frosty silence, seething.

Stephenson's Cash and Carry was a long breeze-block warehouse in Altens: a soulless business park on the southernmost tip of Aberdeen. Inside it was huge, rows and rows of high, deep shelves stretching off into the distance, made miserable by the flicker of fluorescent lighting and the drone of piped muzak. The manager's office was halfway up the end wall, a flight of concrete steps leading to a shiny blue door with 'YOUR SMILE IS OUR GREATEST ASSET' written on it. If that was the case, they were all screwed, because everyone looked bloody miserable.

For someone who'd been dragged out of his bed at four in the morning, the man in charge of Stephenson's Cash and Carry looked bloody awful. Bags under the eyes, blue stubble on his jowly face, wearing a suit that probably cost a fortune, but looked like someone had died in it. Mr Stephenson peered out of the picture window that made up one wall of his office, watching as uniformed officers picked their way through the shelves of jelly babies, washing powder and baked beans. 'Oh God . . .'

'And you're quite sure,' said Logan, sitting in a creaky leather sofa with a cup of coffee and a chocolate biscuit, 'there haven't been any break-ins?'

'No. I mean, yes. I'm sure.' Stephenson crossed his arms, paced back and forth, uncrossed his arms. Sat down. Stood up again. 'It can't have come from here: we've got someone on-site twenty-four-seven, a state-of-the-art security system.'

Logan had met their state-of-the-art security system – it was a sixty-eight-year-old man named Colin. Logan had sneezed more alert things than him.

Stephenson went back to the window. 'Have you tried speaking to the ship's crew? Maybe they—'

'Who supplies your meat, Mr Stephenson?'

'It . . . depends what it is. Some of the pre-packaged stuff comes from local butchers – it's cheaper than hiring someone in-house to hack it up – the rest comes from Abattoirs. We use three—'

He flinched as a loud, rattling crash came from the cash and carry floor below, followed by a derisory cheer and some slow handclapping. 'You promised me they'd be careful! We're open in an hour and a half; I can't have customers seeing the place in a mess.'

Logan shook his head. 'I think you've got more important things to worry about, sir.'

Stephenson stared at him. 'I don't . . . no. You can't think we had anything to do with this! We're a family firm. We've been here for nearly thirty years.'

'That container came from your cash and carry with bits of human meat in it.'

'But—'

'How many other shipments do you think went out to the rigs like that? What if you've been selling chunks of dead bodies to catering companies for months? Do you think the guy's who've been eating chopped-up corpses offshore are going to be happy about it?'

Mr Stephenson blanched and said, 'Oh God . . .' again.

Logan drained the last of his coffee and stood. 'Where did the meat in that container come from?'

'I . . . I'll have to look in the dockets.'

'You do that.'

The cash and carry's chill room sat on the opposite side of the building, separated from the shelves of dry and tinned goods by a curtain of thick plastic strips that kept the cold in and the muzak out. A huge refrigeration unit bolted to the wall rattled away like a perpetual smoker's cough, making the air cold enough that Logan's breath trailed behind him in a fine mist as he marched between the boxes of fruit and vegetables over to the walk-in freezer section.

Detective Constable Rennie stood beside the freezer's heavy steel doors, hands jammed deep in his armpits, nose Rudolf-red, dressed like a ninja version of the Michelin Man in layers and layers of black clothing.

'Jesus,' said the constable, shivering, 'it's fucking perishing in here.'

Logan stopped, one hand on the freezer's door-handle. 'You'd be a lot warmer if you actually did some work.'

Rennie pulled a face. 'The Ice Queen thinks we're all too thick to help. I mean, it's not my fault I don't know what I'm looking for, is it?'

'What?' Logan closed his eyes and tried counting to ten. Got as far as three. 'For God's sake; you're supposed to be looking for *human remains*!'

'I *know* that. I'm in there, standing in a sodding freezer the size of my house, looking at rows and rows of frozen bits of bloody meat. How am I supposed to tell a joint of pork from a joint of person? It all looks the same to me. A hand, a foot, a head: *that* I could recognize. But it's all just chunks of meat.' He shifted, stomping his feet and blowing into his cupped hands. 'I'm a policeman, not a bloody doctor.'

And Logan had to admit he had a point. They only knew the joint of defrosting meat found in the container was human because it had a pierced nipple. Farmers were an odd lot, but not that odd.

Logan hauled open the heavy metal door and stepped into the freezer . . . Holy shit it was cold.

It was like being punched in the chest by a bag of ice. His breath went from mist to impenetrable fog. 'Hello?'

He found Doctor Isobel McAllister on the other side of a stack of cardboard boxes, their brown surfaces sparkling with a crisp film of white ice. She'd traded in her white SOC oversuit for what looked like a couple of dirty-blue parkas and a set of padded trousers, a red and white bobble hat bandaged onto her head with a tatty maroon scarf. Not exactly her usual catwalk self as she picked her way through a mound of frozen mystery meat.

'Anything?'

She scowled up at him. 'Other than hypothermia?' When Logan didn't answer, Isobel sighed and pointed at a big plastic crate stacked with chunks of vacuum-packed meat. 'We've got about three dozen possible pieces. If it was on the bone it'd be a lot easier to spot; cows and pigs have a much higher meat to bone ratio, but look at this,' she held up a pack labelled 'DICED PORK'. 'Could be anything. I'd expect human meat to be redder – based on the amount of myoglobin in the tissue – but if it's been bled and frozen . . . We'll need to defrost and DNA test all of this before we'll know for sure.'

Isobel pulled over another cardboard box, sliced through the plastic strapping, and started picking her way through the contents. 'You can tell Inspector Insch it'll take at least two weeks.'

Logan groaned. 'He's not going to like that.'

'That's not my problem, Sergeant.'

Oh, when she wanted someone to babysit her kid, or suffer through her endless digital camera slideshows of the sticky-fingered dribbly little monster, he was 'Logan', but when she was pissed off at work he was 'Sergeant.'

'And it's not *my* fault he had a go at you, OK?' You think he's bad tonight? I get him all bloody day—' Clunk. Logan froze, eyes sweeping the shelves of frozen goods, hoping to God it wasn't Andy with his bloody camera. Things were bad enough without being caught complaining about Insch on national television. 'Hello?'

'Sergeant McRae?' Mr Stephenson peered around a stack of boxes marked 'FISH FINGERS'. 'I've found the dockets . . .' he trailed off and stared at the pile of meat as Isobel added another chunk to the crate, the frozen pieces clattering against one another like ceramic tiles. 'Is . . . is that all . . . ?'

'We won't know till we test it.' Logan held out his hand, and the rumpled man looked puzzled for a moment, then tried to shake it. 'No,' Logan took a step back, leaving him hanging, 'the dockets?'

'Oh, right. Right. Of course.' He handed over a crumpled sheet of yellow A4, covered with biro scribbles. 'Sorry.'

Stephenson fidgeted nervously as Logan read. 'What's going to happen? I mean if that . . .' He swallowed. 'What am I going to tell my customers?'

Logan pulled out his mobile phone and scrolled

through the contacts list. 'We're going to need names and addresses for everyone who has access to this freezer. I want staff records, customers, suppliers, the lot.' An electronic voice on the other end of the line told him the number he was dialling was busy, please try again later.

The man in the crumpled suit shivered, wrapped his arms around himself and looked as if he was about to cry. 'We're a family firm, been here thirty years . . .'

'Yes, well,' Logan tried for a reassuring smile, 'you never know: the tests might come up negative.'

'I wouldn't go getting Mr Stephenson's hopes up.' Isobel sat back on her haunches, breath a cloud of white around her head as she lifted something out of the box at her feet. From where Logan was standing it looked just like another chunk of pork, and he said so.

'Yes, well,' she turned the joint of meat over in her hand, 'pigs don't usually have tattoos of unicorns on their backsides.'

Cold Granite

Stuart MacBride

Winter in Aberdeen: murder, mayhem and terrible weather.

It's DS Logan McRae's first day back on the job after a year off on the sick, and it couldn't get much worse. Four-year-old David Reid's body is discovered in a ditch, strangled, mutilated and a long time dead. And he's only the first. There's a killer stalking the Granite City and the local media are baying for blood.

Soon the dead are piling up in the morgue almost as fast as the snow on the streets, and Logan knows time is running out. More children are going missing. More are going to die. If Logan isn't careful, he could end up joining them.

'Ferocious and funny'   VAL McDERMID

'A gripping debut'   *Daily Mirror*

'Stuart MacBride goes straight for the jugular . . . tight and thrilling'   *Glasgow Herald*

ISBN 978 0 00 719314 1

Dying Light

Stuart MacBride

It's summertime in the Granite city: the sun is shining, the sky is blue and people are dying . . .

It starts with Rosie Williams, a prostitute, stripped naked and beaten to death down by the docks – the heart of Aberdeen's red light district. For DS Logan McRae it's a bad start to another bad day.

Rosie Williams won't be the only one making an unscheduled trip to the morgue. Across the city six people are burning to death in a petrol-soaked squat, the doors and windows screwed shut from the outside. And despite Logan's best efforts, it's not long before another prostitute turns up on the slab . . .

Stuart MacBride's characteristic grittiness, gallows humour and lively characterization are to the fore in this unputdownable serial killer tale.

'Another brilliant, riveting police procedural. I'm green with envy!'   R D Wingfield, author of *A Touch of Frost*

'Stuart MacBride goes straight for the jugular'
Glasgow Herald

ISBN 978 0 00 719316 5